To her surprise, he placed his hands over hers and said, "How about you join me tonight and find out?"

"Pardon?"

Had he just asked her out on a date? From the smirk on his face, he was loving every minute of her surprise.

After several beats, he asked, "Is it going to be a yes or no?"

"I don't even know your name."

"My apologies." He offered her his hand. "Blake Coleman."

Blake. It was a strong name and it suited him.

"Asia Reynolds." She accepted his handshake and when she did, white-hot heat radiated down to her belly and stole her breath away. The rush of desire she felt was unlike anything she had ever experienced and when she glanced up at Blake, she suspected he felt it too.

"How about it, Asia? Would you accompany me to my aunt's sixty-fifth birthday bash?"

"I—uh..." Asia blanked.

"The only answer I want to hear is yes," he said softly.

An excerpt from *The Marriage Deadline* by **Niobia Bryant**

At the continuing silence, Eve stood up and came around her desk to peek out the door to find Suzi with her mouth agape as she read the card that obviously was delivered with the flowers.

"What?" Eve said, moving quickly to cross the space and ease the card from her friend's hand.

"Oh my, Lucas Cress," Suzi sighed before fanning herself.

"'Every night I dream of making love to you. I want you. You ready for me yet?'" Eve read to herself.

"Oh my" is right.

Eve licked her lips and cleared her throat as she slid the card into the back pocket of the wide-leg jeans she wore. "Let's focus on reality," she drawled even as her heart pounded with ferocity.

Jusqu'à ce que nous nous revoyions, he had promised.

She shivered because he seemed determined to keep his word.

YAHRAH ST. JOHN
&
NIOBIA BRYANT

HER ONE NIGHT CONSEQUENCE
&
THE MARRIAGE DEADLINE

DESIRE

Recycling programs for this product may not exist in your area.

ISBN-13: 978-1-335-45782-0

Her One Night Consequence & The Marriage Deadline

Copyright © 2023 by Harlequin Enterprises ULC

Her One Night Consequence
Copyright © 2023 by Yahrah Yisrael

The Marriage Deadline
Copyright © 2023 by Niobia Bryant

For questions and comments about the quality of this book, please contact us at CustomerService@Harlequin.com.

Harlequin Enterprises ULC
22 Adelaide St. West, 41st Floor
Toronto, Ontario M5H 4E3, Canada
www.Harlequin.com

Printed in U.S.A.

CONTENTS

Yahrah St. John became a writer at the age of twelve when she wrote her first novella after secretly reading a Harlequin romance. Throughout her teens, she penned a total of twenty novellas. Her love of the craft continued into adulthood. She's the proud author of forty-seven books with Harlequin Desire, Kimani Romance and Arabesque as well as her own indie books.

Books by Yahrah St. John

Harlequin Desire

The Stewart Heirs

At the CEO's Pleasure
His Marriage Demand
Red Carpet Redemption

Locketts of Tuxedo Park

Consequences of Passion
Blind Date with the Spare Heir
Holiday Playbook
A Game Between Friends

Six Gems

Her Secret Billionaire
Her Best Friend's Brother
Her One Night Consequence

Visit the Author Profile page
at Harlequin.com for more titles.

You can also find Yahrah St. John on Facebook,
along with other Harlequin Desire authors,
at Facebook.com/HarlequinDesireAuthors!

Dear Reader,

I've been a published author for nearly two decades and it never gets old writing happily-ever-afters. I'm excited to present the third installment in the Six Gems series about the friendship between six incredible women.

Her One Night Consequence continues with Six Gem Asia Reynolds's story. Sparks fly when fun-loving and free-spirited Asia meets sexy billionaire Blake Coleman. The chemistry between them is combustible, but then Asia discovers she's pregnant by her one-night stand. She wants to raise the baby on her own, but Blake isn't going quietly into the night because he knows what it's like to lose his family. He's claiming Asia and his baby, and only marriage will do. I love the passionate yet tender moments between this couple that reveal this isn't just a marriage of convenience, but the beginning of a great love story.

Sit back in a quiet spot with your favorite beverage and escape into the world of Yahrah St. John, where steamy love scenes and family drama abound. I hope you're as captivated by their story as I was. If so, drop me a line at yahrah@yahrahstjohn.com or for more info visit my website at www.yahrahstjohn.com.

Best,

YSJ

HER ONE NIGHT CONSEQUENCE

Yahrah St. John

To my husband, Freddie Blackman,
for being my rock and anchor
during challenging times.

One

"Asia, these pieces are fabulous."

Asia Reynolds was a jewelry designer. But for the past several years, she had been working the retail counter at Yvette's Jewels. She enjoyed the work, but more importantly, the owner, Yvette Sinclair, allowed Asia to sell her original designs in the shop. This particular set was inspired by her recent trip east to visit one of her best friends, Egypt Cox.

"Thank you, Yvette." Asia smiled and placed the items back in the case she'd brought them in. "I was hoping we could sell them here at the store. I know they're not as traditional as you might like."

"Hogwash. When I hired you, I knew you were destined for great things, and these pieces show that," Yvette replied.

"You really think so?"

"I don't know why you doubt yourself, Asia. Look at how well your jewelry is doing online and at the flea markets."

Some weekends, Asia would head to one of the flea markets around Denver to sell her artwork. It allowed her to get a pulse on whether the public liked what she was creating.

"These are much different than the materials I usually use and will demand a higher price point." The lightning bolt necklace she'd made of sliced raw uncut diamonds was one of many pieces in the collection that spoke to her.

When she'd left Egypt in Raleigh, she'd gone on to DC and then to New York to source materials. She'd found what she was looking for at a small family-owned store in New York's Diamond District. Along with the necklace, she'd created a bracelet and cuff bangle, drop earrings, and a ring.

"And that's wonderful," Yvette said. "We have a variety of customers, from all walks of life, and this will be a signature piece for some lucky person."

Yvette always gave the best pep talks and had proven to be an invaluable mentor. As Asia put her case in the back office, she reflected on her recent windfall. Her best friends, Wynter Barrington, Egypt Cox, Teagan Williams, Shay Davis and Lyric Taylor, who with her had been affectionately coined the Six Gems, had inherited a nice sum of cash from Wynter's aunt Helaine Barrington last year, allowing them to start their own businesses.

Wynter hadn't needed much encouragement because

her travel blog was already quite popular. Egypt, meanwhile, had a food truck that she quickly flipped into her own restaurant, Flame. Then there was Teagan, who had her broker's license and was opening her own brokerage firm. Shay and Lyric were making headway opening up yoga and dance studios, respectively, but Asia? She was floundering.

Her trip back east had been twofold: to source new materials for her collection and to get the tea about Egypt's relationship with the handsome amnesiac she'd met. Her bestie appeared to be sprung on Garrett No-Name, but that hadn't stopped her from advising Asia on her business plan. Egypt was able to help Asia identify the steps she needed to take in order to get her brick-and-mortar store off the ground. It wasn't going to be easy.

But had anything in Asia's life ever been easy? She had never had a normal family. She didn't even know who her father was because her mother had been getting busy with many boys in the neighborhood and wound up pregnant at the age of sixteen. Asia grew up alongside her mother and the growing pains had been real. Ava Reynolds couldn't keep a job or a man to save her life and they'd always moved from pillar to post.

But there was a brief period in her childhood when Ava had held a steady job and they were able to stay in one place long enough for Asia to make friends—that's when she met the other Gems. Her relationships with the girls were priceless, so she once made the comment that they were like gemstones. Teagan had agreed and officially proclaimed them the Six Gems.

"Asia, darling. Are you all right?" Yvette inquired. "You look like you were a million miles away."

Asia blinked and forced herself back to the present. "I'm sorry, Yvette. Got lost in the past for a moment."

"Don't stay there too long."

The door to Yvette's Jewels opened and in walked the best-looking thing Asia had seen all day. No, make that all year. Tall, with skin the color of rich butterscotch, the man was sexy *and* handsome. Asia watched him survey the store as if he owned the place. He strolled over to the center display, allowing Asia a chance to really look at him.

His profile spoke of power. His hair was thick and curly, yet cut short in a low fade. His eyes were dark, as were his bushy eyebrows, but it was his chiseled features and strong jaw that drew him to her. He had a sexy five-o'clock shadow combined with firm lips she was certain garnered him an impressive amount of attention from the female population. He wore a black overcoat, but she could see he had on a white button-down underneath, tan trousers that showed off his lean and muscular physique and expensive-looking leather shoes. Asia wondered what he would look like naked, because of course her overactive mind would think of a customer that way.

Suddenly, he looked up and his gaze landed on Asia. His eyes speared hers, then he raked his gaze over her, up and down. A drum beat inside her body, gentle at first, and then louder as he stared at her more intensely. Asia licked her lips, her throat parched. She doubted she was glamorous like the women this man probably encountered daily, but she had her own sense of style.

Today, she wore a leather jacket over a turquoise-blue shirt and a beige flouncy skirt that hit her thighs, along with stiletto heels. Seeing that she was only five feet two, she never went anywhere without her heels.

She walked over to him as her eyes dragged upward. "Good morning."

"Hello." His eyes warmed her face and her body in a way she'd never felt before.

"Is there something I can help you find?" Asia inquired with as much bravado as she could muster.

"Yes, you can." His voice was deep and strong and Asia felt it all the way to her toes. "I'm looking for a gift for my aunt. She's having a birthday soiree this evening and I need something special."

"It's a bit late, isn't it?" Asia asked, quirking a brow. As soon as she said the words, she realized how out of line she was being.

Instead of a snarky comment back, he grinned, and Asia found she rather liked his Colgate smile. "You're right, and I've only myself to blame. I got caught up with work and failed to make time, but I'm hoping you will help me remedy that."

This one is a charmer!

Asia sucked in a deep breath. "Of course. We have some really wonderful pieces. Is there a style you had in mind?"

"At sixty-five, my aunt is bold and daring. It has to be something unique. Sort of like what you're wearing."

Asia glanced down at the raw diamond bangle on her slim wrist. She'd forgotten she'd put it on to show Yvette.

"Oh, this is part of a new collection and I haven't put out all the pieces yet."

His eyes brightened. "You're a designer?"

She nodded. "I am, but there's a lot of other great pieces in the store, if you're interested?"

"Show me."

His words were a command and Asia guessed he was used to being obeyed. She walked over to the display that held most of her work. "Anything in this case is mine. There are different items using onyx, opals and emeralds."

He peered down at her jewelry. "These are very good."

"Thank you." Asia beamed with pride.

"However, I'd like to see the rest of *that* collection." He inclined his head toward her wrist.

Asia glanced over at Yvette, who was eagerly nodding at her from the sidelines. "All right, give me just a minute." She walked to the back office to grab her case. When she returned to the showroom, she found the sexy stranger exactly where she had left him. His eyes followed her as she approached.

"Here we are." Asia placed a cloth down and opened the case to reveal her newest collection.

The sexy stranger picked up her favorite piece, the lightning bolt necklace, and examined it closely. After several moments, he stated, "I'll take this."

Her breath shorted in her chest. "Just like that?"

"I find in life you have to be very decisive," he responded. "How much do you want for it?"

Asia had a general idea of how much she wanted to charge, but this would be much costlier than any of her previous works. She hesitated and he noticed.

One of his bushy eyebrows rose. "Is there a problem?"

"No, it's just…one of my more expensive pieces. Perhaps you want to see something else?"

"That's not a problem," he said smoothly, and then motioned her toward him with his index finger. At first, Asia wasn't going to be beckoned by any man, but this one was different. Very different from the artist and musician types she usually fancied. She leaned forward and he whispered in her ear, "Can I offer you a piece of advice?"

She cocked her head to the side, "What's that?"

"Don't shortchange yourself. If you have a quality product, then the public should be willing to pay the price. Now what's the price on *that* piece?"

Asia's eyes narrowed. "It's fifteen hundred dollars."

"Sold." He handed the necklace back and Asia's hands were shaking as she took it. She'd never sold anything this expensive before. "Can you gift wrap it?." She sneaked a look at Yvette, who gave her a subtle nod of encouragement. Then he slid his black American Express card across the counter, showing her that money was obviously no object.

"A-absolutely." Asia stumbled over the word, picked up the card and went over to the cash register. She put the necklace in a gift-wrapped box with a bow on top. Every now and then, she glanced up and found his eyes probing hers. When they swept down to her lips, a blaze of heat went through Asia. She blinked and forced herself to close the sale. When it was over, she placed the box in a signature Yvette's Jewels bag and walked over.

"I hope your aunt is pleased with the gift," Asia said, handing him his purchase.

To her surprise, he placed his hands over hers and said, "How about you join me tonight and find out?"

"Pardon?"

Had he just asked her out on a date? From the smirk on his face, he had and was loving every minute of her surprise. She looked over at Yvette again, who was doing her best to conceal a sly grin. Some help she was.

After several beats, he asked, "Is it going to be a yes or no?"

"I don't even know your name."

"My apologies." He offered her his hand. "Blake Coleman."

Blake.

It was a strong name and it suited him.

"Asia Reynolds." She accepted his handshake, and when she did white-hot heat radiated down to her belly and stole her breath away. The rush of desire she felt was unlike anything she'd ever experienced, and when she glanced up at Blake, she suspected he'd felt it, too.

"How about it, Asia? Would you accompany me to my aunt's sixty-fifth birthday bash?"

"I-uh…" Asia blanked.

"The only answer I want to hear is yes," he said softly.

"Yes," Asia answered without thinking, because she *wanted* to go with him. Wanted to understand the heat she felt around this enigmatic man she'd just met but somehow was agreeing to go on a date with.

He smiled and it lit up his handsome features, weakening her knees. "Good. If it's all right with you, I'll pick you up here around six thirty. Can I get your number in case anything comes up?" He handed Asia his phone and she typed in her digits on autopilot.

"Thanks." He accepted the phone back. "I look forward to seeing you later." Then picked up his gift and left the store.

She turned toward Yvette. "What the hell just happened?"

"Looks like you got yourself a hot date," her boss cheekily replied.

Did Blake pick up women in jewelry stores on a regular basis? Or was she special? Either way, Asia knew tonight would be a night to remember.

Later, Asia fretted about what to wear to a fancy party with a guy like Blake Coleman. The men she usually dated could barely rub two nickels together, let alone pay for a fifteen-hundred-dollar necklace. Typically, she preferred the artistic type, such as a musician, painter or writer, because they were talented. But Blake was different. From the custom-made outfit he'd worn, she knew he had money.

What could she wear to possibly fit the occasion? It was early April in Denver, which meant the nights were still chilly, so she preferred something with sleeves. Riffling through her closet, she found the perfect dress. Off the shoulder, long-sleeved and with a sweetheart neckline that revealed a bit of décolletage.

It was the little black dress every woman needed in her closet. It didn't hurt that it hit her mid-thigh and showed off a generous amount of leg. Because she was just over five feet, she had to use everything in her arsenal. She opted for pointy heels, chandelier earrings and an oversize ring from last year's opal collection.

Unfortunately, dallying around with her wardrobe, then hair and makeup, left her precious little time to get back to the store. She grabbed her long gray wool coat and rushed out the door. Her Uber arrived at the store just as Blake was knocking on the door.

"I'm here," Asia said with a flourish, sliding out of the back seat of the Uber.

"I was beginning to wonder if you'd stood me up," Blake said, meeting her at the curb.

As if!

He looked absolutely scrumptious in a black tuxedo jacket, black silk shirt and trousers.

She grinned, looking up at him. "Not a chance."

"Shall we?" He offered her his arm.

Seconds later, Blake was tucking Asia into the passenger seat of his luxury Mercedes-Benz SUV. Asia's Hyundai Sonata wouldn't hold a candle to this monster. The soft leather seat felt like butter against her skin, and the dashboard had lots of controls and gadgets she'd didn't have on her basic model.

Soon, they were dashing through the streets of Denver, heading toward where? Asia had no idea. The Six Gems would probably think she was mad for getting into a car with a strange man she knew nothing about, other than what she'd learned during the five minutes she'd taken to look him up online. He was the son of Gil and Daphne Coleman, a wealthy couple who were killed in a car accident when he was twelve years old. Blake was the sole survivor of the accident. His aunt, whose party they were attending, had raised him. As the head of the family real estate development company, Coleman & Sons Construction, he was considered one of Denver's most eligible bachelors.

"You're awfully quiet," Blake said from beside her in the driver's seat.

Asia glanced at him. "That's because I'm not usually picked up by good-looking men in the store."

He hazarded a glance at her. "You think I'm good-looking?"

She raised a brow. "Fishing for compliments?"

"Absolutely."

"Then yes, I think you're attractive, but you already knew that or you wouldn't have asked me out."

"Sassy. I love it!" Blake responded. "I think I'm going to enjoy the evening very much."

To say she was nervous coming to Blake's aunt's home was somewhat of an understatement. Asia would never get used to big displays of wealth. As teens, whenever Wynter had invited Asia over to her family's mansion, Asia had always felt as if she stuck out like a sore thumb. Her mother could never afford the newest fashion, so Asia was often forced to shop at the local thrift stores or sew an outfit herself. In school, everyone thought she was eccentric, when that couldn't have been further from the truth; she was just poor. The one thing Asia had always been good at was faking it. So that's what she was going to do tonight.

She kept her mouth closed when Blake drove through the iron gates and onto the circular drive of a mammoth estate. Uniformed valets greeted them and opened her car door.

"Thank you," Asia said when one of the valets helped her out of the car, but in seconds, Blake was right by her side and circling her arm around his.

He smiled down at her. "C'mon, let me show you inside."

Asia walked alongside Blake with the same self-assured confidence he possessed. He was comfortable in his own skin. Asia wished she were the same, but sometimes she felt as if she was always putting on a show and trying to be more so no one discovered the uneasy, unconfident girl underneath.

Upon their arrival, they were immediately greeted by a butler, who took her coat, and then a slim, salt-and-pepper beauty Asia could only assume was Blake's aunt came toward them.

"My darling, you've finally arrived," the older woman said with a warm smile across her caramel features. Her hair was swept up in an elegant chignon. She wore a floor-length gown embellished with flower appliqués and featuring blouson sleeves. "I thought you were going to be a no-show."

"I wouldn't dream of it." Blake released Asia long enough to place a kiss on her cheek. "Aunt Sadie, please allow me to introduce Asia Reynolds. She's an up-and-coming jewelry designer."

His aunt raised a brow. "A designer?" Her eyes scanned Asia up and down. "It's nice to see you looking for something other than a pretty face." At Asia's crestfallen expression, she added, "Though you are lovely, my dear."

"Uh—thank you," Asia replied to the backhanded compliment.

"Please don't be offended," his aunt Sadie continued, "my nephew is something of a skirt-chaser, and I'm always getting on him to find someone with depth."

Asia glanced up at Blake, who grinned good-naturedly, despite his aunt calling him a playboy. "Aunt Sadie, can I help it if women flock to me? Who am I to turn them down?"

Asia couldn't resist bursting out laughing and so did his aunt.

"Seriously?" Blake feigned being dejected. "You're both laughing at me?"

"I'm sorry to tell you, but yes," Asia replied with a wry smile. "You realize what you said was extremely arrogant."

Blake shrugged. "But true."

"Then I'm surprised I'm here and not one of your flock."

"I like her. She's got spunk!" Sadie replied, looking at Blake. "Try not to do anything to mess it up. Now, if you both will excuse me, I have to mingle." She rushed off to the chat with an elderly couple who'd just walked in through the double doors.

"Your aunt is a pistol," Asia said. "I like her."

"As are you. Do you always say what's on your mind?" Blake asked, moving from the foyer into the living room. When he found a waiter, he procured two glasses of champagne and handed one to Asia.

Asia accepted the glass. "Always. The Six Gems always tell me to look before I leap, but I'm afraid it's not in my DNA."

"The Six Gems?"

"Oh, they're my best friends. I thought we were priceless and so we nicknamed ourselves the Six Gems."

Blake grinned and a swarm of butterflies took up residence in her belly. He moved through the crowds, stopping to make idle chitchat with whomever waylaid him. Standing next to his six-foot-plus figure, Asia felt small, but in a good way, because Blake always introduced her and made sure she was *seen*.

She appreciated that because too often growing up she'd felt unseen. The poor little girl whose mother couldn't be bothered to show up to parent-teacher meetings. Or who never had enough money to go on school field trips. Asia had grown up with somewhat of a complex. She supposed it's why she always made sure her clothes were loud and she was the life of the party—she wanted to be seen.

Her confidence was boosted when Blake mentioned her jewelry to a group of women who wore shimmering designer dresses and whose hair and makeup were works of art. "Asia, show them your bracelet," Blake said.

Asia found herself holding up her wrist, and several people gathered around her, admiring her handiwork.

"It's beautiful," the women gushed.

"Do you have more pieces?" one of them asked.

"I do." And before Asia knew it, she was regaling a crowd with the inspirations for her line and her methods of creation. The women at Sadie's party didn't wear costume jewelry. Instead, they were the customers she would need if she ever wanted to launch her own store with more high-end products. Asia was so engrossed with talking about her work, she completely forgot about Blake and handed out the business cards she'd thrown in her purse at the last minute.

Eventually, everyone retired to the dining room, where they were seated at a long table that easily sat fifty. The room was elegantly appointed with a crystal chandelier, porcelain baroque dinnerware and French-inspired furniture.

Was this how the other half lived? Asia wondered as she sat down and a waiter shook out her napkin and another asked if she wanted wine. The staff began bringing out course after course, from starters to soup. Asia could remember distinct occasions when she'd gone without food because they were out of food stamps, Ava's check was later in the week or just because her mother had forgotten to go grocery shopping.

"Everything okay?" Blake asked from her side after the surf and turf entrée was set in front of her, including an elaborately decorated lobster.

"Yes, I'm just not used to such"—she stumbled, trying to find the right word, until she settled on one—"luxury."

"I guess I take all of this"—he swept his arm around the room—"for granted. I'm glad I have you here to bring me back to earth."

He propped an arm around her chair, moving close enough for Asia to breathe in the spicy scent of his aftershave. It made her senses swim. "You are very lucky. Not everyone is born with a silver spoon in their mouth."

"You think I'm spoiled?"

"No. Maybe entitled," Asia responded.

Blake clutched his heart. "You wound me, Asia."

"Something tells me your ego can handle it."

He chuckled, and that's how they continued the remainder of the evening, bantering back and forth. During dessert, his aunt Sadie finally opened Blake's birthday gift and when she did, her mouth was agape.

"Blake, this is stunning," Sadie said. "I assume this is your work?" She asked, glancing at Asia.

Asia nodded.

"It's outstanding," Sadie replied and turned to her dinner guests. "If you're looking for a jewelry, please consider my dinner guest Asia Reynolds, she's an up-and-coming designer and made this creation." She held up her hand and the rest of the guests ooh and aahed over it, until eventually, it was time to retire to the living room, where a live band was set up and a small dance floor was erected for guests to dance on.

"Care to join me for a spin?" Blake inclined his head toward the floor, where several couples were already swaying to the soft, jazzy tunes.

"Love to."

Blake pulled her into his arms and draped her arms over his broad shoulders, then he placed his hands on her hips and tugged her body into his.

Asia enjoyed the feel of Blake's hands spanning her waist and the muscles bunching on his arm. She rested her hand on his shoulder and felt her skin heat at the contact.

"You're a surprise, Asia Reynolds." Blake said, and she glanced up into his handsome face. Thick dark lashes fanned around hooded eyes that, right now, were peering into her brown ones.

"How so?"

"I asked you out tonight on a whim," Blake confessed as he moved them around the dance floor with ease, "because you intrigued me. You're very passionate about your work, about life in general. It's extremely attractive."

If Asia's brown skin could blush, it would have. "I'm glad, because the feeling is mutual. I'd hate to think I was out here on the ledge all by myself, admiring you."

He grinned. "I like your honesty, Asia. It's very refreshing. So can I be equally honest?"

"Please."

"I want to kiss you."

Two

Heat coursed through Asia's body at Blake's words, and she focused on the sensual line of his lips, which was surrounded by sexy stubble. How would it feel to have his lips on hers? "I'd like that."

He grinned. "Good." He glanced around them. "But not here. I don't want an audience."

Neither did she.

The first time she felt Blake's lips on hers, Asia wanted complete privacy so she could revel in the moment, because the yearning to taste him had been building for hours. The times she'd found his eyes on hers, or those moments when his thigh had brushed hers underneath the dinner table, had been leading up to *this*.

"Let's go," he whispered, and before Asia knew it, he was leading her down a hallway, away from the crowd.

Asia blindly followed because she was ready to extinguish the flames that had been sparking between them all night.

"Here." He led her into a darkened room.

Asia's eyes didn't have time to acclimate to the darkness before Blake was pressing her backward against the door, but she let him. She fit her curves against the hard line of his body, and when he cradled her head, tilting her upward, her breath hitched. She couldn't wait for him to put his mouth on hers, but instead of doing just that, he prolonged the moment, making her wait for it. His thumb trailed a slow, torturous path across her lips, and she shuddered in anticipation.

Only when he felt her surrender did his mouth find hers in a kiss so hot and heavy, Asia let out a sigh of unadulterated bliss. He tasted as good as he looked, and she wanted more. He gave it to her by slanting his mouth across hers and deepening the kiss. It was so hot, she felt as if she were melting from the inside out. When was the last time she'd felt this instant attraction to a man? The answer was never.

Blake's tongue teased and stroked hers, dragging helpless moans from her body. Asia desperately tried to get closer to him because he was hot and warm and everything she wanted. His hands moved to her bottom, molding and squeezing her until he could put her exactly where he wanted her, against his rock-hard erection. Asia wiggled her hips and whimpered in response.

Sexual need was building inside her and Blake must have felt it, too, because then he lowered her dress over her shoulders. He rained a trail of kisses from her shoulders to her breasts. To her utter delight, he began to suck her through the lace of her strapless bra.

"Ah!" Asia threw back her head and Blake grasped her thigh, drawing her leg up to hook it around his waist. Then he pressed his hard ridge against the cradle of her sex. Asia thought she might fly apart, especially when his lips devoured her nipple.

"Jesus, you're so responsive," Blake murmured, lifting his head. "I want you."

"I want you, too."

"Then we need to move to a different location," Blake said, lowering her leg so she could stand on both feet.

Asia glanced around and realized they were in a study lined with shelves of books. This was no place to be getting busy. As she fixed her dress, Asia thought about whether she should be rethinking the sensibility of her actions, but then she looked at Blake and saw the gleam of desire in his eyes. No way was she turning back from this moment. She took his outstretched hand and let him lead her off the edge of the cliff.

Blake took Asia to one of the upstairs bedrooms of his aunt's home. "She rarely comes to this wing," he said, closing the door behind them and blanketing them in the moonlight streaming from the window.

"Asia, I know downstairs we were pretty hot and heavy. And, well, before we take this any further"—he ran his hand over his head—"you should know something."

Her brow furrowed. "What's that?"

He sighed as if it pained him to say the next words.

"I don't want to lead you on that this thing between us might be more…" His voice trailed off.

"More than tonight?" she finished for him. Had she really thought that a guy like Blake might want to see her again? Of course not. He just wanted one night—but so did she.

She nodded, and they reached simultaneously for each other in a whirlwind of arms and limbs. Asia slid her hands underneath his jacket and helped him remove it from his shoulders. Then she tossed it on the floor and her fingers feverishly attacked the buttons on his shirt. She was caught up in a haze of sensual bliss that only Blake could remedy.

Blake was reaching behind her for the zipper of her dress, and before she could finish unbuttoning his shirt, the fabric was sliding down her arms and into a pool on the floor. Asia was left in her bra and panties for Blake's hungry gaze.

He stepped back from her. "Let me look at you for a moment."

Asia wasn't keen on this part. She had always thought her breasts were too small and her butt, too big, but Blake didn't seem to care. He appeared to like everything he saw. "You're beautiful," he said, his eyes hooded.

All she could do was say, "Thank you." Then she moved to him again, resuming her task, but her fingers weren't nimble enough, so Blake ripped the shirt open instead. His broad shoulders and sexy, hairless chest made her mouth water, and she reached for the button on his trousers.

"Let me," Blake said, and had them unzipped and

off, along with his boxers, so fast, Asia had whiplash. But she didn't mind his eagerness, because it allowed her time to study him as he'd done her. Narrow hips, muscular thighs, and there, in the cradle of his groin, was his erection—big and proud. She couldn't wait to feel him inside her, but first she wanted to taste him.

She sank to her knees.

"Asia, you don't have to…" His voice trailed off when she wrapped her hand around the base of his hardness and took him inside her mouth.

Blake released a guttural moan when she stroked him with her hands and mouth. He wrapped his hand in her hair as she moved up and down his length. When she glanced up at him, his head was thrown back and he was arching forward. Asia kept sucking and stroking him in tight motions until she could feel that he was on the verge of release.

"Asia," he bit out, and then strong hands reached down and hauled her to feet, just as she licked her lips.

"You witch!" He groaned. "The only place I'm coming is inside you."

Asia grinned and, reaching behind, unclasped her bra and let it drop to the floor. Then she hooked her thumbs through her panties and eased them down her legs until they were both naked. That's when Blake pounced and picked her up, carrying her over to the massive bed she'd only given a second glance to because she was so focused on Blake.

He came to lie down beside her and, within seconds, his mouth captured hers in a deep, ravishing kiss that had Asia moaning her pleasure and winding her arms around his neck to bring him closer. Blake's tongue swept inside her mouth and tangled with hers while his hands palmed one breast and then the other.

When he finally pulled his mouth from hers to nibble at her neck, Asia felt bereft, but then there were other sensations, including his fingers lightly tracing each of her already puckered nipples. His mouth closed around one nipple and she moaned aloud.

He lifted his head. "You like that, do you?" he asked. "Well, I've a lot more in store." He bent his head to return to the task at hand and Asia lost herself when he boldly swirled his tongue with decadent flicks and licks. It sent arrows of excitement straight to her core and she shuddered in delight.

"More," she pleaded. She was wet and slick between her legs and every part of her was needy with longing.

She was thankful when his masterful lips trailed lower, past her breasts, to her stomach, her hips and on to her thighs. He dropped kisses everywhere he touched, setting off fireworks wherever he went. And when he boldly tasted and licked her where she needed him most, Asia cried out, her head lolling backward as desire rippled through her in wave after relentless wave. He teased and tormented her until she screamed out his name. "Blake!"

Her nails dug into his shoulders as he held her hips and anchored her. Blake kept her in the sweetest of tortures until she pulsed helplessly, but he didn't stop. He increased the pressure of his tongue until she climaxed a second time. Only then, when she was breathless and her heart was thundering, did he move away long enough for her to hear the tear of a wrapper. Then he was back, parting her thighs and driving into her.

At the pleasure of his possession, Asia let out a long, deep moan.

He stilled. "Are you okay?" he asked.

Asia nodded. It had been a minute since she'd been with a man. Her friends might think she didn't discriminate when it came to who she took to her bed, but they were wrong. She needed to feel a connection to them, as she'd felt with Blake tonight.

"You feel so good," he murmured.

She felt her face flush at his openness. "So do you."

He undulated his hips in a way that had Asia's entire body surging, and she arched off the bed. An unguarded groan escaped his lips and his breathing began to get labored as he slowly, yet relentlessly, thrust into her. His grip on her hip tightened as their bodies strained and moved together as one. They were yearning and searching for the ultimate pleasure that was so very near.

And when it came, she cried, wrapping her legs around his waist. "Yes! Oh, yes!" Asia's release was so ferocious and powerful that she splintered into a million pieces.

Her climax triggered Blake to move faster. His eyes grew wild as sweat slicked both their bodies. When his release finally came, she heard her name on his lips as he, too, fell over the abyss into sensual oblivion.

Asia awoke a short while later and felt deliciously sore in all the right places. Then she remembered Blake's words from last night. They would never be more than tonight. She knew it was selfish of her to want more than this one perfect night, but she always wished for the stars, even though she was often disappointed.

She was surprised, however, when she turned sideways and found an empty space where Blake had been. She touched the sheets and they were cold. He'd been gone a while. Had it been that easy for him to walk away from the most amazing sex she'd ever had in her life? Asia had never felt that way with another man. Had never felt as if she'd been transformed and yet reborn.

Hurt, Asia sat upright, clutching the sheet to her bosom. Clearly, Blake had hot sex with the whole flock of women he encountered. Asia was more selective, but she would store this one magical night in her memory so she would have it to hold on to on those cold Denver nights. In the meantime, she had to get up and get dressed. That's when she noticed the note on the nightstand.

Thank you for a wonderful night, Asia.
A car is waiting outside to take you home.

Asia rolled her eyes. What a coward. She couldn't believe Blake wasn't man enough to face her and take her home himself. Maybe he wasn't who she thought he was. The entire evening, she'd thought of him as her Prince Charming in a fairy-tale night, when all along, he'd been the frog.

After dressing, Asia peeked out the door and, finding the hallway empty, quietly stepped out and down the winding stairs leading to the foyer. She assumed she was in the all clear until she heard Blake's aunt Sadie.

"Damn that nephew of mine."

Asia spun around on her heel to find Sadie standing in the foyer in a bathrobe holding a cup of what she assumed was tea. "Sadie!"

"I assume he escaped like a thief in the night?"

Asia couldn't resist a chuckle. "Something like that."

"That's a shame. I had such high hopes. The way he was with you tonight…"

"Was all an illusion," Asia finished. "And it's time I left."

"You might want your coat, my dear," Sadie said and went over to the closet nearby and pulled out Asia's wool coat. She handed it to her.

"Thank you," Asia said, sliding her arms inside. "I apologize for the late hour, ma'am, and happy birthday again." She lowered her head and walked outside toward the car that was indeed waiting to take her back to her ordinary life.

Three

Seven weeks later

"This place is outrageous!" Asia said when she arrived at the Encore Hotel in Las Vegas with the rest of the Six Gems after a short flight from Denver. Egypt and Teagan were in charge of the bachelorette party over the weekend and had outdone themselves. Their three-bedroom villa had panoramic views of the Strip.

When Asia had landed in Vegas, most of the Gems had already arrived, since they'd all planned to get there around the same time. It had worked out perfectly because a limo transfer came with the villa and a uniformed chauffeur had been holding a sign that read Wynter's Bachelorette Party. They'd squealed in excitement before piling into the vehicle, where bottles of Cristal sat chilling in an ice bucket. Teagan had quickly popped open a bottle, and soon champagne had flowed, though Asia hadn't indulged because her stomach wasn't feeling right.

"I agree with Asia on this one. This place is spectacular," Wynter said, glancing around as the butler continued showing them around the villa, which came with a living and dining room, billiard room, exercise room, and several bedrooms, each with its own marble soaking tub, separate shower and walk-in closet. "Thank you so much."

"You're absolutely welcome, diva!" Egypt said as Wynter pulled her into a bear hug.

"You too, Teagan," Wynter, said inclining her head. "Come here." The three women embraced.

Asia glanced at these women who were like sisters to her. They were all so different. Wynter, with her wavy shoulder-length hair, tawny skin and petite figure, was a millionairess now that she'd inherited her aunt's fortune. Then there was Egypt. Restaurateur extraordinaire. She owned being a tall, full-figured caramel-brown woman, and Asia loved that about her.

Next was Teagan. Miss Professional. You would think she would have changed into something more comfortable for traveling, but instead she was in an orange silk button-down shirt, black trousers and pumps. One might assume she was going to show a house rather than attend a bachelorette party.

Lyric, the quiet one in their rowdy bunch, was actually listening to the butler, who was advising them of all the perks that came with the villa. Lyric was stunningly beautiful, with long auburn hair, almond-shaped eyes and a lithe and statuesque figure from years of ballet dancing. Although an injury had sidelined her, Lyric had never given up her love of the art form and was in the process of opening up her own dance studio.

"Are you all right?" Shay asked said from Asia's side. "You're not your usual vivacious self."

"Oh yeah? And what's that?"

"The life of the party," Shay answered. As a yoga and Pilates instructor, Shay was all about fitness. Her smooth toffee skin gleamed from eating right and working out, while her long dark locs had grown longer since the last time Asia saw her. Not to mention, she would kill for Shay's athletic figure instead of her stacked five-foot-two petite size.

"I can't always be turned up," Asia replied. Over the past seven weeks, Asia had been in a funk. She told herself it had nothing to do with Blake leaving her to find her own way home in the middle of the night after sexing her like crazy, but deep down she knew that was a lie. He'd gotten to her and *she,* who prided herself on being immune and never letting anything get her down, had succumbed to his charms.

Shay frowned. "Now I know something's up. You know you can talk to me, to any of us"—she motioned to the rest of the women in the room—"we're family."

"I'm fine. We're here to celebrate Wynter's upcoming nuptials to Riley, not worry about my troubles."

"So you have troubles?"

Asia grasped Shay's arm and pulled her away from the group. "I don't have any troubles. It was the wrong choice of word."

Shay raised a brow. "If you say so, but I'll let it rest for now."

Asia smiled. "Good. Let's do the damn thing!"

As Shay walked way, Asia reminded herself that even though they didn't live in the same cities, the other Gems *knew* her and would know if something was off. And wasn't it? She especially hadn't felt great over the past couple of weeks, which is why she hadn't had any champagne. She'd been battling a stomach bug that wouldn't go away no matter how many ginger ales and saltines she ate. She would power through this weekend by sheer force of will because there's nothing she wouldn't do for these women. As Shay said, they were her family.

The activity slate for the weekend kept them busy. First, there was an elaborate dinner at the chef's table at Restaurant Guy Savoy, followed by first-row seats at the Usher concert. Today, they'd had spa treatments and were now lounging poolside before going out this evening to a famous nightclub.

"Egypt, how much money did you guys spend?" Asia whispered when they were on their way. "Even with me, Lyric and Shay's donation, this had to set you and Teagan back a clip."

Egypt turned to her with a high-wattage smile. "Nothing is too much for my sistas."

Asia couldn't resist grinning back, because that's what these women were to one another: sisters. Asia could recall a time when Claire, a girl in their high school, picked on her in class because she wasn't wearing the latest in fashion. Egypt, bigger and taller than

Claire, stepped in and told Claire that if she didn't back off, she'd have Egypt to deal with. Claire immediately stopped harassing her.

"What are you two whispering about?" Wynter asked, just a little bit wobbly as she held on to a flute of champagne. She'd already had several cocktails over the course of the evening.

"About how much fun we're having." Asia winked at Egypt.

"It's the bomb!" Wynter said rather loudly as she fell forward onto the lounger where Egypt and Asia sat. "You guys don't mind if I sit here, do you?" she asked, glancing at them.

"Not at all." Asia chuckled. "How about I get you some water?" She reached inside the small refrigerator tucked into the bottom of the attached console and handed Wynter a bottle. "Drink this."

"Thanks." Wynter twisted off the cap and took a generous drink. "Where to next?"

"We are going to party like rock stars," Teagan said, "I've arranged VIP access and bottle service at the club."

"Woohoo!" Wynter yelled.

Asia rolled her eyes. It was going to be a long night.

"Blake, darling, it's been so long since I've seen you. Where have you been hiding yourself?" his aunt Sadie asked when Blake finally made it over to her home for dinner that weekend.

"Nowhere, Aunt Sadie." He kissed her cheek. "I've been really busy."

She eyed him suspiciously.

He didn't like the doubtful look she gave him, "What?"

"You know what," she responded. "You haven't been here since the night of my birthday party."

Blake brushed some imaginary lint off his sweater. On weekends, he tended to be in jeans, and today was no exception. "Really? Has it been that long?" When indeed he knew exactly how long it had been, down to how many weeks, days and hours since he was last here with Asia.

"You came with a lovely young woman who I thought you might consider dating," his aunt responded matter-of-factly, "but alas, you messed that up."

"What are you talking about?"

"I saw her, Blake."

He frowned. She couldn't have seen Asia. His aunt was a sound sleeper, especially after several cocktails. "Who?"

Sadie cocked her head to the side and put her hand on her hip.

"Asia?" There. He'd said her name aloud. He'd thought of her often, but forced himself to remove her from his thoughts. Why? Because quite frankly their evening together had scared the hell out of him. The connection he had found with the beautiful spitfire, in and out of bed, had overwhelmed him with its inten-sity. When they'd made love, Blake thought he'd found nirvana.

How was it possible that he, the ultimate serial dater, had been swept up by the magic of the evening? He'd hightailed it out of there as fast as he could, scribbling a quick note and arranging transport so he didn't look like a complete asshole. Though he doubted Asia would believe that. He'd been a coward for running.

"Of course, I'm talking about Asia. I ran into her as she rushed out of my home in the wee hours of the morning."

Blake lowered his head in embarrassment. "I'm sorry, Aunt Sadie. You shouldn't have had to see that."

"And you should have had the decency to take her back home instead of foisting her off on a driver."

Blake released a long sigh. "Listen, do we really have to talk about my love life?"

"What love life? You don't have one. I've been telling you for years not to leave it too late like me or you'll end up alone. As it is, you're already thirty-four. You're not getting any younger, my boy, and good looks fade. Who will be there with you in the end?"

"I think you're being a touch melodramatic, Auntie."

"And you're putting your head in the sand. Asia was by far the most delightful creature I've ever seen you with, so I guess I'll never get a grandniece or-nephew."

"Not any time soon, I'm afraid."

His aunt shook her head in frustration. "You're all I have left, Blake. Losing your father, *my brother,* in that car crash when he was so young was very difficult, but at least I had you. When I'm gone, who will you have?"

"Auntie, you're the picture of health, so can we stop with this morbid conversation and move on to a new topic?" Blake didn't like to talk about, let alone think about, his beloved parents because then he would remember what his life had been like before they'd been taken in a senseless accident. The only reason he'd survived the horrible time was because he'd had Aunt

Sadie. She'd been a rock when he needed one and she hadn't let him draw into himself despite his attempts to do exactly that. He'd had a horrible case of survivor's guilt. Back then, he'd wanted to die right along with them.

"Very well."

Their conversation turned to Coleman & Sons Construction, his legacy, and next steps with the development deal he'd single-handedly brokered for a new piece of land, but Blake's mind wasn't in it. He was thinking about a certain five-foot-two brunette who had wound him around her pinkie finger in just one night. Why couldn't he forget her? What made her so different from the other women he encountered?

It was simple.

There was something unvarnished about Asia Reynolds that he hadn't found in anyone else. He could find other attractive and statuesque beauties, but Asia was interesting and opinionated. Not only was she willing to listen during a conversation, but she could contribute to it. She wasn't afraid to speak her mind, and she had held her own at the party, though he'd sensed it wasn't her usual crowd. She wasn't a pushover and Blake respected that, which was why he was attracted to her.

Just thinking about her again made Blake's mouth tug up in a smile, and he felt a tightening deep in his body. Although he typically never revisited a woman once he closed the door behind him, with Asia, Blake felt like he wanted to. If he attempted to contact to her, how would she respond? Would she slam the door in his face or pull him into her embrace so he could feast on every inch of her delectable body? There was only way to find out—he would have to see her again.

Once they arrived at XS Nightclub, which Teagan and Egypt had selected, the Gems were ushered into a roped-off VIP booth area with full access to the club. Decorated in rich gold, black and bronzes, the club was spectacular. It featured an oversize DJ booth and large dance floor. A waitress immediately came over to introduce herself to their group and let them know she'd be handling their service.

Teagan ordered a couple of bottles of champagne and several other spirits, but, quite frankly, Asia wasn't feeling it. She was going to avoid drinking tonight. The stomach bug she hadn't been able to shake wasn't going away. And if she was being honest, it was more than that. She was heartsick.

It had been almost two months and she'd thought she pushed her unresolved feelings for Blake into a locked box, along with the regrets that their time together hadn't gone beyond that night, but here she was, still mooning over a man who so clearly had forgotten her.

"Asia, honey, what's going on?" Shay asked, coming to her side after Wynter, Egypt, Teagan and Lyric escaped to the dance floor to move to "Black and Yellow" by Wiz Khalifa.

"Nothing." Asia shrugged. "This song isn't my jam."

Shay gave her a sideward glance. "Since when? You love to dance."

Asia was going to have to give Shay some version of the truth because her friend was relentless with the questions and it was starting to grate on her nerves. "If you must know, I have a lot on my mind."

"Want to talk about it?"

"Not really, but since you're like a dog with a bone, I have no choice."

Shay frowned and rose to her feet. "Hey, if you'd prefer to talk to someone else, it's fine with me."

Asia jumped up and touched Shay's arm. "I'm sorry, Shay. Listen." She tugged her friend back down to the couch. "I met someone a couple of months ago who I thought could be special. It was such a fun evening. And later, well—we ended up spending the night together. I thought it meant something, but the next morning, I woke up to find him gone with only a note to remember him."

"I'm sorry, Asia, that's terrible."

"It's not your fault, I had a lapse in judgment. I was fooled by a handsome face and rock-hard abs. I haven't been able to shake off feeling like I lost something important or maybe something that could have been more, ya know?"

Shay nodded. "I understand. I felt that way after my divorce from Kevin. Even though you guys were against it at the time, I thought we were meant to be. I listened to my gut and I was wrong."

Asia raised her hand. "Same here, and look it where it got me."

The waitress returned again with the cocktails the ladies had ordered and Asia felt her stomach roil. All of sudden, the club felt really hot and suffocating. "Asia, are you okay?" She heard Shay's voice, but it sounded far away.

Quickly, with as much energy as she could muster, Asia rushed out of the VIP section and toward the private restrooms that came with their special access. Asia was thankful it was empty because she puked out the remnants of their elaborate dinner. Minutes later, she heard Shay's soft voice.

"Asia, it's me, let me in."

After flushing the toilet, washing her hands and rinsing out her mouth, Asia opened the door only to hear Shay say, "Are you sure you're not pregnant?"

Four

Asia finished out the rest of the bachelorette weekend with half-hearted smiles and forced cheerfulness. No way would she ruin Wynter's moment with the possibility she could be pregnant by a stranger she spent one incredible night with, only to have him leave her high and dry the next morning.

Ever since Shay dropped the bombshell that she could be pregnant, Asia hadn't been able to think of anything else, aside from and the implications the situation could have for her and her dreams of opening her own store. Instead, Asia put on the brightest smile she could at the airport as they all said their goodbyes and gushed about Wynter's upcoming wedding, which was a few months away.

But Shay knew otherwise, and before Asia had boarded

the private jet Wynter had procured to take them both back to her home to San Antonio, she'd whispered, "Please take a test." Wrapping her arms around Asia, she'd said, "Whatever the results, we'll all be here for you."

"Thank you," Asia had whispered back. "I appreciate that."

Asia had been too afraid to take a test in Vegas for fear she wouldn't be able to hide her reaction if the results weren't in her favor. If she was pregnant, she needed to digest the news alone. Although she loved the Gems, they would all have different opinions and viewpoints, none of which she wanted to hear right now. Asia needed to hear her own voice so she could make the best decision for her future.

And so she'd remained mum, hugging and kissing each of them as they'd said their goodbyes. It was only when she was in her economy seat on the plane on her way back to Denver that the enormity of the situation hit Asia. She could be *pregnant*! It had never occurred to her, because her periods had always been irregular. She hadn't thought the stomach bug was anything other than just that. A virus she couldn't shake.

It's not as if she never wanted to be a mother, but she also wasn't eager at the prospect. And most definitely wasn't keen on doing it without the father. Asia knew what it was like growing up without a male presence in her life, and she didn't want that for her child. The thought, though, that she could have created a life from that one night was mind-blowing.

Asia stopped off at the drugstore on her way back to her apartment. She purchased five tests, each from a different manufacturer, to be sure of the results. She'd always been extra careful when she'd been intimate with a man because she'd seen what could happen when you weren't. Once, when she was about ten years old and her mother was seeing one of her string of boyfriends, Asia remembered Ava having a pregnancy scare. Afterward, her mother had drilled it into Asia: if she was going to have sex, she had to be safe and ensure the man wore a condom.

Had the condom broke? Is that why she was in this position?

Because she'd been swept up in the romance of the night, and now, she had to live with the consequences. After dropping her suitcase in the hall, Asia rushed into the bathroom with the brown bag. She'd waited for over twenty-four hours to find out if she was having a baby and the agony of it had nearly killed her. It was time she put herself out of her misery and find out one way or the other.

Ten minutes later, she had her answer.

She'd taken all five tests and they all said the same thing: she was pregnant.

Asia slid off the toilet seat and onto the ceramic tile floor. What the hell was she going to do? She was barely equipped to deal with her own life and it had taken nearly a year to feel prepared enough to start pursuing opening her own jewelry store, but a baby?

A baby didn't factor into her plans. She had so much more she wanted to do in life before becoming a mother, and yet…her hand flew to her stomach. This time, Asia was unable to stop the flood of tears that started raining down her cheeks at the realization that she and Blake created a life in that one amazing night of passion.

Omigod!

Asia bowed her head and cradled it in her hands. She was overwhelmed. She wanted to call the other Gems, but she couldn't. No one could figure this out for her. She was going to have to put on her big-girl panties and make a decision, but it was daunting. Asia never thought she'd be in this position, and certainly not as a single mother.

Did she even want the baby? The alternative was not a possibility she wanted to consider. How could she not have her baby? She was approaching thirty. Who knew if she would get another chance at becoming a mom? But to do so alone was a scary prospect.

She would sleep on it and decide later. She knew she would have to make a decision either way because time wasn't on her side.

The next morning, Asia woke up exhausted. She'd tossed and turned in bed all night, but with the dawning light, she'd come to realize that she wanted her baby. No matter how the pregnancy had come to be, she couldn't get rid of the baby. Although she hadn't planned on becoming a mother this way, she had to accept that fate had other ideas. As soon as the clock struck 8:00 a.m., Asia called her doctor and made an appointment. She had no openings until Friday, so that would have to do.

In the meantime, it was Monday and she had a big meeting at 10:00 a.m. to prepare for. She had an appointment with a bank representative to discuss a loan for the opening of her own store. Determinedly, Asia put her pregnancy thoughts aside and showered and dressed. She didn't own any power suits, but she had a black pencil skirt and black blazer that would work in a pinch. She teamed them with a fuchsia silk shirt that tied at the nape of her neck, simple hoop earrings and her favorite pair of black slingbacks.

Over the past couple of months, Asia had gotten her ducks in a row to be sure she could present a solid business proposal to the bank for Six Gems. When she'd thought about what to call the store, Asia had known that no other name would do but the nickname for her and her sista friends. She was hoping to use the two-hundred-and-fifty-thousand-dollar inheritance she'd received from Wynter's aunt Helaine and her modest savings account as collateral to secure the loan.

After packing her satchel with her business proposal and bank statements, Asia headed downstairs to her Hyundai. Traffic was bumper to bumper, but Asia had allotted herself extra time to ensure a timely arrival to the bank. After parking in the garage, she walked confidently into her meeting with the bank representative.

Despite having all her facts and figures in order, and a solid business proposal that Egypt had looked over, the bank still turned her down.

"What do you mean?" Asia asked, thirty minutes later, after she concluded her presentation.

"I'm sorry, Ms. Reynolds, you have a very sound proposal, but you want us to loan you a half a million dollars for a business that, quite frankly, is a tough market. Jewelry brands succeed based on their reputation, and you're new to the market."

"I've shown you my online and cash sales."

"And they are quite brisk, but not enough to sustain a brick-and-mortar store," the balding middle-aged sandy-brown-haired man stated.

"Let me get this straight. I have over a quarter of a million dollars and fifty thousand in my savings in collateral and you still won't invest in me?"

The man nodded. "I'm sorry. We have very stringent guidelines for start-up businesses."

Asia picked up her bound presentation and pushed it into her satchel. She didn't understand. She had a sound business plan, but they were still turning her down? "Thank you for your time." Asia didn't bother to shake his hand as she left his office. She was devastated.

All her hopes and dreams were going up in flames.

First an unexpected pregnancy, and now this? Could it get any worse? She threw her satchel on the passenger-side seat of her Hyundai and glanced at her phone. The answer was yes. A call was coming in from her mother, Ava, who undoubtedly needed a handout, as she always did. Why did Asia have to be the parent and not the child? All her life, she had been taking care of Ava, not the other way around.

"Yes, Mama, what can I do for you?" Asia asked in a weary tone when she answered the call. It wasn't even noon yet.

"Don't sound so happy to speak to me," Ava Reynolds replied.

"I'm sorry. It's been a bad morning."

"Yeah, well, we all have those days," her mother responded, "me included. Listen, baby girl, I'm a little short on rent this month and I was hoping you could lend me a few bucks until payday."

"Mama, what happened to your paycheck?"

"I needed incidentals," Ava replied. Asia knew what those incidentals entailed. Instead of paying her rent,

Ava had spent her money on new hair, clothes or shoes because she was a notorious spendthrift.

"I've heard that before."

"Don't sass me, Asia. I did right by you, didn't I? When everyone wanted me to give you up, my mama included, I kept you with me."

Sometimes Asia wondered if her mother should have given her up at sixteen, when she'd found out she was pregnant. Maybe then she might have been adopted and had a better life rather than the constant rat race and moving from pillar to post.

"Yeah, Mama. How much do you need?"

"A couple of hundred," her mother replied.

Asia rolled her eyes and sucked in a breath. "A couple of hundred? I'm not made of money."

"What are you talking about? You got all the money from Wynter's old lady. You can't help your mama out?"

Of course she would, because that's what Asia did. She bailed Ava out of her troubles. As for her personal troubles, she was on her own. Ava wasn't the type of mother she could confide in and talk to about her unexpected pregnancy, because she only thought of herself. "Fine. I'll send it once I get to work."

She was tired of being the responsible one. All her life, she'd dealt with Ava's lack of judgment, when it came not only to men, but to finances. Asia didn't know why she thought the situation would ever change. Her mother was a basket case.

Blake headed into the offices of Coleman & Sons Construction feeling accomplished. He had finally made headway with the zoning board on the residential development he wanted to build featuring nearly six hundred homes. It was big deal for the company, which Blake was determined to turn into an empire.

He was proud of the company that had been handed down to him. In the seventies, his grandfather Anthony Coleman had started the company as just Coleman Construction with mostly residential homes. The company flourished after Anthony secured his first lucrative contract with the city of Denver. Once Blake's father, Gil, came aboard, the venture became Coleman & Sons Construction, and Gil grew what had started as a lucrative small-time operation into a multimillion-dollar business. But then both Blake's parents were killed by a drunk driver, ending his father's success streak.

Blake had only been twelve at the time and too young to take the mantle. He was thankful his aunt Sadie, a savvy businesswoman in her own right, running her own chain of soul food restaurants, had taken the mantle. Although unfamiliar with the industry, she'd found the right people to keep the company afloat for nearly a decade, until Blake graduated from Stanford University and was finally able to take his rightful spot at the helm of Coleman & Sons Construction.

It was Blake's birthright, and he was determined to do right by the company. In the past decade, he'd turned the company into a billion-dollar enterprise, branching out from construction to develop residential and retail properties. Business was booming and Blake couldn't be happier, but there were times as he walked the plush carpeted halls, past the pictures of his grandfather and father on the wall, that Blake wished his parents were alive to see his accomplishments.

Who would he pass the mantle to?

Blake was so deep in thought that he walked past his assistant Martha's desk with barely a hello. It was only when he turned on his computer and his calendar came up that he realized what day it was. Rolling his executive chair across the mat, he glanced through the open door to see balloons taped to her chair and a big bouquet of flowers sitting on her desk. Okay, so a call to the florist was out of the question.

And then he remembered where he could go to purchase a gift for Martha: Yvette's Jewels. For days, he'd been telling himself he would go back and see Asia, but he had chickened out instead. Blake would never admit it to anyone, but he was afraid of the effect the pint-size beauty had on him after only one night. He hadn't been able to forget her smile and the way her eyes lit up when she talked about her jewelry. Or the incredible soft moans she'd uttered when he'd been buried deep inside her sweet heat.

If he was going to do this, he needed to go now, before he changed his mind. Plus, he had to get something for Martha, who put up with his mood swings, the late nights, and brushing off unwanted women who might call or stop by the office thinking they might make inroads through her. Martha didn't play that and they were shown the door. So yes, he was going to do this.

He was going to see Asia again. *But how will she react?* She would probably refuse to meet him, but if she didn't, he was certain he was in for a verbal reaming out. Could he blame her? He hadn't ended the evening on the best note. He'd escaped like a thief in the night, and now he had to face the music.

Five

Asia pulled into the store's parking lot just before noon, feeling completely dejected. She hadn't told Yvette where she was going that morning, only that she had some important business matters to address. Yvette had understood and told her she could come in when she was finished, but all Asia wanted to do was crawl under a rock.

As she parked her Hyundai Sonata in her usual parking space, Asia thought about how nothing in her life was going right. Not her career, and certainly not her relationships. And now she found herself knocked up by her one-night stand. Turning off the ignition, Asia took a deep breath and tried to calm her nerves.

It didn't help when she looked at her phone and saw a text from Egypt. How did it go? Asia had forgotten she told Egypt about the meeting with her bank. She regretted it because not only had Asia let herself down, she'd let down Egypt, who had put in a lot of time and effort helping Asia with her business plan.

She'd have to deal with Egypt later. Right now, she had to get to work while she still had a job to support herself. Asia pasted a bright smile on her face as she walked inside.

"Good morning, Asia," Yvette said cheerfully.

"Good morning, Yvette."

"After you settle in, I'd like to have a chat with you, if you have a moment?"

"Of course." Asia walked to the back of the store to put down her belongings. She hoped Yvette didn't suspect that she was thinking of leaving. Asia couldn't afford to lose this job. She needed time to figure out her next move.

When she returned to the front of the store, she found Yvette wiping down the glass displays. "You wanted to see me?" Asia inquired.

"Yes, I was hoping to discuss a proposition with you," Yvette said, smiling as she walked toward her.

"Oh yeah? What did you have in mind?"

"Well, you know I've had Yvette's Jewels over twenty years now and I'm getting on in age."

"Oh, you don't look a day over fifty," Asia said, even though she knew her boss was approaching sixty-five.

Yvette grinned. "I appreciate that, but it's time for me to enjoy life. Recently, I met someone. His name is Melvin. He's a retired navy man who I absolutely adore and he wants to travel the world. So I'm going to chuck it all and go for it."

Asia felt her eyes grow wide with shock. She couldn't lose this job. "But what about the store?"

"Well, that's where you come in."

Asia's brow furrowed. "I don't understand."

"I was hoping you might be willing to take over. Or, to clarify, buy me out."

"Are you serious?" Asia asked. She didn't know why it had never occurred to her that Yvette might retire or consider selling her the store. This would solve all her problems. She wouldn't have to buy or lease her own store, because Yvette paid for the building outright years ago.

"Of course I'm serious," Yvette responded, cradling Asia's cheek with her palm. "I believe in you, my dear. I always have. You have great potential, not only to be a great designer, but a business owner as well."

Tears threatened to fall from Asia's eyes at Yvette's kind words. She'd always looked up to the older woman as a mentor, but the opportunity she was offering Asia was nothing short of miraculous, especially after the week she'd had. "How much are you looking for for the store?"

"Well, since I own the building and the business, I'm thinking about half a million," Yvette said. "Between my late husband's pension and my Social Security, that would set me up pretty nicely."

Asia released a weary sigh. She didn't have enough to buy Yvette's store outright. She was back to square one. How was she supposed to come up with the other quarter of a million dollars? "Can I have some time to figure this out?"

"Of course. I know I'm springing this on you out of

the blue. I wanted you to know where my head is and give you the opportunity before I seek out other buyers."

"I appreciate you, Yvette. Thank you so much." Asia leaned in to give the older woman a hug. She didn't know how she was going to make it work, but perhaps with a little time and luck, she could figure it out. There were always other banks. For now, she would regroup because there was no way she was letting an opportunity like this slip through her fingers.

Blake walked confidently into Yvette's Jewels, but he felt far from it. He didn't usually revisit one-night stands, but Asia was the exception. There was something about her he couldn't turn away from. He had to see her, preferably alone.

However, when he arrived, he found that the store had several customers. The older woman he'd seen before was chatting with two women, and then there was Asia. Her head was bent as she opened a display to show a man one of her pieces. She was so engrossed in their conversation, she hadn't noticed him walk in. It gave Blake time to eat her up with his eyes. Asia wore a bright orange peplum top that stopped right at her waist and allowed him a generous view of her plump bottom, clad in skinny jeans. She'd completed the look with strappy sandals and bold accessories, presumably from her collection. Did she always wear heels?

What Blake didn't like was this male customer taking up so much of her time, or the way Asia smiled at him. And when she flicked her dark-brown medium-length hair over her shoulder, Blake frowned. She was flirting. Could he blame her? If it sold a piece of jewelry, what harm was there?

And it wasn't as if he had a leg to stand on. He owed her an apology for skipping out after their night in bed, but it wasn't something he was used to doing. He might have been a coward that night, but he wasn't one now. Standing up straight, Blake walked toward the duo as they laughed about something Asia must have said.

When she glanced up and saw Blake, her smile faded and she looked if she'd seen a ghost. Seconds later, her eyes narrowed and shot daggers at him. Blake suspected he'd be dead if she had anything to do with it. But then she blinked and resumed speaking to her customer with the fakest of smiles. Blake wouldn't be deterred. He would wait until they were done.

And, of course, it took Asia an extraordinary amount time to help the customer select a piece and ring him up, so much so, that the rest of the store cleared out and the older woman whom Blake had met during his first visit quickly helped him find some earrings from Asia's collection to take back to Martha. When she was finished, she headed to the back of the store.

Blake glanced over at Asia. "Have a great day," she said, handing the customer a bag. "I hope your wife likes the piece."

"Oh, I'm certain she will. You do great work, so you'll be seeing us again."

This time, when Asia smiled, it was a genuine one.

Once the door closed, it was finally just the two of them. "Alone at last," Blake said aloud.

Asia looked at him. "What do you want, Blake? A quick romp in the supply closet?" she inquired.

Ouch. He deserved that.

"Listen…"

She held up a hand. "No. I don't have to *listen* to a damn thing. I think the note you left almost two months ago said enough." He noticed that she stayed behind the counter as if she were afraid of coming near him.

"Did it say I made a mistake?" Blake inquired. "A mistake I've regretted all this time."

"You don't have to feed me that line of bull, Blake. I get it, okay? I'm a big girl. You were looking for a good time and we had it. Plain and simple. So why don't we leave the past in the past and move on."

She turned away and left the counter, giving Blake the window he needed to get in front of her, to *touch* her again, and that's exactly what he did. He grasped her hand just as she walked past him. The instant they touched, a spark flew up his arm, and Blake glanced at Asia.

She felt it, too, but she snatched her hand away. "Don't touch me!"

"Don't be this way, Asia."

"Like what, a woman scorned?" Asia asked, turning to face him. "What did you expect? You left in the middle of the night without a word."

Blake lowered his head. Her derision was warranted. "I'm sorry. I didn't handle things well that night." He glanced around to make sure no other patrons had come in. "We had such an amazing night and hit it off so well, it kind of threw me for a loop, and I ran. But I promise you, I haven't forgotten you. I mean, you're unforgettable." He offered a dashing smile that usually worked with the ladies, but Asia wasn't buying what he was selling.

"Thanks, but no thanks."

She went to move past him again, but he stepped in front of her. "Asia, c'mon. I admit I acted like a complete ass a couple of months ago, but I'm here now, admitting I made a mistake and asking for a do-over."

"No! Don't you get it, Blake? You hurt me and…and I—I can't do this! Not today!" Asia pushed past him and rushed toward the employees-only section of the store.

Blake stared at her retreating figure and wondered what to do next. He was used to things going his way in life. He was Blake Coleman, after all. There were tons of women in this town who wanted him, who would kill to have him here begging for a second chance, but none of them were Asia—the *only* woman he was interested in pursuing.

Lord, why? Asia asked, looking up to the ceiling as she found her way to the closest chair and sank into it. *Why would you send my baby daddy here today to try to make amends when I already have so many pans in the fire?* Wasn't it enough that she'd been punched in the gut by the bank, only for Yvette to offer her a lifeline she wasn't exactly in the position of taking?

And now Blake?

He was here. Or at least he had been before she told him to go take a hike. He was singularly the best lover she'd ever had, but it was so much more than that. The one amazing night they'd spent together had created a life. Asia placed her hand over her still-flat stomach. *She was pregnant with Blake's baby.*

Why did she still feel butterflies in the pit of her stomach at seeing him again? He looked as enticing as ever in a black suit with a crisp white shirt and purple-striped tie. Those dark, smoldering eyes had ensnared hers as soon as she saw him in the store. And those lips. She knew what he could do with them. Jesus, what was wrong with her? She shouldn't feel anything for a man who treated her so callously, but tell that to her hormones, which were firing on all cylinders. Her sex literally clenched when he spoke.

It's not as if he wanted a relationship with her. He probably wanted another night in the sack. Well, she wasn't some booty call he could look up when the mood struck. She was a woman with feelings, which he'd trampled when he told her to find her own way home, albeit in a hired car. Asia couldn't—wouldn't—forgive that. She deserved to be with someone kind, caring and totally into her, like Riley was into Wynter or Garrett adored Egypt. She wanted a love like that, and she wouldn't settle for less, not even with her Prince Charming for the night.

Asia glanced up and noticed Yvette in the doorway.

"Omigod." Yvette sighed. "Don't I recognize that young man I saw leaving? He's absolutely gorgeous."

"We met here," Asia answered, even though a stone was in pit of her stomach. "He was looking for a gift for his aunt's birthday and I sold him a piece from my new collection."

"Oh yes, I remember. He's not a man a woman could easily forget."

"No, he's not." Truer words were never spoken. Unforgettable and totally unavailable. And the father of her unborn child. *What a disaster.*

Yvette came toward her and squeezed Asia's hand. "I told you, you're headed for success. You'll see."

Asia was headed toward something, but it wasn't success. She'd just collided with a meteor in the form of Blake Coleman. Despite her protestations to the contrary, there was unfinished business between them. And not about the baby. She wasn't ready to tell him she was carrying his child, but there was still sexual tension between them that hadn't abated, and something told Asia she wasn't going to come away from this unscathed.

Six

When Asia finally made it home after 6:00 p.m., she knew she had to FaceTime her friends and tell them she was pregnant, but Egypt beat her to the punch by calling her first.

Asia answered immediately and was surprised to see the other Gems on the screen, too. "Hey, ladies," Asia said. "What's going on?"

Egypt held up her left hand. "I'm engaged!" she shouted into the phone.

Asia wasn't surprised; Egypt had been enthralled with Garrett from day one. Why did everyone else get their happy endings and not her?

"Omigod!" While there were cheers and screams of delight from Wynter, Shay, Lyric and Teagan, tears started falling down her cheeks. She remained quiet.

"Asia, sweetheart—" Egypt said. "Is everything okay?" Asia shook her head.

"Whatever it is, you can tell us," Egypt responded.

"I can't! It's your moment."

"Asia, we're all here for you. Just tell us," the other women chorused.

"I'm pregnant!" Asia blurted out, plopping down on the couch. She couldn't hold it in any longer.

Most of the women were silent, except for Shay. "How far along?"

"Ten weeks," Asia replied.

"Is the father the man you had the one-night stand with?"

Asia nodded. "And he's back. He came to the store today all apologetic for how he left things between us two months ago. Told me he handled things poorly and wanted a second chance."

"And what did you say? Did you tell him about the baby?" Shay asked.

"Of course not," Asia responded. "I was so floored to see him I was damn near speechless. I don't know what I'm going to do."

"Do you need us to come?" Egypt asked, "I can be there soon."

"No, you just got engaged," Asia said. "Bask in your happiness. I'll have to figure this out on my own."

"You don't have to," Lyric said. "We can be there. I'll rearrange my schedule."

"Don't," Asia responded. "I just need some time to digest all of this."

"Are you sure?" Teagan asked.

Asia nodded. "I have to go." She quickly ended the

call. She pulled her knees up to her chest and started to cry again, but her cell rang. This time, it was Shay.

"Asia, I'm worried about you, especially with the baby's father back in the picture. How did you leave things?"

"Well…he asked me for a second chance to redo the mistakes of the past."

"And what did you say?"

"I said no, of course, but…"

"But what?"

"Seeing him again…" She didn't finish her thought. She couldn't tell Shay she was scared of the way he made her feel. Scared that she wanted him to touch her again even though she should be pushing him away. But being like a sister to her, she saw it in her face; Shay knew already.

"C'mon, Asia. The guy strolls back into your life months later as if he has a right to be there? That's not right."

"I know it's not. And I gave him the business. I didn't let him off scot-free."

Shay's eyes pierced Asia's from across the screen. "Good—because he deserves it."

Asia understood what Shay was saying, but she couldn't deny that there was still chemistry there. She hung her head low and her eyes watered again. She was normally never this emotional, but she supposed the pregnancy hormones were making her this way.

"Asia. Look at me, please," Shay said. "You're not over him, are you?"

Asia shook her head. "I know it was just the one night, but I haven't been able to forget him, Shay. And now"—she shook her head—"I have a permanent reminder." She touched her stomach. "I'm carrying his child."

"A child he knows nothing about. Are you going to tell him?"

Asia shook her head again. "Not now. I have too much on my plate. I doubt he's interested in anything more than scratching an itch. He probably wants to see if the connection we shared was real or imagined. Maybe he's having trouble moving on, same as me."

"Asia, I fear if you go down this road, you'll only wind up getting hurt. You already have feelings for him."

"No," Asia stated adamantly. "Infatuation maybe, or lust. But that's all."

"I think you're fooling yourself," Shay said. "You need to be careful with your heart, Asia. If Blake is as smooth as you say, who knows what damage he can do if you let him in."

"I won't."

Shay cocked her head to side. She didn't look convinced.

"Thank you for the advice, Shay. I promise to be careful when it comes to Blake."

"If you need me or any of the Gems, let me know," Shay said. "You know we'll be there in a heartbeat."

"I know," Asia said, and ended the call. She may have grown up an only child, but she had the Gems, and they always had one another's backs. Asia suspected she might need them because she doubted she'd seen the last of Blake Coleman.

Later that evening, as he sat at home on the sofa swirling a glass of whiskey in his hand, Blake thought about the day. It hadn't exactly gone as he'd envisioned. He'd known it would be difficult seeing Asia after the way he left, but he hadn't realized how much he'd hurt her with his careless actions.

Maybe that's why he kept things light with the women he dated who knew the score. Asia may come off sassy and worldly, but there was a vulnerability in her that he'd seen today. It wouldn't be easy to get back into her good graces, yet he wanted to discover more about her. Usually, after sleeping with a woman, she lost some of that allure, but Asia Reynolds was special, and he didn't know why.

Work was usually everything for him because it was tied to his family and the legacy he had to continue, but since that night, it hadn't brought him joy. Instead, all he could think about was the storm of passion he'd found with Asia, and from the clench in his gut, he knew there was still a potent sexual chemistry between them. It had been an underlying current in their conversation today even though she feigned disinterest. She wasn't immune to him. She *did* want him. He just had to make her admit it.

If he continued to assault the defenses she put up, surely she would give in and agree to go out with him again? Blake was nothing if not persistent. He remembered the sweet sounds she made as they both sought mindless physical pleasure. And he wanted it again. When Blake wanted something, he usually got it, and with Asia, it would be no different. He would turn on his signature charm until Asia was putty in his hands.

The following day, after a small morning rush of customers had come and gone, the door to Yvette's Jewels opened, but Asia couldn't see who it was because they were hidden by a large bouquet of flowers.

"May I help you?" Asia inquired, coming over and finding a delivery man behind the flowers. He wore a shirt emblazoned with the logo of a local florist.

"I have a delivery for Asia Reynolds."

"That's me."

"Good!" He waved his hand forward and soon several men starting bringing in armloads of flowers by the dozen.

"Stop!" Asia told the men, but they kept bringing in more flowers until, minutes later, the entire store was filled with red and white roses.

"Sign here," the first delivery man instructed, holding out a clipboard to Asia.

"This is ridiculous," she said, signing the order. "You realize this is a place of business."

"I have my orders, ma'am. Here's the card." He handed her a white envelope and then he and his men left the store.

Asia glanced around the store in stunned disbelief. The fragrance of the roses perfumed the air. She didn't need to be a rocket scientist to figure out who had the money to buy out an entire florist. She left the lobby for a moment to open the card and read it in private. It said:

I'm sorry.
Please give me another chance
Blake

Suddenly, her cell phone rang in her pocket and the display read Blake. She'd never deleted his phone number. She answered on the second ring. "What the hell do you think you're doing?"

"Trying to win you back." Asia had heard the words, but not from her phone. She spun around and saw Blake in the doorway with a phone to his ear.

"Listen, I'm not trying to crowd you, but I do like you, Asia," Blake said. "And I know my behavior was appalling, but I'd like to redeem myself, if you'll let me."

Asia couldn't move, because she couldn't believe he was here again. He wasn't letting his foot off the gas in his offensive to win her over. Blake took a step toward her, closing the distance. She wanted to push him away—that's what she told herself was the wise move— but then her traitorous body allowed him to touch her.

It was the merest stroke of his palm to her cheek, but it was enough. That feeling she'd gotten when they'd first met—that he was someone special—came rushing back. It didn't hurt that she found him immensely attractive and devastatingly appealing, with his lean shoulders, dark curly hair and smoldering ebony eyes.

"Asia," he said in that deep tone she liked.

Asia could feel her heart rate increasing, especially when his long fingers tilted her face up and her eyes met his. She drowned in them just as she had that night. Helpless to break his gaze or step away, she knew with every female instinct what was about to happen next. And she let it.

As if in slow motion, Blake's head lowered and his mouth touched hers. Her eyes fluttered closed. His kiss was velvety soft, like silk, and she sighed when his mouth lingered several seconds. Asia didn't want the kiss to stop, but Blake drew away from her. Her eyes sprang open and she met the glint in his. Blood was roaring through her veins and her pulse had quickened from just that single kiss.

"It's still there, Asia," he whispered, looking down at her. "You can feel it, too, can't you? Have dinner with me Friday night and I promise the evening won't end as it did before."

"I…" Asia didn't get to finish because Yvette interrupted them.

"Asia, my darling, I was about to ask how my store became overrun with flowers, but I see you have company." Yvette gazed at Blake questioningly.

"I, uh…" Asia stammered, so Blake stepped forward.

"Blake Coleman, ma'am." He offered his hand and Yvette shook it.

"Yes, I remember you. Pleasure to see you again, Mr. Coleman," Yvette replied, "But I don't allow socializing during business hours and certainly not with grand displays of affection." She motioned around the room at the flowers.

He nodded. "My apologies for the interruption. I'll ensure the flowers are removed." Then he turned to Asia. "Are we on for dinner?"

Blake, and even Yvette, looked at her expectantly. He deserved for her to say no, but there was a part of her—the curious part that had to know if what she felt was real—that was eager to accept. "Yes."

His succulent lips curved into a smile and Asia's stomach dipped. She'd let Blake get to her again. She was in trouble.

"I look forward to it." Blake bowed his head and then he was gone.

"That young man has it bad for you," Yvette said. "Twice in one week, and now this over-the-top gesture? You'd better grab him up quick before another woman scoops him up."

It was Friday. Asia had thought about calling Blake and canceling several times throughout the week, but she had too much to do. She'd texted Egypt to let her know that the bank had turned her down. Egypt had offered her sympathy and told her not to give up. And Asia wasn't going to. She'd reached out to another local bank and set up a meeting for early next week. Her biggest appointment was this morning, when she met with her gynecologist, who confirmed she was indeed ten weeks pregnant. She gave Asia a prescription for prenatal vitamins and set up Asia's next appointment.

Asia was just wrapping her head around the confirmation of her pregnancy when she received a text from Blake asking for her address. She didn't want to give it to him. Didn't want him to know where she lived in case things went south and she needed to make a quick getaway, but Blake was insistent he pick her up and bring her home like a proper date—as if this was going to happen again.

It wasn't.

This was a onetime thing to clear the air between and put aside any lingering feelings that might be between them. Asia needed to get the man out of her system once and for all. She didn't tell Shay about the date because she didn't need a lecture or to hear she had to tell Blake about the baby. She would make her decision based on how the evening went.

When it was time to get ready, Asia made sure not to wear anything over the top. It was warm out for early June, so she settled on a mustard sheath dress that left one shoulder bare. The bodice was plain and cut across her cleavage, and the hemline fell right at her ankle. She added brown strappy sandals and simple makeup. She kept her hair in soft waves around her face.

Her doorbell rang right at 7:00 p.m. sharp, and Asia had to remind herself to breathe as she opened the door. Blake was on the other side looking resplendent in a superbly cut and tailored suit that showed off his impressive six-foot-plus height and lean masculinity. Asia found herself remembering what he looked like without any clothes on. She flushed immediately and glanced up to find Blake watching her.

He took a step back to admire her. "You look amazing, as always."

"Thank you. Let's go." Asia didn't need more pleasantries and suppressed the rush of heat in her veins when Blake placed his hand on the small of her back and allowed her to precede him out of the apartment.

Several minutes later, they were at the curb, and this time, unlike their first date, there was a hired car waiting for them. "I hope you don't mind," Blake said when she hesitated. "I wanted uninterrupted time with you."

Asia flickered a glance over her shoulder. "Of course not." She climbed in even though it was the opposite of what she wanted. If Blake were driving his attention would be divided, but now they had to share the confined space of the rear of the car with nothing but inches to separate them. She sat on the far side of the back seat so they didn't touch. She couldn't afford any slip-ups. She wanted to get through this evening as quickly as possible so she could figure out what she would do next about the baby and the man she had to get out of her system.

Seven

Blake eased back into the rear seat as Denver swirled around them. He was having a hard time sitting beside Asia without touching her. Her delicious scent, a hint of vanilla, flowers and coffee, intoxicated him, but he had to control his impulses. Tonight, he was taking Asia to his favorite French restaurant. The ambiance there was classy and the menu combined French and Mediterranean cuisine. When he had made the reservation, he'd requested one of the few booths available—the best table in the house.

He spared a fleeting glance at the woman at his side, who appeared to be engrossed in the passing scenery. Her averted gaze allowed him a view of her profile, and it arrested him. She was beautiful and sexy. Memories of their earlier kiss assailed him—her dark brown eyes gazing up at him when he cupped her face and tilted her face to his. How sweet she tasted when he placed a soft kiss on her lips. He'd wanted so much more, but they'd been in her place of business and he was still in the doghouse after his behavior months ago.

He had to prove to Asia that she could trust him; only then would she let down her guard and give him a chance. He wanted the Asia from his aunt's party, when she'd been open, warm and receptive to his attention. Right now, her expression was guarded and she was wary of him.

When they arrived at the restaurant, he cupped her elbow and led her inside. She'd softened at his touch, and he felt a satisfying ripple that she'd reacted that way. At least she wasn't as unaffected as she appeared to be.

"Mr. Coleman, so great to see you again," the svelte redhead hostess said when they approached the reservation desk. "Allow me to show you to your seat."

"Thank you," Blake said.

Asia swiftly walked in front of him, not allowing him to touch her again. She could act as if she wasn't interested in him, but her body said otherwise.

Once they were seated, he accepted the menu from the hostess and focused on the woman he'd been thinking about all afternoon. "Le Roux has a great menu. You can't go wrong with anything you order."

"Good, because I'm ravenous."

He remembered from the party that Asia wasn't one of those women who picked at salads, hardly eating when he was around. She was a real woman with a real appetite, and she wasn't afraid to show it.

The waiter arrived and Blake ordered a bottle of Do-

minus cabernet sauvignon, 2017, to go with their baked
Brie and escargots.

"No wine for me," Asia replied quickly.

"Are you sure? They could fix you a cocktail."

"Yes, I'm very sure. Sparkling water is quite enough."

Blake nodded and the waiter returned with her water
and the bottle of wine. After Blake tasted the selection,
he poured himself a glass.

"Tchin tchin." Blake held up his glass and Asia did
the same.

"I've never had escargot," Asia said after she'd
sipped her beverage.

"Trust me, you're going to love it," Blake responded.

Her brows raised at the word *trust* and it made Blake
realize how deeply he'd hurt her by his callous actions.

"I hope to change your opinion of me," Blake said.

"I'm not sure you can," Asia responded.

"Then why did you agree to dinner?"

"Because…" she began and then paused, "because
I'm trying to figure out if the person I met that night
was real or a figment of my overactive imagination."

"He's very much real and wants a second chance
with you."

"So you say, but I don't know anything about you,"
Asia said.

Blake hated this part of a date. The dreaded talk
about family and friends, of which he had very few, but
if it took dredging up the past to change the guarded
expression Asia wore, he would do it.

"All right," he sighed. "My parents, Daphne and Gil
Coleman, were wonderful parents and I had an amazing childhood until I was twelve years old and a drunk

driver plowed into their Mercedes-Benz, killing them both instantly. What most people don't know was that I was in the back seat, but yet somehow, I survived and was pulled from the wreckage."

"Omigod!" Asia's hands flew to her mouth. "I'm so sorry."

"You never looked me up?" Blake was surprised. Women nowadays tended to do a thorough background check online.

"It mentioned the accident, but not much more. I didn't delve too much," Asia replied. "I'm truly sorry for your loss."

"Thank you. And what about your parents?"

"What about them?" she asked a little too quickly.

"I dunno. I shared about mine. I thought you might want to reciprocate." He sipped his wine and regarded her over the rim. She was clearly uncomfortable at the mention of family. Was she hiding something?

The waiter came back with their hors d'oeuvres and, instead of answering, Asia cut into the delicate puff pastry and added some Brie and apples to small pieces of toast that accompanied the dish. When she slid a bite into her delectable mouth and made a tiny little moan of appreciation, Blake felt his trousers tighten in response.

Easy boy, he told himself.

After she finished chewing, she wiped her mouth and finally answered him. "There's not much to tell about my family. My mother is a mess who can't keep a job, an apartment or a man, and not necessarily in that order. As for my father, I have no idea who he is and neither did my mother because she was the neighborhood hottie and hooked up with several men."

He put down his wineglass. "Asia, I'm sorry."

She shrugged. "I'm used to cleaning up after Ava. You see, my mother has trouble taking care of herself. I had to grow up quickly and learn how to fend for myself."

"You shouldn't have had to."

"Yeah, well, that shows how different we are, because there's a lot of Avas where I come from."

He frowned. "Are you trying to pick a fight?"

"I'm just explaining that we don't mesh."

"Except in bed."

The minute he said the words, Blake knew he'd overstepped, because her eyes narrowed. "And you're looking for a redo?"

"No," Blake replied. "Well, yes, but not right now. Jesus, I'm making a mess of this. Asia, we don't have to be on opposite sides. There can be common ground between us. Like the fact that you want to be a businesswoman and I own my own business, or, rather, my family's company."

"I want my own store one day," Asia said, "but it's not been easy to get there."

"Your designs are amazing!"

"The bank doesn't care about that. They see it, or, rather, me, as a risk they're not willing to gamble on."

"Then they're wrong," Blake said. "And who cares what one bank says. There's many out there, and if that doesn't work, you get investors. In no way do you give up on your dreams, Asia Reynolds. If you do, you'll always regret it."

She stared back at him, and for the first time that night, Blake felt as if he'd made a breakthrough. Asia seemed genuinely surprised that he was encouraging her dreams. And he would continue to because she was talented.

Asia was more than a little bit stunned at Blake's impassioned speech. When she looked into his face, all she could see was honesty. No one had ever thought that highly of her. Back in high school, her teachers had always looked at Teagan and Wynter as the smart ones.

Asia had always lagged behind, probably because she wasn't sure what she would be coming home to. Would there be food? Would the lights be on? Or would there be a notice from the landlord for late rent posted on their door for the entire neighborhood to see? Either way, Asia had always felt less than. But not tonight; Blake made her believe that anything was possible.

"Thank you," she said.

He frowned. "For what?"

"For believing in me."

The waiter brought their entrées, interrupting their conversation, and they tucked into their respective dishes, coq au vin for Asia and duck à l'orange for Blake.

Asia glanced in Blake's direction. She felt gauche for never having tried duck, either, and glanced at his plate. He must have sensed her desire to taste the dish because he cut off a piece of meat and held out his fork. Asia leaned over the table and, never taking her eyes off Blake, slid the morsel into her mouth. The orange flavor burst on her tongue.

"That's delicious," she said.

He grinned. "Glad you like it."

Their conversation morphed from food into Blake

telling Asia how his aunt had held the reins of her brother's company until he graduated college. "Sadie is a remarkable woman."

Blake nodded his agreement. "She isn't the only one."

His gaze met hers and held. His expression was intense, and Asia braced herself as his eyes raked over her face. The physical attraction between them was electrifying, like a live spark that sizzled over her skin. Asia's tongue darted out to wet her suddenly dry lips and Blake's eyes narrowed, his pupils dilating. Asia nearly stopped breathing, but then he cleared his throat and blinked because the waiter had returned to the table.

"Dessert, coffee?" the waiter inquired.

"No," Blake said, shaking his head. "I have something else in mind, but I'll take the bill."

And there it was. He wanted to take her bed. The look he'd given her told Asia he hadn't changed. Why had she thought otherwise? She watched Blake close out the bill and then rise to his feet.

"Ready?"

Asia nodded. She was furious with herself for thinking tonight would be different. But could she blame him? By looking at him as if he were a double scoop of chocolate fudge ice cream, she'd sent mixed messages that she was ready for anything on offer. And she was. Her body was saying yes, she wanted this man in any way possible, but her head warned her it would be a mistake. He had no idea of the secret she was carrying, and Asia didn't plan on filling him in anytime soon. Although Blake had said and done the right things throughout the meal, she still wasn't sure she could trust him. She didn't know when the time would be right, but it wasn't tonight.

Once back in the car, she was silent as she thought about how best to tell Blake nothing was going to happen between them, when she realized they weren't on the way back to her place.

Asia glanced at him. "Where are we going?"

Blake turned to her. "There's a great little speakeasy in town. I thought we could listen to some music and talk some more."

As she looked into Blake's molten chocolate eyes, Asia was stunned. She'd assumed that after the lustful glances he'd given her at dinner, he was going to try to take her to bed. Was she demonizing him to avoid repeating their illicit fantasy, which they'd turned into real life one night two months ago?

Lord, she was so in over her head.

Thirty minutes later, after giving the special code, they were shown through two doors, up to the speakeasy, where the staff were all dressed in period attire. The decor was dark, yet included unique vintage furnishings.

The ceiling of the bar displayed art deco murals and the barstools were wrapped in leather. Behind the counter, there was every liquor imaginable and nothing Asia could partake in. That was the hardest part about being pregnant, including the weird cravings. She'd thought there was no way on God's green earth she would ever try snails, but she had and *liked* them. Then there were the intermittent bouts of morning sickness, which weren't a joy.

The host directed them to an area with curtains, which she opened to reveal an enclosed booth. It was private and romantic and exactly what Asia didn't need, with her wayward hormones telling her to rip all of Blake's clothes off and have her way with him.

"This is very intimate," Asia said, taking a seat.

"Is that a problem?" Blake inquired.

Asia inhaled deeply. So, they were playing a game of chicken to see which one of them had the most resolve? Well, she did. "Not a problem at all."

A waitress in a 1920s getup, complete with hair styled in a wavy bob pinned back at the sides, gave them a menu. Since she couldn't drink, Asia immediately went for the delicious-looking desserts. They ordered a fondue platter with an assortment of delicious accompaniments to dip in chocolate, while Blake ordered a drink called Living la Vida Loca. Asia hated to think what happened when you had too many of those.

Blake leaned back on the couch. "Have I proven to you tonight isn't about getting you horizontal?"

Asia laughed. "The night is still young."

"Touché. So why don't you tell me why you aren't drinking? Is there some horrible story about having one too many?"

Asia's stomach dropped. It wasn't as if she could blurt out, *I'm having your baby.* She had to think fast on her feet and decided to go with a version of the truth. "Recently, I had to take care of my mother after she passed out at a bar," It wasn't exactly a lie. It had happened, but that was some years ago. Ava had cleaned up her act, but she still couldn't stay on the straight and narrow. "I guess, since then, I've developed an aversion to drinking."

"Is it problem that I'm having one?"

She shook her head. "Go ahead. It's not your hang-up. It's mine."

Just then, the waitress returned with his Living la Vida Loca and another drink for her. "I didn't order that," Asia said, frowning at the drink.

"It's a virgin of the drink," the waitress said.

Asia smiled. "Oh, okay, thank you," she said, and the waitress nodded before moving on to another table.

Asia locked eyes with Blake. "Cheers." She held up the glass and Blake clinked it against his.

"Has your mother always been irresponsible?"

Asia nodded. "Ava is a spendthrift. She can't save or budget to save her life. As soon as the money comes in, it's going out. When I was, I don't know, six or seven, I started taking money out of her purse for groceries just to make sure I had food because she never remembered how much money she had. If I didn't, who knew if I would have food or the lights would be on when I got home from school."

"That's terrible. I'm sorry you had to endure it," Blake said. "You didn't have any other family to step in?"

"My grandmother disowned my mother when she was pregnant, and she was an only child. It's always just been me and Mama. And sometimes her boyfriends."

Blake sat up, on high alert. "Did any of them touch you?"

Asia didn't answer and put down her drink. This wasn't a topic she was comfortable sharing, but Blake reached across the short distance between them in the booth and grasped her hand. "Tell me," he said, his voice gentle but firm.

She'd never liked people telling her what to do, but with Blake, she didn't mind, because she saw genuine concern in his eyes. "Usually, I didn't have any problems with Mama's boyfriends."

"But…"

"As I got older and started to develop, a couple of her boyfriends thought they were getting two-for-ones. One of them…pushed me down and…" Tears sprang to her eyes. "But then Ava saw them and came at him with a butcher knife and threatened to cut off an unmentionable part."

He grasped both sides of her face. "Thank God you were one of the lucky ones." With the pad of his thumb, he swiped away her tears. The light caress singed through her skin to the most elemental part of her being. Asia lifted her chin and Blake dipped his head, giving Asia time to object, but she didn't, couldn't, because she wanted him to settle his lips on hers.

When he did, she opened her mouth instinctively, letting him in. She closed her eyes and focused on the velvety warmth of his lips. At every lush caress of his mouth on hers, Asia felt her reasoning dissipate and her resistance melt. She craved closer contact. She wanted to meld with him, chest to breast, thigh to thigh, as they had that night. She angled her head and his lips plundered hers, exploring the recesses of her mouth. He sipped at her lips, tangling his tongue with hers until she moaned.

He drew back and she knew her eyes had to be glassy, because she felt dazed. "I want you, Asia, and

I believe you want me, but I need to know you're on board. There's no pressure here. We can end the night with dessert and I drop you back at your place without touching you, without kissing you."

"Or?" she asked breathlessly, knots coiled tight in her belly.

"Or we leave *now*"—his eyes were bright as they burned right through hers—"and we go back to your place and we make love. Every way. Any way. In fact, I know exactly how I'm going to make you come. But if you want me to stop, please say so."

Asia thought about Blake. His scent, his texture, his taste, was so addictive that she didn't know if she could go her entire life without being with him just once more. It was oh so tempting. At least this time, she would be going in with her eyes wide open and not looking at him as some Prince Charming come to life. She was a grown woman with needs and she could own them.

She rose to her feet and held out her hand. "Let's go back to my place."

Eight

Blake had caught the covert glances Asia had given him all night and he'd let them go be because he was focused on undoing the damage he'd done. But with her proposition at the speakeasy, Asia had made it abundantly clear that she wanted him as much as he wanted her. It made the reason they would be together simple. And now, in the rear of the hired car, it was all he could do not to take her right there on the back seat. But he didn't want it to be rushed between them as it had been that first time. He wanted to take his time and savor every inch of her. Still, he had to have a taste. He threaded his fingers into her hair, tugged her head toward him and gave her a kiss, hot, demanding and hungry. As his equal, she plundered his mouth with fervor.

She fired him up and he couldn't wait to touch her, but he had to show restraint. He pulled back.

"What's wrong?" Asia inquired. "You change your mind?"

"Far from it. I'm trying to slow us both down so we don't burn out too quickly." They were both imprisoned together by their desire for each other. He knew what it was like to be buried deep inside Asia and he wanted it again. Ached for it.

"I don't need slow. I want it hard and fast." The honesty and rawness in her voice were evident. It gave Blake the license to feel what he'd felt the very first moment he'd laid eyes on her. No more delays. No holding back. He closed the gap between them and press her backward, against the seat. He held her gaze and then began nipping at her lower lip with light and gentle flicks. She gasped and he swallowed her gasp with his mouth.

Sensations exploded in his mouth. Asia's taste. Her scent was everywhere around him. It didn't stop there. He was drawn to her strength after the calamities she'd endured as a child, to her vulnerability, her sassiness and her sexiness. He wanted all of her. And so he leisurely trailed kisses from her lips to her cheekbones and to her jaw. And when he came to the base of her neck, he licked the soft skin there too, sucking her gently. She moaned, and desire swirled and grew stronger within him.

The car crunched slowly to the curb of her apartment and Blake reluctantly released Asia, but only as long as it took to slide out of the car. She accepted his outstretched hand with a natural elegance. Blake closed the door and nodded a good-night to his chauffeur. It was his cue that he wouldn't be needed for the rest of the night, and he took it.

Hand in hand, they walked to Asia's building, and once in the elevator, they devoured each other with their eyes. Something was starting to form and flow between them, something Blake wasn't used to. All he knew was that Asia was exquisite and so different from any other woman he'd ever been with.

"Asia."

The elevator chimed and she wordlessly led him to her front door. She trusted him, at least with her body, because tonight was on her terms. Blake wanted more than her body. He didn't know why; he just knew that he did.

When she scrambled, with trembling fingers, to put the key in the door, he took it from her. Opening the door, he let her step inside first, still giving her time to change her mind. But rather than change it, she reached for the lapels of his jacket and pulled him inside.

Blake swore under his breath as he kicked the door shut. He wanted to kiss her. Touch her. Lick her. Suck her. Ride her. And he intended to do all the above. All night long.

Asia didn't think about whether going to bed again with Blake was a good idea or not. She just knew she'd dreamed of this very moment for weeks—damn it, for months—and she would enjoy every minute. She didn't waste any time reaching behind her for the zipper of her one-shoulder dress, but then Blake approached her.

"Let me." He took her purse, dropping it in a nearby chair, and then ran his thumbs down her back. Her breathing accelerated when she heard the zipper open and felt the cool rush of air against her skin. The bodice dropped to reveal the lacy bustier she had underneath. She'd never been busty like her best friend Egypt, but her breasts were round and pert. She stepped out of the dress, leaving her in her undies.

"Beautiful." Blake traced the soft swell of her cleavage and then he spun her back around to clasp her face in his palms and cover her lips with his. His kiss was demanding and forceful, but it only sparked Asia into action. She was desperate for him, too, and pushed at his jacket until he shrugged out it. Then she was tugging his shirt out of his trousers, unbuttoning it as she went. She needed to feel him, and when her fingers reached his bare skin, Asia's eyes feasted on the ridged muscles of his six-pack. He was lean and impressively built.

She reached for his belt buckle, but he was quicker. Undoing the zipper, he opened his trousers to reveal tight boxer briefs that were molded to his thick erection. Asia's mouth watered. She wanted him inside her.

He lifted her chin. "Are you sure about this?"

She nodded. "Absolutely. I want to see the rest of you."

"With pleasure." He toed off his shoes and stripped off his boxer briefs until he was standing before her in all his magnificent, naked glory. Her lips curved into a smile. "Now it's your turn."

He came toward her and quickly unhooked the bustier, letting it fall to the floor. Her nipples tightened into brown peaks. Asia faced him again, and this time, it was she who removed the last of her undergarments. The look of naked hunger on Blake's face undid her, and when he dropped to his knees, she was floored. She hadn't expected that.

"I've been wanting to taste you all night long," Blake said, looking up at her. "And I'm going to do just that, but first let's remove these." He helped rid her of her strappy sandals.

Then he hooked one of Asia's legs over his shoulder and buried his face between her thighs. Asia shivered at the first swipe of his tongue against the seam of her sex. She thought she could take whatever Blake could dish out, but as soon as he plunged his tongue inside her, she tried to squirm away. Blake didn't let her.

He savored her like the fine wine he'd had at dinner. He strummed her with his tongue until her back arched and her breath caught in her throat. But he didn't stop there; he kept licking, flicking and nipping at her nub despite her desperate cries. And when that wasn't enough, he slid his finger inside her.

"Blake," she whispered.

"I like my name on your lips," he said, working his finger. "Say it again." He added another digit.

"Blake," she pleaded, her body shaking uncontrollably, but he added yet another.

"Louder." He bent forward and used both his mouth and fingers to torment her mercilessly. His tongue thrust deep and his fingers swirled, but he didn't abate. Asia clutched at his head, and only when she screamed his name and fell apart did he draw back from the exquisite torture.

He rose to his feet, wrapped his arm around her waist and lifted her limp body into his arms. Asia didn't protest. She couldn't wait to have him deep inside her.

* * *

Without any lights on, Blake found Asia's bedroom and laid her down on the duvet and joined her on the bed. If he hadn't left the living room, he would have taken her on *any surface*, just so he could sink into her. Tasting her sex had driven him wild with need.

Now, on the bed, he feasted on her breasts. He cupped her with his hand as his tongue lashed her nipple. She lifted her gaze to meet his and her brown eyes were heavy-lidded, but she wasn't going to fall asleep any time soon. Not with what Blake had in store for her. He continued tugging at her nipples and kneading her breasts until she reached for him, pulling him upward. Gasping, she reached out and caressed the parts of him that she could.

"Don't make me wait any longer," she crooned. "There's a condom in the nightstand."

Blake leaned over and opened the drawer. He tore open the wrapper with his teeth, sheathed himself and returned to her luscious body. "And you can have me now."

He parted her legs and, pushing between them, thrust deep inside her. Asia lifted her legs, locking them around his hips as he slid in farther, until he was all the way to the hilt. Then, ever so slowly, Blake began to move and find his rhythm. Asia was so tight. And wet. She accepted him as if she'd been waiting all night for him, and her sexy sounds of pleasure reverberated throughout the room.

Blake wanted to close his eyes to combat the overwhelming sensation of being inside her again, but he didn't dare look away. His eyes drilled into Asia as deeply as his body did. He stroked her, deeper and deeper, and she arched her hips, widening her legs to take all of him. When she clutched his biceps, he said, "Take what you want, sweetheart."

"I want more," Asia said throatily, and then unashamedly cupped his ass.

Blake reared back and thrust harder than ever. There was no game or teasing in his style. She'd unleashed the wild animal within him, and he was out of control.

Sweat began to slick both their bodies as their movements became frenzied and relentless. He didn't want it to stop even though they were reaching a plateau of pleasure that just might drown him. Blake dropped to his forearms and moved his hips in a circular motion until Asia let out a sharp cry.

"That's it, Asia. I can feel you—"

He didn't stop thrusting, even when her high-pitched scream echoed through the air, because he was right behind her, groaning as he careened toward the avalanche he'd been fighting all along. He bucked against her and Asia squeezed her legs tightly around him until he stopped twitching. Only then did he shift to his side and, taking with her him, fall asleep.

Hours later, Asia stirred, but she kept her eyes tightly closed because she didn't want this feeling of being at peace to end. Did it have anything to do with the man behind her who'd once again blown her mind with the intensity of his lovemaking? After the first time tonight, he'd taken her from the back, in her favorite position, and then, when she'd tried to sleep, he'd slid into her from the side. He hadn't lied when he said every way he could. She was unable to resist him any more than she could the first time they'd been together.

Now she knew it was no fluke. Blake was going to be *the* man she measured every other man against. It was a shame it couldn't last between them. Sure, Blake talked a good game, telling her he was interested in seeing her, but what did that really mean? Going on a few dates that would no doubt end up with them back in bed? Then he'd be on to the next lover. Blake was a serial dater and Asia doubted that would change anytime soon.

However, she knew something Blake didn't. She was pregnant. But did she tell him? He did have a right to know he was becoming a father. How would he react when she told him? Would he be angry and fly off the handle? Or would he feel as if she was trapping him, which couldn't be further from the truth?

Asia could and would raise this baby on her own. She didn't need him. But her baby, *their* baby, at least deserved to know she'd tried. She would tell him in the morning. For now, she wanted to be held in his arms a few more minutes.

Morning came quicker than Asia would have liked, when her stomach rumbled a few hours later. Although her bouts with morning sickness were infrequent, she did have them, and apparently today was going to be no different.

Feeling nauseous, Asia rushed from her bedroom and down the hall to her bathroom. She didn't have time to close the door before she retched the contents of her stomach into the toilet. Why, oh why, was this happening and with Blake here? It was the last thing she wanted, because he had no idea of her condition.

When the bout of sickness was over, she reached across the toilet for a towel to wipe her mouth. That's when she noticed Blake standing in the doorway, wearing his boxer briefs and a scowl—and holding her copy of *What to Expect When You're Expecting*.

"What the hell is going on, Asia?" he yelled.

Nine

Blake had hoped to get a morning quickie in. What he hadn't expected was for the object of his passion to rush from the bed as if her pants were on fire. Rather than follow her to bathroom, he'd decided to go retrieve his underwear in the living room. That's when he'd found the book.

What to Expect When You're Expecting.

Armed with the book in hand, Blake had stalked toward the bathroom, and that's where he was now, watching Asia get up from the floor looking completely miserable. She was still naked and his eyes couldn't stop roving over her curves, even as he looked for answers to the question that haunted him. Her stomach was still as flat as a pancake. Was she really pregnant?

No, he thought. It couldn't be. Asia couldn't be pregnant. Asia didn't strike him as the type of woman who would sleep with him if she was pregnant by some other man. Then it hit him with the force of a Mack truck. *She's not pregnant by someone else.* Blake quickly began doing the math in his head. He didn't know how far along she was, but it was entirely possible—and more than likely—that Asia was carrying *his* child.

Blake's heart began pounding loudly in his chest and he started to feel light-headed. He felt terrible she was going through this, but then again, he was angry. If he was the father, why hadn't she told him?

"Well? Are you going to answer me?" he asked.

Asia rolled her eyes at him. "Yes, but can I have a moment of privacy to put on some clothes and brush my teeth?"

Blake blinked because he realized he'd been staring at her breasts, which looked fuller to him in the morning light—or was he imagining things? "Of course."

He turned on his heel to leave, but not before hearing her slam the bathroom door. It left Blake with nothing to do except pace the halls and think. If he hadn't shown up to the store and demanded another date, would she have kept the pregnancy a secret from him? How long would she have kept him in the dark and prevented him from the chance to be a father to his child?

He heard the water running, but was it a delay tactic for her to come up with a story? Although he wanted to think negatively about Asia, he couldn't. There was no artifice about the woman, as much as thinking so might give him an escape clause. At the very least, he needed to have his pants on when they had this conversation. Blake picked up his discarded clothes and zipped up his pants.

Eventually, Asia joined him in the living room. This time, she wore a knee-length silk robe with a belt tightly cinched around her middle. He could tell she was wearing nothing underneath, because he could see the outline of her nipples. Rather than sit beside him, she sat as far away from him as she could on the sofa.

For a moment, they stared at each other and it was impossible for Blake not to think about how, just last night, in this very room, he'd knelt before her and made Asia scream like a banshee, but there was no time for lust-filled memories. He needed answers. "Are you pregnant?"

"Yes," she said without hesitation.

He swallowed the lump in his throat. "Is the baby mine?"

Asia stared at him for several beats, and at first, Blake thought she wasn't going to answer him. He understood it was her body, but he had rights, too.

"Yes. You're the only man I've been with."

Blake tried to digest that news, but his head was buzzing. He was going to be a father. *A father.* He'd thought about marriage and children, but it was much further in the future. Yet now it wasn't. "Ur...how far along?"

"Ten weeks," Asia replied. "At first, I didn't believe it, because we had been careful that night. I thought I had a stomach virus or something and then when I went with the Gems to Vegas for Wynter's bachelorette party..." Her voice trailed off.

His gaze skated to her stomach. "You were drinking?" He knew he sounded accusatory, but he couldn't help but feel protective.

Her eyes narrowed. "No, I didn't drink, Blake. Couldn't even if I'd tried. I was having a hard time keeping anything down. Shay asked me about my last period, and well, after several tests, the results all said the same thing. I had to accept the truth."

"Have you gone to a doctor? Are you getting prenatal care?"

"Of course I have. I'm not an idiot, you know."

Blake ran a hand through his curls. "That's not what I'm saying. I'm just trying to make sense of this, Asia." He jumped to his feet. "I mean, were you ever planning on telling me?"

The ensuing silence told Blake that if he hadn't had a change of heart and wanted to see Asia, she would have kept him in the dark about their child, *his child*.

"I think I would have eventually told you," Asia started. "It's just…this was such a shock and I've needed time to process it, plus I've had a lot of other pans in the fire."

"Can I assume you've made a decision?"

Asia nodded. "I have. I'm having the baby."

Asia sensed from the impassive look on Blake's face that her answer was not a surprise. She didn't know what she expected, but calm was certainly not it. She expected anger, fear even, but he seemed too serene. Wasn't he shaken by the news that he was going to be a father? If so, his outward appearance belied his inner turmoil. She needed to snap him out of it. "But I don't need anything from you. I can raise the baby on my own."

"Here?" he asked, glancing around her apartment

as if it were some dump beneath his Ferragamo shoes. "You can't bring a baby up here."

"Yes, I can. It may not be the mansion you grew up in, but I make a decent salary, and with hard work, I will be able to take care of me and my baby." A fierce protectiveness came over Asia and she placed her hand over her belly.

"That's admirable, Asia." He said, taking his seat again on the couch. "It really is, but babies need a lot of things, and it's my responsibility to take care of the child."

"I'm not looking for a handout from you."

He frowned. "I wasn't planning on giving you one. With my help, you can get a house, a nanny, whatever it is that you want to make your life easier. Plus, you'll have me."

"What do you mean, I'll have you?" she inquired.

"I intend to be a full-time father, Asia," Blake replied, scooting closer toward her on the couch. "Did you honestly expect me to do nothing after finding out you're having my baby?"

She hadn't really thought that far in advance. Telling Blake had always been in the abstract, but it was happening right here and right now. "I guess I didn't think about it."

"Well, you'd better, because I'm not going anywhere," he responded hotly. "If you're having this baby, I'm going to be right by your side."

"Do you even want kids?" Asia asked, popping up from her seat. She couldn't be this close to him and not touch him. Or want him to touch her. "Or is this some macho pride thing?"

"Does it matter?" Blake said. "We're having a child."

"We're"—she pointed back and forth between them—"not doing anything. I am. I'm the one living through morning sickness. I'm the one that's going to gain weight. I have to give birth, not you."

"You're right. You have to do all those things. I can't trade positions with you, but the facts are what they are and you can't change my role in this baby's life. I'm its father."

"And I'm the mother." Asia didn't like that Blake was trying to insert himself into her life when she hadn't figured out all the puzzle pieces. "And I need some time alone."

"Are you dismissing me?"

"I'm saying you're crowding me," Asia responded, "and I need a little breathing room." It was hard enough as it was just having him near her bare-chested. She could see his six-pack and hairless chest. She wanted to bury herself in him as she'd done last night, but that wouldn't make it all right.

Everything had changed.

Blake knew she was pregnant. And didn't that make it real? She could no longer hide in the shadows of her life as she had been in the days since she'd found out. She was going to be a mother and she had to start putting some plans in place.

"Fine, I'll leave, Asia," he said, putting on his shirt and slipping on his shoes. But this conversation is far from over," Blake said. "*We* have a lot to figure out."

"Asia, honey, thank God you're home," Ava Reynolds said that evening, breezing into Asia's apartment as if she owned the place. Her mother wore skintight black jeans that looked as though they'd been sprayed on, a sparkly top and a leather jacket.

"Hi, Mama," Asia replied, closing the door after her. She was weary. It had been an emotional night and morning. Asia had gone from the highest of highs, an incredible date with Blake, followed by smoking-hot sex, to the lowest of lows as she watched it all come tumbling down that morning.

She recalled the morning sickness and the horrific acidic taste in her mouth as she'd retched the remnants of last night's meal into the toilet. The look of absolute anger on Blake's face this morning when he stood at the doorway holding the pregnancy book. And finally, their argument about whether or not he would be involved with raising their baby. It was all too much.

And now Ava?

She didn't need her mother's troubles today.

"Don't act so happy to see me, Asia," Ava huffed, flopping down on the couch. "I mean, really, after everything I've done for you."

Asia rolled her eyes. *Here we go again.* Her mother's twisted version of the truth was that she was the perfect parent, who had always been there for Asia and never moved from relationship to relationship, who had never forgotten to pay the rent or make sure groceries were in the fridge. It amazed Asia how much her mother could rewrite history.

"What's going on, Mama?"

Ava folded her arms across her ample cleavage. In the too-tight shirt she wore, her C-cup breasts were overflowing from their confines. Why couldn't she act like a normal parent?

"Do I have to have a problem?" Ava asked. "Can't I just come over to see how my daughter is doing?"

"You can."

"There. And what's up with you anyway?" Ava inquired. "You look like death warmed over."

"Thanks a lot," Asia said, taking a seat on the couch. She'd replaced the skimpy robe she'd been in earlier with Blake in favor of some yoga pants and a tank top and had put her shoulder-length brown hair in a ponytail. She hadn't bothered to put on any makeup, because she hadn't been expecting company.

"If you want a man, Asia, you've got to take better care of yourself," Ava said. "Otherwise, you'll end up all alone."

"I'll remember that," Asia replied. When she wasn't with one of her men, her mother preached to Asia about her appearance, whether that was monitoring what she ate to ensure she didn't gain any weight or ensuring she kept up with self-care routines, such as getting her hair and nails done or her eyebrows arched. Physical appearance was everything to her mother. Ava was always getting her normally short hair styled with glamorous and expensive weaves, having her eyebrows arched and her nails and toes painted or buying a designer outfit she couldn't afford. It was all about the upkeep, which is why Ava rarely had any money. "How much do you need?"

A frown marred Ava's brown features, which were very similar to Asia's. When people saw them, they always said they looked like sisters, which pleased Ava to no end. Ava hated to be thought of as "old." "I don't always need something, Asia."

Asia stared at her blankly. Why did her mother persist in acting this way? She did this every time. Act as if she was put out when Asia was giving it to her straight up.

"Don't look at me like that, Asia Marie Reynolds."

"Wow! My full name. I must really be in trouble."

Her mother stood up and pointed her finger in Asia's face. "Don't you sass me. It wasn't easy being a single parent. Everybody told me to give you up. Give you to someone else to raise so you would have two-parent household. But I wanted my baby and I refused to hand you over. When your grandma kicked me out of the house at sixteen, I had no place to go. I found a girls' home for expectant mothers, and they helped me get on my feet and I learned typing skills and became an administrative assistant. But never *ever* did I let someone try to separate us."

Asia sighed. "I know this, Mama." And now she would know it for herself because, somehow, without wanting to, she'd followed in her mother's footsteps and found herself as a single mother. The only difference was, this time, *her* baby's father wanted to be involved. Asia never knew her father. In her opinion, he was a faceless sperm donor who helped Ava become a mom, and nothing else.

"Well, give me a little credit," Ava said, "a little grace. I know I could do better and I do try."

And now, on cue, Asia felt bad because she was being so hard on Ava. "I'm sorry, Mama." She rose to give Ava a hug. She was just tired of being the responsible one. Why couldn't she share her burdens with her mother? Asia would love to be able to talk to Ava about what she was going through. Ask questions about being pregnant and what to expect, but Ava had never been the kind of mother she could confide in.

"Thank you." Ava patted her back. When she released Asia, she said, "And now that you asked, I could use a hundred dollars. I'm a little short on my car payment."

"I don't have any cash on me, Mama. I'll have to Zelle or Cash App you the money."

Ava stroked Asia's cheek with her palm. "Thanks, love. Now Mama has to go. I have a hot date tonight with a man I met in the grocery line the other day." She started toward the door. "And do get some rest, Asia. You're looking a bit haggard."

"I will, Mama. Have fun."

When she was gone, Asia sagged against the door. The more things changed, the more they stayed the same. That's how it was always going to be with Ava, but Asia couldn't take much more. She closed her palm over her stomach. Soon she would have a baby to look out for and she wouldn't have the extra funds to get Ava out of her tight spots.

But what Asia would give this baby was all the love and support and guidance she never received. Her child would always know they could come to her no matter what and she would be there for them. Tears sprang to Asia's eyes. She was starting to think like a mother.

Ten

Pregnant.

Blake was still in disbelief of the situation he now found himself in. He'd knocked Asia up after a one-night stand. Of course, they'd been together more than once now. In fact, they had been together multiple times. Asia had writhed against him like a siren last night. Blake could still feel her breath warm and fast against his skin.

He'd taken his time reacquainting himself with her soft curves and silky skin. They'd moved together as one, as if they'd been designed to fit together perfectly, which had made their second—and third, and fourth—time together just as amazing as the first. Their connection defied definition and left Blake completely satiated. He couldn't remember ever feeling this way.

But in the wake of his realization that he hadn't imagined the way he felt with Asia was the shocking discovery that their first time together had created a life. A baby. He was going to be a father. Blake didn't know how to reconcile that with the life he had. He lived a carefree lifestyle, doing *what* he wanted *when* he wanted to.

That was all about to change. And although he hadn't planned for this scenario, he knew he had to do what was right and be a father to his child. He didn't have any other family, save for his aunt Sadie and an uncle and some distant cousins. This child was his future and would carry on the legacy his grandfather and father had built.

He was thinking about the enormity of the situation he was in as he drove to his good friend Jeffrey Thomas's house. He'd known Jeffrey since they were teenagers. Jeffrey had married his college sweetheart and they had two beautiful kids, Zion, a nine-year-old boy, and a precocious six-year-old girl named Zora. Normally, Blake would have tried to bail on dinner, but he needed to talk to someone about Asia and the pregnancy.

He arrived after 6:00 p.m., carrying a bottle of red wine and a bouquet of flowers for Jeffrey's wife, Mara. She answered the door with a warm smile. Her chic dark brown bob was accentuated by her big brown eyes and round cheeks. "These are for you," Blake said, holding the flowers out to her.

"Thank you, Blake. C'mon in," she said, motioning him inside. Once in the foyer, she said, "I'm surprised you didn't cancel. I know how averse you are to children."

Blake chuckled. He might have been anti-kids once, but not now.

"You know I love my godson and goddaughter." Blake replied, following her from the foyer into the kitchen, where he found Jeffrey at the refrigerator grabbing a bottle of beer.

At six foot two, Jeffrey was nearly as tall as Blake, but whereas Blake was lean and mean, Jeffrey was big and tall, with shoulders a yard wide. He was wearing a Nike tracksuit and sneakers and his hair was closely cropped as always, to match his neatly trimmed goatee.

"You mind getting me one?" Blake asked, indicating the bottle in his hand. He needed something stronger, but Jeffrey had never liked the hard stuff and didn't usually keep it on hand.

"Absolutely," Jeffrey said, opening the fridge once more and pulling out a Bud Light. He screwed off the top and handed it to Blake.

Blake wasted no time in taking a long pull, drinking half the bottle.

"Easy there, buddy," Jeffrey said, but then when he searched Blake's face, he turned to his wife and added, "Honey, we're going to head outside for a bit. Let us know when dinner is ready?"

"Of course," Mara responded. "Go have your men's talk."

"Thanks, babe." Jeffrey walked over to give her a kiss on the cheek before leading Blake outside. When they were in the all clear and seated at one of four Adirondack chairs outside around the firepit, he turned to Blake. "All right, from the looks of it, you have something on your mind. So spit it out. What gives?"

Blake tipped back his beer for another swig. "I think we might need a couple of more of these after I tell you my news."

"Which is?"

"Remember when I told you about the woman I took to my aunt's birthday party?"

Jeffrey sipped his beer. "Yeah, you said it was one hot night. I can only infer you got to know each other better?"

"Yes, we did." Blake sighed. "But there are consequences for that kind of passion. Consequences I never imagined, not when I thought we were careful…" His words trailed off and, suddenly, Jeffrey's eyes grew large with concern.

"Blake…is she…"

Jeffrey was so stunned, he couldn't even say the words, so Blake finished the sentence. "Yes, she's pregnant. But the worst part about all of this is that we got together again and she didn't tell me."

"She kept the news to herself?"

Blake nodded. "Yes, she did. And I think she would have remained silent if I hadn't had a change of heart and wanted to see her again."

Jeffrey leaned back and regarded him. "You don't usually see a hookup more than once."

Blake shrugged. "Asia was different. I knew it that night, which is why I went back to her store to ask her out again. She played hard to get, but I wore her down. Last night we had dinner, and well…one thing led to another."

"So how did you find out?"

Blake put down his beer on a nearby side table and

leaned his forearms on his thighs. "I found out when she bolted out of bed this morning with a case of morning sickness."

"Wow!" Jeffrey's hand flew to his mouth.

"So, you can only imagine how thrown I was, but I thought maybe something she ate at dinner didn't agree with her. But then I found the book. You know the one. *What to Expect…*"

"*When You're Expecting,*" Jeffrey finished. "I remember when Mara got the book. She read it from cover to cover."

"That's how I found out she was pregnant, followed by the one-two punch that I'm the father."

"Dude, I'm sorry how this went down, but why are you here and not with her? How did you leave things?"

Blake rose to his feet. "I told her I wanted to be a father to the baby. You know, play my part. And do you know what she did?"

"What?"

"She kicked me out. Told me I was coming on too strong and that she didn't need me and could take care of the baby all by herself."

"That may be true, because single black mothers do it every day, but she shouldn't have to, not if you're willing and able to step up. You do want to do the right thing, right? You're not just giving this lip service?"

Blake frowned. He didn't like where Jeffrey was going with this. "Of course I meant it. Was I looking to have a baby? Absolutely not. I mean, being a father was far off in the future. I've seen you, my friend. I know how hard it is."

"But Mara and I are together. We're married," Jeffrey said. "You and Asia aren't a family. You've only been together a couple of times."

"Don't you think I know that?" Blake said. "The situation isn't ideal, but this baby is my family, which I have in short supply these days."

"Ah man, I'm sorry," Jeffrey replied, rubbing his goatee. "I didn't mean to imply otherwise. I just want you to have a realistic picture of the situation you're in."

"Yeah, why do you think I'm here?" Blake asked. "I'm scared at the prospect of being a father, but I'm also not one to shy away from my responsibilities. You remember how adamant I was about taking over the helm at Coleman & Sons Construction."

"That's good. That's what you need to keep reiterating to Asia," Jeffrey replied. "She may not be in the headspace to hear you. There's a lot going on with women at this stage. Her hormones. Her body is changing. Give her some time. Don't come on so strong."

"I'm intense?" Blake responded. "Hell, I don't know any other way to be. This is my kid, too."

"It is, but she's doing all the heavy lifting right now," Jeffrey replied.

"True, but I can help her. If she *lets* me."

"She's running scared, same as you," Jeffrey replied, "but if I know you, Blake, you'll figure this out, like you always do."

Blake thought about their conversation all evening, during Mara's delicious dinner of pot roast, potatoes and baby carrots, and afterward, when he sat with their beautiful children, Zora and Zion, who looked and acted like both their parents. Zora was lively and had to be the center of attention, with her big brown eyes and cocoa-butter skin. As the eldest, Zion was serene like his father and was his spitting image in a matching tracksuit, except for his short, curly Afro.

Would his child look like him? Or like Asia? Who would they take after? Even though Blake lost his parents at twelve, he still had memories of his father. Gil Coleman had been tall and lean, much like Blake, but he had worn wire-rimmed glasses, while Blake had twenty-twenty vision. Personality wise, Blake took after his mother, Daphne, who had never met a stranger. She could converse with anyone and make everyone feel at home, and Blake was the same way. There wasn't anyone he couldn't charm when he put his mind to it.

His charm had failed him today with Asia. She could only hear her own voice, which said that *she,* and she alone, would raise this baby. But next time, Blake wasn't going quietly into the night. He would be there for his child and see them grow up. It was a gift and something that was denied him and his parents.

In fact, the more he thought about it, the more Blake's mind went to Jeffrey's earlier comment about being a family. Jeffrey was right in that he and Asia weren't a family like the Thomases. Maybe that was the answer. Sure, he'd never thought about committing his life to another person, but he also had believed fatherhood was in the future. It wasn't. He had a ready-made family with Asia and the baby.

Marriage was the perfect solution. He could give his child the family life he had never had. A mother *and* a father. And the icing on the cake was that he and Asia were compatible in the bedroom. No, correction, they were combustible, if the two nights they had spent together thus far were any indication. All he had to do now was convince Asia that marriage was the best solution for everyone.

His baby's mother better buckle up, because if she didn't give in, they were in for a bumpy road.

"Shay, what are you doing here?" Asia asked, when Shay showed up at her doorstep on Sunday afternoon with a suitcase in tow. When she'd sent an SOS text to her friends yesterday, each of the Gems had called her except Shay. They each listened as she told them the story of how she'd agreed to go out on another date with Blake only to have it blow up in her face because he found out she was pregnant.

"I figured you might need a friend," Shay replied, pulling Asia into a hug. Her dark locs were in a haphazard updo and she had on her usual attire of yoga pants and sneakers, but this time, she had on a zip-up sweater.

"Girlfriend"—Asia hugged her back tightly—"you have no idea." When they finally released each other, Asia pulled Shay inside the apartment.

Shay left her suitcase in the foyer and walked over to the sofa and took a seat. "I'm sorry I didn't call you back yesterday. Had a little issue with my mom that took my entire day."

"Is everything okay?" Asia inquired. She knew Shay's mom, Eliza Davis, suffered from depressive episodes.

"Yeah, she broke up with the man she'd been seeing and it sent her on a downward spiral."

"Shay, what are you doing here? You should be with your mom."

Shay shook her head. "No, I shouldn't. I have a brother who's finally home, so I don't have to carry the load all by myself anymore. We can share it, so Riley and Wynter are there with Mom. *You* need me. You're here all alone."

"I have Ava."

Shay put her hand on her hip. "And? Have you told Ava you're pregnant?"

"Of course not," Asia said. "I don't need to hear her mouth off that I'm making a mistake and I'll ruin my figure. You know all she cares about is appearances and how she looks. I don't need her negativity right now."

"Which is why I'm here," Shay replied, patting the seat beside her. "Come, tell me everything."

Asia plopped down on the sofa. "Thank you for coming. I really appreciate it."

"You're welcome. So have you heard from Blake today?"

"I have," Asia responded. "He called and texted me last night, but I didn't answer. Then, this morning, he sent me a cryptic text that we need to talk."

"So you haven't spoken to him since he found out you were pregnant?"

Asia shook her head. "No, but he's blowing this up out proportion. I don't need anything from him."

"Of course you do. He's the baby's father. And if he wants to step up, let him."

"I don't know," Asia said, "I'm used to doing things for myself. Being dependent solely on me." It was easier that way, because Asia knew she would never be let down.

"I know. You had to be an adult way too early because Ava couldn't get her act together, but you don't have to be alone, Asia. The Gems are here for you in any capacity you need, and apparently so is Blake."

"That's surprising," Asia responded, "after his behavior that first night…leaving me that note. I never expected he'd actually *want* to be a father to this baby."

"Becoming a parent changes you," Shay said. "I remember when I was…" and then she stopped speaking.

Asia stared into her best friend's brown eyes. "Shay? What are you saying? Were you pregnant? When?" Asia knew she was throwing a bunch of questions at her, but this was a shock.

Shay bowed her head, letting her long locs cover her face. When she finally glanced up, tears were in her eyes. "I was pregnant once, briefly," Shay replied, "when Kevin and I were married."

"Why didn't you say anything?"

"Because the doctor told us to wait to share the news until after the first trimester."

Asia rolled her eyes upward. "I guess I didn't do that. I was so stunned, I had to tell you guys. So, what happened?"

"I miscarried after eight weeks. It was heart-wrenching because I'd always wanted to be a mom. It hurt so much I couldn't share the loss with you or the Gems. Kevin and I tried again for another year after that, but each month I wasn't pregnant I felt like a failure. Felt like less than a woman. My lack of fertility sealed the deal on our marriage. We were already so young, and with my mom's depression, we didn't have the skills to cope with the loss, so we went our separate ways."

Asia reached across the couch and grabbed Shay's hand. "I'm so incredibly sorry, my friend. If I had known…"

"You wouldn't have told me you're pregnant?" Shay asked. "Don't do that. Don't feel sorry for me. I have a full life. After all these years, I have my yoga business, thanks to Aunt Helaine, and I have you and the Gems. And now a beautiful baby to look forward to." She touched Asia's flat stomach. "I'm so happy for you and I'm going to be the best auntie this baby has ever seen."

Asia couldn't help but smile. "Thank you for telling me about the miscarriage. I know that couldn't have been easy. It makes me feel silly about fighting with Blake about helping."

"I get it!" Shay said. "I'm here to get you through this and to give you a little perspective. I haven't met Blake yet, but he can't be half bad if he's willing to take responsibility."

Asia nodded. "You think I should hear him out?"

"I do, but ultimately, it's your decision, Asia, and I will support you in whatever you decide."

"How did I ever get so lucky to find you?"

"You sat down at the right table in the high school cafeteria," Shay replied with a wide grin.

They both laughed and continued talking and reminiscing well into the night. When she finally slid into bed, Asia thought she could still smell Blake even though she'd changed the sheets. His scent seemingly permeated her room.

She fell backward against the pillows. What was she going to do? Blake wasn't just a one-night stand who'd stood her up anymore. He was her baby's father and the man she couldn't stop thinking about. Last night, she had erotic dreams about how good it was between them. Surely there would come a point she didn't want him this desperately? It was just a phase. Or that's what she told herself, but Asia wasn't so sure. She was carrying a constant reminder of how good it had been between them. *Still was.*

And that was the most frightening realization of all.

Eleven

Asia woke up Monday not feeling any better about her and Blake's situation, but she also couldn't continue to dwell on it. She had to work on securing the money she needed to buy Yvette's Jewels. Last night, she confided in Shay about Yvette's request to buy her out.

"I know it didn't work out with the bank, but have you thought about asking Wynter for a loan?" Shay had asked. "You know she'd give you the money in a heartbeat."

"Of course she would," Asia had responded, "but I would never ask her." She had too much pride. "Her aunt Helaine already gave us such a generous inheritance. I couldn't possibly ask for more money. It would be selfish and greedy."

"But Helaine wanted you to pursue your dreams," Shay had said.

"And I will," Asia had stated. And she would, once she secured the rest of the finances on her own. She had a meeting with another bank this morning and she was hoping they would see her vision and support her in this endeavor.

Unfortunately, an hour later, Asia was given the same response as from the previous institution. They weren't interested. A high-end jewelry store was a niche market and they didn't consider the venture marketable.

Asia was discouraged. She knew her work was fire because people who bought her jewelry often returned for a second and third time. These banks were being shortsighted because she wasn't a household name. She would keep her head up until she found another way.

She arrived at Yvette's Jewels with minutes to spare for her shift. She hadn't had time to change from her high-waisted black trousers, silk button-down top, black blazer and skinny heels.

"Wow! You look very businesslike, Asia," Yvette said when she walked in.

Asia couldn't help but return the older woman's affectionate smile. "Thank you. I've been working on raising funds to buy you out."

She headed to the back office to put down her briefcase.

"I was going to ask you about that," Yvette said. "Any luck?"

"Well…" Asia didn't want to let Yvette down, but she also didn't have the heart to say she was failing miserably at coming up with the money she needed to take over the store. She'd never been the best student and hadn't gone to college like Wynter and Teagan had, but what she did have was talent, and she just had to convince someone she was worth the investment.

It was late morning when Blake arrived at Yvette's Jewels. He knew it was early for this conversation with Asia, but once his mind was made up about something, there was no talking him down. He'd called and texted her over the weekend, but Asia had given him the cold shoulder. This conversation was too important. His child's future depended on him changing Asia's mind to his way of thinking.

He walked inside and the chime didn't go off indicating a new customer, but he entered anyway. The front of the store was empty, which wasn't the norm. Usually, Asia or Yvette, the owner, was there to greet customers. Blake was rethinking whether he should have come so early when he heard voices. One of them was Asia's.

He couldn't back down from his purpose.

He had to secure Asia's agreement to his marriage proposal.

Blake started toward the back of the store, but something held him back because he caught a portion of their conversation.

"To be honest with you, Yvette, I've be having a little trouble raising all the money I need to buy you out of the store," Asia was saying. "As you know, I received an inheritance which would definitely cover half of what you're looking for, but it's not enough."

"I wish I could take less, Asia," Yvette responded, "but this store is all I have and the extra income will help offset my Social Security and the small pension I receive from my husband's estate."

"I know," Asia said. "All I'm asking is if you could give me a little bit more time to figure this out before you sell the store to someone else? Having my own jewelry shop is a dream come true and I'm ready to work my butt off to make that happen."

"I know you will, dear," Yvette said. "And I can give you another couple of weeks. Melvin wants to head out for the spring on the trip around the world, and I don't want to miss this. When you're my age and you meet someone, well, let's just say I never thought I'd find love again after my Edgar passed. Meeting Melvin is truly special."

"I understand, Yvette, and I appreciate you giving me the extra time," Blake heard Asia reply.

Slowly, Blake backed away and returned to the lobby.

So, Asia needed money to buy out Yvette and take over the store?

That was an interesting wrinkle and could provide Blake with the leverage he needed to get Asia to agree to the marriage. He was wealthy, not just from being majority shareholder in Coleman & Sons Construction, but also because Blake had made some wise investments with Jeffrey, who was a stockbroker. He could easily afford to give Asia the money she needed to buy out Yvette, allowing her the opportunity to be her own boss. But there would be one caveat.

She would have to agree to marry him. As his wife, she would have access to everything she needed to ensure the store and her jewelry line were a success. Blake just had to convince Asia that getting married was best, not only for the baby, but for her as well.

Asia found him when she and Yvette returned to the front of the store.

"Blake!" He could see Asia was genuinely surprised to see him. "What are you doing here?"

Blake's mind went blank and his gaze was riveted to Asia. She was elegantly dressed in high-waisted black trousers and a fuchsia silk button-down top. A narrow black belt was around her still-slender waist, and black patent stilettos were on her petite feet.

"Blake?" Asia's questioning look made Blake snap out of his trance.

"Sorry. I came to see if you would agree to lunch."

Her eyes narrowed. "I thought you were going to give me some space."

"I never agreed to any such thing," Blake responded. "Besides, you and I need to talk"—he glanced down at her stomach—"now more than ever."

Her boss walked into the room again and greeted him. "Good morning. A bit early to be calling, yes?"

Blake couldn't help but smile at Yvette's old-school phrase. "Yes, ma'am. Asia was just agreeing to lunch."

"I did no such thing," Asia whispered.

"I'll be here at eleven forty-five." He ignored Asia's angry glare, inclined his head at Yvette and then headed out. Blake didn't bother looking behind him. He could feel Asia's eyes boring into the back of his skull.

She was angry at his heavy-handedness, but he had no choice. He would use every weapon in his arsenal to convince Asia to marry him. He knew what it was like to grow up without a parent after losing his own in the car crash. He refused to allow his child to be raised without him not when he was ready and willing to be a parent. Soon, she would know that, too, but it wasn't going to be easy. Asia liked her independence and would fight Blake at every turn. As he settled into his car, Blake rubbed his hands in glee. He was ready for the challenge.

Asia was furious!

She supposed Yvette liked that Blake was wooing her, but it was still her place of business. He couldn't come strolling into the store—er, soon to be *her* store—and boss her around. With Yvette standing beside her, he'd known exactly what he was doing. She'd gone along with it, but she would like to wipe that smug smile off his face—a face dominated by attractive features and dark, smoldering brown eyes.

"That young man is quite taken with you," Yvette said from her side. "I wouldn't be too quick to play hard to get. Men like him don't come around every day."

Didn't she know it. Asia had never met anyone like Blake. Her mind wandered to their first kiss in the study. His kiss hadn't been like that of any other man she'd been with. He'd claimed her mouth with total mastery and she'd been unable to resist his fiery passion as he'd boldly swept his tongue between her lips. Ever since then, Asia had been acting uncharacteristically unlike herself.

She wanted to be the exact opposite of Ava, who always *needed* a man. Until recently, Asia could take them or leave them, but Blake? Ever since she'd met him, all she wanted to do was take, take, take.

Fortunately, a customer walked in, jolting Asia back to the present and stopping her from obsessing over

Blake. It would be short-lived because, in a few hours, she had a date with her destiny.

"You know, you didn't have to pick me up," Asia said once she and Blake were seated in an upscale eatery for lunch that specialized in salads, bowls and soups.

"I know I didn't have to," Blake said, "I wanted to."

He sat back and watched Asia's breasts rise and fall with her steady breathing. He liked that she'd kept her hair down lately in soft waves to her shoulders. Her cheeks were lightly brushed with pink, and she wore a hint of gloss on her lips. She looked hot. Blake felt desire tightening low in his belly and swallowed hard.

"Fine," she said, putting down the menu. "We're here. What did you want to talk about?"

"All in due time," Blake replied. He had to ease her into this. He couldn't come out like a bull in a china shop. Otherwise, Asia would run for the door as soon as she could. "Please." He inclined his head to the menu. "Make a selection for lunch. You need to eat. You are eating for two."

Her eyes flashed fire across the table. "I know that, but *you* don't have to worry about morning sickness. What all the books don't tell you is that it's anytime sickness and can affect you throughout the day."

Blake frowned. "Have you talked to your doctor about this?"

"I will."

"There's no time like the present."

"Do you have to be so pushy?" she asked.

He sighed. "Every conversation doesn't have to be

a battle between us either. Can't we find some common ground?"

She lifted her chin and glared at him, but said, "I
suppose you're right."

He was thankful for small blessings. The waitress
came to take their order. A salmon salad for Asia and
steakhouse salad for Blake. He surprised Asia and the
waitress when he asked for them to bring her a large
glass of low-fat milk.

"I don't really like milk," Asia said.

"Are you allergic or is it a preference?"

"The latter."

Blake turned to the waitress. "She'll have the milk."

"I don't need you to order for me," Asia replied. "I
can take care of myself. I've been doing it long before
you entered the picture and I'll be doing it long after
you're gone."

Blake studied her. Asia was a mass of contradictions.
On one hand, she was fiercely independent—or at least
that's what she showed the world. On the other hand,
there was a vulnerability he saw but that she hid from
most people. "I'm not going anywhere, Asia."

"Oh yes, you are. Men always leave when the going
gets tough. I'd rather you start now."

Blake laughed. Her comment told him that Asia had
had a lot of heartbreak in her life when it came to the
opposite sex. He refused to be like those other men.
"Well, I'm here to stay."

She rolled her eyes.

"You don't believe me?"

The waitress returned with Asia's milk and a bottle

of sparking water. After she poured him a glass, she left them alone.

"What do you want, Blake?" Asia surprised him when she picked up the milk and guzzled it. "There. Are you happy?" she asked, placing the empty glass on the table and glaring at him.

"I want you to let me in."

She snorted. "I did that and look where it got me. Knocked up."

Asia was not going to make this easy, but then again, he liked that she wasn't going down without a fight. But he had an ace in the hole. "Asia, we could be a good team together, you and I, if you're willing to give it a chance."

"I don't need to do anything," she said defiantly.

"Are you really prepared to raise our child on your own, with no support system?"

"I have my friends."

"All of whom live in other cities," Blake responded. He'd done some research of his own in the past couple of days. He'd read up on Wynter Barrington and her soon-to-be husband, high-profile divorce attorney Riley Davis, along with yoga studio owner Shay Davis, all of whom lived in San Antonio. Then there was restaurateur Egypt Cox in Raleigh, Lyric Taylor in Memphis and Teagan Williams in Phoenix. Although each of these women were near and dear to Asia, they weren't local and wouldn't be able to help Asia day-to-day. He could.

"Don't presume to think you know everything about me, Blake Coleman."

"I wouldn't dare," Blake said, touching his chest in

mock surrender. "I'm merely stating the facts and that I want to be a full-time father to our child. Surely having two parents is better than one?" Blake took her silence as acquiescence and continued. "I'd like to offer you another incentive, one that might be extremely beneficial to you."

Asia raised one eyebrow. "And what might that be?"

"I understand you're in need of assistance to help buy out Yvette so you can have the store for yourself."

Her eyes narrowed. "How do you know that? Were you eavesdropping?"

Blake ignored her question and got right to the point. "Marry me. In exchange, I'll give you the money you need to buy the store."

Twelve

"Marry you?" Asia had to have heard Blake wrong. He hadn't actually proposed. Had he?

"Listen to me, Asia. I think it's a win-win for both of us. First and foremost, our baby gets two parents. A mother *and* a father. You yourself grew up with a single mother and know the struggles she faced. Second, you get the capital you need to make your lifelong dream into a reality, allowing your boss to retire and ride off into the sunset. And third…"

Her eyes widened in surprise. "There's a third?"

"The incredible chemistry between us," Blake stated, his eyes never leaving her face. "You and I both know that this thing, whatever it is between us, is far from over."

"That's not reason enough to hitch our lives together."

"Isn't our baby enough?"

He had a point. Asia knew what it was like to be raised by a single mother. There were good times, but there were plenty more hard times. Blake was offering her a chance to give her child the two things she'd never had growing up. Stability. Consistency. But was that enough for marriage? She knew what true love looked like because she saw it in Wynter's eyes when she spoke about Riley and the way he looked at her. If she married Blake, Asia would be giving up her chance at finding that kind of love.

"What do you say, Asia?"

She shook her head. "No, I can't do this."

"What about your boss?" Blake pressed. "Didn't she say you need to give her an update in a couple of weeks? Do you really think it's going to be that easy to raise a quarter of a million dollars? I can give you the money, right now, right here, and your worries would be over." He reached across the table and grasped Asia's small hand in his large one. A zing of electricity shot through Asia at his touch. And by the way his eyes sparkled, he'd noticed.

Damn him for making her feel this way.

"You felt it, too, just now, when we touched," Blake said, his voice soft. "You can't deny it, Asia. There's a connection between us. A physical one and now an emotional one. We created a life from our one night together. And our child deserves the very best chance of a happy life we can give him or her."

"I-I..." Asia stuttered. She didn't know what to say to that. Blake wasn't giving her a chance to think. All of this was happening too fast. So much was out of her control, just like when she was younger and her mom would make bad decisions that ultimately affected her.

But could this marriage be a good thing?

Her baby would always be cared for, financially, by Blake and emotionally, by Asia. Even though she had only known about the baby a couple of weeks, she already loved the new life inside her.

"Say yes, Asia," Blake said. "We could be a family. You, me and the little one on the way."

Asia glanced up into Blake's dark brown eyes. "This is crazy. We hardly know each other."

"True, but we can get to know each other and bond during your pregnancy. Think about the great life you could have. You could have your own store and all the resources you need to make it a success. A helpmate and father for the baby. And of course"—he lowered his voice—"an incredible lover in the bedroom. It's all yours for the taking, Asia. All you have to do is accept."

"You drive a hard bargain, Blake."

He leaned back in his chair and stared back at her. "I do when I really want something."

"Why me? Why this marriage? You don't have to marry me to be a father to this baby." Her hand went to her stomach. That's what she couldn't wrap her head around. Blake Coleman could have any woman he wanted. Asia had seen the supermodels he usually dated. She was nothing like them. Who's to say he wouldn't get bored five minutes after the ink was dry on their marriage license?

Blake couldn't believe how hard he had to work to convince Asia marriage was the right fit. He assumed she'd fall in line, because so many women wanted to be Mrs. Blake Coleman, but Asia was nothing like that. She wasn't rushing to say yes to his marriage proposal, and if he was being honest, it kind of stung.

"No, I don't," Blake said, finally responding to her question. "But when I commit and give something or, rather, someone, my word"—he directed his dark gaze at her—"I give them my all."

"So, this marriage would be…" Her voice trailed off, but Blake understood what she wasn't saying.

"Wouldn't be in name only," he finished. "I'd expect"—her eyes flashed that spark he liked about Asia, so he changed his wording—"I'd hope our marriage could be a *real* one. When I commit to you, I do it wholeheartedly, so I would not dishonor our vows by looking at another woman, if that's what you're asking."

He heard her sharp intake of breath and finally felt as if he had her on the ropes. There was nowhere for her to run. No reason for her to say no. Not when everything was laid out so perfectly. So he went in for the kill, pulling at her heartstrings. He knew it was unfair, but he had to secure a "yes" from Asia and ensure that his baby was born a Coleman.

"As you know, I lost both my parents many years ago," Blake began. "Other than my aunt, this baby boy or girl is one of the few family members I have left."

He saw tears well in Asia's eyes, and when one fell, he reached across the space between them and kissed it away.

She was nodding her head, but he needed to hear the words. "Asia, will you marry me?"

"Yes."

Blake had never realized how happy he would be to hear that one word escape Asia's lush pink-tinted lips. He leaned across the table, and in front of the entire crowd, pressed his lips against hers in a soft and tender kiss. When he sat back down, her eyes popped open and she looked dazed, so he reached for her hand again. "You won't regret this, Asia. You can even design your own ring. Whatever stone or stones you want. Money is no object. I just want you to be happy."

"Design my own ring?" she asked, somewhat speechless.

"Absolutely. And who knows," he said, shrugging. "It could be the start of something."

"I can't believe we're doing this," Asia said.

"I can," Blake replied with a grin. "And I can't wait to tell Aunt Sadie. She told me I was a fool for letting you get away the first time."

"She said that?"

"Absolutely, which is why I never make the same mistake twice."

When the waitress returned, he said, "We'd like a bottle of sparkling cider, please. We're celebrating our engagement."

The waitress brought the cider and Blake eagerly began to pour them both a glass, but something still didn't feel right to Asia. Yes, they were marrying for the baby and the marriage would have its benefits, namely Blake as her husband and lover. Asia could live with that. What she couldn't live with was being seen as a gold digger.

The tabloids would assume that a woman like her

was after Blake's money, which wasn't true. She might not have much, but she worked hard creating beautiful, well-crafted pieces that anyone would be proud to wear. And she needed to know she'd gotten there on her own terms, even if Blake was offering his assistance.

"I have one stipulation," Asia added quickly before she lost her nerve.

Blake frowned. He'd probably thought the matter was settled. "And what's that?"

"The money for my store will be a loan. I want it in writing that I will pay you back every cent you loan me to buy out Yvette. So eventually, the store is in my name only. And you also agree to be a silent partner. I make all the decisions when it comes to the store's creative direction and vision."

"Agreed. Is that all?"

Asia was surprised. She'd expected him to put up more of a fuss. Was it really just a drop in the bucket to him? For Asia, having the funds she needed to buy out Yvette was everything. It meant making all her dreams come true.

Something else was bothering her, and her expression must have given it away, because at that moment, Blake's brow furrowed. "Whatever it is, just tell me. We can work through any reservations you might have."

Asia sighed. "All right. It's just that we don't know each other very well."

"That will be rectified once we're married," Blake replied. "Speaking of, I'd rather have the wedding sooner than later, before you start showing."

"Wait just a minute, Blake Coleman," Asia responded, holding up her hand, "Don't try to steamroll me. I agreed to marry you and I agreed it won't be a marriage of convenience. However, I think it's best if we postpone the wedding at least for a couple of months, until we get to know each other, and while doing so refrain from having sex."

Blake was bringing his flute to his mouth, but stopped midstream. "What?"

"You heard me. I think it's best if we leave sex off the table and get to know each other organically."

Asia could see the wheels of Blake's mind turning, as he tried to come up with something to dissuade her, but Asia was resolute in this. Yes, she would be a fool to say she didn't desire him. Whenever he was around, she felt hot and shivery at the same time. No other man excited her the way Blake did and she would like nothing better than to press herself against his whipcord body and burn in the fire they would create together, but she had to be strong. If the marriage was going to work, they had to get to know each other outside the bedroom.

"Fine," he said through gritted teeth. "Is that it?"

She stared at him for several beats, expecting him to change his mind, and when he didn't, she had no choice, but to say, "Yes, yes, that's it."

"Good." Blake handed her a flute of sparkling cider, which she accepted. "Let's toast." He held up his flute. "To our marriage."

Asia repeated the words, but her ears were buzzing. Blake was talking about telling his aunt over dinner in the near future, talking about how long their engagement should be for, but all Asia could think about was that she'd agreed to marry a man she hardly knew after getting impregnated by him.

It didn't seem real. It was such a departure from her life a couple of months ago, when everything had seemed possible. Now she was on a different path. One of motherhood and being a wife, and Asia felt ill-prepared for what came next. How did Blake seem so sure when they'd only spent two evenings together? Didn't he have doubts about rushing into the marriage? If so, he wasn't showing them.

Instead, he seemed ready to leap off the ledge and into the unknown. They had so much to talk about and iron out before the baby came. That's why it was best they take sex off the table and figure out what the hell they were really doing—because one way or another, a baby was coming in little over six months.

Asia wasn't sure what scared her most. Having the baby—or being Blake's wife.

Thirteen

"Are you sure about this?" Shay asked when Asia returned home later that day and spilled the news. "This is insane. You don't even know Blake."

"I knew him well enough to sleep with him," Asia said. "And now we're having a baby."

"Yes, you are, but you don't have to marry him. You can two can co-parent."

Asia shook her head. "Blake is adamantly against that. He doesn't want to miss any moments. He thinks a two-parent household is best."

"And what do you think?" Shay inquired, moving into Asia's path on her way to her bedroom. "All I've heard since you walked in is Blake this and Blake that. What does Asia want?"

"I want a good life for my baby," Asia answered

without hesitation. "I don't want to have to scrape and save to get by. If marriage to Blake is the key to having a partnership, to getting the money I need to open my own store, then so be it."

"What are you talking about?" Shay asked.

"As a wedding gift, Blake will give the money to buy out Yvette, but instead I asked him to draw up papers so that he's loaning me the money. As soon as the store makes a profit, I'll pay him back in installments, until eventually, I own the store outright. And he has to be a silent investor. *I* make all the decisions."

"Wow!" Shay put her hand on her hip and the look of her face wasn't just shock, it was admiration. "I'm really proud of you, Asia, for demanding what you want, but I still think this is way over the top, even for you."

Asia laughed. "You know I never do anything small. It's go big or go home."

"Well, you're marrying one of Denver's most notorious playboys," Shay responded, "so you're definitely going big. Question for you—did he ask for a prenup?"

Asia shook her head. "He didn't, but I don't mind signing one. I don't want him to think I'm marrying him for his money. That's why it was important to me that I pay him back every cent he puts in the store."

"Sounds like you're looking at all the angles," Shay said. "Are you ready to tell all the other Gems?"

Asia exhaled audibly. "I guess there's no time like the present."

Several minutes later, Wynter, Egypt, Lyric and Teagan's faces were on the screen in front of Asia and Shay.

"Shay, you're in Denver?" Teagan asked.

Shay nodded. "Yes, ma'am. Our girl needed us and after you hear her news, you'll understand why."

"Oh, my goodness, Asia," Egypt said. "What have you gotten yourself into?"

"Nothing I'm going to get out of anytime soon," Asia replied with a laugh. She knew the Gems thought she was flighty and the least responsible of the group, but not anymore. She was about to own her own business and marry the most eligible bachelor in Denver. "Ladies, I'm getting married."

"Married!" Egypt shouted. "What on earth is going on out there? Shay?" From the screen, she looked at Shay.

"Why are you asking her?" Asia replied. "Ask me. I'm the one that agreed to Blake's marriage proposal. He made a solid argument about us being a family unit for the baby, plus there's the incredible chemistry between us."

"Asia." She could hear the chiding in Wynter's tone. "Sex is not enough to base a marriage on."

"I'm well aware, Wynter," Asia said testily, "which is why I took sex off the table until we're married. I want us to get to know each other *before* the baby is born."

"Smart move," Teagan responded, "but are you sure about this? Marriage is a big commitment."

It was, and most of her relationships with men had been transient in nature. Once the good times were over, it was on to the next. Asia had no idea what it was like to be in a relationship, let alone a good one. They would have to navigate this together.

"I'll manage," Asia stated. "I want to ensure my baby has the very best in life."

"Our girl is all grown up," Egypt said aloud. "I apologize for doubting you, Asia. I trust your judgment and that you know what's best for you and Baby Reynolds."

After the call ended, they talked for a bit and then Shay retired to bed because she was leaving on an early-morning flight. She had to get back to her yoga studio.

Asia sat up in bed, wondering if she'd made the right decision. She had convinced her sista friends, but inside, she was scared out of her mind. They were right. Marriage was a big deal, and she had no examples to look up to. All of Ava's relationships had been a complete disaster. Speaking of, she needed to tell her mother about the pregnancy, but that would have to wait for another day. She wasn't ready to tackle that conversation just yet.

Was she making a mistake by rushing into marriage with Blake? Asia knew very little about him other than what he'd told her and what she'd gleaned on the internet. It wasn't much of a foundation to build a relationship on, but they had to start somewhere. Asia pulled out her sketch pad from her nightstand drawer and started designing her dream engagement and wedding rings.

Sitting in the offices of Coleman & Sons Construction at the end of the week, Blake felt accomplished. He'd convinced Asia that marrying him was the best solution for their situation. Consequently, it would ensure that he'd be a full-time father and not one of those see-you-on-the-weekend kind of dads. He didn't have much family left, and those he did have, Blake wanted to keep near. His little boy or girl would know their father, and they would have two parents who were hot for each other.

Was it love? No, but Blake feared the emotion. He'd loved his parents, and losing them had hurt so much that he'd buried the feeling along with his parents. At the time, his aunt worried that something was wrong with him because he showed no emotion during his parents' funeral. How could he? He'd lost everything the night they died. He'd recovered from his injuries, but his entire life had changed, and not for the better. He was thankful for his aunt, but that didn't change the fact that he was alone. Blake had vowed then that he would never love anything that much again.

But now?

This baby was about to turn his life on its head. Blake knew instantly he loved his child and would do anything for them, including marrying their mother. Not that marrying Asia was a hardship. They were compatible in the bedroom and that was a start, and friendship would come. He couldn't offer her anything more and he hoped she understood that, because love wasn't on the table. He refused to be that vulnerable again.

He shared his good news with Jeffrey, who was surprised he was going to such lengths to secure a stable future for his child. "You're getting married," Jeffrey said bluntly. "That was your takeaway from our conversation?"

"You said we weren't a family," Blake said. "Now we will be. We'll get married, giving my child both parents. Now I can be a full-time father to my child, same as you."

"I don't know, Blake. You're on dangerous ground,

my friend," Jeffrey said. "I hope things work out how you envision them."

Blake was certain they could. So he'd focused on giving Asia something she wanted desperately: to own her own business. As soon as he dropped Asia off yesterday, he called his bank to draft a check in Asia's name for the amount she needed to pay off Yvette, along with a tidy sum for any renovations the store might need to fit Asia's vision. The next call had been to his attorney. Blake had instructed him to prepare loan and partnership documents giving Asia sole control over the store, thus making him a silent partner.

Rather than go to the store again and risk Yvette's ire, Blake had asked Asia to come to his office. She wanted them to get to know each other better, and by coming here she could understand how much Coleman & Sons meant to him. He would take her around and show her the business his grandfather had started and show her the ways he was keeping their legacy going.

He'd done his best to live up to the family traditions of hard work and perseverance. Blake could only hope his parents were looking down at him and proud of the work he'd accomplished in expanding the business.

Blake was so deep inside his memories. He didn't even notice his assistant, Martha, standing in the doorway until she cleared her throat.

"I'm sorry to interrupt," Martha began, "but you have a visitor. Miss Asia Reynolds."

Blake smiled and rose to his feet, buttoning the jacket to his custom-made gray suit. Since taking over as CEO, he'd had to dress the part. "Please show her in."

Martha opened the door and Asia walked in looking

delightful in a camel-colored coat, a crewneck sweater and a skirt that reached her sumptuous thighs. Rounding out the look were knee-high suede heeled boots. Blake would love to set her on his desk, hike up her skirt and have Asia for lunch.

Instead, he smiled and walked forward, greeting her with a quick peck on the lips. "Martha, I'd like you to meet my fiancée."

Martha's eyes grew wide. "Pardon?"

Blake glanced down at Asia and he could see that she was equally surprised with his proclamation. "We're getting married."

"Wow! Congratulations, Blake. I'm so happy for both of you." Martha gave them a bright smile and then turned to Asia. "Blake doesn't let many people in, so I'm glad you've seen what a good man he is."

Blake was surprised by Martha's statement. "Thank you so much, Martha. Could you give us a few minutes?"

"Of course," Martha said, beaming. "I'm sure you lovebirds would like to be alone." She closed his door on the way out.

When they were alone, Asia spun on him. "We're announcing our engagement now? I'm not even finished designing the ring."

"I see no reason not to. Plus, it'll make it easier when we say you're expecting. I'll have my PR work up an announcement."

"You've thought of everything," Asia responded and plopped down the purse she'd been carrying on one of the chairs in front of his desk.

Blake didn't like her tone. He tipped her chin up

and found himself caught in her beautiful brown eyes. Maybe if he ravished her, her eyes would glow with desire as they had more than once before. However, that wasn't going to be the way to win her over. She'd agreed to marry him, but she was still wary.

"Listen, we're in this together," Blake said. "It's why I brought you here." He motioned around the room. "This is my family's business. It's been in my family for generations, and I'm continuing that legacy."

She nodded. "Thank you for including me."

"Before I give you a tour, you should look these over." He reached behind him to grab the documents his attorney had prepared and handed them to Asia.

"What are they?" she asked.

"The loan and partnership documents you requested. If you read them over, they're all in order."

He watched as Asia glanced over them. "I'll need a bit more time with these."

"That's fine, Blake responded. "Feel free to have your attorney look them over."

"You sure didn't waste any time," she said, moving to one of the seats in front of his executive desk and sitting down.

He reached behind him again, this time for the envelope that held the check his bank had drafted. "And you'll need this."

He held out the envelope. Asia took it, and when she opened it, her mouth was agape. She glanced up at him with bewilderment "Blake, this is too much. I only need enough to buy out Yvette."

Blake shook his head. "Do you honestly want to keep the store looking like that? I assume you want to renovate? Make it your own? You'll need cash for that. Now you have it. Per your request, it's a loan and will be paid back once the store is profitable."

When she glanced up at him again, there were tears in her eyes. "Blake..."

Had he done something wrong?

Blake rushed to her side and, moving her purse, sat in the seat beside her. "What is it?

She shook her head. "Absolutely nothing. You've thought of everything. It's just... I thought all was lost, and now you're helping me get something I've always wanted."

"All you have to do is reach out and take it."

She stared at him for several moments and then she leaned over and hugged him. Blake didn't get many hugs, save for the occasional one from his aunt Sadie. Hugs had gone away when his mother died in the car crash. But the more Asia squeezed him, the more something in Blake cracked open, and he returned her embrace, hugging her tight.

"Thank you so much," she whispered against his chest. "I promise I won't let you down."

He released her and grasped both sides of her face. "I believe in you, Asia."

Asia held a check in her hands that would change her entire future. Aunt Helaine had been the catalyst, but Blake was the final piece of the puzzle. She was finally going to have her own store, Six Gems. Her own brand. It was intoxicating.

"Thank you."

"You don't have to thank me," Blake said. "It's a loan that you will pay back."

She grinned. She appreciated him saying it, but he wouldn't be giving her the money if she weren't pregnant with his child. She mustn't forget that or lose sight of why they were together. Blake had no feelings for her whatsoever, though Asia found that she had caught some for this enigmatic man.

"C'mon." Blake stood up. "I'd like to show you the place and introduce you around."

"Are you sure, Blake?" Asia asked. "Once you tell everyone, it's out there. You can't take it back."

He flashed her a devastating smile and her knees almost gave out. "I know." He tugged her toward the door.

Over the next hour, Blake took Asia around the building, pointing out different departments, introducing her to staff as his fiancée. Asia was amazed at how welcoming everyone was. They seemed genuinely happy for Blake, though she did catch some envious glares from several women because she'd dashed their hopes of landing Blake. All in all, the morning went much better than she'd anticipated. She hadn't known what to expect when Blake told her to meet him at his office, but she was happy she came.

Eventually, Blake stopped in the lobby in front of images of his grandfather Anthony and his father, Gil. Blake favored both men, not just in height but in his commanding presence.

"My grandfather started Coleman & Sons Construction fifty years ago. He used the money that family and friends loaned him. He started out first in construction, building homes. Then he branched out to the commer-

cial sector and constructing office buildings and indus-
trial warehouses."

"And now?" Asia inquired.

"We do all of the above, but I've branched out into
the development sector, buying land and creating master
communities and multiuse complexes," Blake replied.

"That's wonderful, Blake," Asia said once they'd
made it back to his office. She could see how proud he
was of his family legacy. This would be their child's
future someday.

"This is so much different than how I grew up," Asia
said.

He nodded. "I understand, but from what you've told
me, you're a fighter and survivor, Asia. I'm proud to
have you as my fiancée."

"Are you sure about that? My side at the wedding
will be small. I don't have any family except my mother
and the Gems."

Blake came over to her and stroked her cheek with
his palm. "And I don't either. There's my aunt and an
uncle and a handful of distant cousins who I never see.
So don't think I pity you, Asia."

"You don't?" She glanced up at it him, and when
she did, she didn't see pity, only admiration and something else. *Desire.*

And then he brought his mouth down on hers and
all Asia could think about was pleasure. His kiss was
a gentle seduction of all her senses, but that didn't stop
him from increasing the pressure of his lips until hers
parted, allowing his tongue access to the moist heat of
her mouth.

Asia tipped her head back and Blake plundered her

lips with mastery until she was wrapping her arms around his neck to anchor herself. Eventually, Blake lifted his head to look down at her. His eyes were dark and stormy. "I think that's enough sharing for today, don't you think? You should head out. Didn't you say you were meeting Yvette later to talk details of the sale?"

Asia nodded because she was trying to calm down her overactive libido. She was the one who had pulled sex off the table, but right now all she wanted was to feel Blake's mouth on hers once more. To feel his mouth everywhere. She was like an addict, desperate for her next fix.

Once she'd left the building, Asia sat in her car and tried to catch her breath. The engagement, the business, all of it was moving so quickly. She wanted Six Gems to get off the ground, but she hadn't planned on having a husband and baby to go along with it. Despite it all, Asia already loved this little one. She patted her stomach. She would do whatever was necessary to ensure that they had a good life, even if it meant hitching herself to the man whom she could see herself falling in love with.

After leaving Blake's office, Asia deposited the large check into her account and then drove to Yvette's Jewels to tell her mentor the good news.

"I knew you could do it," Yvette said.

She couldn't have without Blake's assistance, but Asia wasn't about to tell Yvette that. She was happy they were both getting what they wanted. Yvette would have her happy ending and go off into the retirement sunset with her new beau, and Asia's dream of owning her own jewelry store would come to pass.

After they discussed the particulars and timeline for the transfer, Yvette stated that she would have her attorney draft the sale documents. She was ready to leave within a couple of weeks, so Asia didn't have much time to prepare, but that was just fine with her. She'd waited a lifetime for this moment.

Fourteen

The next week went by in a flurry of meetings for Asia. Yvette's attorney had the sale documents drafted, but Asia didn't have her own attorney to vet them. One call to Blake later and he'd supplied her with an attorney he recommended, and soon the papers transferring ownership of the store to Asia were signed. A man of his word, Blake was officially a silent partner of Six Gems now and had signed his name beside Asia's when she had asked him to meet her at her attorney's office.

Asia was surprised at how easy it was to ask Blake for his advice. He was a successful businessman, after all, and she was just starting her own journey. He was a great help, but more than that, he was being a great friend. After that scorching kiss in his office, Blake had called or texted her several times to see how she was doing. Asia liked having someone around who cared about her and her well-being.

When she wasn't finalizing the details that came with the sale of the store, Asia was meeting with an interior designer to discuss improvements she wanted to make. At first, Asia had wanted to complete the interior design herself, but during one of his daily phone calls, Blake had quietly suggested that maybe she shouldn't try to do it all herself. She was in the first trimester of her pregnancy, which was known to be a vulnerable time for miscarriages, and since it was her first baby, she should take it easy. Asia listened. She remembered Shay's story and how devastated she'd been after losing her baby.

After speaking with the designer, Asia started to see her vision come to life. She was thrilled when the designer promised to have sketches and color swatches for her by next week. Asia was so into her new venture that she hadn't thought about her mother until Ava walked into the store late on Friday.

As usual, her mother arrived inappropriately dressed, this time in a crop top and leather pants.

"What's going on?" Ava asked, glancing around the store, which was currently in disarray. They'd boxed up the remaining inventory and had taken down much of the decor that was in Yvette's taste. Asia intended to sell any remaining stock at the one of the flea market shows she attended. "Is the store closing? Are you losing your job?"

Asia sighed. She'd known she needed to talk to her mama, but she'd hesitated on filling her in on too many of the details, lest she think Asia was an ATM and constantly ask for handouts. However, she did have to tell her she was going to be a grandma.

"I was just about to close up," Asia said, going to the front door and turning the lock. "Let me grab my purse and we can go out for a drink." A nonalcoholic one for her.

"If you're buying, I'm in," Ava responded. "My money is kind of funny."

Asia rolled her eyes. Of course it was. Wasn't it always?

After locking up the store, Asia drove them to one of her favorite places, La Loma. Lately, she'd been craving Mexican food. Asia didn't bother to ask her mother where her car was. Once they were seated, Ava wasted no time in ordering the Cadillac margarita. When the waiter asked if she wanted a drink, Asia shook her head.

Ava frowned. "You never turn down a drink. Something's wrong, isn't there, baby girl? I saw the store. Is it going out of business?"

"No, it isn't. I'll just have an iced tea," she told the waiter, "unsweetened."

"All right." Ava's dark brown eyes searched hers. "Then what is it? Don't keep me in suspense."

"Yvette decided to retire so I took the inheritance I received from Wynter's aunt and bought her out."

It was a version of the truth, just not the whole story.

Ava's eyes grew large. "You spent it all?"

Asia nodded. "It was just enough to cover the sale."

"You didn't keep any of that money for yourself? For your mama?" Ava inquired, folding her arms across her chest. "Great daughter you are."

"It isn't always about you, Mama. You've known

I always wanted my own jewelry shop. This was my chance, and I took it," Asia responded. "I'm not going to apologize about wanting to build a future for myself."

"You don't know the first thing about running a business."

"You're wrong. I've been learning from Yvette all these years, and I run a successful online business."

"You do? I had no idea."

"That's because you never ask," Asia replied tightly. Her mother never seemed interested in what was going on in her life. It was all about what Ava needed or wanted.

The waiter returned with Ava's margarita and Asia's iced tea. "But I have bigger news than the store."

"Bigger than you owning a store?" Ava chuckled, putting the margarita to her lips and taking a long sip. "Do tell."

"I'm pregnant."

Ava spit out the margarita and Asia had to wipe the spray from her face with a napkin. "What did you just say?"

"You're going to be a grandma."

Ava's brow furrowed. "What are you talking about? Are you seeing someone? How did this happen? Didn't I always tell you to practice safe sex?"

Ava sipped on her tea and counted to ten before answering. "Yes, it's true. I thought I was being safe, but as you know nothing is foolproof. Anyway, you don't have to worry, because Blake has asked me to marry him."

"What? Oh my God, this has gone from bad to worse," Ava said, leaning back in the booth. "First you get yourself knocked up and now you're going to make the situation worse by getting hitched?"

"It's the right thing to do, Mama. I want my baby to have a mother and father—something I never had."

That shut Ava up. She sat back in her seat and glared at Asia. "I'm sorry," she said bitterly. "I did the best I could with you, seeing as how my own mother threw me out when I had you."

"I know this story, Mama," Asia replied. "I'm just telling you that I want more for my baby." She placed her hand over stomach. "And so does Blake. We want this child to have a two-parent home."

"With parents who only married for convenience? What kind of life is that? I think you're making a mistake, Asia."

"Well, I didn't ask you," Asia responded tightly. "I was informing you that you're going to be a grandmother."

"Fine, do what you want." Ava shrugged. "You always do, but don't say I didn't warn you. Now, are you still paying for drinks, or what?"

Asia gritted her teeth. Why did she think it would be any different with Ava? That she would behave like a normal parent and wish her the best? Or say that she would be there for Asia like the Gems? Apparently, she was asking for too much. Asia had to stop hoping, because Ava would never change.

Blake glanced across at Asia in the passenger seat of his Benz. It was Saturday, and they were on their way to his aunt Sadie's for dinner to tell her the news of their impending marriage and baby on the way, but

Asia was unusually somber. Over the past week, he'd made it a habit of checking in with her. It was something he'd never done before in any of his previous relationships. She'd seemed fine on those texts and calls, but now he wasn't so sure.

"Is everything all right?" Blake inquired. "You're rather pensive today."

She glanced in his direction, but he wasn't sure she saw him. "Am I?"

"You are. Is something on your mind?" He didn't know why, but suddenly, Asia's happiness was important to him.

She released a long sigh. "It's just my mother. I told her about the baby and the marriage and she was less than enthused."

"What did she say?"

"That I was making a mistake and I'll regret it."

Blake frowned. He didn't like hearing that. Getting married and becoming a family were the absolute right things to do. "Are you having second thoughts?"

Asia shook her head. "Mama is used to being the center of attention and this time she can't be, so no, I haven't changed my mind."

Blake was glad to hear that. In order for this to work, they had to be on the same page. He gave Asia's hand a gentle squeeze.

Minutes later, they reached the gates to his aunt's estate. He pressed the security code and then pulled into the driveway. Switching off the ignition, he turned to Asia. "You ready for this?"

Asia nodded and Blake exited the driver's side and then came around to the passenger side to help her out of the vehicle. He tucked her arm in the crook of his and led her to the front door. He had a key and didn't bother ringing the doorbell.

"Aunt Sadie," Blake called out when they walked inside the foyer.

"Blake!" his aunt cried from the top of the winding staircase. Of course, the lady of the manor had to make an entrance. She was in a beautiful, ankle-length black sunset tapestry caftan dress with long sleeves.

"My darling, it's so good to see you," Aunt Sadie said when she made it to the ground floor. She kissed both of his cheeks. Then she turned to Asia. "And you, my dear, it's so good to see my nephew knows a good thing when he sees it." She gave him a conspiratorial wink. "Come, I've had canapés set up in the drawing room."

Blake placed his hand on the small of Asia's back as he walked beside her. He couldn't not touch her. She was in a snug-fitting sweaterdress with leopard and cheetah prints across the front and stripes along the side. Blake thought about the last time they'd been here and it made him want to roll that dress up to her waist and...

"Do be a dear and pour us a drink, Blake," his aunt said, interrupting his lust-filled thoughts. "I had some of my famous sangrias made," she said, pulling Asia out of his grasp and toward her on the sofa. "I'm so excited to have you here again. Blake never brings anyone home to meet me. I'm so glad he's considering a relationship."

Blake poured two glasses of sangria and handed his aunt one of them. She froze when she noticed he didn't give Asia one.

"Blake, didn't I teach you better manners?" his aunt asked.

"You did, Aunt Sadie," Blake said, and came to sit beside Asia on the couch. He noticed she was fidgeting and pulling her dress over her knees. He took one of her trembling hands in his and looked directly into his aunt's eyes. "We have some news to share. You see, Asia and I are having a baby, and we're getting married."

"Oh my Lord." His aunt clutched her chest and put down the sangria she'd been about to drink. "This is a shock."

"To us as well, but we are determined to do right by our child. Isn't that right, Asia?" Blake didn't want to do all the speaking.

"Ms. Coleman, Blake and I made this decision together. We want to give our child a family, a two-parent household. It's something I never had and he had for a short time. I hope you'll support us in our journey."

"Oh, absolutely, my darlings," Aunt Sadie responded. "Although I'm taken aback. I am happy for you. I've always wanted my Blakey to settle down with a wife and have some children, so I couldn't be happier for you both. I'm finally going to get that grandniece or grandnephew I wanted." She winked at Blake. "Are you sure this is what you both want?"

"Absolutely," Blake and Asia said in unison.

"Very well, then. Blake, there's some sparkling cider in the bar. Pour your fiancée a glass so we can have a toast."

His aunt was the consummate hostess and they spent the evening enjoying a delicious dinner of rack of lamb with twice-baked potatoes and grilled asparagus while talking about the wedding. Asia wanted something small and intimate since she was expecting, while

Blake wanted the entire world to know he was marrying one helluva woman.

They were still talking about the wedding on the drive home.

"I don't want to make a fuss," Asia said. "It's not like we're marrying for love."

"No one else knows that," Blake replied. "And I want you to have the wedding of your dreams, because I don't intend on getting a divorce." He'd seen what divorce had done to several of his high school friends. They'd hated being shuttled back and forth from one parent to the other. "I want to get married once."

"You sound so final about it all," Asia said. "We're just getting to know each other, and we haven't even lived together yet. What if you decide you can't live with me because I'm a slob?"

Blake frowned. He had a little bit of OCD and liked everything in its proper place. They might have a hurdle to overcome if she was untidy. "Are you?"

She pointed at him and laughed hysterically. "You should see the look of absolute horror on your face." When she finally stopped chuckling, she said, "No, I'm not a slob—*that* would be my mother, Ava—but I wouldn't say I'm a neat freak, either. I'm somewhere in between."

"I can live with that."

They chatted the rest of the way, until they pulled into the parking lot of Asia's apartment building. "Tonight was great," Asia said, turning to him. "Your aunt's reaction is how I wished Ava would have reacted, but..." She shrugged.

Blake leaned across the console and caressed her

cheek with his palm. "It bothers you, doesn't it, that she doesn't approve?"

"It shouldn't. I've always done what I wanted when I wanted because she was never around."

"But she's still your mother."

"There's the rub," Asia responded. She unbuckled herself and opened the passenger-side door. Blake came around to help her, but she was already out of the vehicle.

"I appreciated getting to know Sadie. I suppose you'll be wanting to meet Ava next?"

Blake shrugged. "Whenever you're ready."

She smiled. "Thank you." She leaned toward him as if she were going to kiss his cheek, but Blake turned his head so that her kiss landed on his mouth instead. He'd been dying to put his mouth on hers all night, and when the opportunity presented itself, he'd taken it. Heat slammed through him at the touch of her lips on his.

The kiss was like flicking on a light switch because the next thing Blake knew, she was kissing him back and he was pushing her backward, against the car. Her body was cleaved to his, and he reached behind her and clasped her butt, allowing him to wedge her legs apart so he could push his length against her. She gasped when she came in contact with his erection, but instead of asking him to stop, she ground her hips against him seductively. Their tongues tangled, eliciting a growl from Blake.

He lifted his head and leaned in. "I want you, Asia."

She planted both hands on his chest and, to his surprise, pushed him away. "I know you do, and although my body wants you, we agreed to wait. I need to know you want me for me, not just because I'm carrying your baby."

"Asia, where is this coming from? I've wanted you from the first moment I saw you in the store, and it's why we ended up creating a baby together."

"Maybe, but I think we should still stick to the agreement," Asia responded.

"If that's what you want," Blake replied, stepping backward.

"It is."

"I'll walk you to your door."

"I think it's best if I go there alone," Asia said. She gave him a small smile and then walked into her building.

Blake understood her reticence. She was looking at the long game and not immediate gratification. He vowed right then that he would temper the attraction he felt toward Asia even though she was the most exciting lover he'd ever had—and he'd had a fair number since his teen years.

He was still coming on too strong. He needed to assure her that a marriage between them would work even though they were relative strangers. He had to show her he could be the man she needed, a man she could rely on and count on, because Asia had had so very little of that growing up. Only then would she be willing to bring their passion back to the forefront.

Fifteen

Asia was impressed. Ever since the night they'd told Blake's aunt Sadie of their marriage and she requested they stick to the no-sex agreement a couple of weeks ago, he'd been nothing but the most charming fiancé. When she'd finished designing the ring, he'd sent it off to a jeweler, who had had it ready within days. Then he had surprised her one night with the ring box and slid the ring on her finger. Asia was officially an engaged woman.

He continued calling her several times a day to be sure she ate, was getting enough rest or working on expanding her collection, which she was. He even introduced Asia to his friends Jeffrey and Mara over dinner at their home. As an added bonus, Blake was starting to open up to her. One night, he'd confided in her about his parents and what it had been like growing up. How his mother had baked cookies for him and his friends, how he and his father would tinker with old cars in the garage. Or how his father had taught him how to shave.

Blake was doing everything she asked, but he didn't kiss her and rarely touched her anymore, except to help her out of the car or place his hand on the small of her back for support. She almost wished she hadn't said anything about cooling things off between them. It wasn't that she didn't want Blake—she did, and now she wanted *more* from him because, deep down, she was starting to fall hard for her baby's father.

Instead of focusing on the lack of passion in their relationship, Ava had thrown herself into getting Six Gems ready. After selecting a layout and a palette with the designer, construction drawings had been created and sent to Coleman & Sons. It was the one thing Blake had been insistent upon: his company doing the construction. That way, he could oversee the project and be sure the work was done to the highest level of quality. Seeing that she had very little knowledge on the topic, Asia had acquiesced on this point only.

The store's doorbell chimed and Asia came from the back office to find Blake casually dressed in jeans and a white button-down shirt, but looking as sexy as ever. His low-faded curly hair, sexy five-o'clock shadow and sensuous lips called out to every female instinct in her.

"Blake, what are you doing here?" Asia asked. If she'd known he was coming, she would certainly have dressed better than leggings and a large graphic tunic, which on her petite frame was oversize. Although she was only fourteen weeks pregnant, she'd already gained a few pounds despite the morning sickness. Her clothes were usually fitted, so she was quickly running out of options—thus today's poor man's attire.

"I brought lunch." Blake held up two large bags. "Since the work you wanted done was minimal, I fast-tracked the pricing for construction, and I have it with me." He held up a folder, which Asia tried to jump up and grab, but he smacked her hand away. "But first, you have to eat lunch."

Asia pouted. "Can't we eat and work?"

"We could," he responded, "but we're not going to. Let's head to your office." Rather than brook an argument, Blake headed straight to the rear, where the office held a desk, chair, and a small table and two additional chairs.

Blake set the bags on the table and took out the clear containers with chopped salads. A Cobb salad for her and a Southwest salad for him. He handed her a fork as well as a bottle of fruit juice.

"Thank you," Asia said, curling up into the chair to dig in.

"You're welcome." Blake poured vinaigrette on his salad and commenced digging in. "You know, we've talked about the store, but we haven't talked about the wedding or even where we'll live afterwards."

Asia was doing her best not to think about that. Being responsible for the store while being pregnant was enough.

"Are you going to tell me what's wrong?" Blake asked while eating his salad. "Are you having second thoughts about marrying me?"

Oh, she was having second and third thoughts, but

she didn't want to say that. "I have a lot on my plate. The pregnancy, the store and now you want me to plan a big wedding."

He put his fork down, "If it would be easier, we can have the small, intimate wedding you want for close family, and when we're ready, we can have a larger one. How does that sound?"

"Thank you. I appreciate your willingness to compromise."

"It's not my usual modus operandi, but for you, I will. But I think you should move into the penthouse. We can look for a house before the baby is born."

Asia laughed as she ate a bite of her salad. "You mean you don't want to move into my cramped one-bedroom apartment?" It might be good enough for Asia, but she knew they needed a nursery with a place for all the baby's things.

"Not a chance," Blake replied. "Now on to the timeline for the project."

"Yay!" Asia rubbed her hands together in glee.

"Based on the drawings, the work you want is minimal and should only take about four to six weeks. You should really start thinking about planning your grand opening."

"That's it?" Asia assumed it would take more time.

"Six Gems is my top priority."

Asia beamed. Blake understood the importance of the store, and it warmed her heart. "I guess I'd better start pulling together my collections and what I want to showcase?"

"I think so," Blake said, taking several more bites of

his lunch. "You never told me, how did you get started with designing?"

Asia shrugged. "I don't know. I think I was twelve or thirteen when I started sketching clothes. I really wanted the latest fashions like other teenagers my age, but Ava couldn't afford it. She would take me to thrift stores and I would take those clothes and reinvent them into my own creation. Once I met the Gems in high school, I no longer cared what everyone else thought, so I moved on to jewelry. I started out with beads. I would hang out at the bead store and make endless bracelets and necklaces. Eventually, it led to me creating my own jewelry with other materials."

Blake screwed off the cap of his sparking water and took a sip. "Was your mother supportive?"

"Ava? Be supportive?" Asia snorted. "That's a joke. Wait until you meet her, you'll see."

"And when might that be?"

Asia stared across the table at him. She was hoping for never, though she doubted that was possible. They had to meet, but she wasn't looking forward to it. "You don't know my mother. She'll probably make a pass at you."

"Which I will politely decline. There is only one woman I'm interested in." When Blake said it, Asia believed him, because his eyes were glittering with an emotion she couldn't define. "I wouldn't jeopardize our relationship."

"Good answer." Asia couldn't resist smiling at him. Blake had that effect on her. "And I promise you will meet her. But how about you meet your baby girl or boy first?"

"What do you mean?"

"My next doctor's appointment is in two weeks. I was hoping you might join me, because the doctor will be performing an ultrasound to check on the baby's health and development. They might even be able to tell the gender."

His mouth curved into a smile. "I would absolutely love that."

Asia wanted to cry with relief when Blake leaned over and claimed her mouth with his in a hungry kiss. Since that night outside her apartment, Blake had kept his hands to himself and not made any untoward moves on her. It had left Asia worrying that she might have made a mistake with her no-sex rule. She had been starting to wonder if the chemistry and passion between them was waning. But this kiss obliterated any of Asia's doubts and made her realize that she wasn't just falling in love with Blake. She was already there.

"I never thought I'd see the day you wanted to meet me in a children's store," Jeffrey said when Blake met up with him that weekend.

Ever since Asia asked Blake to go to the ultrasound appointment, he'd been filled with joy. He was finally going to see his baby. Hear their heartbeat. It made Blake realize that he needed to start thinking like a father. Who better to help him than Jeffrey, who already had two young children?

"I wouldn't have believed you if you had told me this six months ago," Blake said, "but there's no way I'm not going to be involved in every aspect of my child's life. I heard this store was the place to go."

"Then why didn't you bring your baby's mother? I imagine she would like this."

"Because I want to surprise her with a nursery," Blake said. "I've been reading up a lot and I already reached out to a top-notch nanny agency, who gave me a laundry list of things we would need for the baby."

"I can see how excited you are about the baby," Jeffrey said, "but what about Asia? Last we spoke, you were talking about getting married. I haven't heard anything about a wedding. Has anything changed?"

Blake shook his head. "Not at all. We've just been focused on getting her store going, but we did agree that we would have an intimate ceremony with family and friends."

"You're doing an awful lot for a woman you barely know."

Blake frowned. "Asia and I have grown closer the last few weeks."

"I know how you work, Blake," Jeffrey said with a smirk.

Blake couldn't resist smiling as well. "And usually you would be right, but Asia took sex off the table. We've been completely platonic. In fact, dare I say it, we've actually become friends."

Jeffrey clapped his hands. "Well done, my friend."

After the death of his parents, Blake decided he would never become a hostage to his emotions again. It was why he'd pulled away after their kiss yesterday. Plus, he respected Asia and he wanted her to know she could trust him.

"But it begs the question why you're going through all the trouble," Jeffrey said.

"Asia's going to be my wife. I want her to be happy. The relationship can't just be on my terms."

Jeffrey turned around and did a double take. "Are you sure you're Blake Coleman, because the Blake I know is always in charge."

"Can't I evolve? I'm doing what's best for everyone."

"I can see that," Jeffrey said. "And I'm calling you out that you might have an ulterior motive, one that you don't even realize."

"Which is?"

"That you've developed feelings for the mother of your child. And if you have, that's a good thing, Blake. It will only strengthen your marriage and give you a solid foundation."

Blake shook his head. "It's not like that, Jeffrey. We're not like you and Mara. You guys fell in love, got married and had children. We've done completely the opposite. We're having a baby and decided to get married. Love isn't an option."

"Who's to say there can't be love?"

"I say," Blake stated vehemently. "I can't endure losing another person, Jeffrey. Losing my parents was hard enough."

"All right," Jeffrey replied, holding his hands up in defense. "I'm just telling you, from the outside looking in, it appears as if there's more going on between you two. I encourage you to dig a little deeper and explore it. Who knows what you could unearth?"

*

Later that day, Blake thought about Jeffrey's comments as he put together the crib he'd bought at the children's furniture store. He could have paid for the installation service, but for some reason, Blake wanted to do it for himself. He did work for a construction company, after all. How hard could it be?

Four hours later, he glanced at his handiwork. Blake was proud that he'd put together the beautiful pebble white stone Evolur baby crib with a full headboard and solid molding that could convert into a toddler bed one day. He didn't know whether they were having a boy or a girl. All he knew was that he felt protective over their unborn child and wanted to give them everything he'd never had, namely, the stability and sense of home that had been brutally taken away from him because of a drunk driver.

Having a child with Asia would forever link her life with his. It made sense for them to marry. Jeffrey was wrong about him developing feelings for her. He was going the extra mile with Asia so she felt secure about their arrangement, and to make their relationship seamless. He wanted Asia to be happy, but all he could ever give her was passion because he wasn't capable of any other emotion—especially love.

"I have to say, you've landed yourself a whale," Ava said, bursting through Asia's apartment door Sunday evening in a leather jacket and skinny jeans. She tossed her purse on a table in the foyer.

Asia was in no mood for her mother's shenanigans. She'd had a great day. She and Blake had signed off on the contract for Coleman & Sons to begin renovating the store and their relationship was headed in the right direction. She couldn't be happier.

"What's up, Mama?"

"Why didn't you tell me your fiancé is Blake Coleman, a wealthy developer? I read up on him. He comes from old money and his company has been around for decades."

"What does that have to do with anything?"

Ava put on her hands on her hips. "It means, young lady, that he can help take care of you and your mama."

"No, it doesn't," Asia replied. "Blake's responsibility is to me and this baby."

"Ah, don't be like that, Asia. Now that you've got yourself a rich beau, he can afford to give you a spending allowance. All you have to do is ask. I mean, look at that ring." Her mother grasped Asia's hand and ogled the six-carat diamond atop her left ring finger. Asia hadn't meant for the rock to be that huge, but Blake had told the jeweler to find the biggest diamond he could and put it in her design.

"I'm not begging Blake for money," Asia retorted hotly. "I take care of myself, always have. I don't need Blake to do it for me."

"Then why are you getting married if not for stability?" her mother asked.

"That's part of it, but the stability is that our child will have two parents living in the same house who will love and support them."

"That's all fine and good," Ava said, "but does Blake love you?"

Damn Ava for asking the question that had been stuck in Asia's craw this entire time. No, he didn't love her. The only reason marriage was on the table was because Blake wanted his child and felt duty bound to marry her. Asia was happy he wanted be a father to her unborn baby, but she was worried that a marriage without love might not work.

But then again, Blake never failed to look at her with desire. There was always a gleam in his eye that set her pulse racing. Asia had never had that kind of passion with any other man, but was it enough? Could a marriage based on hot sex and a desire for a family succeed?

"We will love our child," Asia answered. "And we want what's best for them, and that's giving him or her the life we both longed for as children."

"Was it really so horrible growing up with me?" Ava asked. "Would you have rather I given you up so you could have been adopted?"

"You did your best."

"Which wasn't good enough," Ava surmised correctly.

Asia remained silent.

"Asia, you've always had your head in the clouds, wanting things that weren't within your reach. Maybe it's because you were surrounded by friends with easier lives than you. I may not have been the best mother, but I can tell you this—money can't buy you love or happiness."

Ava picked up her purse, which she'd thrown on the hall table in the foyer, and left. Asia thought about going after her, but what she could she say? That she was right? Yet on the other hand, Asia knew she couldn't turn her back on Blake. Their relationship may not be perfect, but they were making strides. It was always possible he could fall in love with her. She had to hold on to that hope.

Sixteen

"The day is getting closer, Egypt," Asia said from inside the store. Blake hadn't been lying when he said he would fast-track construction once she removed all her belongings. A week later, they'd demoed the entire store, down to the concrete. A week after that, they'd had it framed with drywall.

"Look at this place." Asia turned the phone around so Egypt could see the progress. It was finally starting to look like her vision.

"Omigod! It doesn't even look like the same place," Egypt replied.

Asia turned the phone back around so she could see her best friend. "It won't be. It's a whole new fresh design that will allow my pieces to shine."

"This is wonderful, Asia. I'm so glad to see everything

you worked on coming to life," Egypt said. "I wasn't sure what to think when the bank turned you down."

"I couldn't have done it without your help on the business plan."

"You're absolutely welcome."

"And how is Sexy Chocolate?" Asia inquired. Egypt's new man was exactly the type of man she needed. Tall, dark and handsome and could handle her bold personality.

"Garrett is doing amazing. I still can't believe all three of us are engaged," Egypt said, "or that Wynter's wedding is next month."

"I'll probably have to get my bridesmaid dress taken out," Asia responded, "thanks to my ever-expanding tummy."

"That's what happens when you're pregnant. How've you been feeling, by the way? Has the morning sickness subsided?"

"It's starting to. I'm actually going to see the doctor today for my very first ultrasound."

"Oh, Asia, that's wonderful. I can't wait to see images of Baby Reynolds."

"Doesn't she mean Baby Coleman?" Blake asked from behind Asia. She spun around to face her fiancé, who had a smile on his face.

"Is that Mr. Blake?" Egypt inquired. "Let me talk to him. Hand him the phone."

Asia scrunched her face into a frown. "Bossy much? Here"—she handed Blake her iPhone—"Egypt would like to speak with you."

Short of eavesdropping, she couldn't listen in on their

conversation, because Blake walked to the far side of the room. When he returned, he handed her back the phone.

"Well?" She raised a brow. "What did she say?"

"Egypt told me that if I didn't treat you right, she was going to fly all the way the Denver to give me a beatdown."

Asia laughed out loud. Now that sounded like Egypt. "I guess you have your marching orders. Are you ready to go? My appointment is at eleven."

"Let's go."

They chatted on the way to her doctor's office about how his new residential community was going. They'd finally broken ground and were working through the permit process. Asia liked that Blake shared his work with her. When they arrived at Dr. Speaks's office, Asia signed in and waited for her name to be called.

She noticed that Blake was not only very quiet, but his butterscotch skin looked pale. "Is everything okay?"

Everything was far from okay, Blake thought. Yes, he knew Asia was pregnant. He'd seen evidence of it in the way her body was starting to change. He didn't know if she had noticed, but her breasts were becoming fuller and her skin glowed. But today, here in the doctor's office, he'd gotten a reality check.

Everywhere he looked, there were pregnant women. Some had small rounded bellies. Others looked as if they were ready to give birth at any moment.

"You've had a lot more time to wrap your head around this," Blake said. "And you've had to deal with the physical ramifications. I guess you can say, in this moment, it just got real for me."

Asia nodded. "That makes sense. How do you feel?"

"Scared," Blake answered honestly. He didn't want to make a mistake raising his child, but didn't all parents make them?

Asia reached across the space between them and threaded her fingers through his. "So am I. It hasn't been easy going through all these changes, physically as well as emotionally. I'm just thinking about the end result—a beautiful boy or girl."

"You're right." He placed his free hand on hers. "That's the most important thing."

"Asia Reynolds?" A nurse was in the doorway with a clipboard, waiting for them.

Asia stood. "C'mon."

They held hands walking to the examination room. Blake's senses were assaulted with all things baby, from images on the walls to pregnant mothers walking in the corridors. He felt as if he were in an alternate universe. He could kiss his bachelorhood days goodbye, because they were being replaced with fatherhood.

After taking her vitals and asking a few questions, the nurse told Asia to get on the bed and a technician would be in shortly to perform the ultrasound.

"Nervous?" Blake asked as she sat on the bed.

"A little. You know, we never talked about if we want to know the gender. Personally, I'd like to know now, so we can plan," Asia said. "How about you?"

Blake smiled. He appreciated Asia asking for his input. "I'd like the same."

"Good."

The technician came in shortly afterward and explained that the ultrasound procedure was used to locate the pregnancy and to check the overall health of the baby to make sure it was developing normally. Blake sat in a nearby chair to watch it all unfold.

Asia lifted her shirt and the technician placed some ultrasound gel on her stomach and then began moving the wand across. An image popped on the screen and Blake could just make out the shape. He heard the technician talking, but he was mesmerized by what was on screen.

"We can see the baby's chest and the heartbeat," the technician said, and pointed the wand's cursor to an area for them to see. "I'm going to enlarge the image so you can hear the heartbeat. Let's listen now."

Blake felt his throat constrict as he listened to the thump, thump of his baby's heartbeat. Tears welled in his eyes as he looked at the screen, and when he hazarded a glance at Asia, tears were streaming down her cheeks. He reached for her hand and squeezed it.

"That's our baby," she said through her tears. All Blake could do was nod. He was overwhelmed by the experience. He had never imagined this day would come, but now that it was here, it felt like the most magical thing on earth.

"If the baby cooperates, we can usually get a profile picture, which is always nice to take home especially with this new HD format," the technician continued.

On the screen, the baby looked so lifelike. The technician pointed out several features. "This is the forehead, nose and upper lip." She moved the wand. "Now we're looking at the bones and limbs, and I'll measure them as well. If you want to know if you're having a boy or girl. I can get everything teed up for the doctor."

"We want to know," Blake and Asia said simultaneously.

After the technician concluded the ultrasound, Dr. Speaks came in to talk with them. Dr. Speaks was an older gentleman with a shock of white hair. He looked like he'd been delivering babies for a long time.

"How's our baby?" Asia asked the doctor.

Dr. Speaks looked at Blake. "I assume you're the baby's father?"

"Oh yes, I'm sorry, Dr. Speaks. Blake will be at all the appointments going forward. You can speak freely," Asia replied. She appreciated him respecting her privacy.

Dr. Speaks nodded and then directed his attention at Asia again. "Very well. Then to answer your question, the baby is doing just fine, Asia. Everything is progressing normally," Dr. Speaks said. "But I understand you want to know the baby's gender?"

"Yes, we do," Asia said.

"Then you both should be pleased, because you're going to have a boy." Dr. Speaks moved the cursor on the screen and an image popped up. "You can see he has an extra appendage."

Blake closed his eyes and took such a deep breath, it nearly hurt his chest. When he opened them, he saw the image on the screen and it felt as if an arrow had pierced his heart. He didn't know it was possible to feel such instant, all-consuming love. It made him weak in the knees.

A son.

"Thank you, thank you for this precious gift." He bent his head and brushed his lips against Asia's.

He was so thankful Asia had come into his life. If she hadn't, he wouldn't have a son. Blake would do everything in his power to ensure that his baby boy had the very best in life. He would be raised a Coleman and he would carry on the legacy of the Coleman name. Now, all Blake had to do was get Asia to the altar.

Asia had known the ultrasound would be life changing, but she hadn't realized how much it would affect her. Seeing her baby on the screen, hearing her son's heartbeat, was everything she could have hoped for. But, quite honestly, it was Blake's reaction that touched her the most.

He was right. She'd been living and breathing the pregnancy, but he was on the outside looking in. Today, he got to be a participant, and she was so happy for him. She knew he was thrilled to have a son. Asia knew how important family legacy was to Blake.

Eventually, they left the doctor's office with a slew of pictures she could show the Gems, and even her mother. Asia knew Ava wasn't thrilled with how the situation came to be, but surely, once she saw the 4D images of her grandson, it would change her outlook. It had certainly changed Asia's.

She was going to have a son. A little boy. And little boys loved their mamas. Asia hoped to be the best mother she could be. She would be there for her son, to guide him through all that life had in store, and show him the difference between right and wrong. She couldn't wait to start the journey of motherhood. And she was excited to share that journey with Blake.

"That had to be the most singularly best moment of my entire life," Blake said once they were in his car.

Asia didn't know where they were headed and she didn't care. She was on cloud nine. "You mean meeting me wasn't the best?"

Blake chuckled. "I'm sorry, but no."

"Wow!" Asia's said, laughing. "Say how you really feel."

Blake kept one hand on the steering wheel and used his other hand to grab one of hers. "Seriously, though, if I hadn't met you, we wouldn't have our baby boy."

"No, we wouldn't."

They were both silent until twenty minutes later, when Asia noticed they weren't at her apartment, but pulling into the garage of a tall, modern building.

She turned to Blake with a raised brow, and he said, "Thought it was finally time you came to my place. I've had dinner ordered, so we can relax and catch some Netflix. And I've got a surprise for you."

"You do?"

"I do," Blake said, parking his SUV, "and I can't wait for you to see it."

They took a private elevator from the garage to the top floor, where it dropped them off inside a luxurious penthouse apartment. There, she was greeted by a spacious great room, which featured a coffered ceiling, a beautiful formal dining room with views of the mountains and a large balcony that looked as if it wrapped around the entire penthouse.

In another part of the apartment, a well-designed kitchen overlooked a bright casual dining area, equipped with a large center island, breakfast bar and plenty of counter and cabinet space, as well as an ample walk-in pantry.

"This place is yours?" Asia asked, glancing around. "It's pretty spectacular."

Blake grinned. "Thank you. We developed this piece of property, so I decided to take the top floor."

"If this is what Coleman & Sons Construction is able to accomplish, then I can't wait to see what you do with Six Gems."

He held out his hand. "I want to show you your surprise."

Asia took his proffered hand and followed him down the hallway's marble floor, passing by a powder room, an office and a guest bedroom before Blake stopped in front of a door.

"Go ahead and open it," Blake said.

Asia glanced at him curiously before turning the handle.

Her hand flew to her mouth. "Oh my…" She glanced around and couldn't believe her eyes. Blake had outfitted the entire room, complete with a crib, a changing table and an armoire. There was a ton of natural light in the room, allowing Asia to see a rocking chair with matching ottoman for her to cuddle their little one in. He'd even thought of a bookcase filled with children's books, while cute little framed animal photographs hung on the light gray walls. "I… I have no words."

He frowned. "Is that a good thing? Or a bad thing?" he asked. "I mean, I know it might have been presumptuous of me. You probably had your own ideas of how you wanted the nursery to look, and we didn't know the sex when I…"

Asia walked over to him and lifted her mouth to his. The sensation of his mouth on hers sent desire coursing through her veins. Blake must have felt the same way, because he took over, becoming the marauder and demanding a response from Asia. She eagerly gave it, clinging to his broad shoulders as wave after wave of pleasure crashed over her.

Why had she denied herself—or them both—*this?*

Because she had wanted to be sure that the man she'd fallen in love with wasn't just with her for the baby and the hot sex. But at the moment, Asia didn't care about any of that. She needed him to fill her more than she remembered needing anything in her life.

Blake lifted her into his arms and carried her down the hall to his bedroom. It had an oversize bed with a black comforter and silk sheets. He laid her on the bed and then started kicking off his shoes and stripping off his clothes as he went, causing buttons to clatter to floor. Asia echoed the sentiment, flicking off her heels and lifting her sweater over her shoulders, tossing it to the floor. Her skirt was next, but she fumbled with the zipper.

"Let me," Blake said, unzipping the garment and sliding it down her hips. And then his mouth was on her, on her neck, sucking in *her spot.* She angled her head to give him better access as he devoured her. His hands came around to the front to mold and shape her breasts in her bra, then he undid the clasp, allowing it to fall to the bed.

This felt right. More than right.

Because she loved him. The emotion was strong and pure and filled her with elation, but she wouldn't say the words to Blake now, for fear that it would spoil the moment. Instead, she thrust her breasts upward, back into his palms so he could caress her, gently at first, and then harder.

"Put your mouth on me," she cried.

A guttural groan broke from Blake and then he was turning her around and pushing her down on the bed. As he came toward her, bare-chested, she got a great view of his rippled torso. She planted her hands high on his pecs and her palms tingled from his hot flesh, but she only had a moment to register the contact before Blake gave her exactly what she wanted.

With his tongue, he licked, flicked and teased her chocolate nipples before taking one in his mouth and sucking on it. When he was finished with one, he paid the other equal homage.

"You know exactly where my erogenous zones are."

"I look forward to finding more." Blake gave her a sexy smile and then continued kissing his way down from her breasts to her belly. Then he stopped.

He placed one large hand across her stomach and his dark eyes were transfixed on her. "You're carrying our child in here. I don't want to hurt you."

Tears welled in her eyes. She felt treasured and cared for. "You won't. The doctor said I can have a normal sex life. It won't harm the baby."

If it were possible, his eyes turned darker and then Blake was dropping to his knees. She felt his hands slide up her bare legs, hook inside the waistband of her panties and pull them down, flinging them aside. The sight of his head between her thighs and his hot breath on her skin had her tied in knots, waiting for the inevitable.

When he dipped his head and pressed his lips to her center, her body convulsed. It hadn't been long since they had been together, but it felt like forever. Another stroke of his tongue and her legs began to tremble.

"Easy, love, I've got you," he said. Then he parted her legs wider and had his way with her, stroking her with his lips and tongue, and when she began to cry out in ecstasy, he added his fingers. She clutched his shoulders, trying to anchor herself from the storm, but she couldn't. Blake was a maestro, playing her body this way and that until she began to tumble and see flashes of white light.

Asia took in deep gulps of air, and as she did, she watched Blake finish undressing, removing his pants and boxers in one fell swoop.

"I need to be inside you," he said, moving back up the bed.

"Then take me," Asia said.

He plunged one hand into her hair, holding her to him, so he could claim her mouth once more. The kiss went on and on, but Blake was a multitasker and she found he'd positioned himself at her entrance and then he was entering her with one deep thrust. As he sank deeper inside, her body welcomed him. Then, ever so slowly, he began to move. It was exquisite torture.

"Harder!" she yelled, and Blake surged in, hard and fast.

"Yes. Just like that."

She wrapped her legs around his waist and he surged in again, increasing the pace and friction, and she breathlessly urged him on. His palm slipped beneath her bottom to tilt her exactly where he wanted her, and when his fingers delved lower between their bodies to stroke her clitoris, Asia shattered as her climax struck. His own release followed hers, and he thrust deeply once more before pitching forward with a primal growl of pleasure.

They stayed connected for several long moments, with his face buried in her neck and Asia cradling him. She was overwhelmed with the knowledge that they'd shared something special. After seeing their son, they'd made love. She wanted to confess her feelings for Blake, but he wouldn't welcome them. He had made it abundantly clear that love wasn't on the table in their marriage. She would have to pack it away in her mind and mark it Do Not Open. But for now, she would bask in the love she had for him as she drifted off to sleep.

Seventeen

Blake was distracted. Usually, when he was at work, it was all business because that's all he had to keep him going. Things weren't so simple anymore. He was going to be a father. Asia was having his son, and that changed everything. When she'd seen the nursery, he'd watched her and she'd opened up like a flower when it came in direct contact with the sun. Something had stirred and eddied within his chest at her effervescent smile. He was developing feelings for the woman. He'd assured himself he could remain detached and unfeeling toward the mother of his child. He'd been wrong.

Last night, when they'd come together, it had been earthshaking. They'd never made it out of bed and ended up eating the meal he'd ordered there. Consequently, all morning, he hadn't been able to get the taste of her, the feel of her, out of his mind. She tasted so damn delicious that he was addicted to her. And she'd taken him to heaven this morning when she'd woken him up by pleasuring him with her lips and tongue. He had no willpower when it came to Asia. How had she overridden his common sense? He'd thought marriage would bind them together for the baby and sex would be a bonus.

But it kept getting better each time. What was he supposed to do with these unwanted feelings? In the past, he was always the one who walked away and never looked back. But he could never walk away from his baby boy. He was his family. As for Asia, the thought of leaving her made Blake feel sick to his stomach.

It was only going to get worse once they were married and Asia moved in. This morning, in bed, she had mentioned hastening the latter. She was finally ready to be in his bed every night, and Blake welcomed it, but it also made him nervous. He didn't want her to start thinking love was on offer. He wasn't prepared to give it. He couldn't bear to lose someone else like he'd lost his parents. Their deaths were why he'd become who he was, a man incapable of love and emotion, but could he change that?

Did he want to?

No. He shook his head. Love was a recipe for disaster—or at least that's what he told himself.

"So, what do you think?" Blake asked Asia when he arrived at the store two weeks later. The construction for Six Gems was nearly complete and he was here so they could go through the punch list items and make sure everything was ready for the grand opening the following Saturday.

Asia didn't know how Coleman & Sons Construction had managed to finish the project in four weeks, but they had. She was impressed with the quality and craftsmanship of their work. "It's wonderful, Blake." She whirled around to look at her dream come to life. "I can't believe this is happening. All because of you."

"No." Blake walked toward her and took both of her hands in his. "Because of you. You had the vision. This is your dream. I'm only helping facilitate it. I've seen you working your fingers to the bone to add to the new collection you started with that first piece you sold me months ago."

Asia had expanded her raw diamond collection to include more pieces that would complement the necklace. "True, but you were a big piece of the puzzle. Thank you." She stepped up on tiptoe and placed her lips against his. She mated her tongue with his in a dance that sent shivers up and down her spine. She couldn't get enough of this man. Ever since the day of the ultrasound, they'd been inseparable, in and out bed.

Her decree of no sex until they got to know each other had gone out the window after that day. She was madly in love with Blake and *wanted* to be with him every day. He thrilled her to the core of her being. However, she did sense that Blake was holding back. Asia didn't know how she knew, but she did.

Was he as passionate in bed as before? Yes, but that night, as they'd lain in each other's arms, Asia thought she'd seen a shift in Blake that gave her hope he might be falling in love with her, too. But then recently, she'd thought she imagined it. Was she projecting because she wanted so badly to believe he could love her, too?

"You're welcome," Blake said. "Do you feel like you have everything you need for the party?"

Asia nodded. "The party planner you suggested has everyone staged and ready for Saturday. Food will be high-end canapés. Music will be a soft harpist playing in the background, and my jewelry will be spotlighted so everyone can see the new collection. And the best part? All the Gems are flying in for the event. You'll finally get to meet them."

"I can't wait to meet the women who have been such an integral part of your life."

"Neither can I." She was eager to have all five women here to help advise her if she was making a mistake, because she was in such deep waters with Blake, her feet couldn't even touch the bottom.

"You look stunning, Asia," Blake said the night of the grand opening. She'd been staying at his apartment the past few days because it was easier than shuttling back and forth to her place.

"Thank you for the dress." Blake had had a slew of dresses sent over for Asia to choose from. She'd decided on a strapless embellished Dior Haute Couture gown. Asia liked the light gray dress because it was wrapped in sleek fishnet and tulle fabric. What made it stunning was the staggered rows of tulle and crystal-beaded ribbons that gave it sparkle, and it covered up her baby bump.

Although she was barely showing, there was definitely a swell to her stomach. As for her hair, she'd opted to have her shoulder-length do done in sideswept 1930s waves. She had a smoky eye and dark red lipstick, but otherwise, the rest of her makeup was minimalistic. The true star was the diamond necklace she'd made for the event, which she'd paired with a matching baguette bracelet.

Although they were spending an extraordinary amount of time together, Asia still wondered if Ava had been right. Was a marriage without love doomed to fail? Blake told her she would want for nothing in life and he would support and care for her. But love? She knew he would love his son. She'd seen it in his eyes when he saw the ultrasound. He loved him already, but her? He didn't love her. The question was, would he ever?

She felt Blake's hands on your shoulders. "You all right? You were daydreaming. Are you nervous about tonight?"

She shook her head. "Not at all. Having you and my girls here is all the reinforcements I need." Even Ava said she would swing by, especially when Asia had had a designer dress couriered over for the event. She couldn't risk her mama showing up in one of her tawdry ensembles.

Blake offered her his arm. "Then we had better get you to the ball, Cinderella."

A limousine was on hand to drive them to the event so Blake could enjoy a drink if he wanted to. Asia wished she could have one. She was all nerves, wondering how many people would show up. With Blake's connections and the help of the publicist she'd hired, she'd reached out to all the major news outlets and invited several movers and shakers in town, but she still had no idea how things would turn out.

It was a big deal for Asia. Six Gems was her baby. She'd put everything she owned and her blood, sweat and tears into this venture. It had to succeed.

A half hour later, Asia and Blake arrived to find several photographers outside the store, waiting by the red carpet. Was that a good sign?

Blake squeezed her hand. "It's going to be all right. You got this." He leaned over to kiss her cheek and then he was climbing out of the limo and waving at the press. He held out his hand and helped Asia exit.

"Blake, are you really going to settle down with one woman?" one of the photographers yelled out.

"How does it feel to snag one of Denver's most eligible bachelors?" another shouted.

The press knew about their engagement, but that's the way Blake wanted it, so Asia wasn't going to fret. She smiled and waved but didn't speak as she entered the store. When she arrived, she was happy to see that Six Gems was bustling with guests. She wished Yvette could be there, but she was off on a world cruise with Melvin. She did see her favorite five women huddled in a corner, sipping martinis.

Shay saw her first and screamed, "Asia!" and rushed toward her. Blake released her hand as the rest of the women followed suit, enveloping Asia in a hug.

"It's so good to see you, Asia," Wynter whispered, when they finally parted. "I've been worried about you, but I don't know why—you're looking fabulous."

"I have to agree with Wynter," Egypt said. "Motherhood looks good on you."

Asia couldn't resist blushing. "Thank you." She tried to keep tears from falling because she didn't realize how much she'd missed these women, how much she *needed* these women, until now.

"And are you the illustrious Blake Coleman?" Teagan asked, walking up to Blake. Teagan was sizing him up from head to toe.

"One and the same," Blake replied, and offered his hand. "I take it you're Teagan."

"How can you tell?" Teagan inquired, shaking his hand.

"I've seen pictures, and Asia's description fits you to a tee," he responded.

"Oh, I love a man that can give it back to me," Teagan said. "We should chat."

"I agree," Shay and Egypt said in unison. They each circled an arm around Blake and led him away from the group with Teagan on their heels.

Lyric reached out and grasped Asia's hand. "Since they"—she glanced over her shoulder at Shay and Egypt, who were no doubt about to grill Blake— "have Blake covered, how are you doing, my friend? I mean, this place"—she glanced around—"looks nothing like it did before."

"I agree," Wynter said. "You've done a complete three-sixty, and it looks wonderful. And you've got a great turnout tonight."

"Thank you, ladies, but if you'll forgive me, I do need to mingle," Asia said. She saw several of the women whom she'd met months ago at Sadie's birthday party come in. "But I'm in desperate need of some girl talk. Are you guys free later?"

"Oh, absolutely," Lyric said.

Asia gave her friends a smile and headed for the wealthy group. Finally, she could talk freely about her feelings to her *sistas*, who understood her. Asia hoped they might help give her some clarity on what to do next.

Blake wasn't afraid of talking to Asia's friends. He was confident in who he was and knew he was doing the right thing by Asia. Whether the Gems thought that way was another matter entirely.

Once they were some distance away from Asia, Blake turned to them. "What do you want to know, ladies?"

"Everything," Shay responded, folding her arms across her chest. Her dark locs were arranged in a hap-hazard updo, but it worked for her, and she was just as athletic in her fitted jumpsuit as Asia had mentioned. "Why did you propose to Asia?"

"What are your intentions toward our girl?" Egypt asked. She, too, was exactly how Blake had envisioned her. Buxom and bold and nearly meeting his height in the heels she wore with a black sheath dress.

"Are you ready to be a husband and a father?" Teagan fired off. Teagan was an all-work-and-no-fun kind of gal in a red power pantsuit, but he could take her.

Blake held up his hands in defense. "I can only answer one question at a time, so I'll start first with yours, Shay."

He sensed that the yoga instructor wasn't his biggest fan. Asia had mentioned that Shay had flown to Denver when he'd proposed and hadn't been keen on the marriage. "I proposed to Asia because I want us to be a family. Her, me and my son."

"Son?" Shay asked, her eyes wide.

Blake glanced at each of the women. "Asia didn't tell you?"

They all shook their heads furiously. "I'm sorry," he said. "I assumed, given how close you are, she'd have shared the news. Maybe she wanted to tell you in person? Anyway, I know what it's like to have two parents and have a happy life and to have it all snatched away, because my parents were killed by a drunk driver when I was twelve years old. I grew up without my parents and I don't want that for my son. Asia and I want our son to have everything we never had, which is two parents who love him."

"That's commendable," Shay replied. "And I appreciate your honesty. I, too, I know what it's like to have a missing parent."

"Then you can see my intentions are honorable," Blake continued. "I'm doing the right thing. Making an honest woman out of your girl"—he looked directly at Egypt—"and taking responsibility for the new life we created."

"True," Teagan said, "but are you ready for it?"

Blake shrugged. "Is anyone truly ready to be a parent? We could read all the books in the world, but honestly, I think you have to follow your gut," he said, pressing his hand to his stomach.

Egypt and Teagan both nodded their heads, but Shay was the holdout. "How do you feel about Asia?"

Her question was direct and not one he could answer easily. "I care for Asia a great deal. I think she's beautiful, sexy, funny and talented. I want to support her dreams and protect her. She'll want for nothing. I'll make sure of that."

"And love?" Shay pressed, looking Blake directly in the eye.

Fear clawed at Blake's insides. Fear that whatever answer he gave wouldn't be good enough. He'd told them everything he was capable of, same as Asia. He hadn't lied to anyone.

Egypt touched her friend's shoulder, "Easy, Shay."

"I think it's a valid question," Shay replied, her eyes drilling into his. "And perhaps you might want to give it a little thought before you take vows. Marriage is a commitment and not something you should take lightly."

Without another word, Shay stalked off.

"I'm sorry," Egypt mouthed, and then she and Teagan left Blake alone.

Blake moved some distance away from the crowd to get in control of his emotions. He knew Shay meant well and only wanted the best for Asia, but she'd tried to push him to say three words he'd never said to another living soul except his parents and his aunt Sadie. The Gems wanted him to say he loved her, and he suspected Asia wanted the same thing, but he couldn't do it. He had to stay in control of himself and his feelings. He couldn't—*wouldn't*—make himself vulnerable to heartbreak again.

Asia was having an amazing night. The grand opening was going fabulously. The food was divine. Asia munched on a couple of spinach and mushroom tarts as she flitted around the room from one group to another, making sure everyone was enjoying themselves. She stopped and talked shop with several people who wanted to talk about the inspiration for her collection and was thrilled when she saw purchases being boxed discreetly at the back counter. Several of the women from Sadie's party had bought one of her pieces.

It was beyond fabulous to have Wynter, Egypt, Shay, Lyric and Teagan on hand for her big day. Every now and then, she would stop to check in with them and they would give her an enthusiastic thumbs-up, but Blake had been suspiciously absent for most of the night.

The few times she'd seen him over the course of the evening, their eyes had connected from across the room and he'd smiled, but there had been something missing. She had thought he'd be by her side the entire night, but he hadn't been. Had his conversation with the Gems not gone well? Shay, Egypt and Teagan had remained mum when she asked, but she knew there would be a post-mortem, if not tonight, then tomorrow, since her friends planned on having brunch before leaving the next day.

Asia tried to tell herself it was nothing. This was her big night, but it was Blake's, too. He'd been instrumental in seeing her vision come to life. She wanted to go find him to talk to him, but then she felt a tap on her shoulder.

Asia spun around and saw Ava dressed in a fashionable black gown with one dramatic sleeve that draped to the floor. Her hair was swept up in an elegant chignon. "Mama, you look fabulous."

Her mother grinned broadly. "It's easy to do that when you're dressed in couture." Ava leaned over and gave Asia's shoulders a gentle squeeze. "Congratulations, baby girl. You said you were going to open your own store and you did it!"

Asia beamed with pride. "Thank you, Mama."

"And you look stunning in the dress—I can hardly tell you're preggers," she whispered conspiratorially.

Asia didn't know how to take that comment, so she remained silent.

"So," her mother said, glancing around, "where is my soon-to-be son-in-law? I can't wait to meet him."

"C'mon, I'll introduce you," Asia said, moving them across the store until they came to Blake, who was chatting with a group of women. With his thick, dark brows, square jaw and sculpted lips, he looked handsome in a custom black suit. All of the women in the group were tall, gorgeous and looked as if they'd just walked off the runway. They were Blake's usual type.

"Excuse me," Asia said. "Do you mind if I steal Blake away?"

"Not at all," one of the women said. "Congratulations on the store. I love your work."

Asia feigned a smile, when, inside, she was crazy jealous. She didn't like seeing Blake with beautiful women, especially not *thin* beautiful ones. Her arm around Ava's shoulders, she grasped his arm with her other one, and once they were a discreet distance away, she said, "Blake, I'd like you to meet my mother, Ava Reynolds."

"Ms. Reynolds, it's a pleasure to finally meet you," Blake said, taking her mother's hand and kissing it. "I've heard a lot about you."

Ava was momentarily stunned into speechlessness. Asia was certain she wasn't used to a man as charming as Blake. "Umm, thank you. I appreciate everything you've done for my baby girl."

Blake turned to Asia and she caught a glint in his eye. One she hadn't seen all night. "No thanks needed. Asia is a very special lady."

Asia believed that Blake cared for her. She did, but how much? She loved Blake. She loved his integrity. His commitment to his family legacy. But was her love enough to build a marriage on? Could she commit her entire life to a marriage knowing he might not ever love her back? Asia wasn't so sure, and that frightened her.

Eighteen

The event ended on a high note. Asia had sold a huge number of pieces from her new collection and was feeling really good about herself. Once she was assured that the planner had everything under control to get the store in order for the soft opening on Monday, Asia came toward Blake, who was waiting for her. After a quick appearance, her mother had departed, claiming she had a hot date. The Gems had also retired to their hotel, with plans to meet up with Asia the next morning for brunch.

"Ready to go?" Blake inquired. "You must be exhausted. It was a big night."

She nodded. She wanted to talk to him and find out what was going on with him, but Asia was afraid to. She wasn't sure how the conversation would go, so she decided to remain silent. "Yes, I'm ready."

They walked outside, only to be greeted by several reporters.

"Blake, when did you find out Asia was pregnant?"

"Is that the reason you're having a shotgun wedding?" another screamed.

Asia's hand instantly went to her stomach in a protective gesture and Blake ushered her into the limo. After being accosted by the press, she was somber in the limo on the way home. That was not how they wanted to announce her pregnancy. How had they discovered she was pregnant? They'd told no one but their immediate family and friends, but maybe someone had overheard her tonight with the Gems or her mother?

And that wasn't the end of her troubles. Instead of the conversation Asia had hoped to have with Blake about his feelings and their future, Blake stayed on the phone the entire ride home.

When they got to the penthouse, Asia was so tired that she took off her makeup, showered and went straight to bed. Sometime in the night, Blake must have come to bed, because she'd felt his lean, strong body curl around hers, and then she'd drifted back to sleep. All had felt right in the world again.

This morning, however, was a disaster. The image of her holding her stomach was the exact image she'd woken up to, as her phone started blowing up with notifications. Blake's side of the bed was empty. The press was having a field day with the news. Asia had no idea what to do. This was out of her wheelhouse. Blake, however, knew exactly what steps to take. Thankfully, she found him in the kitchen on the phone with his PR team, making sure they could do damage control.

Returning to their bedroom, Asia lay in bed and glared at the image of her. The photo had been splashed across several Denver outlets and was making its rounds on social media, too. People were commenting that she had gotten pregnant on purpose to trap Denver's most eligible bachelor.

There were other reports about her mother. Her mother, for Chrissake! They found out that Ava was bankrupt. When had that happened? Asia knew her mother needed money all the time, but she had no idea it was this bad. Some were saying that she and her mother had concocted this elaborate scheme to dupe Blake into sinking money into her store.

God, what a nightmare! This fake story would trump her grand opening! The press cared more about salacious news than an upcoming jewelry designer. There were texts from the Gems asking how she was doing and there was even one from her mother, with a 911 to call her immediately, but Asia wasn't interested in any of them. She needed to talk to Blake.

Wrapping a robe around her nightgown, she padded down the hall to find Blake sitting at the island with a mug by his side and his phone in his hand. He didn't look up when she entered the room.

"Blake?" She walked toward him and he finally glanced up. His expression was clouded and he looked as if he'd gotten very little sleep. She pulled up a barstool and sat across from him. "I'm sorry about all this." She motioned to the phone in his hand.

"Why? It's not your fault," Blake said, rising to his feet and taking his empty coffee mug to the sink.

Then why was he moving away from her? Asia tried

not to be hurt by his lack of warmth. "I honestly don't know how they found out."

His brow furrowed. "Don't worry. My PR team is handling it," Blake responded. "We'll be issuing a statement later on, announcing our upcoming wedding and your pregnancy. They should be sending me a draft shortly."

"Is that what you want?" she asked quietly. It was a valid question, but from the stormy look in Blake's eyes, he clearly didn't like it.

"What do you mean, is this what I want?" Blake asked. He couldn't believe Asia was still questioning his motives. After everything he'd done? He'd been breaking his back to prove to her that he was worthy of her, and she still didn't believe him?

"Given everything that's happened, I think it's a fair question." She rushed to her feet and glared at him across the island.

"Really?" Blake asked, coming around the island toward her. "After all we've been through together? Haven't I done enough, Asia, to prove you can trust me? What more do you want?"

He watched her face crumple and then he saw tears leak down her cheeks. *Damn!* He felt like a jerk for yelling at a pregnant woman. "Asia, I'm sorry." He started toward her again, but she backed away.

"No!" She held up one hand and brushed away her tears with the back of the other. "I think it's time we finally have a talk."

"Talk? We've done nothing but talk the last two months, Asia. You wanted to get to know me. We did that. You wanted to spend time together. We've done that. You pulled sex off the table, so I agreed. But then we couldn't keep our hands off each other, so it was back on. I've been playing by your rule book the whole time, Asia."

"And I've been playing by yours," Asia replied. "You're the one who said we needed to get married."

"Because we do! We're having a child together."

"We don't need to be married to parent our child," Asia replied.

"Jesus!" Blake ran his hand through his low fade. "Are we really back to that? I thought we agreed on this."

"Agreed? Or did you browbeat me into agreeing?"

Blake was furious. He'd never had to convince a woman to be with him. "Browbeat you? Is that really what do you think? If so, why did you agree?"

"Because"—her shoulders shook and tears started flowing again—"you're charming and you can be very convincing. And because I…"

"And you what?" Blake said.

"Because I love you!" Asia yelled back at him tearfully.

Blake reared back on his heels as if she'd slapped him, but rather than shrink away from him, Asia leveled him with a stare.

"I know you don't want to hear it, Blake, but I love you. I don't know when it happened, but somewhere along the way, I fell in love with you. And I guess I thought that if we got married, in time, you would fall in love with me, too."

Blake shook his head. "Asia, stop this. You don't know what you're saying."

Asia walked toward him until she was standing in front of him. "Yes, I do. I know that I love you and nothing would give me greater joy than if you said you loved me, too. Then we could raise this baby"—she reached for his hand and placed it on her stomach—"together. That's what I want. A loving and happy home. That's what our son needs."

Blake stared at his hand on Asia's belly, which was swelling with his child. He knew she wanted him to say he loved her, too, and if he did, all would be right with the world. But he'd never lied to her and he wasn't about to start now.

Slowly, he pulled away his hand. "I'm sorry, Asia, but I can't give you what you need. What I've offered is all I'm capable of. If you can accept the marriage I'm offering, which includes me being a husband who will be there with you to help raise our son, a lover who will please you in ways you've never known, then I'm all yours."

Her eyes misted over and her expression hardened. "You'll give me everything except what I want the most. Your love."

Blake didn't like where this conversation was headed. Pain wrapped itself around his chest, squeezing the air from his lungs. "Asia, please don't do this. Don't draw a line in the sand we can't come back from. We can be good together. Hasn't the last month shown that?"

"It has, and it's made me want more," she responded. "It's made me want a man who loves me. It's made me want a soulmate, a companion that I can spend the rest of my life with. And I guess that's not you, is it?" After pausing a few seconds, she said, "I can't marry you, Blake. I can't commit myself to a loveless marriage, no matter how much I might want to."

"So you would leave me instead? Leave our son to grow up in separate households?"

"Don't try and emotionally blackmail me, Blake. It won't work."

"Do you need more time?" Blake asked, grasping at straws. He couldn't lose his son or Asia. The prospect of either scenario was like a stone in his stomach.

"Why? So I can waste time waiting for you to fall in love with me? I could spend years of my life waiting, wanting, wishing for something that might not ever happen. I can't marry you, Blake." She let out a long sigh and, to Blake's horror, pulled off her engagement ring and handed it out to him.

Blake shook his head. It couldn't end like this; he wouldn't let it. "Is this how you show you love to someone—by walking out on them?" If so, he could definitely do without the emotion.

"It's because I love you that I have to. I want our son to know love and to never look for it in the wrong places. I'll be that example, starting now."

"Is this your final decision?"

"Yes," Asia said, nodding. "I'll go pack my things, and then I'll leave."

As she turned on her heel, he said, "What about the baby?"

"I won't keep you from him," Asia replied, not turning to face him. "You can have as big or as little a presence as you would like. And you're welcome to come to all the doctor's appointments. I'll send you calendar invites."

"Fine," he said through clenched teeth.

She walked away and he could hear her moving around in his bedroom. Blake found himself walking over to the window, and for the first time, he didn't see the amazing view of the mountains. All he could think about was Asia leaving him and how he would no longer feel her electrifying touch on his skin. He wouldn't taste her sweet lips or feel the boundless passion between them.

She'd told him what she wanted and she wasn't willing to accept anything less. As much as he wanted her to stay, he couldn't give her the love she craved. He'd already behaved more out of character for Asia than he had with any other woman. Blake had gone from confirmed bachelor to an engaged man in a heartbeat. He'd done it for the baby, and, if he was being honest, for Asia. If she couldn't accept what he had to offer, then so be it.

Twenty minutes later, Asia emerged from the room fully dressed, with a small bag in tow. She stopped in front of him at the windows. They stared at each other for what seemed like an eternity, Blake willing Asia to stay with his eyes. Instead, she leaned forward, pressed a kiss to his cheek, and then she was gone.

Poof!

Gone, as if she hadn't played a big part in his life for the better part of two months. What was he supposed to do now? Go back to being a footloose and fancy free bachelor with a stream of endless women gracing his arm? The idea repulsed him because in five months' time, he would be a father.

The Gems were already waiting for Asia when she arrived back at her apartment. Before she showered at Blake's place, she sent them a text informing them that the wedding was off and she and Blake were over. She needed the support of her friends right now.

As soon as Asia opened her door and saw them sitting on her couch, she dropped her bag and began bawling. Shay and Wynter rushed over, sweeping Asia into a hug.

"I'm so sorry, Asia," Shay said, rubbing her back. "I know how badly you wanted things between you and Blake to work out."

"You must be devastated," Wynter said, wiping her tears away with her hand.

Asia nodded, and once they released her, she walked over to the couch. On her coffee table were some teacups, no doubt set up by Shay, who swore by the stuff.

"I have decaf for you," Shay said, pouring some water into a teacup with a bag.

Asia gave her a half-hearted smile. "Thank you," she said, but she couldn't drink anything.

"What happened?" Egypt asked. "Last night you both seemed like you were in harmony. When we talked to Blake, he was committed to you."

"He was. He is. To the marriage. To the baby," Asia replied, "but not to loving me."

"Are you sure?" Wynter asked. "I saw the way he looked at you. He looked like a man in love."

"You could have misread the situation, sweetie, because you're so in love with Riley, you want it for Asia, too," Teagan said.

"Did you tell him how you felt? Lyric chimed in. "Did you tell him you loved him?"

"Yes. I thought about what all of you said from the beginning, and even Mama asked if I could live with a loveless marriage, and I thought maybe I could. Blake was committed to being a husband and father. Said he would never cheat on me. And I could see how much he loves his son already. How can he love his child, but not love me?"

"It's not always easy for men to tell you how they feel. Unlike us," Shay said, glancing at each of the women. "We're open books and wear our hearts on our sleeves. Except maybe you, Teagan."

They all chuckled, but Teagan said, "Hey, I have a heart, too, and it's breaking for you, Asia. I mean, you're carrying his child."

"And now I'm going to be a single mother," Asia cried. "I thought I could handle it before, but having Blake there with me at the ultrasound and then the nursery… Did I tell you he already created a nursery for our baby boy?"

Asia pulled out her telephone and showed the ladies the pictures of the nursery.

"It's gorgeous," Teagan said, and the others concurred. "The man has a good taste."

"He's going to be a great father," Lyric said.

Asia thought so, too, and it made her start bawling again in earnest. "He's clearly capable of love. He just doesn't love me."

"Oh, Asia." Shay came beside her and Asia curled into the fetal position.

Asia knew she deserved better than what Blake was offering, which was why she refused to compromise and lose a part of herself in the process. She'd thought she could take losing him, but a wave of pain filled her chest, making her cry harder, and it was too much. Even with the other Gems hugging her tight, it wasn't enough, because Asia hadn't just lost a fiancé, she'd lost her best friend.

"You look a wreck," Jeffrey said when Blake showed up to his house the day after his argument with Asia. Blake was dressed uncharacteristically in sweats. "What's going on?"

"Asia left me." Blake replied, sweeping past Jeffrey and into the house. He glanced around but didn't see Mara and the kids. "Are we alone?"

Jeffrey nodded. "Yeah, they're at a birthday party. And I'm glad for it. Tell me what happened."

Blake began pacing in the living room. "I don't know, Jeffrey. I mean, last night everything was going fine, or so I thought. Asia had her grand opening and it was a hit. I met her five friends who are like sisters to her."

"How did that go?"

"They were hard on me," Blake responded. "And I get it. They were looking out for her. I answered honestly and I think I passed muster."

"So how did you get here, with Asia breaking up with you?"

"Have you seen social media?" Blake asked.

Jeffrey nodded. "But I figured your PR team would

handle it and put out some sort of official announcement to quash all the haters."

"That was the plan until this morning," Blake said.
He stopped pacing and put his hand on the mantel. "Asia
came at me, Jeffrey, talking about this love thing, man."

"What did she say?"

"She said she couldn't live with a loveless marriage
even though she'd agreed. I told her months ago what I
was capable of giving. I thought she understood."

"And what happened next?"

"She told me she loved me."

"Ah"—Jeffrey rubbed his goatee—"now I understand."

"You understand what?"

"Did you tell her you loved her?"

Blake huffed. "Of course not," he said. "I don't do
that love thing. Never had. Never will."

"Did you say that to Asia?"

"Not in so many words," Blake replied. "Do you
think I'm daft?"

"You must be to let a woman like Asia get away. And
she's carrying your child."

"You think I don't know that?" Blake said, his voice
rising. "Why do you think I'm going out of my mind?"
He ran his hands through his hair.

"I don't know. I thought you might feel the same.
You've been spending a lot of time together. When you
guys came over for dinner, I was certain you had feelings for her."

"I care about Asia. I do, but love?" Blake held his
head down. He had strong feelings for Asia, but he refused to equate that with love. Love hurt. Love was
knowing he would never see his parents again. Love

was knowing he couldn't save them. And now, Asia was doing the same thing. Taking his son away from him. He was going to be a part-time father, something he'd never wanted.

"Why not? If you could just open your heart, Blake..."

"So it can be trampled on?" Blake asked, throwing up his hands. "*She* left *me*!"

"Because she can't live without your love," Jeffrey responded quietly.

"Then we're at an impasse," Blake said. "And we have no future."

And that made Blake angry. He was used to things going his way, but not this time. Asia would rather be a single mother than marry him. She'd rather spend her nights alone than in bed with him making passionate love. It was a blow to his ego, but deep down, he knew it was more.

It was a blow to his heart.

Nineteen

Asia was on her own.

Her friends had gone back home to their respective lives, with plans to meet up at Wynter's wedding in a couple of weeks. Asia was happy for her bestie, truly she was, but it was going to be hard to put on a smiling face and listen to their vows when her own heart was breaking. But that's what you did for those you loved.

Instead, she put on a brave front and went to her store on Monday. Asia had blocked her social media and didn't answer her phone unless she recognized the phone number. Thankfully, there was no press skulking about Six Gems early in the morning, so Asia was able to sneak in undetected. When she did, she took a moment to look around. Six Gems looked completely different than it had under Yvette's ownership.

She'd hired some temporary help to run the store during the soft opening, until she found a suitable right hand, who would complement her as she'd done for Yvette. Asia had hoped Blake would be here on her opening day, but that wouldn't happen. She was trying her best not to think about him, but it wasn't easy. As soon as Blake learned she was pregnant, he'd been by her side, making sure she had everything she needed. Now he was gone. But as much as that hurt, it would hurt more to be in a marriage with him knowing he didn't—couldn't—love her.

Last night, she'd dreamed of him and his killer smile and sensual touch. Her body craved his because only Blake knew exactly what buttons to push to make her go nuclear. She would have to forget him, but tell that to her heart. She'd opened up to Blake in ways she never had with any other man. Asia had given herself to him completely and he'd made love to her in a way that said he understood her, but he hadn't.

He didn't want her, or at least, not in the way she needed him to—as part of a foundation built on love. He wasn't interested in building a future with her, and she wasn't going to stay with him and pretend she didn't love him. She had to accept that what they had was gone and he was never coming back.

Blake sat in his office the following Monday and stared out the window. He hadn't been able to sleep all week because he didn't have Asia by his side. Had it already been a week since they'd broken up? Hell yes, because he'd felt every minute of it. In just a short time, the petite brunette had clawed her way through all the roadblocks he'd put up to protect himself, and he was angry. Angry that he missed her. Missed her smile and her sassy ways. Missed sharing about his workday with her and having her give him sound advice. Missed watching her as she sketched designs on the couch while they watched television together.

He had been so dazed during his morning meeting that Martha had had to correct him on several key points. This was madness. He couldn't go on like this. *Get it together*, he told himself.

Maybe a change of scenery would do, but the thought of going back into the dating scene sickened him. He wasn't interested in sleeping with anyone but Asia. He couldn't imagine feeling the kind of desire he felt for her with anyone else. Without him realizing it, Asia had changed him.

Martha knocked on his office door, interrupting his thoughts.

"I know you're in a mood," she said, "but the final figures for the Six Gems construction came in. I assume you'd want to look them over?"

"Of course. Thank you." He accepted the folder and placed it on his desk.

His and Asia's personal relationship might be over, but they were still joined in business. Fortunately, Coleman & Sons work on the Six Gems project was complete, but he, although silent, was still part owner of the store, and that wasn't going to work. If they were going to break up, he needed it to be a clean break.

Asia wouldn't have the money to buy him out outright for a couple of years, which is why Blake needed to *give* her the store. He didn't need the money. She was the one who had insisted on a promissory note, but he was going to forgive it, making her sole owner. It was the least he could do.

She wanted to be free of him.

He would give her wish.

He would give her Six Gems.

A lump formed in Blake's throat at the thought, but he was doing what he thought was best.

"How are you holding up?" Shay asked when she called to check in on Asia late Monday afternoon, one week post-breakup.

"I'm all right. The first week for Six Gems was a hit. Between the grand opening and this week, it's off to a good start."

Shay rolled her eyes. "I'm not talking about the business and you damn well know it. I'm asking how *you are* doing?"

Asia shrugged. "As well as can be expected. I mean, if nothing else, this entire experience has made me grow up. I'm no longer flighty Asia. I have two purposes in my life. The store and this baby."

"Yes, you do, but will that be enough?"

"It has to be, Shay," Asia answered honestly. "Give me a moment." She placed her phone down when a delivery courier stepped inside the store. She signed for the package and ripped the envelope open.

She scanned the document, and that's when she realized what it was: Blake was dissolving the partnership between them. And if she read it correctly, he was *giving* her his 50 percent, making her the sole owner of Six Gems. She should have been thrilled, but instead all she felt was horror, because until their son was born, the store was the one tie to Blake she never thought would be severed, at least for a long time.

Blake was cleaning house and wanted nothing more to do with her.

"Asia?" She heard Shay's voice calling to her, but it was being drowned out by the loud drumbeat in her head.

She picked up the phone. "He wants nothing to do with me, Shay. He's ending our partnership in the store. He already signed the dissolution papers."

"That's not true, Asia. You guys share a son. Blake will still be a part of your life even if you don't own the store together."

"On what? A part-time basis?" Asia cried. "When he comes to pick the baby up and drop him off?" Tears flowed down her cheeks and she started hyperventilating.

"Asia, you need to calm down."

"How—how, c-can I?" Asia could barely get the words out. "Blake wants to be rid of me as if the last couple of months meant—meant nothing!"

"Asia, please calm down. This can't be good for the baby."

"I-I can't." Suddenly, a sharp pang went through Asia's stomach and she clutched it. "Oh!"

"Asia, what's wrong?" Shay asked on the other end of the line.

Tears sprang to Asia's eyes. "I don't know, but something's wrong. I think it could be the baby. Ouch!" Another pain struck her straight in the abdomen and Asia fell to the floor. She could see Shay on the other end.

"It's okay, sweetie. Hang up. I'm calling an ambulance," Shay said.

As she lay on the floor clutching her belly, all Asia could think about was the baby. This baby meant everything to her, and she hoped she wasn't losing him.

The papers had been delivered.

Blake had just received confirmation that the dissolution of his partnership with Asia was under way. He'd wanted to exorcise her completely from his life and he'd done just that. So why did it feel as if he'd just ripped out his own heart?

He hadn't wanted to do it, but Asia had thrown down the gauntlet. He was just picking it up.

He needed to talk someone and, unfortunately, Jeffrey was out town for work. So, in the middle of the day, Blake left the office and drove to the countryside to visit his aunt Sadie. She had just gotten back from one of her whirlwind European trips.

He pulled his Mercedes-Benz SUV into the driveway a short while later and used his key to enter. "Auntie?" Blake called out as he closed the door.

"In here, Blake." He followed the sound of her voice until he found her in her craft studio behind a pottery wheel, with wet clay on her hands. He didn't recall Sadie being into pottery.

He frowned. "What are you making?"

"I'm not sure." She laughed. "I recently took up pottery when I was abroad and found it was very relaxing." She kept adding more water and sticking both her hands into the clay. "I need to slow the wheel down a bit." He watched her tap her feet and soon the piece of clay became rounder.

"I think it's going to be a bowl," Sadie announced and kept stretching the bowl out farther and farther, until it became an oval. "So, what's on your mind, Blakey boy? I don't imagine you came all this way to watch me make pottery."

"No, I don't suppose I did."

She glanced up. "Where's my girl. Where's Asia?"

Blake exhaled deeply and shook his head. "We're no longer together."

Sadie stopped the pottery wheel immediately. "What do you mean? She's having your baby, Blake. She's having a future Coleman."

"Don't you think I know that, Auntie?" Blake said, getting up to his feet. "I tried to talk her out of it, but she refused to budge."

She stood up and went over to the sink to wash her hands. "And why not? What's the problem?" She kept an eagle eye on Blake as she wiped them dry.

"Why are you looking at me like that, Auntie? I asked her to marry me. I gave her a ring—which she gave back to me, by the way."

"Because?"

"Because she wants love, which I'm not capable of giving her."

"That's a load of hogwash and you know it, Blake," his aunt said. "I saw you with Asia and I know a smitten kitten when I see one."

Blake rolled his eyes. "You're getting older. Your eyesight must be going."

She swatted his thigh. "Don't make fun of an old

lady. I saw it the first night you two met. You were drawn to each other like magnets and you couldn't take your eyes off of her. It's been that way ever since. Why can't you see that?"

"I…" Blake didn't know what to say because his aunt was right. He had been fascinated by Asia from the start. "But love hurts, Auntie. Don't you remember how I was when Mom and Dad died?"

"Yeah, you were a shell of the former happy boy I used to know."

"That's right." He pointed at his heart. "It hurt so much losing them. Do you know how hard it was watching my parents die in front of me?"

"I know, Blake. I can't imagine what you went through."

"I couldn't save them," Blake said, his voice raspy.

His aunt walked over to him. "I know you couldn't. No one could. Their injuries were too severe."

"I never want to go through that kind of pain again," Blake said. "I couldn't bear it.

"So the alternative is choosing to never love again?" his aunt inquired. She stroked his cheek. "That's no way to live, Blake. You have to let love in again, here." She touched his heart. "You can't be afraid of what you might lose, or you might lose what's right in front of you."

Blake shook his head. "I don't know if I can."

"I know you can. You might be scared, but I have always believed in you, Blake, even when everyone told me I was a fool for turning over Coleman & Sons Construction to a twenty-one-year-old fresh out of college, but I did. I have never stopped supporting you and

I won't now. Not even when you make stupid mistakes by letting the woman you love get away."

Suddenly, Blake's phone rang. The display read Shay Davis. When he and Asia were together, she made certain he had stored each and every one of the Gems' phone numbers in his phone in case of emergency, but why would Shay be calling him? Had something happened to Asia?

His heart nearly stopped beating. He answered on the second ring. "Hello?"

"Blake, it's Shay." Her voice sounded somber. "I have some bad news."

"What's happened?" Blake asked.

Color drained from his face at Shay's chilling words from the other end of the phone. When she ended the call, the phone hung limply from his hand.

"Blake, was it?" his aunt asked.

"It's Asia. She's in the hospital. She could be losing the baby."

"Let's go." his aunt said.

As they raced toward the hospital, all Blake could think was, *Please, God, please, don't let me lose Asia and the baby like I lost my parents.*

Beep. Beep. Beep.

Slowly, Asia opened her eyes. She was in a hospital and her mother was sitting by her bedside. She immediately began to sit up. "The baby!"

"Is okay," her mother said quietly, pushing her back down. "The baby is okay. Look, there's the heartbeat." She motioned to the other side of the bed and Asia could hear her son's heartbeat on a fetal monitor.

"Oh, thank God." Tears misted Asia's eyes. "I didn't lose the baby."

"No, Baby Reynolds is just fine," her mother said.

Asia's brow furrowed. "What are you doing here? How did I get here?"

"Shay thought you might need some reinforcements and called me right after she called the ambulance. You passed out at the store."

"I did?" Asia asked. "Is everything okay?" Suddenly, the baby's heartbeat started beating in earnest.

"Asia, darling, I need you to calm down. Right now, stress isn't good for the baby or you," she replied. "The doctor gave you some medication to stop the contractions, but you need to rest. As for the store, I got there just as the ambulance arrived and was able to lock up. Everything is fine. You don't have to worry about it."

Asia took a deep breath. "Okay, okay." She tried to calm her nerves. "Thank you for being here, Mama."

"Where else would I be? My daughter and grandson are in the hospital. I'm so thankful Shay called me. I know I haven't always been the best mother, but I'm determined to be a better grandma. Or shall I say, *mimi*, because I'm too young to be a grandma to the little man."

"You know it's a boy?"

Ava grinned widely. "The doctor kind of spilled the beans earlier. I hope that's okay?"

"It's fine. We know."

We. There was that word again, but there was no longer a *we*, just a her. It was up to Asia to ensure that the baby was healthy and well cared for, because Blake was no longer a part of her life. And, thus far, she was doing a poor job of it if she was in the hospital a week after they'd broken up.

"You mean, you and Blake?" Ava asked. "Where is he, by the way?"

"He's right here." Asia heard Blake's voice and her heart turned over in her chest when she saw him standing behind Ava with terror in his eyes.

"Sorry it took me so long to get here. I was driving as fast as the law would allow."

"I can vouch for that." His aunt Sadie was with him. She looked disheveled in overalls covered in some sort of residue. "It is so good to see you both." After leaning over to give Asia's shoulder a reassuring squeeze, Sadie turned to her mother. "Ava, right?" she asked, and Ava nodded. "What do you say I treat you to a cup of coffee while these young people chat? We can talk about how we're going to spoil our grandson and grandnephew."

"I'd love that." Ava gave Asia a wink and vacated the seat by her bedside.

"May I?" Blake asked, indicating the empty seat.

Asia nodded and he sat down. She watched him glance at the fetal monitor at her side. "The baby's okay," she blurted aloud before he could speak.

"I'm glad. Really glad to hear that, Asia, but I was going to ask you, how are *you* doing? How are you feeling?"

She was surprised he cared, given that he felt nothing toward her and had dissolved their partnership. "Honestly?"

"That would be a start."

"Scared. Nervous. All of the above," Asia said. "When I thought I might lose the baby…" Her voice trailed off and she reached for Blake's hand, clutching it, and he let her. Tears slid down her cheeks at how close she came to losing their son.

"It's okay, Asia," Blake said. "I thought the same thing. I was making all kind of promises to God—that if he spared you and the baby, I would be a better man. The kind of man you need."

Asia pulled her hand away from his. "Don't make promises you can't keep, Blake."

"I meant them," Blake replied, but he understood why Asia would be hesitant to believe anything he said. He'd given her every reason to be wary of him. Time and again, he'd told her that he wasn't capable of being the man she needed. That he couldn't offer her anything but a loveless marriage.

Aunt Sadie's words had already struck a chord with him, and he'd realized that no matter whom he loved, there was a risk of losing them one day. He couldn't be afraid to love—otherwise, he would miss out on loving the best woman he'd ever known. And then Shay had called him and told him Asia was on her way to the hospital. He had been worried about the baby, yes, but all he could think about was Asia. Was she okay? Would she pull through?

The drive to the hospital had been terrifying because he'd realized he could lose them both, Asia and the baby. The thought had terrified him, but Blake was more terrified of spending the rest of his life without Asia.

"I need to tell you how I feel," Blake said.

Asia shook her head. "Don't. I can't handle any more discussions, Blake. I'm in this bed fighting to keep our baby inside my womb. I can't be on this merry-go-round with you."

"And you don't have to be," Blake said, patting her hand. "But you have to know that I lied to you when you asked how I felt about you. From the start, you touched something deep in me, Asia. I don't know if it was your beauty, your smile, your refreshing honesty or the incredible passion between us. All I know is that I'd never felt this way about another person and it scared me. It's why I ran that night. I thought I could go back to my playboy ways, but there was no way I could be intimate with another woman when I couldn't get the taste of you, the scent of you, out of my mind."

"You expect me to believe that?" Asia asked. "You're a serial dater."

"Who became celibate when we were apart. After our first night together, I felt like my head was spinning and I felt out of control...it made me feel how I did when my parents died. When I couldn't pull them out of the car. When I lost them, it crushed me. It crushed a part of my soul that I had never gotten back, until you awakened me."

"Don't say stuff like this, Blake, not when you don't mean it. Yes, we have incredible chemistry, but that's all it was."

"Asia, you're right. We do have an amazing chemistry, but that's because, when I'm with you, we're making love."

"I felt that way, but as you said, you don't do love."

"And in my head, I thought that was true," Blake said, "but it was a lie I was telling myself to protect my heart. Because, the truth of the matter is, the more time we spent together out of bed, thanks to you, I realized I not only liked you, but respected you. And as each day passed, I found myself developing feelings for you, so I tried to deny them and push them down, but I can't anymore. I love you, Asia. On the drive here, all I could think about was that I couldn't lose you, too."

A slight smile crossed Asia's beautiful features, and Blake realized he was making headway, but then the smile fell. "Are you sure you're not pretending to be in love with me so I'll marry you for the baby's sake?"

"I love our son, and he is a precious gift," Blake said. "But I'm not saying I love you because of him. I'm saying I love you because I want spend the rest of my days with you. I'm saying I was a fool to let you leave when I'm head over heels for you."

Tears slipped down her cheeks. "Say it again."

"I love you," Blake said, feeling the words vibrate from the depths of his chest and radiate outward. Rather than feeling scared, he felt free for the first time in his adult life. "You've captured my heart and my soul. I tried to fight it, resist it, push you away, but in the end, I can't deny what's in my heart. I want you to be my wife, Asia. Will you please do me the honor of marrying me?"

Asia threw her arms around Blake's neck and lifted her face for a kiss. Blake bestowed one to her, kissing her deeply and holding her close, but not too tight, because of the baby. He felt the dampness of her tears against his cheek.

"I'm so sorry for hurting you, Asia," Blake said when he pulled back. "I almost lost you and I didn't know if I could bear it."

Asia cupped both sides of his face. "No one has ever

made me feel the way you do, Blake Coleman. I think I fell in love with you, too, when you walked into the store all cocky and arrogant. Our first night together was magical, and because of it, we created a life." She placed his hand on her stomach. "I know getting pregnant wasn't what either of us expected, but it led us to each other and allowed me to fall in love with you. I love you, too, Blake, and I would love nothing more than to be your wife *and* your partner. So, what do you say we rip up those partnership dissolution papers?"

"Hell yes." Blake cradled her face in his hands and kissed her with bone-shaking tenderness. He hoped it convinced her that his love would last a lifetime.

When they finally broke apart for air, Blake said, "You have my heart, Asia."

"And you're mine and I'm yours," Asia said. "Forever."

Epilogue

Three weeks later

Asia was profoundly in love with her amazing husband. They hadn't been able to wait. As soon as she was released from hospital, Blake found the nearest justice of the peace and they'd married in a private ceremony, with her mother and his aunt as their witnesses. There would be time for a larger celebration later. For them, it was about sealing their commitment to each other.

Asia hadn't told the Gems, because she didn't want to upstage Wynter. Today, her best friend and sister had been the most beautiful bride. Wynter had worn a beaded off-the-shoulder lace ball gown with sequined appliqués adorning the bodice, and she'd held a simple bouquet of white peonies. She and Riley had stood up before God and over three hundred guests and pledged their eternal love for each other.

Asia had loved Wynter's and Riley's personal vows because they mirrored the ones she and Blake had said to each other just a short while ago. For now, their marriage would be their little secret. She would tell the Gems *after* Wynter's wedding.

In the meantime, Asia was having the time of her life with Blake, who looked all kinds of hot in a Giorgio Armani tuxedo. The black textured suit jacket and matching trousers fit him like a glove. Asia couldn't wait to rip his clothes off when they got back to the hotel. It was definitely true about what they said about pregnant women. She couldn't get enough, wanting her man morning, noon and night.

"Why do you look like the cat that got the cream?" Egypt asked, sidling next to Asia when she left Blake's side to mingle.

"Whatever do you mean?"

"Don't be sly with me, sis," Egypt responded with a smirk. "I call it like I see it, and you've definitely got a secret."

"Not here. And not now," Asia whispered conspiratorially. "Don't you have enough to keep you busy? Your man"—she glanced over at tall, dark and chocolate Garrett, who was killing it in a dark navy tuxedo jacket and trousers—"looks a little thirsty."

"Oh, I've got him covered," Egypt said. "But don't think this conversation is over." She gestured with her index and middle fingers to warn Asia that she had her eyes on her.

Suddenly, Shay was tapping Asia's shoulder. She had

a handsome man in a dark gray suit by her side. He had dark brown eyes, a close-cropped hairstyle and a five-o'clock shadow, much like the one Blake had. And he looked oddly familiar.

"Do I know you?" Asia inquired.

Shay laughed. "You don't remember Colin? He went to high school with us. Anyway, I'm helping him get back in tip-top shape."

"Ah yes, now I remember. You were dating Claire Watson." Asia's face bunched into a frown and Shay tried to hide a smirk.

"We broke up in college," Colin replied.

"Shame," Asia responded. Claire had been one of the girls who bullied her for not wearing the latest fashions. "You're in good hands with Shay. If anyone can fix you, it's her."

Asia winked at her best friend before making her way to the dance floor for "The Cupid Shuffle." Former ballerina Lyric gracefully stepped her way past the rest of the crowd, showing everyone how it was done. Meanwhile, Teagan was on the sidelines with her phone, as usual. Sometimes that girl couldn't get out of her own way.

Eventually, the song ended and the music changed to something slow and sexy. That's when Blake pulled Asia into his arms. Asia would never get tired of the way he held her.

"You've been a hard woman to nail down today."

"I'm sorry, babe. When we girls get together, it's madness and mayhem, but in a good way," she said with a smile.

"I'm here to slow you down," Blake responded. "You know what the doctor said—you have to take it easy."

"Not too easy," Asia said, squeezing his bum.

"Why, Mrs. Coleman, are you trying to put the moves on me?" Blake asked, his ebony eyes gleaming with desire.

"Yes, I am," she said unabashedly. "How am I doing?"

Blake whispered several naughty things in her ear, and when they returned to their hotel room much later that evening, he did all the things he'd promised to. He made such passionate love to her that her blood sang in her veins.

"You've opened my heart to love, Asia, and I can't thank you enough," Blake said, and there was no denying the love she saw shining in his eyes.

"How about you spend a lifetime showing me?" Asia asked, and then she pulled him in for a searing kiss.

* * * * *

*Don't miss any of the Six Gems novels
from Yahrah St. John!*

Her Best Friend's Brother
Her Secret Billionaire
Her One Night Consequence

Dear Reader,

This is a bright hello *and* a sad goodbye.

I'm thrilled to present book five in my Cress Brothers series, *The Marriage Deadline*, but it's the last. How fitting that it's for the youngest brother, Lucas—the undisputed "favorite" of the family. Since childhood he is used to having his way—including enough decadent desserts to make him fifty pounds overweight. Five years ago, he lost weight and gained a bevy of beauties vying for his new chiseled physique.

His desire to have what he wants lingers—especially at seeing his old crush, mean girl Eve, at their high school reunion. Although he's tired of being the only single brother and *determined* to wed before the end of the year, Eve is not on his list of candidates for the bride because he believes she hasn't changed. Will he forgive her treatment of him in school to see her as more than a one-night stand—his one true love?

Gather everything you need to comfortably sink into a brand-new "Sexy, Funny & Oh So Real" romance...

On your mark. Get set. Go!

Happy reading, y'all. :)

N

THE MARRIAGE DEADLINE

Niobia Bryant

As always, this one is dedicated
to the wonderful thing called love.

One

Lucas Cress took a sip from his flute of champagne as he stood before one of many massive poster-sized black-and-white photos hanging in the entry hall of Manhattan University Prep as the sound of "Low" by Flo Rida and T-Pain loudly blared from inside the gym. It had been the number-one song from the year he'd graduated from the prestigious private school for the city's wealthy and famous. He was currently at his fifteen-year high-school reunion.

The photo?

A reminder of what he used to be.

He frowned as he took in the chubby kid with curly hair who was over fifty pounds overweight. Not the favorite of the girls or the jocks. Not as popular as his brothers when they'd attended the school before him.

Not comfortable in his skin. Shy and reserved. So unsure of himself.

He felt sad for the kid.

For me. The old me, anyway.

Now he was an acclaimed pastry chef and an executive at Cress, INC., his family's successful culinary empire. He had worked hard five years ago to lose the extra weight put on during decades of indulgence in the food he and his entire family created. He was no longer out of shape and lacking confidence. With his good looks and chiseled frame, he enjoyed a level of popularity with the ladies that he'd sorely lacked in high school.

"Luc Cress?"

He took another sip of his champagne as he turned at the sound of his name. His heart skipped a few beats and a warmth of nervous energy radiated over his body as he eyed the woman standing there with a soft smile and surprise-filled eyes. Eve Villar.

Even with her once long jet-black hair now cut into a short pixie style, she hadn't changed very much. Medium brown complexion. Thinly shaped eyebrows. Deep-set eyes. High cheekbones and the most luxurious full mouth covered with a deep maroon lip gloss. Very akin to the singer Teyana Taylor. Very intense and sultry without even trying.

Still as beautiful as ever.

He remembered her well.

He remembered a lot very well, unfortunately. The memory caused him to clutch the stem of his flute just a little tighter...

Lucas and one of his older brothers, Coleman, had been sitting on the wrought-iron bench of the quad of their high school dressed in the school uniform of navy cardigans and khaki pants with white shirts and striped ties. They were both looking across the courtyard at a group of girls gathered atop a wooden table with their legs crossed as they talked, laughed and drew the eyes of those who either wanted to be them, or be near them.

Like Lucas.

As he sipped from a bottle of fruit juice, his dark eyes locked on Eve Villar as she dragged the tips of her pink glittery nails through her long dark brown hair streaked with auburn. She moved with an awareness of her beauty. Every move seemed to be the pose of a model. Every expression was meant to please or tease.

The very sight of her made Lucas feel nervous energy. His heart beat faster and his palms sweated whenever they were in the same junior classes. There was nothing about the beauty that didn't tempt him in his dreams. The idea of barely seeing her over the summer made him regret the coming end of the school year... and made him feel emboldened to finally reveal his adoration.

"I'm going to do it," Lucas told his brother, who was a year ahead of him and graduating in a few months.

Coleman smoothed his long fingers over his close-cropped hair as he shook his head. "I don't know about that, Luc," he advised. "Eve Villar and her crew are a piece of work."

"Beautiful work," Lucas countered, as he handed his brother the bottle of soda, then picked up the plastic container of strawberry-shortcake cupcakes he'd prepared the night before.

Just for Eve.

Being from a culinary family—and enjoying sweets from a very young age—Lucas was already a capable pastry chef with plans to attend culinary school upon graduating high school next year.

"More like beautiful chaos," Coleman warned with another shake of his head as he eyed her.

Lucas felt his eyes widen a bit as Eve tilted her head back to laugh, exposing her neck. As his heart pounded in excitement, he wondered if she smelled of candy or flowers—either way, he knew it was sweet.

And if she was his girl, he could plant a kiss there.

Lucas picked up the clear plastic container holding the half-dozen strawberry-shortcake cupcakes he'd created for her. He wasn't as popular with the girls as Cole, who was already lean and chiseled, but he was cute and knew it. And he was one of the Cress brothers, chubby or not, and with those things going for him he felt he had a chance.

For Eve, I'll take that chance.

He felt he had no choice. He was too distracted by her to do anything else.

Coleman gave him a comforting clasp on the shoulder. "Good luck, little brother," *he said.*

Lucas nodded and began walking. His palms dampened the container as each step across the manicured grass brought him closer and closer to Eve.

"What's going here?" *one of Eve's friends asked as he neared their table.*

"Definitely the wrong Cress brother," *another said in a tone meant to mock.*

The girls all giggled.

Lucas paused and he felt uncomfortable even as he focused his gaze on Eve's face.

"What's that?" she asked, notching her chin toward the container he was carrying.

He loved the husky timbre of her voice. He wanted nothing more than to hear her say his name.

"I m-m-m-made you some cupcakes," he said, extending his arms to hand them to her.

Eve shifted her eyes down to the treats without moving her head at all. She arched her left eyebrow high before frowning.

"Th-th-they have a fresh strawberry filling and are topped with cotton candy," he explained, hating the stutter that appeared when he was nervous.

Eve glanced back over her shoulder at her friends, then faced forward again as she rose from the tabletop. She stood before him with her hands on her hips. "Do I look like I sit around and scarf down cupcakes?"

Alarm filled him as he shook his head. "No. I thought you would enjoy them—"

Eve gave him a tight little smile as she took the cupcake container from him. "If you knew like we all know, you would stop eating these," she said, then turned to drop the container into a wrought-iron garbage receptacle. She at stared him, giving him a withering look, from his dark curls down to the soles of his Air Jordans. "It's the last thing you need."

As her friends began to laugh at him, enjoying her ridicule, Lucas stood there as his heart shattered into a million tiny pieces. He lowered his head, unable to do otherwise, and turned to walk away.

"Oh, hell no," Coleman said, suddenly beside him.

His brother had pressed one hand to Lucas's chest and had tipped up his chin with the other. "You're a Cress..."

As the memory faded, Lucas smiled a bit at how his brother had skewered the entire lot of them with harsh words and profanity that sent them running from his reproach. Back then, he had needed Coleman to defend his honor. Not anymore. That had been sixteen years and over fifty pounds ago. That Lucas was long gone.

Eight years ago, he had lost weight via exercise, chiseled his frame with weights and claimed the title of the family's Lothario, with plenty of willing candidates for his attention.

Life was great.

Eve stepped closer to give him an air kiss. "You look amazing," she said.

Lucas tilted his head to the side as he took in the emerald-green strapless jumpsuit she had on, along with strappy copper heels. Her physique was toned but still curvy and her cinnamon-brown complexion gleamed. "So do you," he said, before taking another sip of his drink.

She glanced over at his reunion photo and then back at him, giving him a hesitant look. "I'm glad you're here, Luc," she said, reaching to squeeze his wrist.

He glanced down at the connection and felt warmed by her touch. Like a spark.

"I just can't believe how much you've changed," Eve said with a shake of her head and a deeper smile.

Luc's eyes searched hers and he clearly saw her appreciation of his looks. Perhaps even desire. One skill he had honed since his weight loss was how to read a woman's level of interest in him and Eve Villar definitely liked what she saw.

And maybe enough for me to woo her right out of that jumpsuit.

With a slow smile he knew dazzled women, Lucas covered her hand with his. He felt her slight tremble—another telltale sign of attraction. And desire.

"And I can't believe how much you look the same," he told her, infusing his voice with the same deep warmth that he felt.

"Thank you," she said.

They fell silent and shared a long look filled with sexy intentions.

Oh, this is happening.

"Listen, I wanted to apologize for my behavior back in high school," she said, her thumb lightly stroking his.

He remembered her words. *"It's the last thing you need."*

"That's in the past," he said, pushing aside the remnants of embarrassment that lingered even after all that time.

"But there's so much that's—"

"Eve!"

They both looked over at the trio of women excitedly walking up to her with champagne flutes in their hands and the desire to celebrate brightening their eyes and smiles.

Lucas and Eve released each other's hands. He stepped back as the same friends she'd had in high school rushed to surround her with excited chatter.

"Look at you, Eve!"

"Eve, how have you been?"

"It's so good to see you, Eve!"

He turned away from them and looked at the photo of himself as he raised his glass in a toast, then took a deep sip and walked away with one last glance at Eve. He found her looking back at him as her friends steered her deeper into the party. He gave her a wink and smile and promised himself that he would bed Eve Villar—something he would have never been able to do in the past.

Even though he knew with his fame as a celebrity chef—a Cress nonetheless—that many of his classmates had seen him in the press, coming to his reunion had been the opportunity to show off his muscular physique that he'd worked so hard to obtain. Making Eve Villar see him and regret turning down his tender offer of love had been a hope, but the opportunity to get in bed and fulfill a high-school fantasy was more than he could wish for.

The chase is on.

Eve entered the restroom of the school and released a sigh of relief that it was empty, and she was free of the cloying attention of her high-school friends, Claudia, Ashanti and Lorn. She set her metallic clutch atop the marble counter. She used the tips of her gold glitter-covered nails to tease her short haircut, then opened her purse to refresh her sheer hot cocoa lip gloss in the ornate wood-framed mirror. Like everything at Manhattan University Prep, the design of the lavatory was embellished with plenty of carved woodwork, hinting at its century-old history.

There was plenty of history she wished she could forget.

She closed her eyes, wishing she could erase the memory of her mean and judgmental behavior.

I was an awful human being. Just vain and cruel.

During the last year, she had left so much of her past behind, and fought hard to do better and be better. Her only reason for even attending the reunion was to show her former schoolmates that she had changed and to make amends to those she'd hurt in the past with her snobbery.

Like Luc.

Eve grimaced, remembering her harsh words to him.

"If you knew like we all know, you would stop eating these. It's the last thing you need."

He had poured out his heart and she'd taken it and crushed it in her grip, then slammed his delicious-looking cupcakes in the trash like LeBron taking it to the rim with force. Even as his brother had laid out in brutal clarity what he felt about her treatment of his brother, she had feigned boredom because Eve Villar never let anyone see her as anything but cool and composed.

"Luc Cress," she said aloud.

The chubby teenager had morphed into an even more handsome version of Regé-Jean Page, the handsome actor from the TV series *Bridgerton*. Shortbread complexion with dark close-cropped hair and the faint shadow of a beard that emphasized his high cheekbones and soft mouth. Deep brown eyes that were slanted and intense were framed by lush, long lashes. Tall. Broad. Fit. Strong.

She had known he and his brothers had gone on to

be just as famous as their parents, Nicolette and Phillip Cress, Senior, in the culinary world, but she had not given them any of her real attention over the years. Seeing the new Lucas Cress had been quite a shock.

An arousing one. She pressed her hand to the pulse of her opposite wrist and found it pounding at the thought of the long look they'd shared. It had made her swoon a bit, but she hadn't been able to look away.

Never would she have imagined that she would be in a bathroom having naughty thoughts about Lucas Cress. She'd envisioned him being bigger and sadder than in school.

Boy, was I wrong!

The door to the bathroom opened and the blare of "Better in Time" by Leona Lewis entered along with her old friend Lorn, who was wearing a smile that Eve returned. "We wondered where you disappeared to," she said, setting her crystal-adorned, heart-shaped clutch on the counter before leaning against the edge as she crossed her arms over her chest in the sequin pantsuit she wore. "Can you believe Luc Cress?"

"Not at all," Eve admitted.

"He's won most improved, that's for sure!"

Eve just smiled as Lorn began to give a salacious rundown of the scandals of their former classmates. Who was sleeping with whom? Who was on drugs? Who faced financial ruin? And on, and on, and on. So much had changed in the five years since she'd last spoken to or seen her friends. And she was okay with that.

It was a reminder of who she used to be.

Lorn fell silent as Eve didn't serve up the usual oohs and aahs to the catty gossip.

The bathroom door opened again. Eve leaned to the left to look past Lorn as a woman she didn't recognize entered.

Lorn turned and gave the woman a frigid smile as she turned her by her shoulders to guide her back out of the restroom.

"Lorn!" Eve gasped in horror.

"Could you find another bathroom? We're having a private chat. Thanks," Lorn said, pushing the woman out into the hall as she sputtered in disbelief.

"Sorry!" Eve called out to the stranger just before Lorn pressed a hand to the door to shut it.

Wham!

Eve hung her head as she pressed her fingertips to the spot just between her eyebrows.

"I was hoping to catch a moment alone with you, Eve. We haven't spoken since Aaron's death," Lorn said, lightly touching her elbow.

She shook her head a bit as she fought the instinct to shy away from her touch…and from a clear mirror of just who she used to be. "Not now, Lorn," she said softly, gripping the edge of the counter as she released a long, ragged breath that still did nothing to empty her of the emotions that had arisen.

The grief and the guilt.

"I called you—"

Eve gave the woman a forced smile. "Thank you for that. Seriously," she said. "But I'm not ready to talk about it."

Lorn nodded, her emerald eyes filling with pity, then she turned to face the mirror and smooth the edges of her red hair pulled into a sleek ponytail. "That's under-standable," she said.

Eve felt like a specimen under a microscope because of Lorn's hawklike stare at her reflection in the mir-ror. "Listen, it's been nice catching up with you and the other ladies," she said, having had her fill. "But I'm going to have a quick chat with someone and then head home."

Lorn frowned.

Eve picked up her clutch and tucked it under her arm, then leaned in to give an air kiss to each of the woman's cheeks. "Get home safe," she said, before moving past her to open the heavy wood door.

"Why does this feel like a very polite 'get lost'?" Lorn asked.

Eve paused and looked back. "Because it is," she said, then stepped into the hall and let the door slowly close behind her—slowly enough for her to hear her former friend's gasp of shock mingle with the sound of Santana's "Into the Night" as the DJ continued to re-mind them all of 2008 with his music selection.

She made her way down the wide hall, with its pol-ished black tiles, and reached the auditorium at the cen-ter of the main hall of the campus. With a pause, she allowed her eyes to adjust to the dark interior that was lit by colorful beams of flashing lights. She opened her clutch to check the time on her phone. It was just after nine and she really was ready to head home. She had an early start in the morning with an onsite class for CPR recertification for the entire staff of her pri-vate lifeguard company, Aquatic Safety Solutions. Her days of late nights *and* early mornings were no more.

She looked at the gyrating bodies for the sight of Lucas Cress. By the stage, she spotted a small crowd gathered around someone and headed in that direction. As she approached, she saw the crowd was women, and their centerpiece was none other than Luc. She stopped just on the edge and looked on as he signed a stack of yearbooks with flourish, then flashed a smile that was charming and disarming.

He's enjoying this, she thought as she continued to watch his eyes brighten as a woman whose bright blond hair and massive bosom defied realism leaned in to press a kiss to his cheek, leaving bright pink lipstick behind.

He looked up and locked eyes on her just as a beauty with waist-length braids whispered something in his ear. Eve bit down on her bottom lip as she raised both eyebrows at him. His smile was bashful as he held up both of his hands.

He's a flirt!

She watched him closely as he rose to ease through his fans. She missed not one detail about the man. His height. The breadth of his shoulders and the leanness of his hips. The navy suit he had on was tailored to fit his frame and suited his shortbread complexion, which seemed a bit darker than when he was younger. The chubby kid had morphed into one sexy man. It all worked for him.

And he *knew* it.

It wasn't ego or cockiness. Just bold confidence.

She released a breath that shook with her awareness of him. He came to stand in front of her and towered over her by at least four inches, just upping the intensity. "I wanted to talk to you…if your fans don't mind?" she said, looking past him at the dozens of eyes piercing into them.

He looked back and gave them all a wave. "Sure," he said when he refocused on her.

"In private," Eve added.

His face filled with interest as he smiled. Slowly.

"Seriously," she insisted, winning the fight not to return his smile.

He made a show of straightening his designer silk tie, standing taller and clearing his throat as he gave her a mock-serious face.

Eve turned and led him through the crowd as some other 2008 rap song played. She felt eyes watching them and ignored them all. She was sure many of them remembered the massive blowout of her embarrassing Lucas before his brother, Cole, had put on a show that led to him being suspended for a few days. To see two of the key players now strolling together across the gym was enough to get tongues wagging.

In the hall, she turned just as he leaned his back against the row of lockers.

"I need to apologize to you," Eve began, nervously raking her fingernails through the short hair on her nape.

"For?" he asked, watching her closely.

"How I treated you back in high school," she said. "Especially the day you tried to give me the cupcakes you made for me."

He looked down at the tip of his polished handmade shoes and then back up at her with a glint in his eye. "No worries," he said. "It's in the past."

Eve wasn't sure what to make of the moment.

"Then again, dinner and drinks at my place might make the lingering hurt go away," he added. The look in his eyes was one of appreciation and attraction.

"And why does 'drinks' feel more like my panties on the floor by your bed?" she asked.

His eyes lit with fire. "If you're attached to them, I can just ease them to the side," Lucas said, pushing off the lockers to take a long step toward her.

Eve stiffened her lower back and her knees to keep from stepping back from him and his overwhelming presence. She refused to run. With a notch of her chin, she was thankful her heels gave her added height as she looked up into his eyes. "I'm offering apologies, not sex," she said.

"Damn," he said in obvious regret.

She chuckled, unable to help herself as she shook her head at him. "It's good to see that you are doing very well, Luc," she said.

"I could be better," he said, raising his hand to lightly touch her upper arm. "For both of us."

Eve closed her eyes for a moment at his heated touch. "My plans for the night are for a long and hot bath before climbing into my bed *alone*. Good night, Lucas," she said, then turned away from him.

"Eve?" he called behind her.

She stopped and looked back.

"Okay. I pressed too hard, and I forgot my manners," he said, his voice echoing in the hall along, with the steady bass-line thump of the music. "Thank you for your apology."

She held her clutch with both hands in front of her.

"Thank you for hearing me out," she said, before turning away from him again. "And good night again, Luc."

"Tu es encore plus belle qu'au lycée," he said.

Eve paused as his deep voice speaking French echoed in the hall.

"You're even more beautiful than you were in high school," he said.

"You speak French?" she asked fluently in the language as she met his gaze yet again.

Lucas shook his head and laughed. "We were in class together all through high school, Eve," he said.

"Right. I forgot that," she admitted.

Or I was too caught up in myself to see anyone outside my bubble.

"I better go," Eve said, turning one last time to walk down the length of the hall. Her heels hitting against the tile echoed until she reached the double doors.

"Jusqu'à ce que nous nous revoyions," Lucas called behind her.

Until we meet again.

Eve felt like it was a promise.

Two

Lucas took a sip of his cup of coffee and smiled as he looked at his entire family scattered about the private family dining room of the Cress, INC. corporate offices, which were located on the entire fortieth floor of a towering Manhattan office building. He used his free hand to smooth his silk tie, which he wore with a hand-tailored suit from his favorite designer. He was a man who enjoyed the finer things in life, from what he wore on his back to the women he had in his bed. He enjoyed luxuries and felt no shame about it. Unfortunately, it was his love of indulging that had led to him being overweight for most of his life.

And that weight had been far harder to shed than it had been to gain.

It had taken a steady regimen of eating less and working out more. He still ran five miles on the treadmill every morning so as not to start gaining back those fifty pounds. He couldn't eat many of the sweets he still enjoyed baking because they were such decadent creations.

Although everyone in his family was able to make desserts, he was the pastry chef, or pâtissier—although he had yet to top his mother's crème brûlée. But, of course, she was Nicolette Lavoie-Cress, a world-renowned award-winning chef, as was his father, Phillip. After meeting and falling in love in culinary school, the couple had gone on to establish restaurants across the country, written more than two dozen bestselling cookbooks and culinary guides, and won prestigious Michelin stars and James Beard awards. After lengthy careers, they shifted to creating their nonprofit, The Cress Family Foundation, and Cress, INC., a powerful culinary empire.

Each of the Cress brothers, all acclaimed chefs as well, held executive positions within the conglomerate. Gabriel headed up the restaurant division that oversaw the thirteen CRESS restaurants around the world. Coleman controlled marketing, and oversaw the digital magazines, websites and social media. Their oldest brother, Lincoln, his father's newly discovered heir who'd been born in England before Phillip's marriage to Nicolette, was thriving as the president of sustainability. Sean had expanded his reach from starring in syndicated cooking shows to launching the company's own network, CRESSTV. Lucas ran the popular cookware line that was sold worldwide. It was top-rated, and had been included as part of Oprah's Favorite Things for the second year in a row.

Lucas shifted his eyes to Phillip Junior and studied him, taking note of the change in his brother since he'd been appointed CEO a year ago. There was more confidence and far less edge. Without the pressure to compete with his brothers for the position he always felt he deserved as the eldest Cress brother—before the discovery of Lincoln—Phillip Junior was easier to be around *and* was thriving in the position.

Today, the entire Cress family had gathered and nearly everyone was dressed in different textures of linen as they chatted and waited for the photographer and his staff to set up his equipment. Gone was the normal round table, large enough to fit their parents and brothers in the past. It was replaced by a long and wide table set for fourteen with an array of colorful Cress, INC. cookware adorning the middle, along with floral arrangements.

Lucas eyed his entire family, smiling because they were growing in number with each passing year.

Lincoln and his wife, Bobbie, were standing near windows, both dressed in winter white. Lincoln held their soon-to-be one-year-old daughter, Poppy, who was named after his deceased mother.

Phillip Junior looked across the room at his wife, Raquel, giving the ponytail of their eight-year-old daughter, Collette, some last-minute attention before she straightened her oval-shaped rose gold spectacles.

Two-year-old Emme climbed down from the lap of her mother, Monica, to take wobbly steps and press both of her palms against the glass of the floor-to-ceiling window that displayed Manhattan. Gabriel ended a call on his phone and moved over to the window to kneel beside their daughter, then motioned with a raise of his chin at his wife to join them.

As Jillian sat in one of the dozen club chairs in the dining room, Coleman stood behind her gently massaging her neck and shoulders. Lucas smiled when his brother bent at the waist to press a gentle kiss on his wife's forehead.

Morgan, the two-year-old son of Sean and his wife, Montgomery, sat on the polished hardwood floors laughing as he pushed a truck in the shape of a dinosaur—two of his favorite things combined into one toy that he took everywhere with him.

There was so much love in the room.

And his parents sat together with joyful smiles and their hands lingering on each other. Ever since his father's heart surgery and subsequent retirement, the two had spent the last year leisurely traveling and rediscovering their love of food in each exotic locale. Their decades-long marriage had survived many difficulties, and somehow, they loved each other more than ever.

Lucas frowned a bit as he eyed everyone in the room again. He was the lone single Cress in the room. His frown deepened. All his brothers were married. Happily so.

Hmm...

As the youngest Cress brother, "The Favorite," as his brothers teased him, it was natural he would be the last to get married, but perhaps the time had come to join his brothers in becoming a husband. Stability. Children. A home. Family.

Lucas looked down at the bare ring finger on his left hand. He imagined a wedding band on it. *Diamonds, of course.*

And the wedding would be massive. Bigger than any of his brothers'. The best of the best.

Of all his brothers, Lucas enjoyed material shows of wealth the most. He reveled in it all. Designer clothes. Expensive cars. A luxurious lifestyle. First-class everything.

Before the end of the year, I will be married, too.

"Now I just need a bride," he said softly, barely above a whisper.

Women? He had plenty of conquests. Someone suitable to join the Cress legacy? Not one.

The women he attracted since acquiring his muscular, fit frame, and losing the chubbiness of his face for a more chiseled look, had greater bra-cup sizes but smaller intelligence quotients. That made for great fun, but not finality. At all. Most of his most recent entanglements lasted no more than a night.

"Not now, Sean. Your parents are looking."

At the whispered plea of a feminine voice, Lucas shifted his gaze over to Sean pressing kisses to Montgomery's neck as he tried to covertly steer her toward the hall that led to the private bathroom. Of all the brothers, Luc was closest to Sean—even with Gabriel and Coleman cushioned between them in age. Seeing them be so openly affectionate, he thought of the late-night conversation they'd had when Sean first discovered Montgomery was pregnant. Theirs had not been a love connection. The marriage was because of the pregnancy, but somehow, they had found their way to love.

They're all in love.

He studied the couples again.

Whether by lingering touches, long looks, or smiles that spoke of sexy secrets, each radiated that they loved the other.

He scowled.

The love, he could do without—he saw it as a weakness. An open door for someone to glide through and deliver unbelievable pain. Love meant placing your heart in someone else's hands. The last time he followed his heart it led him directly to hurt and embarrassment.

And my cupcakes slam-dunked in the trash.

Eve Villar.

Lucas picked up his phone from the edge of the leather club chair just as Coleman strode over to sit in the empty chair angled beside him.

"You finished Poppy's cake?" his brother asked.

His newest niece was turning one and her parents were throwing a huge birthday party to celebrate. As he had in the past for the birthdays of his nieces and nephew, Lucas was making the cake. And everyone in the family had asked him about the cake since his arrival. "She'll love it," he said, sparing Coleman a quick look before refocusing his attention on opening an email.

"I don't doubt it," his brother said.

"'Your floral arrangement has been delivered,'" Lucas said, reading the message aloud. Then he set down the phone with a satisfied smile. Every day since the reunion, he had sent flowers to the address of Eve's business, which he'd discovered when he'd searched for her name online.

Coleman shifted in the black suit he was wearing—completely against the color scheme and ever the
rebel—before removing a leather cigar case from the
inside pocket of his tailored blazer. "Flowers?" he asked
as he removed a sixty-ring cigar. "That's not your style.
Who's the lucky lady?"

Lucas smiled as he picked up his phone and pulled
up the photo he'd covertly taken of Eve at the reunion.
He handed the phone to his brother. "Recognize her?"
he asked, quickly taking one of the cigars in the case
before Coleman snapped it shut and slid it back into
his inner pocket.

"Wait," Coleman said as he used his fingers on the
screen to zoom in. "Is that…?"

"Eve Villar," they said in unison.

Lucas's tone was one of satisfaction.

Coleman's was astonishment.

He took back his phone. "She was at our high-school
reunion," he explained.

"She still looks the same," Coleman said, biting
down on the end of the cigar. "And still the same beautiful chaos?"

"Undoubtedly," Lucas said, looking down at the
photo. "Although she did apologize."

"She did?" Coleman asked, seemingly more aston-
ished by that than he had been by the picture. "She owes
you more than that."

"Damn right," Lucas agreed.

Coleman leaned back in his chair to eye him. "What's
your endgame?"

"To sweet-talk Eve Villar into my bed," Lucas said
without missing a beat.

"Like a dog with a bone about that one, huh?" Coleman asked.

Lucas just shrugged one shoulder. "Trust me, she's game," he said, thinking of the desire he saw in her eyes when she looked at him. Saw him. The new him.

It was a look of interest that he had become very good at recognizing.

"*N'allumez pas ce cigare*, Coleman," Nicolette said across the spacious room in her native tongue of French as she stood behind where their father was sitting with her hand stroking his nape.

Lucas looked on as Coleman gave their mother a slow smile and a wink before looking over at his wife with a question in his eyes.

"He just likes to bite on them these days, Nicolette," Jillian added, unbuttoning the blazer of the satin rose gold suit she had on. She crossed the room to come and stand beside where her husband was sitting, then exposed her small, rounded belly. "He hasn't lit one since we discovered we're pregnant!"

Everyone in the room gasped in shock moments before there was thunderous applause and exclamations. Coleman beamed with pride and Jillian preened as hands were carefully pressed to her womb. A circle of love, family and support was created around them.

"Congratulations," Lucas said to them before rising to ease to the back of the crowd.

As he watched the pure happiness of Coleman and Jillian, Lucas knew he was ready to find a suitable and compatible woman to wed and start his own family.

There was a break in the crowd as their patriarch, Phillip Cress Senior, stepped forward with Nicolette close at his side. Physically, his parents were opposites. He was a tall and broad Englishman with a deep brown complexion, while she was a slender Parisian with a pale complexion and hair that was far more silver than blond, but they had forged a large family and an empire together with love and passion.

"A blessing," Phillip Senior said, his deep voice heavy with his British accent. He bent down his more than six-foot frame to press a light kiss to Jillian's temple.

It was a marked difference from his parents' first reactions to both Monica and Jillian shifting from being former staff of their luxury townhome to being their daughters-in-law.

"A girl or boy?" Nicolette asked with a prominent French accent. She clasped her hands together under her chin and happiness danced in her blue eyes.

Coleman and Jillian shared a look. "It's twins," they said in unison before looking back at the family.

Lucas bit back a smile—everyone looked doubtful as they cast covert glances at Monica and Gabriel. Early in Monica's pregnancy, they'd announced they were having twins. The family later discovered that her "instincts" said twins even though the obstetrician said there was no sign of that on her ultrasound. Ultimately, the obstetrician was correct and little Emme was born into the world sans a twin sibling.

"Confirmed?" Nicolette asked before gently biting down on her forefinger as she pointed it at the couple as well.

"What?" Monica said, rubbing circles onto Emme's

back as their daughter played in her curls. "I really *thought* I was having twins."

Gabriel pressed a kiss to his wife's cheek. "In my wife's defense, there are such things as a hidden twin and women giving birth to twins without both showing on the ultrasound."

The family jokingly teased Monica, who could only smile and hide her face against Emme's neck, causing the toddler to giggle.

"Ours is confirmed," Jillian said. "No offense, Monica."

"None taken," she mumbled against Emme's neck.

More laughter ensued.

As the family eventually took their positions to pose in front of the beautiful Manhattan skyline, there was a celebratory mood with laughter and smiles that could only make the photos better. The last shot of the day was the entire family seated around the table.

"Excuse me, everyone," Phillip Junior said, rising from his seat.

All eyes fell on him.

"While we are all gathered here in the offices of Cress, INC., where the tradition of love, family and business has been created by our parents and further strengthened by the contribution of not just each Cress brother, but also the support of their beautiful wives, I wanted to thank you for the belief you have all placed in my as the new CEO this last year," he said, extending his hand for Raquel and Collette to come stand beside him. "The future is bright here at Cress, INC., but only because of the foundation laid by the past."

"He really wanted it," Sean said, leaning in closer to Lucas where they were sitting beside each other with

Montgomery on the other side of him. "More than any of us."

Lucas nodded in agreement. "That's for sure," he said. "And the brothers are better because of it. The war is over."

Sean grunted in agreement. "You finished the cake?" he asked, almost offhandedly.

"No," Lucas lied.

Sean's face filled with shock, but the look of sarcasm on his youngest brother's face immediately caused his broad shoulders to relax.

"In honor of the past, I thought it was time to bring back one tradition that we haven't experienced since our parents began their world tour," Phillip Junior said with a smile at their parents. "Continuing the tradition started by our mother, there will be freshly prepared lunch for the family and our support staff cooked by me once a week…starting today."

He turned and opened the double doors leading into the company's test kitchen. Moments later, he returned with a large, wide frying pan of paella that he had set on a large trivet on the center of the table. "And I thought, what better meal to fix today than the one and only lunch prepared for us here at work, Dad."

Sean, Lucas, Gabriel and Coleman all shared looks as Phillip Senior eyed the dish of tomato-infused rice filled with lobster, mussels, clams and shrimp. Their father had made the dish as a show of his disappointment in no one garnering a James Beard Award nomination in both the journalism and the restaurant-and-chef categories. He expected from his sons the same flawless execution it took to properly make the Spanish dish.

An unspoken message. Their father expected perfection and nothing less.

Lucas was sure his brothers wondered just what message Phillip Junior was trying to get across as he began to serve everyone from the still steaming pan. As he dug into the meal, he did not hold back a grunt of pleasure. It was just as good as their father's. Exquisitely seasoned. Perfectly cooked rice, tender seafood. A slight crunch at the bottom of the paella.

"Dad?" Phillip Junior asked, looking at their father.

For a moment, it reminded Lucas of all the brothers' attempts to garner the approval of their father, who had been far less stern since his heart surgery two years ago.

"Job well done, son," Phillip Senior said, raising his glass of spring water to him.

It was clear he meant the dish and his performance as the new head of the conglomerate.

Message received.

Collette surprised them all by rising to her feet with her goblet of lemonade in hand. *"À la nourriture. À la vie. À l'amour,"* she said, already fluent in French.

Nicolette beamed with pride as she raised her glass of white wine. It was her favorite saying in her native French tongue, and it was also branded across every Cress, INC. product.

To food. To life. To love.

"À la nourriture. À la vie. À l'amour," the entire family said in unison.

Eve leaned in the doorway of her home office in her modest home on Swan Lake in East Patchogue, New York. Within the eighteen hundred feet of the ranch-style home she both lived and ran her business, Aquatic Safety Solutions. At the moment, it was looking like a flower shop. Nearly every inch of the space was filled with vases of flowers of all colors, scents and varieties.

Every day for the last two weeks a new bouquet had arrived that was larger than the one delivered the day before. Each one was meant to tease her and remind her of him. The April sun glared through the curtainless window to highlight the variety of bright colors and intensify the fragrant scents.

Lucas lay-it-on-thick Cress.

It had been hard not to think of him when he made a point of sending daily reminders ever since the reunion. She closed her eyes and released a breath as she remembered every detail about him. Every single thing that made him so different from who he had been in high school. The looks. His confidence. The sex appeal.

"What does he want?" she asked aloud.

"We both know the answer to that."

Eve sighed heavily as she turned to find her office manager and best friend, Suzi, sitting at her own desk in the last empty bedroom directly across from her. The woman, with her ebony hair cut into a bob that framed her round face and her large blue eyes, was an invaluable asset to her. "And I think it's wasteful to cut flowers that will survive two weeks at best and pay thousands of dollars for it," Eve said, turning to walk into her office to pick up the massive three-foot bouquet of more than fifty long-stemmed vibrant blooms.

She carried them out of the office and across the polished hardwood floor of the hall, then set them on the edge of Suzi's cluttered desk. "For you," she said, after leaning to the left to see beyond the flowers. "And donate the rest."

"Even the tulips? They're your favorites," Suzi said, biting back a smile.

True.

"Okay, not the tulips," Eve mumbled.

Suzi smiled and rose from her seat. She leaned in and smelled a green flower that was shaped like a trumpet. "And the man…is he up for a donation as well?" she asked with mirth in the depths of her bright eyes.

Eve paused in her walk back to her office to look over one of her shoulders. "You're ready to give him a go based on flowers?" she asked with humor.

Suzi was very tongue-in-cheek as she leaned over to swivel her computer around to reveal Lucas's photo on the screen "One sexy pastry chef," she said.

Yes. Yes, he is.

Eve eyed him. Her reaction was swift. Quickening heart rate. Pounding pulse. The awakening of the fleshy bud of her femininity.

In high school, Lucas had been chubby and cute—just a hint that beneath the weight was a stallion waiting to be revealed.

And ridden.

With a small gasp at her salacious thought, Eve turned and reentered her office. The scent of the flowers he sent awaited her. Teased her. Pleased her. Their very existence was a promise of far more than a brief reacquainting at a reunion.

She crossed the sun-filled room to stand behind the desk as she moved all the flowers except the tulips to the floor against the white-painted wall. There was work to be done and no attention to be spared for whatever she-nanigans Lucas was up to. It was just a few weeks from May Day, signaling the start of the peak busy season in all the hamlets and villages of Southampton and East Hampton. Bookings had already been made months in advance for Eve and her staff to work as lifeguards at private beach and pool parties, give swimming lessons and supervise some aquatic school events. Eve also provided training for new lifeguards and provided substitute lifeguard services for those businesses needing to replace one of their lifeguards on staff who could not make a shift. Even during the off-season months, there were bookings with owners of indoor pools.

All of it kept Aquatic Safety Solutions busy year-round.

Thank God.

What had started as a labor of love had become a business that thrived and provided a stable income. Eve was proud that she had started it all on her own without the financial backing of anyone. That had been more important to her than anyone could ever know.

Eve released a deep sigh and forced herself to focus on any new online bookings. There were more than she expected. "Suzi, I know we're fully staffed, but perhaps we should consider adding one or two more lifeguards this season," she called out to her.

At the silence, Eve paused.

She and Suzi generally spoke to each other with raised voices rather than by intercom or any other communication because of the close proximity of their offices. All the work of the lifeguards was essentially mobile, with them traveling to private homes or beaches. There had never been a customer to enter the home and force them to stand on formality.

At the continuing silence, Eve stood up and came around her desk to peek out the door to find Suzi with her mouth agape as she read the card that obviously had been delivered with the flowers.

"What?" Eve said, moving quickly to cross the space and ease the card from her friend's hand.

"Oh, my, Lucas Cress," Suzi sighed before fanning herself.

"'Every night I dream of making love to you. I want you. You ready for me yet?'" Eve said, reading the note.

"Oh, my" is right.

Eve licked her lips and cleared her throat as she slid the card into the back pocket of her wide-leg jeans. She was also wearing a sheer black long-sleeved frilly top over a lace bralette. "Let's focus on reality," she drawled even as her heart pounded with ferocity.

Jusqu'à ce que nous nous revoyions, he had promised.

She shivered because he seemed determined to keep his word.

"I have quite a few applicants for you to interview," Suzi said, reaching to pull a green folder from one of the many stacked on the edge of her desk. She handed the folder to her boss of the last five years.

"Thanks, Suzi. What would I do without you?" Eve asked, turning as she quickly scanned the stack of applications printed from their online portal.

"Hopefully not the same thing you have done with your libido?" Suzi said behind her.

Eve froze in the doorway.

"Forget all about it," Suzi added.

"I figured that's what you meant," Eve drawled.

"It's been six years, Eve," Suzi said with the gentleness of someone who knew the ins and outs of Eve's struggles. "Just how long are you going to punish yourself?"

That made Eve turn to face her friend. And in the depths of Suzi's big dark eyes was all the compassion anyone could seek. "Su-zi," she said, begging her to understand.

"Listen, I looked him up. He's exactly what you need. All the fun with none of the ties," Suzi said. "A nice little bridge to get you over to the other side of your grief and guilt."

It had been six years since she'd shared her bed with anyone, and the joy of her vibrator was not the same as the feel of a warm male body pressed atop her. Below her. Inside her.

"Jusqu'à ce que nous nous revoyions."

She turned and said nothing as she walked back into her office to drop the folder on her neat and orderly desk, then pulled the card from her back pocket. She read his words again. And again. She could hear his deep voice saying them to her in her ear.

"You ready for me yet?"

Eve quivered as she opened the top drawer of her desk and dropped the card atop the others she had kept.

Perhaps I am.

Three

The atmosphere of the midtown Manhattan venue was bursting with the excitement of an event—a Cress family party. The theme of an enchanted forest transformed the space, with grass covering the floor and towering faux trees. The ceiling was draped with dark silks and twinkling lights, with a glistening moon dangling from the rafter. Entertainers dressed as winged fairies dangled from above. Even the tables around the perimeter of the ballroom were covered in green taffeta adorned with leaf petals. Candles and floral decor were surrounded by mini tree stumps and there were recreations of small garden areas throughout.

It was beautiful and magical, offering realism and the feeling of walking through the woods for the partygoers there to enjoy the first birthday of the youngest Cress heir, Poppy.

Upbeat music blared through the speakers. There was a candy bar, an ice-cream-sundae station and a decorated table towering with both cupcakes and mini cheesecakes. The hundreds of kids of all ages in attendance enjoyed the indoor games, slides, laser tag area, jumping castle and ball pit. The adults had plenty of themed drinks. And everyone enjoyed heavy appetizers, courtesy of both of the New York CRESS restaurants.

"All set, Luc?"

Lucas turned from the birthday cake he'd created for his niece to find Lincoln standing in the doorway to the kitchen with his hands over his eyes. He removed the chef's coat he had on to reveal the V-neck sweater he wore with dark jeans. "All set," he told them.

"Can I see it now?" Lincoln asked, his British accent still prominent.

"In about a minute, with everyone else," Lucas said, walking over to steer his brother out of the kitchen.

"What if Poppy doesn't like it?" Lincoln asked.

"First, *I'm* Luc Cress," he said with extreme confidence. "Second, she's one, big brother. Relax."

Lincoln released his disappointment in a heavy breath a moment before Lucas gave him a gentle push back into the hoopla of the party that was costing him plenty. On his way back to the kitchen, he pulled his iPhone from his back pocket to once again check that Eve's flowers for the day had been delivered. He smiled at the notification.

This time he had included the details of the party and an invitation to attend.

Will she?

Only time would tell.

He was beginning to believe that he would never woo the woman into his bed when she wouldn't come within a hundred miles of him. He even considered driving to the Hamptons, but felt that bordered on stalking and had quickly abandoned that idea. Flowers were one thing. Driving three hours for a surprise pop-up was just cause for police involvement. Thus, the invite for *her* to come to *him*. To do so was a clear sign that she was intrigued and wondering if he could deliver on his promises.

I damn sure can...and I damn sure want to.

He was curious if the snobbish beauty dropped the pomp and circumstance in bed. Was she wild or reserved? A talker or silent? Either way, he wanted Eve Villar, and he was going to have her—even if only just once. Her interest in him was an opportunity he would not squander.

Not when I've waited fifteen years...and back then I only wanted a kiss.

Back in the kitchen, Lucas made sure to place a box of gloves and a cutting knife onto the cart he was using to roll the cake out to the party. Once he reached the double doors, he used his left elbow to press the pad that automatically swung the door opened. He stepped out long enough to give the DJ a thumbs-up signal, the way they'd planned. He waited patiently as the music switched from Kidz Bop covers of music to the version of "Happy Birthday to You" from the YouTube show *Gracie's Corner*. The kids immediately began to stop to follow the instructions in the song as the lights darkened and colorful strobes flashed.

He was thankful for the neon velvet ropes the event planner provided as he made his way to the spot in front of the elaborate balloon structures at the front of the room. The family awaited him, with Lincoln and Bobbie in the front as his brother's wife held a squirming Poppy in her arms. There were gasps and sighs, and applause for the cake, but his eyes stayed locked on his niece, waiting for the first moment she got sight of her life-sized unicorn cake, complete with a gold saddle on its back, and the unicorn bent down to drink from a puddle of water surrounded by grass. He was rewarded with wide eyes, a gleeful smile and claps as she squirmed to be free of her mother's hold, seemingly uncaring of the entire party singing "Happy Birthday to You" to her.

Perfect, he thought, stopping the cart in the spotlight and putting down the foot-lock brake before moving to take his niece into his arms.

Poppy, who was the spitting image of her mother, complete with a curly afro, hugged his neck so tightly that he fought not to tear up with all the love he felt for her exploding in his chest. He didn't even care that her pudgy hands were sticky as they pressed against his designer sweater.

"Good job, Luc!" Bobbie sighed, squeezing his arm in excitement. "It's perfection."

"It's really bloody good!" Lincoln said, giving his shoulder a resounding slap.

"The middle is carved rice Krispy treats so she can sit on the saddle," Lucas told them. "And we'll cut the pond first before taking it into the kitchen to slice up. The kids don't need to see us eviscerate the unicorn."

"Exactement," Nicolette said as she reached up to softly pat the cheek of her favorite son.

Every Cress brother had a role. Lincoln had become "The Eldest" with his addition to the family. Phillip Junior reigned as "The Responsible One". Sean was "The Star," while Coleman loved being "The Rebel" and Gabriel was unproblematic as "The Good One."

Over the top of Poppy's curls, Lucas noticed a familiar face aiming a beautiful smile at him.

Lana Ariti.

She was the socialite daughter of Italian billionaire real-estate magnate Apollo Ariti. Beautiful. Accomplished. And staring at him with open appreciation.

Hmm...

Lucas handed Poppy to his mother, who eagerly took her step-granddaughter into her arms to press kisses to the cheeks of the child. He slid his hands into the pockets of his jeans as he made his way through the crowd with his eyes locked on Lana—a beautiful darkhaired beauty who resembled actress Sophia Loren in her younger years.

Lana gave him a slow smile as he came to a stop before her. "Long time no see, Lucas," she said, with only a slight hint of an Italian accent.

"It's good to see you," he said, bending to press a light kiss to her cheek.

"Same," she agreed with warm eyes. "I away was overseeing the sale of my family's winery in Tuscany."

He took in the casual but chic outfit she was wearing with polished leather flats. She somehow balanced being sexy with more reserved clothing. She was very different from the women he normally favored—flashy, and not the type he would risk introducing to his mother. It would not be worth sitting through the tirade.

"I'm surprised to see you here," he said. "Unless there's an update I missed."

Lana tucked her long hair behind her ear and smiled at him. "No husband. No children. Your mother invited my niece, Naya, so I brought her on behalf of my family," she explained, pointing a finger over to an exuberant eight-year-old zooming down the slide. "In fact, your niece Collette is invited to Naya's party next week."

Lucas looked over and chuckled as her niece landed in a steep pit of balls with glee.

"A little birdie also told me you were looking to be wed this year, Lucas," Lana said.

He faced her again with his head cocked to the side as he gave her a warm look. "That's the plan...if I find the right woman to be my bride," he said.

Lana nodded in understanding. "That's ambitious," she said, reaching up to gently swipe something from the sleeve of his sweater.

"And I plan to succeed," he assured her.

Lana shifted her hand up to lightly grip his shoulder, then continued up, to gently press her hand to his cheek. "Then let me be clear, Lucas Cress," she said. "I plan to be your bride."

With one last smile as she stroked his chin, Lana moved to walk past him.

Lucas slowly turned to watch her walk over to where her niece was making her way out of the pit. He would have never expected such boldness from the heiress. He liked it.

A lot.

The afternoon spring sun made the lake glisten as Eve lounged on her cedar swing glider on her deck, sipping a glass of freshly squeezed lemonade. She adored the lake for its beauty more than she desired to sink beneath its depths and slice the water with her arms as she swam. She preferred the ocean or a pool.

It was those particular bodies of water that had been her redemption.

Physically and mentally.

Her grip on her glass tightened and her view of the lake was blurred by the tears that gathered.

With a small shake of her head, she closed her eyes. Tightly. Tears raced down her cheeks. She freed a shaky breath.

Her life was so different than it had been in the past. Deliberately so. She was relieved for the transformation but still deeply scarred by the events that had led to it, as a memory overtook her...

"All drinks on me!" Aaron Marks hollered.

As the bass of the music seemed to pulse against the dancing bodies in the club. Eve tossed her long, flowing black hair over her shoulder as she looked up at her boyfriend, Aaron, who was standing atop *a clear acrylic table at the luxury club with his hand raised high in the air clutching a soon-to-be empty magnum of champagne. She clapped her hands and bounced up and down excitedly on her seat.*

Aaron was a sought-after software developer who had just sold his app to the tune of forty million dollars. There were plenty of reasons to celebrate. It was not his first successful launch of an app and Aaron enjoyed his wealth—and lavishing it on Eve. She lived as one of the elites of Manhattan. Her taste for nothing but the finest things had been cultivated as the privileged daughter of her high-profile, entertainment-attorney father and neurosurgeon mother. Upon meeting Aaron three years ago, right after he first sold his first social-media app, he was more than happy to spoil her endlessly.

Aaron stumbled off the table to unceremoniously drop down on his seat beside her on the leather bench as the strobe lights flashed against them. She laughed with glee as he pulled her close and pressed kisses to her bosom in the rose gold strapless dress she had on. She grabbed the sides of his face to pull his head up to lick wildly at his mouth.

"We're flying to Dubai tomorrow," Aaron told her, his eyes intense and glassy from his excitement, the flowing alcohol and perhaps a snort or two of cocaine.

"Yes!" she exclaimed, about to fling her arms around his neck, but then pausing. "Private?"

Aaron gripped her thigh in the short dress. "Nothing else," he promised her.

Eve envisioned another round of shopping sprees, luxury spa treatments, decadent food and wild partying. It was her turn to grab the magnum from his hand to drink the rest of the champagne, not even caring when some overflowed to drip down the sides of her mouth and onto her dress.

To hell with it.

She didn't care. She never wore any outfit twice. She wouldn't dare. She loved every bit of her life and always wanted more.

They danced and partied until the high-end club closed. Together, they laughed and stumbled their way to the red Ferrari he'd purchased just earlier that day. There was no wish or dream they did not enjoy. Nothing was denied. Not one bit.

As soon as she slid onto the passenger seat, she kicked off her sequined heels and dropped her clutch to the floor beside them. Aaron started the car and accelerated out of the parking lot with a squeal of the tires against the street. The sun was just starting to rise and break the darkness of the sky. He lowered the convertible top as he gave her a look.

"This is your car, babe," Aaron told her with a dimpled grin. "I want a black one for me."

Eve squealed in surprise before leaning over to press kisses on his cheek as he sped the sports car down the nearly empty streets of New York. She pressed her hands against the dashboard and stroked it lovingly before leaning forward to press a kiss to it. "Her name is Candy," she said, loving that her hair blew in the wind and the alcohol in her system had her so relaxed.

"Whatever you want, baby," Aaron said—just like always.

"Where we going?" she asked when she noticed he didn't take the turn to go toward their penthouse condo in Tribeca.

Aaron gave her a wink. "The airport. Dubai. Remember?" he said, getting onto the highway.

"With nothing?" she asked, being coy.

"Nothing?" Aaron balked. "Never! We're never nothing."

"Damn right," she agreed, snuggling back against her seat with a smile.

"I'm going to open this thing up," he told her. "Let's see just what Candy can do."

Neither had a care about a speeding ticket.

Life was theirs to do with as they pleased. Nothing was to be denied them.

"Faster, baby! Faster!" Eve exclaimed, reaching to massage and grip his thigh as he shifted gears.

He obeyed with a rev of the motor as the vehicle seemed to sit lower with the acceleration.

"This our world," she said.

"You better believe it!"

Eve didn't want their life to slow down, either. She enjoyed the rush. She craved it.

"'You can have whatever you like.'" Aaron sang the hook of T.I.'s song "Whatever You Like."

"I. Like. More!" she screamed at the top of her lungs as she squeezed her eyes shut.

He shifted another gear.

Suddenly, the car slid across the lanes. Eve had released a high-pitched squeal as she felt her body slam against the door as the car began to rotate in circles. Aaron's screams had matched her own, before the car was hit head-on by a tractor-trailer.

Darkness...

That was all Eve remembered after that. Weeks later, she awakened in the hospital to discover both her hips and legs were broken, and Aaron had not survived the crash. That had been six years ago. Her grief and guilt rose as if it had been just yesterday. It pierced her. Deeply.

Her regrets were many.

Her shame, even more.

Eve had accepted that she had been a deplorable person. Rude. Ungrateful. Mean. Entitled.

It was hard to run from the truth while trapped in a

bed and having missed the funeral of the man she loved. In facing her truth—her faults—Eve had decided to drastically turn her back on wealth and excess, believing her and Aaron's desire to obtain more of everything had been a major cause of their reckless accident. Foolishly, they had believed wealth made them invincible.

We were so very wrong.

She never went back to their condo, which she still owned. Never collected anything from it. Never checked on the status of the car.

With the pain of her boyfriend's death, and coming close to her own, she'd felt compelled to change her entire way of life—be more kind, thoughtful and giving. Every day she tried to atone for her behavior. She fought to forget the person she used to be and the guilt she couldn't overcome.

That version of me is gone.

The use of aquatic therapy to recover from her injuries had led to a rediscovery of her love of swimming from her childhood—before she hated that it ruined her hair. And in the water, she had found physical healing and a cleansing of her old ways. She cut the hair she once cherished. Forsaken her inheritance, to the dismay of her parents. Lived a simple lifestyle with solitude.

She was out of the elitism of Manhattan, leaving her old friends and old ways behind.

It's why she had been determined to attend the reunion and apologize to Lucas.

"Do I look like I sit around and scarf down cupcakes?"

Eve shook her head and bit her bottom lip.

"If you knew like we all know you would stop eating these."

The memory of her slamming the container into the trash replayed like it was on a loop in her mind.

"It's the last thing you need."
"It's the last thing you need."
"It's the last thing you need."
"It's the last thing you need."

"What a bitch," she mumbled into her drink before taking a deep sip.

Five years ago, she came to the Hamptons for the summer and advertised as a private lifeguard, being sure she was insured and had all the necessary certifications—American Red Cross lifeguard, ocean lifeguard, scuba diving, first aid and CPR/AED. She knew it was the right decision because everything fell into place so effortlessly. She acquired enough clients, and she recruited another lifeguard to help her with her bookings. With each summer season, her business grew. Two years ago, she purchased her home in East Patchogue, which was less than an hour's drive from most of the areas she served and much more affordable than living closer to the Hamptons.

The irony was not lost on her that she now served the very people she had once relished being—the wealthy and influential. She preferred being on the other side of the velvet rope. It was there that she found her soul.

Thankfully.

Eve checked the time on her phone. It was still early afternoon. More than enough time to drive into Manhattan. It would be one of her last free Saturdays until Labor Day. Although she hated that her parents kept her old room just as she'd left it—like an homage to the Eve she was in high school—she would love to see her folks and appease their requests for her to come home more often.

Fine.

Eve gave the lake one last glance before rising to enter her house through the sliding glass door. Sitting on the counter next to the white porcelain farmer's sink was the newest floral bouquet from Lucas in shades of white, rose and lavender. She eyed the card sitting beside it. It was an invite to his niece's birthday party with his cell phone number.

A nice gesture that was definitely not as sexual as the others.

Unless it's just a maneuver to get me near him.

She remembered walking down the hall of their old high school as his words floated to her with far too much confidence.

"Jusqu'à ce que nous nous revoyions."

"Definitely not," she said aloud as if convincing herself.

But when she walked to the hall, she paused and looked back at the card, allowing herself to imagine just what might happen were she to dare to attend. She slowly raised an eyebrow at the image of him sneaking her away to a closet to ravish her as he used to do to cupcakes. She imagined him devouring *both* treats. Quickly at first, as if starved for it, and then slowly to finish, to savor it.

Bit by bit.

"You ready for me yet?"

Eve released the breath she had been holding, but it did little to relieve the pressure of her desire for Lucas Cress.

Neither did thinking of him as she showered.

Now, when she slid her satin-and-lace underwear onto her body—her one luxury—she wondered if his touch was just as soft.

She set aside the jeans she had been going to wear for a spring dress bursting with flowers because she wondered what Lucas would think if he saw her in it. She found it very matronly. So she switched from that to a green one that was more form-fitting but still sedate and settled on a red one that she knew flattered her frame.

In the mirror, she shifted her head to the left and then right as she studied the deep *V* of the women's cotton dress and how it gave her small but plump breasts the push they needed. The calf-length wide skirt—with pockets—emphasized her ankles and gave her more of an hourglass shape. The color seemed to make her medium brown complexion gleam and contrasted in the best way with her short jet-black hair.

She convinced herself her parents would enjoy seeing her in something so lively and upbeat. And that gold jewelry was the best accessory. And why not finish it off with wedge sandals? And, of course, a bold red lip gloss.

"Just the right outfit for a trip to Manhattan to see my parents," Eve told her reflection before turning to leave her bedroom.

During the almost two-hour drive, she unintentionally listened to that type of slow and sultry R&B music that evoked visions of two people lounging together on a couch sharing kisses as the rain softly hit the window.

Two people lost in each other. Enjoying each other and their physical connection.

I miss that.

As she sat behind the wheel of her modest late-model sedan at a red light, softly singing along with Muni Long's "Hrs & Hrs," she wished it hadn't been years and years since she had been satisfied. She looked up at the towering buildings of the city. The sun was just beginning to set, and the skies were deepening in color. Even with the music playing inside the car mingling with the familiar sounds of the city just outside her window, the pounding of her heart echoed above both.

It was fueled by her desires and her nervousness about what she was considering.

"He's exactly what you need. All the fun with none of the ties."

"Get out of my head, Suzi," Eve muttered as she looked to her left—the turn to reach her parents' Upper East Side penthouse apartment—and then to the right, where there was a cluster of hotels for several long metropolitan blocks.

When she paused in her decision to go visit her parents or seek pleasure, the driver of the car behind her blew its horn. She jumped in surprise and made the turn to the left, driving for sixteen blocks until she reached the thirty-nine-story, century-old apartment building where her parents had owned one of the penthouse apartments for the last thirty-five years. She double-parked.

With her heart pounding even faster and her nerves making her hands tremble, she picked up her phone and dialed a phone number she really shouldn't know by heart since she'd never used it before.

It rang several times.

"Luc Cress."

What am I doing? she asked herself as the sound of loud music, the chatter of adults and the gleeful laughter of children echoed through the phone line.

"Hello?" he asked.

"Luc," she said, licking her lips as she looked up at the reflection of her eyes in the rearview mirror. "This is Eve. Eve Villar."

She instantly felt foolish for saying her full name, as if the man hadn't sent her flowers every day for the last two weeks.

"Eve?" he said, his deep voice filled with surprise and pleasure. "Are you here?"

"I'm in Manhattan, but not for the party," she said, rotating the gold bangles that she wore around her wrist. "Thanks for the invite, though."

"You called just to let me down?" he asked, sounding bemused.

The bridge to the other side.

"Are *you* ready for *me* now?" she asked, leaning closer to the driver's-side window to look up at the well-lit art deco building.

There, I said it.

"When and where?" he said without missing a beat.

She giggled. She couldn't help but do so at his eagerness. "I thought we could meet up after the party is over," she said, already pulling away from the building to merge with the light traffic as she began her trek to circle the block to go back toward the cluster of hotels.

"I'm getting a hotel room. I'll text you the info. I'll see you after the party."

She ended the call before she lost her cool and changed her mind.

As she chose a hotel, parked, paid for the room and texted the info to Lucas, she began to feel the excitement of going on an adventure. That mix of anticipation and trepidation of the unknown. Particularly after she'd had a moment of sticker shock at the cost of the room for one night. There was a time when she hadn't asked how much something cost and just whipped out a credit card, paid for by her parents or Aaron, to get whatever she wanted.

Those days were long gone, but still, she opted to splurge.

She had just begun to undress when there was a knock at the door. She stopped undoing the side zipper of her dress, walked across the junior suite and looked out the peephole. A gasp escaped her lips as she stepped back to unlock and open the door. "Luc," she said, looking at him. "I wasn't expecting you so soon."

"I left the party early," he said as he strolled past her inside the hotel.

Eve felt light-headed as she closed the door. She rested her head against it as she allowed herself a very slow count of five.

"Get it together, Eve, you asked for this," she said under her breath, then turned to press her back to the wood.

Lucas stood just a few feet from her, watching her closely. *"Jusqu'à ce que nous nous revoyions,"* he said, closing the gap between them with one long step. He eased a strong arm around her waist and lightly jerked her body forward against his.

"Et nous voici," Eve replied in a whisper as she pressed her hands to his broad shoulders before gripping them.

And here we are.

Four

Lucas locked his eyes on hers as he dipped his head to cover her mouth with his own. Slowly. He savored every moment of finally—*finally*—kissing Eve Villar. And it was everything he used to dream about. Her sweet scent as he drew nearer. The first spark he felt was at the softness of her lips. The feel of her hands gripping his shoulders. How she met his lips with hunger.

For me!

He knew that thought was seventeen-year-old Lucas surfacing. He mentally pushed his inner child back into his subconscious as he stayed focused on the present moment and raised her off her feet. He shivered at the feel of her hands releasing his shoulders to ease her arms around his neck to stroke his nape.

He shivered from her touch.

"Wait," Eve said, tipping her head back to look up at him.

"What? What's wrong?" Lucas asked, his eyes searching her face.

"Condoms," she said with a look of embarrassment.

"Right?" he said, setting her down on her feet to reach into his back pocket for his wallet. He removed a row of several foiled packets. He smiled. "I got some."

Eve locked her eyes with his. "Some?" she asked, taking them from him before she moved across the room to sit on the side of the bed.

He watched her, loving the way the skirt of her dress swayed as she moved and then splayed as she crossed her ankles. "I stay ready so I don't have to get ready," he told her, following her steps to the bed to stand before her.

"You *are* the perfect bridge," Eve said, almost in wonder.

Lucas frowned a bit in confusion. "Huh?" he asked.

"Nothing," she said, looking up at him with a smile. "You really are a handsome man, Lucas Cress."

He pressed a hand to his chest and slightly bowed his head in thanks.

She patted the bed beside her, indicating that he should join her.

He did, and was surprised at the nervousness that streaked through him as she moved to straddle his lap. His eyes fell to her mouth—it was plump, full and designed for kissing. Tempting him. He gave in to the impulse, lightly tracing her lips with his tongue as he brought his hands up to splay against her back.

She deepened the kiss, catching the tip of his tongue between her supple lips, and gently sucked.

Eve Villar!

With her knees straddling his hips, Lucas was able to reach and remove her shoes as they kissed. He reveled in the feel of her soft skin as he trailed his fingers from her ankles, up to her calves, and then to the outside of her thighs. Her moans of pleasure gave him the urge to drag his hands across the top of her thighs and back to grip her buttocks. The feel of the lace and satin hardened him, but slipping his fingers beneath them to palm her cheeks filled him with *such* hunger.

Eve lightly gripped his chin in one hand as she looked into his eyes. In those depths, he saw her desire and a spark of something else. It intrigued him as she held her stare while leaning in close to lick at his lips. That simple move packed a punch.

"It's been so long," she admitted in a whisper between kisses.

Lucas's eyes widened a bit at her confession.

"So very long," Eve gasped.

His fingers deepened into the soft flesh of her bottom. She released a soft moan with her lips agape and her eyes half-closed with a backward tilt of her head. He watched her in awe at the freedom she allowed herself to show her pleasure. No shame. No reservation.

"I *need* this," she sighed.

Lucas dipped his head to press a kiss to her cleavage and felt the wild pounding of her heart vibrate against his lips. What he felt at that moment could be exhilaration. Every tremble in her touch. Every shaky breath she released. The desire she professed fueled him. Made him not just aroused, but joyful to be the one to give her such release. He deeply inhaled the sweet scent of her skin, then gave her a gentle lick. And then another and another, each drawing deep gasps from her.

Curious, he brought his hand down between her thighs to palm her intimacy. Not even the cover of her sheer panties kept her warmth from him. His gut clenched. She was throbbing.

"Oh, God you're so wet," he moaned against her before raising his chin to nudge hers for another kiss.

As their lips collided once again and their tongues slowly danced with one another, he heard the familiar tear of the foil and felt conflicted. As badly as he wanted to bury himself deeply within her, he just as much wanted their foreplay to continue. He wasn't yet ready to begin what could only lead to an ending…no matter how explosive.

"Eve," he moaned, as she set each foot on the floor and rose with the corner of one of the condom foils in her mouth.

She tilted her head to the side as she raised the hem of her dress to ease down her panties, which fell on top of her shoes.

He looked down at them and then back up to her face. She kneeled between his open legs and began to undo his belt and pants until his hard inches gently tugged free. The first feel of her soft hands on him made him draw air through his teeth in a hiss as he arched his hips forward and clenched the embroidered coverlet of the bed into his fists.

Lucas was used to taking the lead in the bedroom, but Eve was in control. And the way she stroked him with both of her hands from root to tip pushed him close to releasing a high-pitched squeal that would have shamed him later. So he bit down on his lips as his thighs quivered and he felt close to reaching a climax far too soon.

Releasing the covers, he covered her hands with his own to stop. "Please," he begged, his voice deep but still vulnerable that his high-school crush was about to push him over the edge with ease.

She smiled as she sat back on her haunches and removed the condom from its foil. "Please what?" she asked.

He couldn't lie that he almost dared to ask her to taste his hardness with her luscious lips. Almost. Instead, he rose and worked his jeans and boxers to slide down his legs. His hard curving length created a shadow across her face.

"This is what I missed out on all those years ago?" she asked as she gripped the base of him.

Lucas nearly cried out again and bit down on the side of his tongue. He didn't dare speak, amazed that she was rattling him in his shoes. Was it their history? His crush on her? His desire to finally have her after so many years, when he thought he would never get the chance?

Slowly, she unrolled the latex to sheathe him. "You might need a bigger size," she said.

Lucas just nodded, feeling a level of nervousness he hadn't experienced since he'd lost his virginity.

What is wrong with me?

With his dick still in her grip, Eve rose to her full height and pushed him down onto the bed with her free hand, never letting *him* go. "Eve," he moaned.

She shook her head as she climbed onto the bed, her knees straddling his thighs. "Sssshh," she said, looking down at the smooth tip of him as she stroked him slowly.

She really is beautiful.

The short haircut emphasized her high cheekbones and full mouth. Her eyes glistened with desire and were framed by lush black lashes as she watched him carefully as she lightly licked her bottom lip before gently biting down upon it.

So damn sexy without even trying.

"Can I go for a ride?" Eve asked him.

Get it together, Luc.

He took a deep breath and tried to draw on the lover he had become over the years, seeking his confidence. Needing boldness. His eyes searched hers and he feasted on the desire he found in the dark brown depths.

Her desire for me.

Lucas used his hard-earned abdominal muscles to sit up, bringing them face-to-face. Again. Their eyes locked and their breathing was inaudible. "Can you handle the ride?" he asked her before pressing a kiss to her chin.

With the skirt of her dress covering both their laps, she rose and reached behind, holding his inches upright as she guided her core down onto him. So slowly. His eyes feasted on the subtle expressions on her face as she adjusted to the thickness of him.

"Easy," he advised.

She released a tiny cry and lowered her forehead to his as she continued her descent upon him. "It's hard, Luc," she gasped, even as she gave her hips a tiny circular moment as she navigated his curve. "So *hard.*"

Her walls gripped him as tightly as the condom.

Lucas wrapped his arms around her and held her. She did the same to him.

And when all of him filled her, she shivered and dropped her head to his shoulder.

"You okay?" he asked, knowing his size could be formidable.

Her kisses landed on his neck. "You?" she whispered.

That tugged at him—and that was surprising. It was a one-night stand. A victory for him that he had not been able to secure years ago.

Nothing more.

"I'm good," he lied.

Lucas was far from innocent, but with Eve there was excitement and nervousness combined with the tight feel of her. The warmth and the wetness. Him tottering on the edge of an explosive climax. The tenderness he felt as he stroked her back and enjoyed the feel of her breasts pressed to his chest.

And then she suckled that spot just beneath his ear as she indeed began to ride him, sliding up and down the length of him. Slowly, though. As if she was savoring the ride.

Lucas leaned back, wanting to see her face as he felt his pleasure.

There was no denying what he saw. She was enraptured. Eyes closed. Mouth opened. Pants. Gasps. Moans.

"Good?" he asked, releasing his own pants as he lowered his hands to grip her buttocks and gently slam her down against him.

She cried out.

He did it again, watching with intensity—he was almost afraid to blink and miss a moment.

Another cry.

"So good," she admitted.

And so he did it again. And again. And again.

And each time she vocalized how much the move shook her.

"It hits my spot," she admitted, gripping his chin to lick at his mouth again.

"Oh, yeah?" he asked, massaging her bottom before gripping it and slamming it down again.

"Yes," Eve gasped into his mouth.

Lucas locked her hips in place, keeping her from riding him. He relished the annoyance that filled her pretty face because her desire was being denied. He enjoyed the steady clutch and release of her walls against him regardless. It was enough to make him climax…if he allowed it. He closed his eyes and fought like hell for it not to…come.

"Luc."

He shook his head, still focused on curbing his desire.

"Luc," she said again.

His eyes shot open when Eve forcefully swiped his hands away from her and then pressed down with both her hands to his chest to ease him back, flat against the bed. "No!" he groaned when she began to ride him in earnest.

"Yes," she answered him with simplicity before biting down on her bottom lip. She moved her body in a snake-like motion with a pop of her hips when she eased her core up to his throbbing tip.

Lucas arched his back, having no care about how

he looked and succumbing to how she made him feel. Blindly, he slapped both his hands against her buttocks before massaging them. The combination of her clutching her walls as she rode him and then circling her hips as she reached his tip while he felt the vibration of her bottom made him widen his eyes. "Whoo-oo-eee!" he howled.

Eve Villar!

She was relentless.

As she drew sweat from him, he wished they were naked, but didn't dare stop her so. He didn't care when she gripped his sweater so tightly that he knew the cashmere would lose its shape. He was quite sure he would ever be the same again!

"I needed this," she gasped as she gave his tip another twerk.

Lucas dared to look up at her, finding her face lined with such intensity. "Need what?" he asked.

"Sex," she moaned before she quickened the pace.

Oh. Okay. Straight to the point.

Eve leaned down to kiss him. "Thank you!" she enthusiastically whispered into his mouth.

"You're, uh, welcome?" he said with hesitance and a bit of confusion.

But those feelings were *quickly* forgotten.

"I'm coming, Lucas. I. Am. Coming!"

His body was led into bliss by hers. He kissed her deeply as she rode them to a fiery climax that made him tremble from his toes to the longest strand of hair on his head. The squeal he released would not be contained. Thankfully, Eve's high-pitched cries mingled with his own.

It was intense.

And explosive.

He looked up at her in awe as she continued to slowly ride him until he was spent and limp, with his toes curled, as he struggled not to release another shriek.

Have. Mercy.

Eve sat up to look down at him before she stretched her arms high above her head with a smile of pure contentment. "That was *amazing*," she sighed, rising from the bed and stretching her arms out wide and then above her head again.

Meanwhile, I'm shivering like a leaf in the wind, and not sure my legs wouldn't wobble beneath me if I stood.

He raised his head to watch her as she scooped up her panties and made her way to the bathroom.

Did she skip?

The sound of water running echoed.

"Are you headed back to the party?" Eve called out to him.

Lucas frowned. Visions of them undressing and cuddling in bed before another round of sex were slowly beginning to fade. He sat up and looked down at his member, still encased in latex. "No, I wasn't planning to," he answered.

Eve stepped out of the bathroom with not even a hair out of place and her panties no longer in her hand. "Well, I'm headed out," she said. "My parents are expecting me."

Lucas tilted his head to the side and watched her in shock. "B-b-but—"

Eve went to him and kissed away the complaint he was struggling to formulate. "Definitely worth it, Luc," she whispered as he felt something plastic pressed into his hand.

It was the key card to the room.

"Just drop it at the front desk on your way out, okay?" she asked, then turned and strode out of the hotel room without a look back or a wave of goodbye.

Well, I'll be damned!

Outside of the joy Eve found in swimming, there was very little she allowed herself to do with enthusiasm anymore. Sex with Lucas Cress could now be added to the list. She smiled as she dragged her index finger across her bottom lip, remembering the feel of his kisses from the night before.

She still couldn't believe she had gone through with it.

Or that I didn't hang around for more.

It was clear that Lucas had been surprised at her sudden exit, and when she was on the other side of the closed door, she had clutched that doorknob and fought the desire to return to him. But attending family gatherings and sharing a night together was not a part of her plan. In fact, she was surprised *he* wanted those things. It was his unavailability—and his sex appeal—that made him the best candidate for a one-night stand.

Or two.

She looked around at her very pink bedroom suite from high school, complete with sparkle, frills and sequins. The Eve of the past had reveled in such vain luxury, but now it made her want to run screaming from the room while yanking her hair from her scalp. It was a reminder of the self-involved person she used to be.

A person I am ashamed of.

Her eyes landed on a photo of Claudia, Ashanti, Lorn and herself on a private plane headed to Paris for fashion week. A gift from Aaron. One of what seemed like a million.

She took a long, deep inhale through her nose and exhaled through pursed lips. Nice and slow. After the accident, she learned the technique as a part of her recovery to control the pain and her anger. Now she sought it to relieve her grief. To relax. To forget.

She failed.

With her arms crossed over her chest, Eve eyed her iPhone sitting on the edge of her gold-gilded dresser. She moved across the wood floor to retrieve it. Her heart pounded a bit as she dialed. She was seeking a distraction and wondered why she was lingering in the city, since her parents had already left for the day to attend church and brunch.

She dialed. It rang endlessly. Her disappointment stung.

I could use a Lucas fix.

With a tiny grunt and a shake of her head, Eve craved the excitement again.

I started something I'm not ready to finish.

The man was built to please.

Who knew?

"Lucas Cress. Lucas Cress," she said aloud in a singsong fashion in praise.

Bzzzz.

She looked down at the phone vibrating in her hand.

It's him.

Eve answered the call, placing the phone on the speaker. "Hello, Mr. Cress," she said with a smile.

"Mornin'."

"Last night was fun," she told him, turning to look out the patio doors at the first signs of spring, with green on the trees, and birds fluttering their wings.

"Very much so."

"I have a little free time before I head back home," she said, moving over to the mirror to study her reflection and play with her short ebony hair. "Maybe I can come by and see you really quick on my way out of the city."

"Quick or quickie?" he asked, his deep voice amused.

"Yes. And *yes*," she said, turning to eye the jeans and T-shirt she packed in her overnight bag. It was no match for the red dress she'd worn the day before.

It will have to do.

"I'm home. I'll text you the address," he said.

Excitement coursed through her veins. "On the way," she promised, then ended the call.

Ding.

Lucas's text.

She was surprised the address was in the Chelsea section of Manhattan and not the Cress family townhome in the prominent and historic Lenox Hill section of the Upper East Side.

"New digs, huh?" she asked aloud, reaching for her jeans.

She had already enjoyed a leisurely bath and her parents' chef had made her breakfast a strawberry cheesecake crepe. Within ten minutes she was dressed and retrieving her car from the valet. As she drove, she fought hard to stay focused on the traffic and not let her mind wander.

Bzzzz.

She glanced at her phone and then reached for it as she steered with one hand. "Suzi!" she exclaimed, feeling happier than she had in years.

"Hey, you. I dropped by the house to surprise you with a pan of homemade buttermilk biscuits," her friend said. "I used my key to leave them on the stove."

"Thanks, I will have enough of an appetite by the time I get home to eat six, back to back," she said, slowing her car down as she made a right turn.

"Doing what?" Suzi asked, sounding distracted.

"Lucas Cress," Eve smoothly replied.

"Ye-e-sssssssssssssssssssssssssssssssss!" Suzi enthused. "Wait. You do mean what I hope you mean?"

"Yes. And it was so good I'm headed to his place for round two," she said.

"No!" Suzi exclaimed.

"Yes!" Eve answered back.

They both laughed in delight.

"I want as many details as you're willing to share when you get home," Suzi said.

Eve slowed down and made the turn into the underground parking garage of the building. His instructions included the number of his visitor parking spot. "I'm parking right now," she said, pulling into the spot next to an all-black Bentley Bentayga Speed W12 with the personalized license plate: YES CHEF.

The thought of her giving Lucas such a response as he bent her over the back of a sofa made Eve move a bit quicker toward getting to him.

Lucas released a yawn as he opened the wrought-iron gate and stepped off the elevator onto the library section of the second floor of the Cress family ten-thousand-square-foot townhouse. "Hello, family," he called out to everyone gathered in the leather reclining chairs of the movie theater in the front section.

He paused before joining them. The entire back of the five-story home was a glass wall, and he wanted to enjoy the magnificent view of the large tree in the backyard whose leaves were turning to a deep emerald as the sun's rays burst through the branches. He missed it—particularly in the winter, when the snow flurries made it seem he was looking into a massive snow globe.

Unfortunately, six months ago his latest attempt to sneak a bedmate into his suite of rooms on the fourth floor had been discovered and had led to his father gently suggesting he locate his own playpen in which to frolic. His mother had not liked that yet another of her sons had moved out of the family home, but if there was one thing the beauty loved more than her favorite son, it was her privacy, and she absolutely hated that Lucas continued to bring wayward women into her home.

Lucas had purchased his condo in Chelsea and made sure to visit his parents often.

All's well that ends well.

Reluctantly, he turned and made his way past the bookshelves lining the walls and leather club chairs to the front, where there were twenty leather recliners in front of the movie screen. He paused at the snack station against the wall to treat himself to a box of chocolate-covered peanuts, then claimed a seat at the rear.

The family was gathered to screen the new documentary on his parents' complete journey in the culinary arts produced by Sean and to be streamed on

CRESSTV. Everyone was present except Gabriel, who was away preparing for the upcoming grand opening of the newest Cress, INC. restaurant, CRESS XIII, in Dubai. The entire family was prepared to attend.

"All right, family, settle down," Sean said from the front of the room.

Lucas gave him an encouraging smile, knowing that his desire to please his parents with this film was paramount.

"First, I want to thank all of you for participating in this project that is a labor of love," Sean said, clasping his hands as he looked to where his parents sat in the center seats of the front row. "I present to you the newly titled documentary, *Nicolette and Phillip: Love, Family and Food*."

"À la nourriture. À la vie. À l'amour," everyone said in unison as if on cue.

Lucas looked on as their father raised their mother's hand and warmly kissed the back of it just before Sean used the iPad to close the curtains on the rear glass wall and darken the lights.

Lucas tried his best to focus. That was hard to do when he was completely distracted by recollections of Eve suddenly appearing in his life and seducing him before leaving him shaken and spent after their climax.

The day of Poppy's birthday.

The next afternoon at his condo.

And then early this morning, a week after not hearing from her—and not answering his calls or texts—suddenly she texted him that she was in Manhattan and wanted to see him.

See me? More like sex me.

And they never even made it past his foyer. He opened the door, and she stepped inside, pushing him against the wall by the door with deep kisses. Everything after that was a fiery blur of loud moans, dirty talk, hard strokes and then rough cries as they climaxed together.

Not long after that, she gave him an excuse of having a work responsibility and exited his condo just as quickly as she'd arrived, leaving him feeling used.

Bzzzz. Bzzzz. Bzzzz.

"S-sh-hh, Uncle Luc," Collette whispered to him from her seat in front of him.

"My apologies," he whispered back before pulling his phone from the back pocket of his gray open-legged sweatpants. It was a text from Eve.

He frowned as he placed his phone on silent and set it face down on the empty seat beside him. He tossed candy into his mouth and focused on the screen. But even after many minutes had passed, his eyes kept going to the phone. Even in the darkness, he could see it. It called him. His curiosity was piqued and memories of the explosive chemistry he shared with Eve were not to be denied.

But then he felt like a desperate seventeen-year-old again, craving the attention of the beautiful Eve Villar. Like a flunky.

That's not me. Not anymore. Never again.

But then the screen lit up with another text notification. He stared at it. Long and hard. His pulse was racing. His gut was clenched. His grip on the box of peanuts was tightening so much that the sides buckled in his hand.

Damn!

Lucas reached for the phone, hating how desperate he felt to hear from her again but unable to deny himself. The screen lit his face in the darkness as he silently read the message. This morning was amazing, Luc. Can't even focus on my work. Another drop-in later on? I should be done in an hour.

She can't get enough of me!

He had a clear vision of the look on her face when he made her climax.

Becoming addicted to making Eve Villar come was not a part of the plan.

Getting married before the end of the year? Yes.

Running like a lost lapdog every time Eve snapped her fingers? No.

One had nothing to do with the other and it was clear that even if he became foolish enough to want to wed Eve, that all the vain vixen wanted from him was sex. No conversation. No real connection. Nothing more than pure physical release.

And the thought of that sent warmth radiating over his body. Like a rush.

Lucas rose and made his way across the front of the recliners to head for the stairs. He paused on the steps to text her back. I'll be waiting.

"Luc!"

He looked back to find Sean coming down the stairs toward him. "Where are you going?" he asked.

"To get a woman out of my system," he said before continuing down the stairs.

"I thought you were on the hunt for a bride?" Sean asked.

"*Not* her," Lucas said, stopping to turn on the bottom step of the first floor. "But before I find the right woman to marry and propose I must make sure my future bride and I are not haunted by this woman."

Sean's face filled with sudden understanding. "Great sex," he said.

"Exactly," Lucas grumbled. "Best ever."

Sean chuckled. "Good luck with that, little brother," he said, then turned and jogged up the stairs to leave behind a perplexed Lucas wondering just what he'd meant.

Five

At the echo of a splash, Eve focused her gaze on the Olympic-sized pool of the nearly sixteen-thousand-square-foot, six-story Manhattan townhouse. She was serving as a last-minute private lifeguard at an indoor mermaid-themed pool party for twenty-five little girls. The elaborate decor had transformed the already beautiful space into an "Under the Sea" theme and each of the girls was given metallic mermaid bathing suits adorned with their names.

Thankfully, the eight-hour daytime party was nearing an end and soon she would be headed to Chelsea for another taste of Lucas Cress.

I am so ready.

The first of May would mark the official start of her busy season. Her weekends were booked until Labor

Day. There would be no time for last-minute events in Manhattan or spontaneous sex pop-ups with Lucas.

This next time will be the last time.

Eve shifted from her seat at the edge of the pool when one little girl didn't immediately emerge. She relaxed when the freckled redhead cutie broke the surface.

"See. I told you I could hold my breath!" the little girl proclaimed, to her friend's delight.

I gotta keep my eye on that one.

The parents were in the adjoining room enjoying conversation and cocktails, thus making Eve lifeguarding the party necessary. She rose to her feet, sliding her hands into the pocket of the dark blue tear-away track pants she wore over a matching bathing both embossed with the Aquatic Safety Solutions logo. She walked the length of the pool, ensuring all the girls were accounted for and safe.

"Thanks so much for this."

Eve turned to find a beautiful dark-haired woman holding a flute of champagne. Everything about the woman spoke of wealth and affluence, including her demeanor. "No problem," she said with a smile that she prayed didn't look as forced as it felt. "Your daughter, Naya, is a beautiful little girl."

"No, I'm her father's sister, Lana," she said, turning to point to a tall man slowly pacing back and forth as he talked on his phone.

"My apologies, I misunderstood," Eve said, being sure to redirect her attention back to the girls playing in the pool.

"I'm not a mother *yet* but I'm working on it," Lana

said before taking a deep sip of her champagne and arching one of her eyebrows.

"Good luck," Eve said, knowing it sounded more like a question than a statement.

With another smile, she began to continue her walk around the pool. She frowned a bit when Lana fell in step with her.

"Listen, a little birdie told me you went to school with Lucas Cress," the woman said.

Eve wasn't surprised at being recognized. She used to be a well-known member of the New York social scene of spoiled socialites spending their days shopping, getting spa treatments and lunching where they would be soon in their new exclusive designer wear. At one point, Eve Villar felt like the queen of New York.

Until it all crashed.

In her mind, she could hear the squeal of the tires, the loud clang of the collision and the echoing cries of metal being mangled. Their lifestyle and the need for more had propelled both her and Aaron right into that tragedy.

Their screams still echoed inside her head. Eve shook it to free herself from the violent memory. "Um, yes, we were in the same graduation class at Manhattan University Prep," she said, eyeing the pool and longing to be deep in the water, where everything was silent and peaceful.

"Were you friendly?" Lana asked.

Then? No. Now? We're friendly with benefits.

"We didn't run in the same circles in school," she said.

Lana nodded in understanding as she took another sip of champagne.

Eve shifted her gaze to the woman. "Do you know him?" she asked, allowing her curiosity to be fed.

"Not as well as I'd like," Lana said. "But I'm working on it because he's on the hunt for a new wife before the end of the year and he is one hell of a catch."

"He is?" Eve asked, having to catch herself from showing too much shock at the revelation.

"A catch or on the hunt for a bride?" Lana asked, eyeing Eve over the rim of her glass and truly looking at her before her eyes filled with a different glint.

It was proprietary.

"Don't get any ideas," Lana said, her demeanor changing and her face hardening. "As if *the help* could have a chance with a man like Luc, anyway."

For a moment, her anger and annoyance were triggered, and the old Eve rose to slay the woman with an insult that would make her question her entire life. But Eve took a deep breath instead. She took pity on her, knowing fear and insecurity were the root cause of her sudden insulting behavior meant to make herself feel superior to Eve.

She needs self-confidence, not verbal annihilation.

"I'll just be getting back to…*helping*," Eve said, before walking away from her.

For the rest of her time at the party, she felt such unease. She couldn't stop the barrage of questions conquering her thoughts.

Lucas wants to get married?

Does he think I want to get married, too?

Does he already have a fiancée?

Am I a damn sneaky link?

Eve was grateful to gather her things into her duffel bag, pull on her black ankle-length puffer coat and leave the party that would shift to a sleepover for the little girls with the pool closed. As she sat in her car, she was rethinking her pop-up to Lucas. Suddenly everything felt far more complicated than she intended.

She held her phone and looked down at it as she tapped the screen with her natural fingernail.

They had no relationship—no ties at all. Still, just blocking his number and steering clear of him felt more like a move of the old Eve. *And I need some clarity*, she thought, setting the phone down on the console before starting her car. She made the fifteen-minute drive to eventually pull into the empty spot next to Lucas's Bentley.

A clear show of his wealthy status. Just like the six-figure vehicles both her parents drove. It was a lifestyle she was ardently and deliberately avoiding.

"As if the help *could have a chance with a man like Luc, anyway."*

Lana's words struck a nerve. Not because of Eve's demotion in economic standing—that was a choice—but because it was a reminder of how wealth and status had made her feel superior. Judgmental. Hateful. Cruel.

Everything she fought hard not to be anymore.

She left the car and crossed the garage, taking note that her car stood out like a sore thumb next to the more costly vehicles of the building's residents. Thankfully, the elevator was empty as she rode up to the penthouse. She tried to figure out just what and how to say what she had to say as she made her way to the door. It opened and Lucas filled the doorway before she could knock.

"I do not want to marry you," Eve said, throwing all her perfectly laid plans out the window.

Lucas crossed his arms over her chest and looked at her. "Okay," he said, before stepping back and opening the front door wider. "Still dropping by?"

Eve cocked her head to the side. "Are you engaged to be married?" she asked.

"No."

"Girlfriend?"

"Nope."

Eve's face filled with curiosity as she looked up at him, then entered his condo. For perhaps the first time, she looked around at his home, decorated in browns, tans and cream, with lots of African art and sculptures. The ceilings were high. The view of the Hudson River was magnificent. And the glass doors leading to the private terrace were inviting.

"I love your apartment," she said, setting her keys on the table behind the brown leather sectional before coming around it and looking down at the tricolor rawhide rug beneath a tinted glass table. "There's so much character and texture. And the flow is excellent, Luc."

Lucas chuckled. "This is your third time here, Eve," he said.

"The first time I was bent over your couch, and the second—"

"We never made it past the foyer," he added.

Eve was looking at a wooden sculpture of a female form sitting atop a clear stand. "This is beautiful," she said, looking over at him.

Lucas was dressed in a T-shirt and cotton sleep pants, with his feet bare.

"It's a little early for bed," she teased.

He smiled. "I was making it easier for your drop-in and drop-out," he said, holding up both hands. "Easy access."

Eve removed her coat. "I feel judged," she said.

Lucas eyed her bathing suit and track pants with a chuckle. "I still can't believe you're a lifeguard," he said. "I can't imagine Eve Villar risking ruining her hair. In high school, you got out of physical education all the time."

Eve forced a smile. "I'm not that shallow anymore," she said.

Lucas released a laugh filled with disbelief.

She gave him a chastising look.

"Sorry, I just can't imagine you've—"

"What? Changed?" she asked with a bit of a bite as she motioned her hands toward his new body. "Fifteen years was a long time ago, Luc, and a lot has happened since the cupcakes."

Lucas gave her a nod of acquiescence. "Right," he said.

They fell silent.

He came across the living room to pull her close, and rested his chin atop her head.

Eve closed her eyes and allowed herself to be comforted by his embrace. She took a deep inhale of the fresh scent of the soap still clinging to his skin. It warmed her and not in a sexual way. Just comfort. Ease.

And that surprised her.

"As if the help *could have a chance with a man like Luc, anyway."*

Lana's words had provided a mirror of the old Eve

and she was still grappling with it. As Eve brought her hands up to press against the strong muscles of his back, she somehow found *her* strength. "I *had* to change, Luc," she admitted, needing to be freed of her emotions. *My demons.*

As she began to reveal her past Lucas her past— her arrogance, her lifestyle—she took some comfort in his arms tightening around her. She leaned into him— physically and emotionally—and felt grateful for his support.

"After Aaron's death, being in the water gave me so much time to think. It felt like washing away all my sins," she said softly. "All of the obsession with wealth. All the greed. No matter how much we had there was a hunger for more. No matter how many millions he had, it was never enough for either of us. Always. No matter who we had to betray or hurt. It didn't matter."

Eve inhaled deeply and then released an exhale that seemed to go on endlessly. At his silence, she stepped back out of his embrace and turned away from him, afraid of being judged. "I had no choice but to change. I was so lost that when I discovered Aaron had ripped off his investors I didn't blink an eye about it," she said, looking out at the sun setting above the river in the distance. "I just feel horrible that it took something as drastic as Aaron's death for me to free myself of the trappings of wealth. I wouldn't have changed had he lived."

"Eve," Lucas said.

She felt his presence when he came to stand behind her closely. The first feel of his hands on her bared shoulders surprised her, but she didn't step away. "It feels as if he had to die so that I could shed my old ways," she admitted, perhaps for the first time, the root of the guilt that lingered and clung to her.

Lucas released a soft curse as if her words touched him, then he turned her into his embrace again. "Don't do that to yourself, Eve. Don't torture yourself like that," he told her, his deep voice impassioned. "That is not how life works. We are not meant to suffer."

Eve shook her head, denying his reason.

"Hey," he said, leaning back to tilt her head back by her chin. "Choose to be thankful *you* are still alive. If you live in such regret of that blessing, it's as if you wished you did, too, and stewing in that kind of negativity over time can do just as much harm physically as mentally."

Eve felt doubt.

Lucas smiled. "You should be thankful every day to be alive," he told her. "I'm thankful you are."

Eve felt a bit of lightness as she looked into his warm eyes. "I'm really not in the mood for a quickie, Luc," she drawled.

They shared a laugh.

Eve stepped away from him with reluctance, but out of necessity. His presence had become far too comfortable. She didn't want to miss him when it was over. "I think I'll head home," she said, moving to the sofa to pick up her coat and then grab her keys from the table.

She quickened her steps at feeling sad about leaving his home.

And him.

Lucas moved quickly to lean past her to open the door for her.

"Thanks," she said, pulling on her coat and sliding the keys into one of its deep pockets.

"Eve," he said.

She looked up at him and didn't give him the chance to say whatever was on his mind. "Word on the street is you have a marriage deadline," she said.

He looked taken aback, then he shifted his eyes away from hers for a moment—a very revealing one.

So it's true.

"Was I even in the running?" she asked, not sure she even cared but loving seeing him squirm.

"You made it pretty clear that I was relegated to drop-ins and pop-ups only," he replied.

Eve smiled.

He did not answer my question and that was as good as a no.

"Well, this would have been the last drop-in," she told him as she stepped into the hall. "My busy season in the Hamptons starts Thursday and you're on the hunt for a bride. So…"

"This is goodbye," he said, leaning his tall frame in the doorway.

Eve saw the regret in his eyes. It mirrored how she felt as well. But still, she nodded.

"Good luck with work," he said, the light in his eyes dimming. "Be safe."

"And good luck with finding a bride," she said. "And you be safe because there's a barracuda on your trail."

Lucas flung his head back to laugh.

Her eyes dropped to his throat, and she wanted so very badly to kiss him there.

And for him to kiss me everywhere.

Eve felt flutters in her belly.

Lucas looked at her. She didn't hide her desire and soon his eyes darkened as they searched her face. "Eve," he said in warning.

"Maybe one last drop-in," she said, already taking a step toward him. "After I take a shower."

Lucas looked intrigued. "You mean I get to see you naked?" he asked.

"And do everything else to me," she promised as she passed him to enter the condo. "And then I'll do the same to you."

Lucas raised both eyebrows.

Eve pulled him into the condo and closed the door.

One month later

Lucas stared into the flames of the elaborate fireplace in the den attached to the kitchen's east side in his parents' Victorian townhouse. Around him, his family was chatting away and the children played on their tablets. Felice, the live-in housekeeper, served light appetizers from a tray. Outside the patio doors, light rain fell. Lost in his thoughts, he took a deep sip of the aged brandy in his snifter.

Memories of the shower he and Eve shared a month ago *still* had him in a trance.

He shivered at the memory of holding her nude body close as he stroked her deeply to a climax. "Woo," he said under his breath, with a shake of his head.

"Did you say something, Luc?"

He stiffened at Lana's softly spoken question near his ear. The move was from guilt and surprise—he'd forgotten she was sitting in the light gray chair beside him. Or that she had been there at all. He'd invited her to dinner with his family to gauge if she would be a good fit as his wife.

Lucas looked over at her. "No, nothing," he said, giving her a warm smile.

Lana returned it with one of her own.

She is beautiful. And smart. And cultured. And my parents love her.

His smile weakened a bit.

She checked all the boxes for a life mate and made it clear she wanted him, but…

Lana leaned in and pressed a kiss to the corner of his mouth.

It contained none of the spark he got from Eve.

"Good luck with that, little brother."

Lucas shifted his eyes to land on his brother Sean, who was pouring himself a glass of sparkling water from the wide glass-and-brass bar beneath the seventy-inch television on the wall. "Excuse me," he said to Lana, rising to his feet and causing her hand to fall away from him. He made his way toward his brother and best friend.

"Sean," he said, near his ear.

His brother visibly jumped before turning with a shocked expression to find him so close.

Lucas bit back a smile and took a step back. "I need to talk to you," he said. "Follow me."

He led him over to the adjoining dining room, where they had feasted on the wild salmon stuffed with crab, lobster and shrimp dressing atop a white wine and lemon risotto prepared by Chef Carlisle. He stopped at the long dining room table, with its charcoal leather top and suede armless chairs in the same steel blue accent that was found throughout the home.

"What's up?" Sean asked, taking a sip of his drink.

Lucas felt his face become pensive as he stared out the glass doors at the lit waterfall fountain at the end of the paved garden area. In front of it was a long concrete table beneath the arched framework covered with bamboo leaves that ran the length of the full thirty-two-foot backyard. The structure offered the shade and privacy the towering tree did not.

"The day of the screening for the documentary, when I told you I was going to get Eve Villar out of my system—"

"Eve Villar!" Sean exclaimed with a low whistle. "You did not say who the woman was, but Eve was a beauty."

"Still is," Lucas offered.

Sean looked across the space at Lana. "What's this desire to be married about any damn way?" he asked.

"It's time. I'm the last one single," Lucas explained.

Sean turned his mouth downward and gave him a look as he shook his head. "Not good enough," he said. "We all got married for love—not for something to prove, Luc."

"Says the man who got married as a publicity stunt," Lucas countered. "Love had nothing to do with it."

"At first," Sean insisted, shifting to look over at Montgomery as she stooped down to pick up their son, who was tugging at the hem of the bright orange knit dress she wore. "But now they both are my everything and I love her more every day."

THE MARRIAGE DEADLINE

Lucas eyed Lana.

"Can you say the same?" Sean asked.

"Why can't love come later, like it did for you?" Lucas asked, distinctively feeling his role as the baby brother—young and foolish.

"It's possible," Sean said. "But—"

"But what?" Lucas asked.

"Montgomery and I had attraction before the love," Sean offered. "It's how we ended up making the baby first. We couldn't keep our hands off each other."

A heated memory of his first coupling with Eve flashed.

"Oh, God, you're so wet."

He cleared his throat as his words of praise to her echoed in his mind. "And?" he asked.

"And you have more chemistry with sweets than you do with Lana Ariti," Sean drawled.

"Can I go for a ride?"

Eve's words taunted him still.

"Why did you wish me good luck that day?" Lucas asked.

Sean released a weighty breath as he looked his brother directly in the eye. "Because sometimes love begins with attraction. It is the chemistry—that first spark of awareness—when you know there is *something* between two people. The thing that makes you pause when you cross paths," he said. "People judge sex being the original impetus for a relationship as if chemistry doesn't matter, but sometimes what begins as a physical connection shifts to an emotional one."

"And I may not be able to shake my attraction for Eve," Lucas said in understanding.

Sean chuckled. "Exactly," he said. "Bobbie believes that every person has a soul and that instant attraction, that desire, we feel for someone could be the soul's way of alerting us that we have met our match."

Lucas scowled. "I'm not looking for a soul match, just someone to make a suitable bride and fit into this family," he explained.

Sean shrugged one shoulder as he held up one hand. "First, don't worry about the woman you love fitting in. I don't think any of us picked someone that made *the* Nicolette Lavoie-Cress happy. Take note," he began, ticking off each finger. "Second, fall in love. Third, why not Eve? If nothing else, you'll have years of great sex—the best you ever had, if I recall right?"

Her cries as he made her climax came back to him. *"Luc!"*

Every nerve ending in his body went on high alert. *"I do not want to marry you."*

Lucas felt like chuckling at Eve's declaration.

"Eve was never an option. Our history is murky," he said.

"If you let it," Sean offered.

"Plus, she's grappling with a lot of emotional baggage from the death of her ex," he offered, remembering the emotions she shared that were palpable.

"Still?" Sean asked. "It was six years ago."

"You know about it?' Lucas asked.

"Aaron and I used to run in the same circles," Sean said. "Wild dude. Money-hungry."

Lucas nodded. "That's what Eve said and she admitted she was no better," he said.

Sean finished his water. "I heard she donated her

trust fund to the families of the other people killed in the wreck," he said.

"She did?" Lucas asked.

"I had to change, Luc."

"She did," Sean said, clasping his brother's back before walking away and leaving him alone.

Lucas eased his hands into the pockets of his slacks as he turned to look out the windows. The rain had ceased. The night sky was clearing, and the moon's light broke through the limbs of the tree.

I wonder what Eve's doing?

He shouldn't care.

He didn't mean to give a damn.

But he did.

He thought of her often and dreamed of her even more.

"Penny for your thoughts."

He focused on the reflection in the glass of Lana walking up behind him. She slid her arms around his waist. He covered both of her crossed hands with one of his own as he looked back over one of his shoulders at her. "Did you enjoy dinner?" he asked.

"I did. Thank you for the invite," Lana said, looking up at him with a smile. "Perhaps we could go back to my place and have dessert."

Lucas broke her hold on him and turned to wrap his arms around her. "Dessert?" he asked, looking down into her eyes.

They had done nothing more than kiss so far.

And that had been lackluster.

Sean was not wrong. They had no chemistry. No spark. He hadn't even pressed her for more. His focus had been on having her as his wife and the mother of his children. The image they would present. Her fit in his family. Her background. Her prominence. Her love for her niece and the rest of her family.

He thought of all those things.

But there was no passion. There was no chemistry. Even if there was love that would grow one day, would the chemistry?

I want passion.

I want my wife's touch to make me tingle.

I want her kisses to excite me.

I want to make love to her for pleasure, not just to procreate.

He looked away from her to take in his family. His brothers—even his parents—had it all. Love. Passion. Companionship.

Yes, he wanted to wed, but he wanted it to last. To flourish. To not feel like an obligation.

Lana is not my bride.

Lucas took one of her hands in his and pressed a kiss to the back of it. "Let's head out," he said.

She smiled. "Okay," she said softly.

They said their goodbyes and Lucas took note that his mother, who was normally reserved with people outside their family, gave Lana a kiss on each cheek and a warm hug. He also noticed all the daughters-in-law shared long looks and raised eyebrows in surprise. That made him smile. He loved them all and knew his mother had given them each their type of hell for loving a Cress brother.

"Drive safe," Nicolette said when he bent to press a kiss on her cheek.

"I will," he said.

"Luc, *elle est la perfection*," his mother whispered to him of Lana's perfection, her blue eyes filled with excitement. *"Je ne voudrais personne d'autre pour mon petit garçon."*

"I would want no one else for my baby boy."

Lucas just gave her a weak smile, then led Lana out of the townhouse.

Six

Two weeks later

Eve was exhausted.

She was lounging on her back porch looking out at the light of the moon sparkling against the lake as she kicked up her legs and propped her crossed feet atop the wood railing. She had shampooed her hair to get rid of the chlorine of the pool, and it was now slicked down with wrapping lotion and drying by air. She took a sip of her strawberry float, made of strawberry soda poured over strawberry ice cream.

It had been a long day spent in the Hamptons, where she'd not only completed her bookings, but also filled in for one of her lifeguards who was sick, and dealt with a client whose attitudes and demands had triggered memories of her own past behavior. It all left her feeling depleted. She was thankful for the solitude, so she could recharge and get ready for the next day. She had come to love her little home and its surroundings on the lake. The smell of the earth, the rustle of the trees and other sounds of nature were pure and loud, as opposed to the hustle and bustle of Manhattan.

It was here she had begun to find inner peace.

Bzzzz.

She picked up her phone from the small wrought-iron table beside her swing glider. She smiled at the photo of her mother on the screen—an older version of herself with longer hair and far more sophistication. "Hello, Joan," she said as she answered the FaceTime call.

Her mother gave her a stern look.

Eve chuckled. "Mama, how are you?" she asked, taking note of the strapless burnt orange evening gown her mother had on, and a background she didn't recognize. "Better yet, where are you?"

"In the ladies' room at the Plaza," Joan said, pushing the long bangs of her beach-wave bob back from her face. "Your father received an award for entertainment lawyer of the year."

Eve felt unease knowing what was coming next.

"We both wish you were here," Joan said with the guilt only a mother could dole out.

And there it is.

"*But* we both understand," Joan added, her eyes soft and loving.

"Thanks, Mama," Eve said, giving her a smile as a lightning bug flew past her face that she swatted away.

"We were thinking of you and I told him I would

sneak away to give you a call," Joan said. "He just wants to know his baby girl is getting better."

Eve looked away from the screen and back out to the lake.

"We miss you," her mother added. Softly. Gently.

Once Eve had begun dating Aaron, most of her time was spent with him, and then in the days after his death, Eve clung to her grief, and it created even more distance between herself and the people she truly loved more than anyone in the world. They had understood her desire to change and did not even blink an eye when she gave away her trust fund. They, too, had wanted their child to change from the spoiled and privileged woman she had become.

Her parents had given her so much grace in how she chose to heal. They'd been so supportive.

"We all have regrets, Eve," the brilliant and highly honored neurosurgeon continued. "Perhaps we could have spoiled you less. Not given you so much. Not paid so much attention to our careers that we missed you needed more than our affluence, but our time and love."

Eve looked back to the screen; her face filled with alarm. "No, the person I became is on me. It's my life. My journey. My choices," she said.

Joan's expression revealed she didn't agree, but as always, her parents would deny her nothing, not even a complete renouncement of their lifestyle. "Okay," she said. "I have to get back. I don't want to miss his speech, but text your father something to make him smile."

"I will," Eve promised.

Joan panned the phone down to show her dress.

"How did Mama do? Because your father says I look *muy caliente*," she said.

Her mother was African American and her father was a Cuban-born American. She smiled as she remembered how much it frustrated her mother when they would speak Spanish in front of her and she could only decipher some words or phrases. They did it to tease her.

I miss that, Eve thought with a pang.

But Dr. Joan A. Ellis-Villar, one of the top neurosurgeons in the world, was not to be topped and learned the language.

"Las pilates te quedan bien, mamá," Eve said, telling her mother that Pilates looked good on her.

Joan preened. *"Gracias,"* she said, raising the hem of her dress to do a kick.

"Dr. Ellis-Villar!" some unseen woman in the restroom exclaimed in shock.

Her mother shrugged one shoulder and gave Eve a playful wink.

I miss them.

"Don't forget to text your father, Eve," Joan said with her finger already nearing the screen. "Love every bit of you."

"And I love you even more," Eve answered, just as she had done since she was a child.

The call ended.

She immediately sent her father a congratulatory text and lots of heart emojis. Before hitting Send, she promised to carve out time to see him really soon.

She had not been back to Manhattan in six weeks.

For her mother's hugs and fun nature.

Or eating one of the delicious Cuban dishes her father prepared during his limited downtime.

Or to see Lucas.

Eve closed her eyes and softly smiled as she remembered their last time. Her body warmed and her pulse came to life as she thought of *him*. Missed *him*. Craved *him*.

The things they did to each other in that shower had created mind-blowing wonder at what they shared mixed with such bliss that she also forgot large parts of what they'd done. Now, she was just left with sexy recollections.

Of what was and will never be.

She pushed her foot against the edge of the railing to gently shift the glider back and forth. She chuckled to think what fun they could have on the swing as she straddled him with his hard inches deep inside her.

If only...

They could have more pop-ups and drop-ins.

They didn't live hours away.

He wasn't intent on keeping his marriage deadline and marrying another woman.

That made her feel jealous and uneasy.

She wasn't looking to wed, but she could admit that she enjoyed their chemistry. It had been explosive.

And fun.

"I could use some fun," she drawled into her glass, then took a deep sip that left the sweet froth on her upper lip.

"So could I."

Eve's eyes shot up to find Lucas standing at the foot of the steps leading up to her deck. He looked handsome in a dark linen shirt with the sleeves rolled up and vintage jeans that were distressed. Casual and always sexy. "Luc, what are you doing here?" she said, lowering her legs and rising to leave the swing.

"I need something from you," he said, sliding his hands into the front pockets of his pants.

She moved across the deck to lean against the banister and crossed her arms over her chest in the red T-shirt dress she was wearing. "Sex, huh?" she asked, pretending to judge him.

How could she when she had just been lost in spicy memories of him?

"No, actually," he said with a shake of his head as he looked down at his sandal-covered feet and then back up at her. "I want more."

Eve's heart slammed against her chest. "More?" she asked.

"Of you. Your time. Your smile. Your energy," he said with a smile. "I want more of you. Not just sex."

Eve looked past him to the trees surrounding Swan Lake. "I'm not looking for love or marriage, Luc," she said.

"Neither am I," he said. "But I want to get to know *you*, Eve."

Her eyes shot back to him. "What about your deadline?" she asked, surprised at how breathless she felt. By his presence. His words.

"That's done," Lucas said. "I'd rather be happy than married."

Eve took one step down. "And you think I can make you happy?" she asked, wondering if he could do the same for her.

"Damn right," he said without hesitation.

She came down another step. Closer to him, as if he drew her to him. "Nothing serious," she began.

"But more than sex," he stated.

"Fun," she said as she stepped down on the step just above him, giving her the extra height to look directly into his eyes.

Lucas smiled at her. "You are hard to forget, Eve Villar," he admitted.

"Am I?" she asked, resting her hands on his broad shoulders.

"Since ninth grade," he said with a chuckle as he freed his hands from his pockets to settle on her hips.

"And which do you prefer—young Eve or now?" she asked, loving their flirtation.

"Now," he said without missing a beat. "Time has served you well, Eve Villar."

She studied his eyes and then his handsome face. All she knew for sure at this moment was that it felt good to see him and be near him. She leaned in to that feeling and toward him to kiss him. Lightly. Beneath her hands, she felt his body tremble as her body did the same.

There was no denying their physical connection.

And why should we?

"Wait," she said just before they kissed again. "Um, how'd you know where I live and that I'd be home—"

"Suzi," they said in unison before sharing a laugh.

"I called your cell earlier today and she answered," he explained, sliding his hands across her bottom. "She gave me directions."

"So that's why she was giggling all damn day," Eve

said. "Makes sense. She thinks I deserve a good time and she believes you can deliver, Mr. Cress."

"Suzi and I became the best of friends," he told her with a wink.

"Really?" Eve asked, enjoying him raising the hem of her cotton dress to massage the backs of her thighs just below her buttocks.

"Tomorrow, she's coming over to meet me in person and bring us breakfast before I head back to the city," he said.

"Tomorrow?" Eve asked.

Lucas nodded. "More of you. Of us. Remember?" he asked.

"Isn't this a pop-up?" she asked, easing her hand around his neck.

He pressed his face to hers. He grunted his agreement. "But I am not driving back to the city tonight after making love to you," he said. "*And* we can enjoy several rounds."

"All night?" she asked, hearing the hope and excitement in her voice.

Lucas chuckled against her throat as he lifted her.

Eve wrapped her legs around his waist and locked her ankles while he began to climb the stairs with an ease that deepened her desire to have every bit of his strength and power in her bed. "Sometime tonight we are coming back out to swing," she said, remembering her earlier thought as they passed the glider on their way inside the house.

"The bed," Lucas demanded in his deep voice near her ear.

Eve shivered as she guided him across the kitchen,

through the living room and down the hall leading to her bedroom. He lay her down atop the queen-sized bed in the softly lit room and pressed his body down over hers as they brought their lips together to deeply kiss. She didn't think there was anything more delicious than Lucas gently sucking the tip of her tongue.

"Wait," she said, pressing her head back into the pillows to look up at him.

"I have condoms," he told her before lowering his head to claim another kiss.

She slowly smiled.

He did the same.

They kissed. Slowly. There was no rush. Not this time.

Lucas made space to relieve her of her dress, and then the sheer fuchsia panties she was wearing. Naked, she arched her back, meaning to tempt him with the taut tips of her breasts. He roughly pulled his shirt over his head, causing the top buttons to fly off and bounce against the wall. She gasped when he undid his belt and pants. And when his hard length was freed from his boxers, she reached for him. Sitting on his haunches between her open legs, Lucas thrust his hips forward as she stroked him.

His strong thighs trembled and he clenched his jaw with a grunt from deep in his gut. "Damn," he groaned as she lightly dragged her thumb across the shiny tip.

He shocked her by swiping her hand away, but she brought both hands up to clutch her pillows into her fists as he bent and lowered his head, and tasted her intimately. With his lips and then his tongue.

Eve felt a million darts of pleasure swell in her nerve

endings and cried out as she pressed her feet into the bed and rolled her hips. "Yes, yes, yes," she sighed, feeling electrified.

And when he sucked her throbbing and swollen bud into his mouth, she covered her face with a pillow and bit down into it to keep from screaming as he slowly sucked her to a fiery climax that coated her body in sweat. The pillow was snatched from her face, and she opened her eyes to Lucas sitting up and staring into her eyes as he stroked his own hardness.

Oh. Oooh.

She liked his boldness, His freedom in the bedroom. It made her want to match his abandonment. To not have one care. Quickly, she shifted her body to be on all fours in front of him. She dipped her head to taste him with her tongue.

He released a fierce swear.

She smiled with him still in her mouth before taking in a good bit of him, then eased him out as she circled his thickness with her tongue.

"No," Lucas cried out, freeing himself.

He moved from the bed to retrieve the condoms from his wallet. She dared herself not to look away as he held one hand to the base and used the other to unroll the latex down the length of him. The bed sank as he pressed a knee onto it. He grabbed her ankles and pulled her body down to the edge before spreading her legs.

Eve gasped.

Lucas looked into her eyes and used his hips to guide his sheathed tip inside her. And with a bit of a scowl, he bit down on his lip with one thrust and filled her.

She cried out as shivers wracked her body at the

feel of him against her rigid walls. He took each of her breasts in his hands as he delivered deep thrust after deep thrust, and kept his eyes locked on her face. She shook her head and sat up, wrapping her arms around his neck and using her strength to raise her upper body against his. They locked lips as she worked her hips to match his thrusts. Staring at one another, she and Lucas rode the waves into an explosive climax that left them shivering and gasping for breath.

One month later

Lucas was lying beside Eve on a large blanket on the grass beside Swan Lake. He looked up at the night sky, which seemed to be scattered with a million stars, but all he could focus on was the sweet scent of Eve. "What exactly are we doing again?" he asked, rolling over to his side and propping his head up on his hand to take in the sight of her frame in the sports bra and cut-off jeans she was wearing. Her body was toned and fit from her athletic career, and she also had plenty of curves, from the breadth of her hips to her full breasts. Just perfection to him.

"We are enjoying the peace of just being still, Lucas," she told him with her eyes closed. "I have learned not to always be on the go and live life like I'm scared to miss something. What I learned during my recovery is that I was missing peace. Rest. Stillness."

He gave in to the urge to touch her. He was not to be denied. He traced her navel.

Eve giggled before swatting his hand away. "Peace,

not the other *P* word, Lucas," she said, never opening her eyes.

He smiled and lay on his back again, crossing his ankles and looking up to the sky.

"Listen," she urged him. "The sound of nature is better than music sometimes."

Lucas frowned. He'd been driving to East Patchogue to spend nearly every Saturday night that she wasn't working with her. Stargazing was not a part of *his* plans.

"I felt your body tense up," she said.

He looked over at her to find her eyes still closed. "It's quiet, Eve," he said.

Now she opened one eye to look at him. "It's quieter than Manhattan, but it is not quiet, Lucas Cress," she said, then rolled over to straddle him.

He reached for her hips, but she shook her head and eased his hands away, then held them against the blanket as she looked down into his face. "What a waste of a good position," he said.

Eve smiled. "Close your eyes, Luc," she said.

He did, feeling excited at her closeness. It was what he sought as often as her time, and the distance between them, would allow.

"Hear the crickets," she said, her voice barely above a whisper.

He did.

"And the owls."

He nodded.

"And the rustle of the leaves from the wind."

Lucas tilted his head to the side a bit.

"Good," she said, releasing his arms. "I can feel you

relax. Now just take deep breaths and clear your mind as you *listen*."

As Eve shifted to lie back down beside him, Lucas did not stop her. He took a deep inhale and let his arms fall to his side. He smiled at the croaking of frogs and then something broke the surface of the water with a small splash.

"This peace and swimming saved me, Lucas," she admitted, her voice soft but filled with relief. "Sometimes you just have to tell the rest of the world and all the things you think are important to pause while you reset."

He took an even deeper breath before releasing it slowly.

"For me, sex is amazing," she said. "But just lying here with you—like *this*—means much more to me."

There was an intimacy to the simplicity of just lying together in stillness. He leaned into the nothingness of not chasing a thing—sex, work, events, commitments, noise—and allowing the sounds of nature to soak into him. It would breathe new life and energy into him. Rejuvenate him.

He dared to reach out for her hand and hold it in his own. Softly.

His heart pounded and his body felt alive when she didn't break the hold.

They got lost in the bliss of stillness. Together.

Eve awakened the next morning with a long stretch in her bed beneath the sheet covering her nudity. Lucas was not in bed, and for a moment she thought he had left for his ride back to the city. Last night had been the first night they'd shared a bed and had not made love.

Still, his holding her from behind throughout the night had brought its own kind of peace.

Perhaps for him, it wasn't enough.

She felt a pang of hurt, but then saw his leather duffel bag still on the recliner in the corner. She smiled as relief flooded her. Their weekend nights had come to mean a lot to her—more than she had ever wanted.

And then her smile faded as she bent her legs and pulled them to her chest. Somewhere in the weeks since he'd popped in at her home, more had developed than just a need for the diversion of explosive sex. The nightly phone calls. Texts—some sexy and others funny. The never-ending flower deliveries. The laughs. The talks.

Waking up together.

It hadn't been the plan, but it felt good. And Eve was siding with Suzi that she deserved a little goodness in her life.

Who knew that one day she would be completely enthralled by little chubby Lucas Cress?

Eve heard a noise coming from the kitchen and flung back the sheet to rise from bed. She grabbed a woven cotton robe, pulled it on and tied it at the waist. Barefoot, she made her down the hall and to the kitchen to watch Lucas as he moved around in nothing but a damp towel slung low around his waist. He was searching through her cabinets and finally noticed her standing there watching him.

He stopped and looked over at her with a smile. "Hungry?" he asked.

She barely heard him because she was eyeing his

hard chest and rigid abdomen, which were covered with the flat chest hair that she loved. "Huh?" she asked.

"I cooked breakfast," he said, tossing a floral hand towel over one of his shoulders.

She moved over to the counter. "What's on the menu?" she asked, feeling her stomach grumble.

"Cinnamon-raisin scones with a champagne glaze, ricotta pancakes with homemade raspberry syrup, sliced ribeye steak, a Gruyère cheese omelet and ly-onnaise potatoes," he said, then took a bow and bent down to check her lower cabinets before standing with a pitcher in his hand. "And, of course, mimosas."

Every bit of it was worthy of a spread in a cook-book, or a food magazine like *Bon Appétit.* "You must be starving," Eve said. "This is a lot of food for the two of us."

Lucas looked confused. "I was gonna make me a to-go plate for the drive back home this morning," he explained. "I thought you'd like to call Suzi over and y'all enjoy it before you have to work."

Eve shrugged one shoulder and gave him a bashful look. "Did I forget to mention I got another lifeguard to cover that beach party for me today?" she asked.

"You did?" Lucas asked.

"I did. I thought we could spend some extra time to-gether since you'll be in Dubai next week. Unless you have to hurry back," she quickly added.

"Hmm," Lucas said, looking out the bay window over the sink. "Now what should we do all day?"

"Definitely breakfast," Eve said as she came around the counter and wrapped her arms around his waist.

"And then?" he asked with a feigned innocent expression.

Eve chuckled. "Maybe a little nap, or...*something*," she suggested as she undid his towel and let it drop to the tiled kitchen floor.

"Or something," he said.

"Definitely something," she said, bending down in front of him.

His length grew hard in anticipation.

Eve swiped it from tapping against her cheek and rose with his towel in her hand. "After we grub. I'm starving," she said.

Lucas looked disappointed. "Hell, so am I," he said with a look down at his erection.

"Okay. Fine," she said, taking his hardness in her hand. "But we go for a run around the lake later."

"Deal!" Lucas said with enthusiasm as she gently pulled him behind her and out of the kitchen.

One week later

Aboard the family's private jet, Lucas swiped through the images of the fall line of Cress, INC. His final approval was needed on the design and new colors of cookware, bakeware, kitchen gadgets and tableware. He used his stylus to circle and initials his selections. "Phillip, I thank you for backing me on expanding Cress, INC. into linens and textiles," he said without looking up. "Phillip Senior held off for years."

The brothers and their wives had all flown to Dubai for the week for the grand opening of CRESS XIII. Phillip Senior and Nicolette had kept all the children, allowing the adults to enjoy the "City of Gold." Without a beautiful woman on his arm, Lucas had focused a lot of his attention on work.

"It's an innovative idea," Phillip Junior said.

"I agree, Lucas," Raquel said. "Delicious food cooked in Cress, INC. cookware should be enjoyed on table linens that are beautiful."

Lucas glanced up to give her a smile of thanks. She was sitting next to Phillip Junior as he smoked a cigar and swirled the brandy in a glass. "It's going to be all about the design choices to make sure we stand out and draw the eye of the consumer," he told her.

"I agree," Raquel added, taking her husband's glass to sip from his drink. "It's all about quality textiles and the design. Classic is key. It will make the discerning customer think of longevity."

"Exactly," Lucas agreed, circling the new deep magenta color before he suddenly looked up at Raquel. He took in the simple white tank she was wearing with high-waist, wide-leg orange taffeta pants and gold sandals. He had to admit that of all the sisters-in-law, he loved her classic fashion style the best. "Wait. Don't you have an art degree?"

Raquel and Phillip Junior shared a brief look before they both looked at him. "I do. From Wellesley," she said with a nod and a look of curiosity in her eyes.

"Would you mind taking a look at some mock-ups I have?" he asked, already pulling up the file.

"Me?" Raquel asked, obviously surprised.

Ding.

She picked up her phone from where it was sitting on the seat.

"Absolutely," Lucas said. "I just air-dropped you the file."

"Yeah. Yes, I can do that," Raquel said. "Thank you for thinking of me."

Phillip Junior leaned closer to kiss her neck. "I wish I had thought of it first," he admitted.

"Just pay her a nice consultation fee, big brother," Lucas offered.

At that, Raquel gave Lucas a nod of thanks and took her husband's cigar to take a deep inhale. Then she tilted her head back and blew a smooth stream of silver smoke upward.

Everyone on the plane chuckled at the move.

Lucas reopened his previous file and looked down at the digital color sample of the deep and rich magenta color. It reminded him of the lip gloss Eve wore the night of their high-school reunion. He tapped his finger against the screen as he thought of her. He missed her—had missed their usual Saturday night and Face-Time was just not the same.

Another week to see her again?

He released a heavy breath and looked out the window at the evening sky. The sun was just beginning to set, and the sky seemed painted in hues of red, orange and deep blue. He smiled, knowing Eve would want him to just enjoy the beautiful view.

He used his tablet to take a picture of it and then texted it to Eve.

Lucas looked around at each of his brothers snuggled up with their wives. Content and secure.

Not alone.

Bzzz. Bzzz. Bzzz.

He looked down at the incoming text.

It's almost as beautiful as you, he read, feeling as if he could hear her voice saying it.

Couple of hours later they landed at the New Jersey airfield where they housed the private jet. It was after eleven.

Hell with it.

"Good night, everybody. Get home safe," he said, then bolted off the plane, strode over to the parking lot and climbed behind the wheel of his SUV.

He made the trip to East Patchogue in record time and was thankful he'd done so safely. With his heart pounding in anticipation, and not caring that he would have to get on the road back home in a few hours, he parked in front of her house and got out of the vehicle. Before he reached the first step, the front door opened, and Eve stood there fresh-faced, in an oversized T-shirt, with her hair wrapped down beneath a print silk scarf.

He took the stairs two at a time, crossed the front deck and pulled her body up against his. "Right now, you have never looked better to me," he said.

"Luc," she gasped, gripping his neck as she pressed kisses to the side of his face.

He carried her inside with plans to make love to her up to the very moment he had to leave.

Seven

Two weeks later

"Amazing," Eve sighed as she stood on the edge of the deck of the cottage and looked out at the clear waters of Bimini, Bahamas. In the distance, the water seemed to meet the sky, and the sun blessed it all.

In a white bikini, she stretched her arms high above her and then arched her back. She closed her eyes and listened to the sound of the ocean, but there was also an incredible silence that warmed her soul. She felt so completely grateful for viewing such grand beauty on the other side of her transformation.

The new version of Eve was humbled by it.

She longed to dive into the ocean, but turned to ease into the edgeless pool instead, because Lucas was inside sleeping and she didn't want him to awaken and not find her. With her arms at her side, she used her feet to propel her forward, pretending for a moment that she was a mystical mermaid. She loved the water just as much as one.

She lost count of the laps she swam, only surfacing long enough to grab air before going back down in the pool that was tiled in a mosaic of dark blue, turquoise and sea-green. She didn't care. She felt at home in the water. As she twirled her body beneath the depths and then pushed her feet off the bottom to break the surface, she smiled at how foolish she had been to give up swimming because she wouldn't dare ruin a perfect hairstyle.

She swam length of the pool and pushed her hair back to shake off the water, then settled her arms atop the edge as she looked out at the ocean.

When Lucas had offered her a long weekend in Bimini, Bahamas, she'd resisted. Instantly, she had imagined Lucas Cress renting a luxury villa with a private staff and all the amenities, near plenty of nighttime activities.

Eve turned in the pool to eye the beautiful but small two-bedroom cottage on a private island. There was just Galy, an older woman with knowing eyes that twinkled, weathered skin as dark as fudge and a sweet disposition. She had a boisterous laugh and cooked them the most delicious meals.

I will miss her—and her conch chowder—most of all.

Although Eve had once traveled all over the world and seen amazing locales, she felt an affinity for the island just fifty miles from Miami—the closest Caribbean island to America. The history, the food, the people and the peace it gave her were indescribable.

Is it possible to fall in love with a place?

"Good morning, gorgeous."

She closed her eyes and smiled as her entire body tingled at the sound of Lucas's deep voice. She turned in the water. Lucas was standing on the deck that surrounded the home and was wearing white swim trunks. She sank beneath the water and swam to him using a slow and easy backstroke that she knew gave him a full view of her body in the skimpy bikini.

"Where's the bikini I brought for you in Alice Town yesterday?" she asked him, looking up at the sun framing his sleek frame.

Lucas chuckled. "There wasn't enough coverage," he told her. "I'm sure Ms. Galy does not want to see that kind of wardrobe malfunction."

Eve laughed with him.

"Having fun?" he asked, his hands on his narrow hips as he looked down at her.

She nodded earnestly, then climbed from the pool, wrapped her arms around him and pressed kisses to his chest. "I'm going to hate leaving," she admitted, turning to lean her back to his body and draw his arms around her as she looked out at the view.

"Maybe I should buy a house here?" Lucas asked. "The we could boat down whenever we wanted."

Eve stiffened.

The ease with which he spoke of spending money was a reminder of his wealth—a part of him she tried her best not to think about.

"He's not Aaron and you are far too hard on yourself—back then and now," Suzi had said when Eve confessed her unease about a weekend getaway to the Caribbean.

He's not Aaron.

Eve pushed away her concerns and turned again to look up at Lucas. "Let's walk down to the ocean," she said, easing her hand into his.

It was a comfortable fit.

"Thank you for taking the weekend off for me…well, for us," Lucas said as they moved down the steps of the deck to the white sand. "I needed a break from work."

"Me, too," she admitted, pressing a kiss to his upper arm before leaning against it. She looked out into the ocean again. "Everything okay at work?"

"I have an idea to expand the Cress, INC. line into textiles and linens," he explained. "My father had always been against it, but now that Phillip Junior—"

"You call him Phillip Junior?" Eve asked.

"We all do, and my father is Phillip Senior," he said.

"Very formal," she observed.

Lucas chuckled. "Trust me, that suits both my father and my brother," he said.

"I remember Cole and Gabriel from school, but I don't really know your other brothers," Eve told him as they came to where the ocean met the sand.

As they sat down on the beach and let the water cover their feet, Lucas told her about his brothers, and it was clear there was a lot of love for them. She was intrigued that they all were world-class chefs and now worked together with their parents in continuing to develop a culinary empire.

"Why pastry?" Eve asked.

Lucas picked up a broken piece of shell and used his strength to throw it high into the air. It landed in the water and created rings on the surface. "I attended culinary school in Paris like everyone in my family, but I wanted to be different and chart my own path," he said, before looking over at her. "And I have loved sweets since before I could walk. My mother spoiled me—but don't tell that to my brothers because I will deny it."

"So you're her favorite?" Eve asked.

Lucas looked a bit bashful. "According to my brothers," he said.

"I don't blame her. You're my favorite, too, Lucas Cress," she said.

"Now," he said.

She looked at him. There was so much weight of the past in that one spoken word. So much hurt. And the reminder that she had once been so cruel to him stung her with guilt, shame and regret.

Eve moved to straddle his lap and held his handsome face in her hands. *"Yo era una tonta, Luc,"* she whispered as she looked into his dark eyes before leaning in to kiss him. *"Me perdí un gran sexo e incluso mejores bollos."*

Like his brothers, Lucas was fluent in several languages, including Spanish, and he laughed at her admitting to being a fool and missing out on great sex, and even better scones.

"Trust me, if I knew then what I know now, I would keep those cupcakes and then eat them off your body," she told him against his mouth, then continued to kiss him.

Lucas leaned back with a look of disbelief. "Off the body I had back then?" he asked.

Eve held his chin and locked her eyes on his. "Yes," she told him truthfully. "Because now I don't just see all the sexy, but who you are inside. I was too self-absorbed to notice that before."

He kissed her, but Eve could feel his lingering doubts and understood them, although they also triggered her. She stood up and ran into the water, splashing away with her arms, then turned to wave at him as he remained sitting on the sand. "Come on, Luc!" she called, then spread her arms wide and fell back into the clear blue water to let it envelop her.

She allowed herself to swim out far before turning and doing strong freestyle strokes to reach the beach. As she walked toward him, she loved the way Lucas's eyes devoured her. She knew the effect of the water dripping off her bikini-clad body and he was loving it.

"There are benefits to a private beach," he said, reaching to touch her thighs as she stood before him.

"Yes, like swimming in a beautiful ocean," Eve said, dropping down to her knees in the sand.

"Um," Lucas began, then cleared his throat. "Ah, I can't swim."

Her eyes widened. "Huh?" she asked.

"I just never learned," he said.

Eve eyed him and her instincts went on high alert when his eyes shifted away from hers. "Lucas, that was a whole lie," she said.

He squinted hard as he looked down the length of the beach.

Eve sat back on her haunches. "Now, I'm not asking for perfection in this situationship we have going on, because I am not perfect, but I do humbly request you not play in my face."

"Play in your face?" Lucas asked.

"Lie to my face," she explained.

"I like that," he said with a nod of appreciation.

"I didn't coin it," she said.

They stared at one another.

Eve tilted her head to the side.

"Okay!" he exclaimed, as if unable to take the pressure of her stare.

"I never learned to swim like my brothers did because I was self-conscious of my weight growing up and didn't want to undress," Lucas said with rushed words that almost slammed together into one chaotic word.

"Oh, Luc," she sighed.

"No pity," he said.

Eve removed the angst from her face and gave him a smile that felt like it might be frightening-looking. She rested a hand on one of his knees as she looked past him right into the kitchen of the cottage. She remembered Ms. Galy guiding her on how to make traditional johnnycakes—cornmeal pancakes.

"Are you afraid of the water?" Eve asked him.

"Not at all. I even do water sports *now*," he said.

Eve smiled and reclaimed her seat on his lap, resting her elbows on each of his shoulders. "Then I am going to teach you to swim," she said.

Lucas's brow furrowed a bit as he leaned past her to look out at the water. "Uhhh," he said.

"Let me give you an incentive," Eve said, pressing kisses to both sides of his neck.

He cupped her buttocks.

"We will take advantage of the benefits of this private beach first," she said with a lick of her lip. "And then start your swim lessons."

Lucas considered her offer. "Can I make a counteroffer?" he asked.

She looked skeptical.

"Reverse cowgirl," he said.

Eve arched an eyebrow. "You sure?" she asked. "The last time I thought you had a stroke, the way your mouth twisted."

"Don't pretend I haven't given you a few convulsions my damn self," he told her, entwining their fingers.

"Right—I was damn near to the pearly gates," she replied. "I had to step away from the white lights."

They laughed together.

"Worth it, though," Eve added with several grunts in the back of her throat.

Lucas pressed his face to her neck.

She shivered and massaged his broad back, loving the feel of his muscles. "Luc!" she gasped when he drew circles around her pounding pulse with his tongue.

Eve gave in to the passion, reveling in the feel of his touches as he slowly removed her bikini and then kissed away the salt of the ocean. From her neck. Each breast. Her taut nipples. Slowly. As if he was luxuriating in the taste of her.

But Eve had a hunger of her own.

She pressed him to his back on the sand and shifted her body down his to feast on him with licks and kisses. She tried not to miss any of the deliciously contoured body that he had worked so hard to obtain. Each broad shoulder. His hard chest. Those abs. And then every thick inch of his length until it was shiny and wet.

"Good?" she asked, looking up at him as he raised his head to stare at her work.

He nodded, clearly speechless.

With one last lick and then a deep suck of the tip that made his legs jump beneath her, Eve rose and turned to straddle him backward. Lucas lightly slapped each of her buttocks as she rose on her knees to ease down onto his hardness. As she rode him and leaned forward to grip his ankles, Eve wore a soft smile. She was enjoying the feel of the sun warming their nude bodies as she inhaled the scent of the ocean deeply, surrounded by nature and claiming every bit of her bliss.

"Luc, I'm still not sure about this."

He glanced over at Eve sitting beside him in the back of one of his family's chauffeur-driven SUVs. She looked astoundingly beautiful in an emerald satin strapless evening gown with her short ebony hair in large finger waves and a diamond flower-shaped hairpin over her left ear. "I would like you by my side, Eve," he said, reaching to take one of her hands into his.

She released a shaky breath as she stared out the tinted window at the brightly lit New York theater of the Directors Guild of America. There was a crowd and plenty of press hoping to catch a glimpse of the celebrities scheduled to attend the world premiere of *Nicolette and Phillip: Love, Family & Food*.

She looked over at him with a weak smile. "This is the type of attention I would have craved in the past," she admitted, clutching his hand tighter.

Lucas saw her unease but pushed it aside. "I think it's time to not let the past control you anymore," he said. "No more running, Eve."

Lucas had asked her to carve out time in her hectic schedule to attend the premiere with him. And he was excited about it. On those nights they lounged about her house making love, taking a night run, or chancing a skinny-dip in the lake, Lucas felt relaxed just being with her, spending time together and laughing. Eve.

"You've changed," he reminded her. "There's no going back."

Eve nodded as if reassuring herself of it.

Just a few days ago they had been in the Caribbean and now they were making their world debut as a couple.

"Ready?" he asked.

She leaned it to kiss him and then retrieved a napkin from her clutch to wipe his lips free of her shiny peach-tinted gloss. "Ready," she said.

As they stepped out of the rear of the SUV and onto the red carpet, Lucas felt Eve's hand gradually tighten on his as the camera flashes went off around them. But as they walked the red carpet and posed for pictures, it was clear that Eve could not be comfortable back in the spotlight. Her body was stiff and her smile stiffer.

Normally, it was during public spectacles that Lucas would smile through his own discomfort being in front of the cameras. Being seen. And judged. The chubby kid of his past was always with him. Always feeling not quite good enough. Or fit enough. Or handsome enough.

And then it hit him.

He had cajoled Eve right into a scenario that *he* rarely found comfortable.

Lucas pressed a kiss to her temple, and she looked up at him. He smiled at her and she did the same. For a moment, everything around them faded to nothing. It was just them and he felt her ease return.

But it was short-lived.

The roar of the crowd and the press broke through their bubble.

Eve forced a smile as she leaned in close. "No more photos for me," she said.

He held on to her hand, but she eased out of his grasp and walked away to stand at the end of the red carpet. Out of the spotlight.

"Beautiful woman, Luc!" someone yelled.

He nodded in agreement. "That she is," he agreed.

"Who is she?" someone called.

Lucas down the length of the carpet to where Eve was standing. "My girl," he called back, giving her a smile.

Eve returned it with one of her own.

"Let's get some with the entire family," the family's publicist said, guiding them all to the center of the step and repeat background imprinted with all of the Cress, INC. logos and the other sponsors of the event.

Nicolette held the hand of Phillip Junior with one hand and slid the other around one of Lucas's arms. "And where is Lana?" she asked through her smile.

"Hopefully somewhere as happy as I am," he said.

As the entire family posed for pictures, Lucas kept checking to make sure Eve was okay as she waited for some of the hoopla to die down. He was thankful when they all began to move toward the entrance, and he could take Eve's hand in his to draw her back close to his side.

"I'm glad that's over," Lucas admitted to her as they entered the lobby, where their guests were enjoying a pre-premiere soiree, complete with an open bar and heavy appetizers.

"You look good," Eve assured him as she smoothed down the lapels of his black tuxedo jacket.

Over her head, he saw his parents eyeing them.

Phillip Senior's retirement had been brought on by a heart condition and subsequent cardiac surgery two years ago. That had served as the impetus for both of his parents to soften their approach to their children. To demand less and accept more.

But as they made their way over to him and Eve, he wondered if they had reverted to their old ways—his father was demanding and their mother was controlling.

"It seems introductions should be made," Nicolette said, looking stunning in a gold metallic one-shoulder gown that brought out the blond highlights of her silver tresses.

"Of course," Lucas said, clearing his throat and smoothing his hand down the front of his jacket. "Eve, these are my parents. Nicolette Lavoie-Cress and Phillip Cress Senior. *Maman* and Dad, this is Eve Villar."

"Nice to meet you both," Eve said, extending her hand.

"Villar?" Monica said as she walked up to them with Gabriel following behind holding Emme in his arms.

"Yes," Eve said.

Lucas felt the shift in her energy and wondered if she was concerned if Monica was about to bring up her past.

"Any relation to Marco Villar?" Monica asked. She

was glowing in a white strapless dress with her hair bone-straight.

Eve smiled and nodded. "Yes, he's my father," she said with obvious pride.

"And an excellent attorney," Monica said, extending her hand.

Eve took it. "I agree," she said with a laugh.

During their exchange, he noticed Nicolette's demeanor change at the mention of Marco Villar. Her stance noticeably softened and the smile she gave Eve was suddenly welcoming.

Of all her sons, Lucas was the closest to Nicolette and her most ardent defender, but in truth, most times he saw what they saw. A woman who loved deeply but also just as firmly wanted to grip the reins of the lives of those she loved. She, at times, put the show of perfection above all else. And at times, her elitism made her judgmental.

But Lucas viewed Nicolette and her often bad behavior as a woman struggling to run from a past burdened with poverty. To feel above her upbringing. In their closeness—he'd been her last child, and the one who clung to her side the longest—Lucas had asked her a million questions as she'd fed him endless sweet treats.

Lucas finished introducing Eve to the family, and he loved the way she bent down in the designer dress he'd given her to interact with the toddlers.

"Votre épingle à cheveux est jolie, Miss Eve," Collette said, telling her that her hairpin was pretty.

Eve promptly removed it and then bent at the waist to place it in his niece's curls. *"C'est encore plus joli sur toi,"* she said with a soft smile.

Lucas looked on as Collette beamed at being told the pin was even prettier on her, then ran off to show her new accessory to her mother, Raquel. He turned to Eve, smiling down at her. "I don't know which version of you I like best. In a swimming suit or like this," he told her just as a server walked up to them with flutes of champagne on a tray. He took two and gave her one.

"I don't drink, Luc," she said in a tone that suggested he should understand that.

"I didn't know, Eve," he told her, stopping another server to set both flutes on the tray she carried.

She visibly softened. "I'm sorry," she said, pressing a hand to her cheek. "I'm adjusting to being in the midst of this again."

"I'll go to the bar and get us both a nonalcoholic cocktail," he said, briefly holding both of her upper arms before he turned and walked away.

He paused as he spotted Coleman and Jillian standing and laughing together before sharing a kiss. "Could you keep an eye on Eve for me?" he asked.

"Hard pass," Coleman said.

Jillian swatted his arm. "Cole!" she exclaimed.

"What? You weren't in school with her," Coleman said with a shake of his head. "Hell on heels."

Lucas stiffened. "She's changed. Respect her the same way I respect Jillian," he said, his voice stern.

Coleman's eyes widened. "Jillian is my wife," he countered.

"Boys," Jillian admonished.

"And it wouldn't matter. Either way, she always got my respect and you are going to give Eve hers," Lucas countered, taking a step forward.

"Look who is trying to grow up," Coleman said, taking a step of his own until they were nearly face-to-face.

"Fully grown, big brother," Lucas countered.

"Gentleman!" Jillian snapped under her breath, then looked to see if they were drawing attention.

"I used to put you in headlocks, little brother," Coleman snapped.

"Try me now," Lucas warned with a slight flex of his shoulders.

Jillian eased in between them and began to plant soft kisses on her husband's mouth. "Hey, hey, hey. Look at me," she said softly.

Coleman reluctantly shifted his hard stare from Lucas to his wife. Soon, he began to kiss her as well, as they wrapped their arms around each other. "I'm going to check on Eve for my brother-in-law," Jillian said in between kisses. "And will you please get me a virgin sex on the beach from the bar *with* your brother?"

"*Sex* on the beach?" Coleman asked with a suggestive look, grabbing her hips in the lavender-draped sequin gown she was wearing that emphasized her pregnancy.

"Plenty of it," she told him with a meaningful wide-eyed stare.

"Get a room," Lucas grumbled, then turned away.

Soon Coleman fell in step beside him as they made their way to the bar in the corner. "My wife saved you," he said.

Lucas gave him a side-glance. "From hurting you," he drawled. "Yes, she did."

"Whatever, man," Coleman muttered.

"Yeah, whatever," Lucas returned.

They reached the bar.

"Let me get two seltzers with fresh fruit of your choice," Lucas ordered.

"Virgin sex on the beach and then a double scotch on the rocks for me," Coleman said.

"Right away," the female bartender said, giving them both an appreciative smile.

They both ignored it as they stood there in stony silence.

"You must be serious about her," Coleman finally said, breaking the ice.

"I am," Lucas said, softening his stance.

The Cress brothers didn't always get along, but their disputes never lasted for long.

"I thought your endgame was just to sweet-talk her in your bed?" Coleman asked, just as they retrieved their drinks.

"What?"

Lucas's heart slammed in his chest as Eve and Jillian walked up to them. It was clear from the stricken look on her face that she had overheard his brother.

"Shit," Coleman swore.

"Eve," Lucas said, turning to set the drinks back on the bar.

By the time he turned around, he saw nothing but her back as she weaved her way through the crowd with the speed of a track star.

"Really, Cole?" Jillian said with obvious disappointment.

Lucas left them behind and rushed behind Eve, feeling panicked. By the time he reached the street, he looked left and then right, and spotted her walking fast, already nearly to the next long block.

"No more running, Eve."

He pulled out his phone and called his driver for the night, then took off behind her.

"Eve!" he called when he saw her heel twist, then she fell to the ground.

What tore at his gut was that she lingered on the sidewalk as if too broken to gather the strength to rise.

"Get up off this street, Eve. This is still New York, baby," he told her as he held her under her arms and lifted her to his feet. "Mess around and have a rat in your hair."

She instantly pushed against his chest. *"You're* the damn rat in my hair!" she snapped.

He took a step forward to replace the one he'd lost from her push. "Eve, let me explain," he said, eyeing her.

"Sweet-talk me into your bed, Lucas?" she said with clear bitterness, her eyes filled with fury. "I guess you got brownie points with your brother for the blow jobs, huh?"

He winced. "Definitely not," he said. "Neither one of us wanted something serious at first, Eve."

She had been pacing as best she could on one broken heel, but stopped to glare at him. "Yeah, but I was *always* honest about my intentions," she told him.

"And so was I," Lucas told her, reaching for her.

Eve leaned back to avoid his touch. "You're playing in my face again, Lucas?" she asked.

Their driver arrived and double-parked in the street.

"You have come to mean so much to me, Eve. Please believe me," he begged.

She shook her head. "Never again," she said. "To

hell with you, Lucas Cress, and this time I have every right to say it."

He tightened his jaw.

Eve limped over to the car.

The driver quickly exited the vehicle and moved around it to open the passenger door. "Find a ride home, Luc," she said over her shoulder.

He said nothing, admittedly stuck somewhere between their past and the present, where the younger version of him was triggered by her harshness, but still understood the role he'd played in hurting her.

"Mr. Cress?" the driver said with the door still open.

"Take her home," Lucas said, eyeing Eve sitting rigidly in the back seat as she ignored him.

"Yes, sir," the driver said, finally closing the door.

The rear window lowered.

"Tell me, pastry chef, is revenge sweet?" Eve asked, her eyes brimming with pain and soon-to-be-shed tears.

A piece of him was thankful when she raised the window, blocking him from seeing the hurt and pain he'd caused with his foolish pride.

What have I done?

Long after the vehicle pulled away, Lucas felt desolate as he stood there on the street. The blend of emotions nearly weakened his knees until he thought he might replace Eve in the spot where she had fallen.

Eight

One month later

Eve never thought she would come to feel uncomfortable in the home that had become her refuge. Now it was a constant reminder of the time she'd shared with Lucas. Although she had slam-dunked anything he left behind into a box, his presence lingered. Like an imprint.

Mocking me.

Even after four weeks, she still felt foolish. Not just because of what she'd overheard Coleman say, but because even after that, she still thought of him. Still missed him. Still wondered what he was doing.

Still cried.

An ache radiated across her chest. It had become familiar.

So had the image of Lucas standing on that street with his head hung low. She had turned on the rear seat to watch him until the distance made him disappear from her view. There he had remained.

That had struck her even as her anger and embarrassment had consumed her until her neck and ears had felt hot. Her parents had been surprised at her sudden appearance at their door in a stained evening gown and carrying a shoe with a broken heel. She offered them a vague truth of falling, but omitted that her heart had just been shattered.

But it was her father—ever observant and wise—who had brought a cup of soup to her old room to check on her.

She smiled as she recalled the tender moment…

Knock, knock, knock, knock.

Eve had been sitting in the window seat looking down at the traffic on the street without really focusing on it. Her silent tears flowed with too much ease and still failed to purge her of the hurt and disappointment she felt. Using the edge of the satin pajamas her parents had kept, Eve wiped away her tears as she crossed the wide space to open the door for her father. She knew it was him because her mother would have cracked the door open and peeped in without invitation.

And sure enough there he stood. Marco Villar. Tall and portly with a shiny bald head and thick black-framed glasses still in the black vest of the three-piece suit he preferred to wear during rare appearances in court. Man of brilliance and power—a pillar. Love of her mother's life. Preparer of delicious Spanish food that reminded him of home. But to her, just simply her dad who made her soup, even though she knew he had plenty of work on which he could be focused.

"Hola, Papi," she said, hoping her eyes were not too puffy from her tears.

"I made you some caldo gallego," he said. He was carrying a *steaming oversized ceramic mug.*

She smiled as he entered and set the mug on the gold-trimmed nightstand. "You just made that, didn't you?" she asked of the Spanish white-bean soup he filled with collard greens, ham hocks, potatoes and sausage. He had taught her that it took ninety minutes to make.

Marco gave a little shrug and splayed his hands. "Soup is always good for the soul," he said. Her father was a large man with a deep voice, but a slow cadence that was calming.

Eve sat down on the side of the bed as her father slid his beefy hands into the pockets of his slacks as he walked around the large bedroom and studied it. "There have been times I have come to stand in the doorway and wish you were a little girl again," he said, picking up an antique porcelain flamenco doll. "Back then, I could save you from hurt."

Eve looked up at her father. "I'm fine, Papi," she lied with softness.

Marco put the doll back on the shelf and turned to face her. "I know that what I saw tonight in your eyes was far more damaged than your dress or shoes," he said.

She shifted her eyes from his steady all-too-knowing gaze.

"Ah," he said.

She had given herself away.

"Did someone physically hurt you, Eve?" Marco asked.

She shook her head. "I really did fall in the street after I twisted my ankle," she said.

"¿Y tu corazón, mi hermosa, mi hija?" he asked, crossing the room to squeeze her shoulder after asking his beautiful daughter about her heart.

It is broken.

She knew from the depth of her hurt, which far outweighed her anger, that she had come to love Lucas Cress. As she looked up at her father, a tear raced down her cheek.

"Ah," he said again as he captured it with his thumb.

Eve jumped to her feet and pressed her face to her father's barrel chest, then she wrapped her arms around him to hold him so tightly. Marco swayed their bodies and slowly rocked her—just like when she was young. She smiled a bit when he began to hum a tune.

Eve had allowed herself to accept her father's strength and comfort because it may have been the only way to free herself of the emotions that had been weighing her down...

Unfortunately, the weight of her hurt and sadness lingered.

She had never revealed to Suzi what happened, but it was clear that whatever had been between her and Lucas was done. Thankfully, her friend had let the matter rest, and life returned to some semblance of normalcy. They were just a week shy of their busy season ending with the coming of Labor Day. The Hamptons and the surrounding areas would find some quiet as Manhattanites brought their summer to an end and returned to the hustle and bustle of the city.

"A hundred dollars for your thoughts."

Eve looked away from her computer to find Suzi entering her office carrying two glasses of the fresh squeezed lemonade she'd made earlier. "They're not worth that much," she said, taking the glass offered to her before enjoying a deep sip through the paper straw.

"Here's to making it through another season," Suzi said, briefly raising her glass in a toast.

"What are you going to do with more free time?" Eve asked, wiping away a speck of lint from the white sundress she wore with flip-flops.

"Nothing much," Suzi said, claiming the chair in front of Eve's desk and shifting far too much in it to find comfort.

Eve eyed her. "What?" she asked. "We're keeping secrets now?"

"I've met someone," Suzi said.

Eve smiled. "Who? No, first, why not tell me, *friend*?" she asked.

"You've been so sad about…" Her words trailed off.

"True," Eve said, stiffening her spine. "But that doesn't mean I can't also be happy for you."

Her friend looked hesitant. "Really?"

"Really," Eve insisted.

"Well, it's Hank," Suzi admitted, her eyes twinkling.

"Hank the fisherman?" Eve asked, envisioning the tall, broad man with a full beard.

Suzi nodded eagerly. "He's been crushing on me for years and I finally decided to give him a try…especially after seeing how happy you are—*were*—with Luc," she said.

"Well, it was fun until it wasn't, but hopefully you

have a nice normal guy with a good heart who just wants to love you because that's what you deserve," Eve said, reaching across the desk to extend her open palm to her friend.

Suzi gave her a warm, dimpled smile and squeezed her hand with her own. "Thanks, Eve," she told her.

"I uprooted my entire life to move to East Patchogue for a regular life," Eve said. "Maybe I need to find myself a fisherman or mechanic or real-estate agent. And leave the Aaron Markses, Luc Cresses and the like alone in their privilege."

"I was rooting for you," Suzi admitted.

Eve gave her hand a squeeze of her own before sitting back in her seat. "You know what? So was I," she admitted.

"Have you heard from him?" Suzi asked.

Eve shook her head.

"Not a phone call or flowers or anything?" she asked in disbelief.

"It's for the best," Eve said, even though she wasn't quite sure of that. "I learned he just wanted to sweet-talk me into bed. Sometimes it's all about the chase."

"And fun," Suzi reminded her.

Eve gave her a look.

Suzi set her drink on the corner of Eve's neat desk. "Listen, I don't know what the ending was, and I don't need to know, but the beginning was just me encouraging you to use him for sex and fun. So if there was some chasing, it went *both* ways," she said.

Eve drummed her fingertips on her desk as she eyed her friend.

"I love you, but the truth is truth, and we don't dwell in the house of lies," Suzi reminded her.

"Well, maybe honesty isn't the best policy," Eve countered.

"You do not believe that."

Eve smiled at her. "I really don't," she said.

They shared a laugh and then fell silent.

"Any chance that things got more serious for Lucas the same way your feelings snuck up on you?" Suzi asked.

Eve recalled the desolate image of him standing on the street again. Even now, weeks later, it pained her. It had not been a man victorious in his revenge, but one regretful in his actions. Possibly even embarrassed.

And then it hit her, and she gasped at the revelation.

Watching him on the street that night as she was driven away in the SUV reminded her of the way he walked away with his head hung low from her mockery that day in high school.

"Suzi, I honestly don't know," Eve said, releasing breaths that were as shallow as she had once been.

Bzzzz.

They both eyed her cell phone.

Eve reached for it and she gaped in surprise at the name of the caller. Her heart pounded as she answered. "You are just the person I need to talk to," she said.

Lucas looked out at the view of New York as he ran on his treadmill at full speed. He enjoyed the workout and pushing himself to stay healthy even as his brain tried to convince him that giving in to his sweet tooth would make everything better.

It wouldn't, so he didn't.

As he finished the five miles and slowed the machine so that he could switch to a normal pace, Lucas grabbed his water bottle to replenish himself. The workout was great for his body, but had little effect on his mind. It was still preoccupied with Eve.

They hadn't spoken since the night of the movie premiere.

Whether it was her present anger or his past hurt, Lucas was running from facing either one.

Bzzzz. Bzzzz. Bzzzz.

He eyed the screen of his phone as he stepped off the treadmill and patted the sweat from his bared chest with a plush black towel. It was Sean. He answered FaceTime.

Sean's face on the screen scowled. "Are you naked?" he asked. "Are you having sex?"

Lucas laughed as he flung the towel over his right shoulder. "Trust me, if I was I wouldn't have answered," he said as he picked up the phone from the cup holder on the treadmill and left his home office.

"Thank God," Sean said.

Lucas eyed his brother's background. He didn't recognize it as one of the rooms in his and Montgomery's home in Passion Grove, New Jersey. "Where are you?" he asked as he went down the hall and entered the open living space.

"Out to dinner with everybody. I stepped out to call you," Sean said, turning the phone to show him the luxurious interior of CRESS X in Tribeca. "Join us."

"Another night of playing the spare wheel? No thanks," Lucas said, envisioning the couple sharing kisses while he was left to swipe on social media or entertain the kids if they were present. "I'm regretting giving up my hunt for Mrs. Lucas Cress. Then I could play footsies—and God knows what else—under the table during couples' night."

Sean began to walk back into the restaurant. "We all just wanted to check on you, Luc," he said. "Say hello to Luc, everybody."

"Hello, Luc!" all his brothers and their wives said in unison as Sean flipped the phone to show them all gathered in one of the rooms used for private parties.

He forced a smile that he hoped looked real enough. "Enjoy your dinner, everybody," he said, using his free hand to open the double-sided, glass-front fridge to remove a bottle of water. "Have the citrus pana cotta for dessert. Best ever."

Best ever.

Best ever.

Best ever.

He distinctly remembered saying that very thing to Sean about sex with Eve.

It haunted him.

She haunted him.

"Have a good night," Lucas said, then ended the call and dropped his phone on the island in the center of the kitchen.

Best ever.

He gripped the water bottle, then turned and flung it into the farmhouse sink with a swear before turning to lean against the counter.

He missed her.

Life was not as fun and vibrant without Eve in it.

And no other woman had claimed his attention. She had made him view the world differently. Finding even the smallest moment of joy in everything.

But now it's over.

He had never thought it would last a lifetime and never imagined it would crash and burn the way that it had.

Bzzzz. Bzzzz. Bzzzz.

Lucas flipped over the phone to see who was calling. "Wendi," he said, taking in the contact picture of his sultry redheaded neighbor from the fourth floor hoisting her plush bosom nearly under her chin as she licked out her tongue.

She consistently delivered a good time, with nothing off-limits.

He had no doubt she had the skills to make him forget anything. But once it was done and he ushered her to the front door, he knew he would still be left with his sadness. Sex was no better a vice than drugs or alcohol. None of it truly healed the trauma. Although he had not made love to anyone since Eve, he flipped over the phone again and let the call—and, undoubtedly, an invitation for crazy sex—go to voice mail.

Lucas was cleaning up the water that splattered on the quartz countertop when his doorbell chimed. "Wendi?" he asked aloud with a slight frown. "She wouldn't? She would. Hell, she has."

One time he had barely gotten her inside his condo before she'd dropped to her knees and unzipped him.

Setting aside the kitchen towel he had been using, Lucas made his way across the kitchen, past the dining area and through the living room to the front door. "Look, Wendi—"

"Who is Wendi?" Eve asked as she stood there in a white summer dress with her short ebony hair in curls and her lips painted red.

Lucas took a step back in shock at her reappearance. "Hello, Eve," he said calmly, even though his heart was hammering, and his gut was clenched.

"Hi, Lucas," she said.

He had to fight the urge to pull her body into his embrace. He just wanted to smell her unique, sweet scent and feel her body closely. To get lost in that unique energy of hers that had given him both peace and excitement.

"Can we talk?" Eve asked.

He nodded and kept his lips pressed together as he stepped back to allow her entry. He was shielding showing how happy he was to see her again. His entire body felt alive.

Eve paused to look up at him. "If *Wendi* doesn't mind," she said.

Lucas looked down at her, knowing he could stare at her for hours, and was thankful that the sadness and anger he feared she must have felt was not evident. "Wendi was not invited," he said.

Eve just gave him a shrug of one smooth brown shoulder before she continued into the foyer and then the living room.

Lucas eyed her frame in the short dress she was wearing, loving the wideness of her hips in comparison to her smaller waist. Her short haircut left her neck free, and he licked his lips at the urge to plant kisses there. "How are you, Eve?" he asked, crossing his arms over his bare chest.

She turned. "Better," she said. "A call from your brother Cole apologizing helped."

"Cole?" he asked, not keeping the surprise from his face.

She nodded. "Yes. For what happened that night of the premiere and for holding on to a grudge based on who I was and not who I am," she said.

"Cole called you tonight?" he asked, still trying to make sense of all the surprises being dropped in his lap, so to speak.

"Yes, from the restaurant," Eve said, turning to move about his living room.

He watched her like a hawk.

"They were making sure you were still home," she said, pausing at a copper statue of an elephant with its trunk raised before giving him a small look over her shoulder. "I guess they didn't think to ask about *Wen-di*."

Lucas bit back a smile at her cattiness. It was cute. "Wendi is an old friend hoping to reconnect and I turned her down," he explained, not wanting anything else to come between them.

If we are reconciling.

He acknowledged that was an assumption he shouldn't make.

"Poor Wendi," Eve said, then opened both patio doors and stepped onto the private balcony.

Intrigued, Lucas removed the towel still over his shoulder and tossed it onto the sofa before slowly following behind her to stand in the doorway. Eve stretched her hands across the railing, then turned to lean back against it and look at him with her head tilted to the side. It was one hell of a sight—the city lights and the Hudson River behind her, in all white.

"Cole is not the only one who owes giving an apology," she said.

He nodded in agreement. "I—"

"No, not yet," she said with a small shake of her head.

He slid his hands into the pockets of his basketball shorts and continued to watch her. Be enthralled by her.

"I apologize for using you for sex," she said with a deep lick and bite of her bottom lip. "I gave you the same consideration I would a vibrator."

His desire stirred and he cared more about the growing hardness tenting his pants like a perv than the truth she'd just given him.

"In the beginning, it was all I wanted," she said, turning again to face the view, but giving him a little look over her shoulder. "Not very different from you, I guess."

Lucas took a step out onto the balcony. "Eve—"

She gave him another shake of her head. "And that night—I apologize for making you feel the same way I did all those years ago back in high school," she said with her gaze on the skyline.

Now that made him pause in his movement forward. He couldn't deny that he had felt transported back to that same moment she'd embarrassed him and crushed his heart. "I know that wasn't your intention, Eve," he admitted aloud.

She turned again. "Good, because it wasn't," she said, looking at him.

Lucas balled his hands into fists inside his pockets

to keep from reaching for her and to billow his shorts more, so that his oncoming erection didn't show. "I apologize for my immaturity in pursuing you just to prove I could now because I couldn't then," he said. "But it's you. You're Eve Villar. I could hardly breathe around you. You were *everything* to me in high school."

Eve pushed off the railing and took one long step toward him.

The late summer wind swirled around them, offering some relief from the evening heat.

"And now?" she asked, looking up at him.

Lucas looked up at the dark sky and took a deep breath that expanded his chest. "You still mean everything to me. More than ever," he confessed, with his eyes on the moon. He was giving in to his vulnerability.

He felt Eve move past him and he turned to find her standing just inside the living room.

She reached behind herself to unzip her dress and let it fall into a puddle around the white leather Converses she was wearing. She was nude and her body gleamed as if she had rubbed it down with oil.

Lucas gasped and didn't care that it sounded as if it had been pulled from the deepest part of his gut. Eve was a goddess.

"Come," she said, beckoning with her finger before turning to head toward the rear of the condo.

And just like that, he was back on her trail—this time at her invitation.

Lucas reached her in the hall and used one arm around her waist to lift her body against his. She rested the back of her head on one of his shoulders as he kissed her neck and cupped her breasts in his hands. He carried her that way to his owner's suite that lined the rear of the condo. The bed was in the center of the room, and he paused long enough to illuminate the king-sized structure with just the fixture above it—it was like a spotlight.

After he laid her upon the bed and stood at the edge of it, he stepped out of his shorts—he felt she deserved it. She arched her back and gently eased her legs apart as she feasted on his body with eager and appreciative eyes. Boldly, she patted the plump lips of her femininity before opening them to expose her fleshy bud. Their explosive chemistry was stoked.

It had been thirty days.

He was starved for Eve. Not just in his bed, but in his life.

"Marry me," Lucas said fiercely, taking his hard inches in his hands to please himself as she did the same.

She paused. "What?" she asked, her glazed, desire-filled eyes now widened with surprise.

"Marry me, Eve," he repeated.

"Luc," she said with a hesitant smile. "Really?"

"Absolutely," he asserted. "I do not want to go another day without you in my life."

Eve shifted on the bed to stand in the center of it.

He watched the brown beauty in wonder as she walked to reach him. She offered him her fingers to taste her juice.

"Yes, I'll marry you," she said softly as she watched him suck them clean with a deep guttural moan.

Bursting with excitement and trembling with need, Lucas lowered their bodies to the bed and entered her swiftly with one hard thrust. Filling her. Her gasps fueled him as he held her body closely around the waist with both of his arms and suckled one of her breasts in his mouth. With deep kisses and even deeper sighs, they mated with hunger and passion. A mindless and electrifying connection with promises of many more such unions to come. He slow-stroked them to one climax and then another that left them both shivering and coated in sweat as they clung to one another with whispered promises to never let the other go.

One week later

"Time to make it official," Lucas said as he slid the engagement ring on her finger as they stood in the jewelry store on Fifth Avenue.

Eve looked down at the heart-shaped five-carat solitaire on a five-carat band of bead-set diamonds. It was flawless. Beautiful. And obviously costly.

"Don't you like it?" Lucas asked.

Yes!

But she felt that she shouldn't. It was the type of flash she had craved when materialism ruled her life—something she had deliberately stepped away from.

"I do love it," she admitted, looking up at him and smiling at the salesclerk. "But let's do a smaller center stone. I wouldn't want to worry about it while I'm swimming."

Lucas gave her a warm smile. "Smaller?" he asked, sounding amused.

"Yes," she said as she spread her fingers and took in the flawless diamond under the light.

It is beautiful, though.

"Eve," Lucas said.

"Huh?" she said, feeling conflicted because she loved the ring but didn't think that she should anymore.

She forced her eyes from the ring to look up at him.

"It's okay to love it. Keep the ring, just as it is," Lucas insisted. "I'll have it insured, so no worries."

"May I offer a compromise," the salesclerk, Doris, said.

They both looked at the stylish, middle-aged woman dressed in all black.

She offered them a smile and reached inside the glass case to remove another ring in a suede case. "Same design. Total carat weight is six. Three for the heart-shaped center stone and three for the band," she said.

Eve and Lucas shared a look before she removed the ring and set it back on the suede display pad as Lucas took the new ring from Doris.

"Better?" he asked, then took Eve's hand in his own and slid the bauble onto her finger.

"Yes," she said with a smile.

And it was. Just as beautiful. Just as flawless.

It even fit her perfectly without sizing.

"If I could offer a young couple some advice," Doris said with a motherly smile. "Compromise is a huge key to a happy marriage. Give and take...*both* ways. Trust me on this."

They both nodded in agreement.

As Lucas completed the purchase, Eve continued to admire her ring and was still trying to wrap her brain around them being engaged to wed. Doris's advice was timely. There was so much to still decide and discuss.

Where will we live?

What will our lifestyle be?

What will Lucas expect from me as the wife of a Cress brother?

What will I be willing to give up to make him happy?

"Ready?" Lucas asked, sliding his billfold inside the navy blazer he had on, with a matching shirt and denims.

"Yes," Eve said, sliding her hand into the one he offered her as they made their way out of the store and across the sidewalk into their waiting chauffeured SUV.

"I still can't believe it didn't need sizing," Lucas said.

"Me, too," she said.

"Will your father be upset tomorrow to meet me *and* discover we're engaged all at once?" he asked as the driver safely merged the car into the busy weekend afternoon traffic.

"My father will give me the world...if I let him," Eve assured him as she rested her head against his shoulder and gently played with her fingers. "It's my mother you might have to worry about."

"Same for mine," Lucas admitted.

They shared a chuckle before falling into a comfortable silence as they headed back to his condo with plans for them to cook dinner and enjoy her weekend in town. No one knew of their engagement. Neither had been willing to step out of their bubble of bliss, but Lucas had insisted on getting her a ring. Eve had insisted on being there to help select it.

"Let's have an engagement party to make the big announcement," he offered suddenly.

"Maybe a dinner with just family would be nice," she countered.

Lucas chuckled. "Compromise, huh?" he asked.

"Yes!" she stressed, tilting her head up to look at him.

He kissed her.

"Promise me we will always put each other first, Luc," Eve asked, feeling fear that anything but that would happen.

"I promise," Lucas said. "This is just about the life we are building together."

Her smile was hopeful, but as she looked down at the brilliant sparkling ring, it wasn't just Lucas she was worried about. Would marriage to a man like Lucas Cress find her gleefully sliding back into being her former self?

As she remembered her instant love of the bigger ring, Eve had her concerns.

Nine

Two months later

Eve stared at her reflection in the floor-to-ceiling mirror covering one wall of the London bridal salon of Alonuko, the brand of Nigerian designer Oluwagbemisola "Gbemi" Okunlola. It was her final fitting on an express order and Eve felt magical in the strapless beaded gown that fit her body like a second skin, with a detachable overskirt that gave it the right touch of being a bride.

It's divine.

Eve felt poignant.

"Eres hermosa, mi hermosa hija."

In the mirror, she locked eyes with her father and found his glassy with emotion, after he'd just told her that his gorgeous daughter was beautiful. She gave him an indulging smile when he raised his thick-framed glasses and swiped away a tear before it could fall. Beside him on the cream sofa were her mother, Joan, and Lucas's parents, Nicolette and Phillip Senior.

They had all traveled to London on the private jet for the final fitting of her gown.

"When I saw the dress the designer did for Danielle Brooks it was a moment. I knew she was the designer for your dress.," Joan said, taking a sip of the prosecco in her flute. She rose and crossed the patterned hardwood floor to stand beside Eve. "*This* is a moment. Just stunning."

"Danielle Brooks? The actress?" Nicolette asked with her French accent.

"I have a picture of it. It is so delicious," Joan said, reaching into her crocodile tote to remove her phone.

Nicolette, in a turquoise suit, rose and joined Joan. "Yes, let's see," she said. "Perhaps I will have to design an evening gown for me."

Marco and Phillip Senior shared a bemused look, both doting husbands to their wives.

"Here it is," Joan said.

Nicolette gasped. "The way the sheer fabric matches her deep brown complexion!" she said, using her fingertips to enlarge the photo.

"And this is a stunner," Joan said, circling Eve on the round platform she stood on.

"It really is beautiful, Eve," Suzi said.

Eve shifted her eyes to look at her best friend in the mirror. Suzi was sitting on a separate club chair and Eve was so grateful she was there. "But?" she said, wanting Suzi to be as honest with her as she always was.

Joan, Marco, Nicolette, Phillip Senior and the bridal consultant all turned to stare at Suzi, who gave them a nervous smile. "But…it's so glamorous for a wedding by the lake," she said.

"Outside in the grass?" the bridal consultant asked.

"The lake? What lake?" Joan asked, swiveling to look up at Eve on the platform. "By your house in *East Patchogue*?"

Marco just looked confused.

Eve turned to face her friend. "With it being a December wedding because Lucas is insisting on getting married before the end of the year, everyone thought it would be more comfortable inside…at the Plaza," she added.

"Oh! I didn't know, Eve," she said, rising to her feet and crossing the floor to reach her. "When you first told me you were engaged you kept talking about a small wedding by the lake. I didn't realize things had changed, I'm sorry."

"Yes, lots of things have…changed," Eve admitted, pressing a hand to her belly as it felt a bit uneasy.

Nicolette and Joan had met and aligned to ensure the only daughter of the Villars and the favorite son of the Cress family had a grand wedding. And she could not deny that every bit of it would be a showpiece. She loved the choices being made.

Suzi took her other hand in both of hers. "Eve, it's your wedding day. Enjoy it," she enthused.

Eve looked over her shoulder at herself in the dress.

I am marrying Lucas Cress.

The thought warmed her and her smile became more genuine, but her hand remained on her flat belly.

"I really think you should get hair extensions and then have it pinned up for the veil," Joan said, tilting her head to the side as she studied her daughter.

Eve shook her head. "Lucas loves my hair in waves and I have already purchased a rhinestone headband," she said.

"But—"

"No *buts*," Eve said, releasing Suzi's hands to turn to her mother. "I have made many concessions for this wedding. The few times I insist on something, please respect it, Mama."

"But—"

"Es su boda, esposa. Déjalo ser," Marco said, telling his wife that it was Eve's wedding and to let her be. He rose to cross over to press a kiss to his wife's cheek. "Be thankful she is giving *you* the wedding *you* want, Joan."

"Same for you, Nicolette," Phillip Senior added.

"I didn't say anything," she said, eyeing him.

"It's written all over your face," he told her.

Eve was thankful for her father and her future father-in-law. "I think we are set," she said to the consultant. "We'll take it with us."

Joan and Nicolette both looked prepared to protest, but thankfully, neither said anything.

As the bridal consultant helped her down off the pedestal and toward one of the fittings, Eve looked back over her shoulder. "If someone could call Lucas and let him know we should be headed back to the hotel soon," she said. "I think he wants to grab lunch before we fly home."

"Of course, we'll go to CRESS VII," Nicolette said,

speaking of their restaurant in the Westminster section of London, as she reached for her phone.

"Of course," Phillip Senior agreed.

In the dressing room, Eve continued to study her reflection. It was exactly the dress she would have chosen years ago. "I am not her anymore," she whispered to her reflection.

"Did you say something?" the consultant asked.

"Just reminding myself of something important," she said.

Two weeks later

November in New York was brutally cold.

As Lucas looked at Eve standing on his private balcony wearing just a bulky sweater with a pair of his sweatpants, he wondered if she even felt the chill as she stared out into the distance at the Hudson River.

What's on her mind?

He grabbed the blanket draped over the corner of his sectional sofa, but paused as she looked down at her wedding ring for the longest time before looking back out at the view of the river. The doors were closed but he could tell she'd just released a sigh by the slow rise and fall of her shoulders. When the screen of her cell phone lit up and her hand gripped the device, he *knew*.

It was the pressure of both their mothers about the wedding that was weighing down on her.

Lucas reached for his phone on the edge of the leather steam trunk used as a side table. He called her phone and looked on as she looked down at the screen and then turned to him with a curious expression. "Answer," he said while motioning for her pick up.

"Yes, Luc," she said into the phone as they stared at one another through the glass of the French doors.

"No wedding plans today. No phone calls from our mothers or the wedding planner," he said. "None of that."

Eve smiled. "Tell them that," she said.

"I can and I will," he promised her.

She bit her bottom lips as she glanced down at her slipper-covered feet before looking back at him.

The simple move made every nerve ending in his body jolt to life.

"Can we go to my house this weekend?" she asked.

And in her eyes, he saw her desperation.

"I just need to reconnect to me," she said. "I'm feeling a little lost in all this. You know?"

Without another word, Lucas ended the call, dropped the blanket, and retrieved their winter coats before walking over to the French door to hold her shearling coat out for her. "Let's go," he said.

She turned to slip each arm into the coat and then leaned back against him as he wrapped his arms around. "Thank you. I know I said we would stay in the city this weekend, but I just want to go home," she explained as they entered the condo. "My home. I guess. I don't know. What are we going to do about that? The wedding is in a month, and we still haven't agreed—"

"Or compromised," he interjected.

Neither wanted to move to the other's home full-time.

"Okay, we haven't compromised on where we will live," she said with a nod. "But we have to decide. We can't start our marriage going back and forth."

"Why not?" he asked.

Eve eyed him as he grabbed his keys from the metal table in the foyer before they stepped out into the hall. "Huh?"

"I know I requested for the wedding to happen before the end of the year—"

"Requested?" Eve drawled. "That's putting it lightly. It's the one thing you insisted on. You agreed to wear whatever, have it wherever and do whatever as long as you were married before the New Year."

They stepped onto the elevator together.

Lucas chuckled as he pressed the button for the parking level in his black full-length shearling leather coat. "I'm very goal-oriented and that was a goal," he said, smiling at her as she leaned against the wall of the elevator opposite him.

"Really?" she asked with a bemused look.

He shrugged.

"Okay, then set a goal to find our home in a place where we both are comfortable and that we both could afford alone without the other," she said. "Can you do that?"

The elevator slid to a slow stop before the doors opened.

"Impossible, because that limits me because I can afford…more," he said delicately.

"Shade!" Eve exclaimed with a shocked expression as she playfully pushed his arm.

"I'm not throwing a shady comment," he said as they walked toward his two parking spots. "I am only speaking fact."

"You are bougie, Lucas Maël Cress," Eve said, stopping in her track.

"Full name, though?" he asked as he paused as well.

"You love designer, designer, designer," she said.

"Okay," he agreed.

"You have to have the best of the best...of the best," she added.

"Again. O-kay," Lucas said.

Eve walked away from him and paced a few steps before she returned, pulling her keys from the pocket of her coat. "Let's take my car," she said, very tongue-in-cheek.

Lucas looked over at it and then at his luxury vehicle. "Um...see, it's winter in New York," he said.

"I have heat," she said, walking over to unlock the driver's-side door.

"Not in the seats, though," he added, using the fob to unlock all the doors of his vehicle.

Eve covered her mouth so he wouldn't see her laugh. "Prove you are not bougie, Luc," she said. "Prove that my lifestyle is not beneath you."

He twisted his mouth as he frowned. Several times he opened his mouth but no words emerged. "Is this a test?" he asked.

"No. It's not," she said.

"Then I'd really rather take *my* whip," he said.

She threw her hands up in exasperation. "Exactly!" she exclaimed, closing the door and swiveling to open the passenger door of the Bentley. "Wait! No."

Lucas paused in climbing inside the SUV. "What?"

"I always cave," she said, looking at him across the hood. "I always give in. Not this time."

He looked on as she unlocked her car door again.

"If my car isn't good enough, then my house isn't good enough, and maybe I'm not good enough for you," she snapped. The she climbed inside her car and started it before Lucas could take a step out of the spot where he was standing.

"Eve," he said, although he knew she couldn't hear him. She reversed out of the spot and pulled away.

"What the hell?" he exclaimed as he got in his vehicle.

Lucas didn't speed. He didn't try to keep up with her. He didn't even call her phone. When he pulled into the driveway in front of her house, Eve was still sitting behind the wheel. He exited to come over and open her car door. She looked up at him.

"You good?" he asked.

She nodded.

He extended his hand and she took it. Together they climbed the stairs onto the porch.

"Hey," he said before she could unlock the front door. He touched her chin and raised her head so that their eyes met. "Our home is wherever we are. Wherever you are I am, wherever I am you are."

"Yeah. Yes," she agreed. "But promise me we will honestly try to compromise."

"I promise," he said before bending to lift her in his arms to carry her inside.

Three weeks later

Eve eyed the dress hanging on her side of the closet that Lucas had made room for her to leave some clothing at his house. "Luc?" she called out to him.

He appeared in the doorway carrying an apple.

"Yes?" he said before taking a bite of the fruit with a loud crunch.

"What this?" she asked, taking in the strapless dress with sheer 3D butterfly embroidery.

"I thought you could wear it tonight," he said, leaning in the doorway.

"Babe, it's freezing outside," Eve said, walking over to lightly touch one of the colorful butterflies atop a sheer back bodice.

"True, but Sean and Montgomery have heat," he said. "Wait. We're not about to argue about heat again, are we?"

Eve chuckled. "No, we're not, but we are going to compromise."

"About?" he asked before taking another large bite.

"This is too much for dinner at your brother's…but I think it's perfect for our rehearsal dinner," she said, reaching up to take down the dress to hold up to her body. She caught sight of the designer and her eyes widened. There was a time she would have known the designer and the season with one look—she also never *used to* worry about the price. "How much was this?"

Lucas shook his head. "I'm not stepping into that trap. It's a surefire argument and I have plans for us when we get back home later tonight," he told her. "I refuse to give you a reason to climb in bed in full gear with your back to me all night long laying stiff as a statue."

"Luc?" she said, walking over to him. "How much?"

"Look. I was on Fifth Avenue. I saw it in a window and thought of you. I want you to have it. To wear it. To like it. Do you?" he asked.

"I love it," Eve admitted, coming to stand in front of him. *"But—"*

"Compromise," Lucas reminded her. "I don't want to spoil you, because you won't let me, but you have to let me do nice things for you sometimes, Eve. The goodness of gifts is not just receiving them, but giving them, too."

She looked back at the dress. "How do you always seem to pick something I can't help *but* love?" she asked as her gaze lingered on it.

"Guess it just means we're a perfect match."

Eve faced him. "You think?" she asked, wrapping her arms around his waist and resting her forehead against his chest in the red T-shirt he had on.

"Definitely," he assured her.

"Good thing we're getting married next week," she said, looking up at him.

"I'm ready," he told her with a serious look in his eyes.

"I never imagined attending my high-school reunion would lead to this," Eve admitted.

Lucas chuckled. "Me, either," he said.

"You know," Eve said, lifting his T-shirt and pressing kisses to his chest, "we have enough time for a quickie before heading out."

Lucas looked down at her as she began to slowly lower herself before him. He stopped her. "If we go down that road, we'll miss the dinner altogether," he told her.

She pouted in disappointment.

They shared a long look ripe with sexy possibilities, then moved apart from each other with reluctance.

"Later?" Lucas asked.

"Definitely," Eve agreed.

That subtle dance of temptation continued as they got ready. Visions of the other in the shower. Touches. Long looks. Shakes of heads in regret. Teasing smiles.

Even as Lucas drove them through the streets of Manhattan, they lightly played with each other's fingers or reached to stroke each other's cheek. They never lost contact with each other. Touch. A connection.

It seemed to fuel them both. A subtle energy that was alive and well between them.

Eve felt warm and comforted by it.

She had just looked away from savoring Lucas's profile when she noticed the small town they were entering. "Passion Grove, New Jersey?" she said, reading the well-lit bronze sign declaring the name of the town they were entering. She took note of the atmosphere that was more relaxed than the hustle, bustle and sometimes chaos of Manhattan. It was a small town, but it was clear from the landscape and the mansions lining the street that there was affluence. Very much so.

"Montgomery's hometown," Lucas explained as they soon drove down a quaint Main Street lined with businesses with matching black canopies. "They live in her grandparents' home that she inherited. Sean completely renovated it for her without her knowing and now they live quite happily here."

"Without her knowing!" Eve exclaimed.

"Yes. Montgomery will gladly tell you all about causally mentioning plans she had to renovate the house to Sean and he remembered every detail and delivered," he said, sounding proud of his older brother and best friend.

Eve eyed Lucas as he spoke.

"I never thought my 'Sean Cress,' the partying playboy—"

"The Star," she interrupted, remembering the roles they all played in their family dynamic.

"Right," Lucas agreed with a nod as he turned down a tree-lined, brick-paved street that was named after flowers. "Well, I never thought he would settle down, especially in a small town, but I think Passion Grove is a nice..."

"Compromise," they said in unison, sharing a look.

"Wait a sec," Eve said, reaching for her cell phone to check the distance between East Patchogue and Passion Grove. "Just under two hours. Not too much more than Manhattan."

"And Sean commutes every day into Manhattan," Lucas said, reaching with his free hand to grab hers. He rubbed his thumb against her engagement ring.

Eve lowered the window. "Listen to how quiet it is," she said, not even minding the crisp cold weather as she stuck her head out the window.

Her eyes widened as they passed long driveways— some gated—leading to beautifully landscaped mansions. Some were even sprawling megamansions. All were beautiful.

"Eve," Lucas exclaimed, reaching with his right hand to ease her back in the car to raise the window.

She laughed. "It is cold," she said, leaning close to the heating vent.

Luke suddenly did a U-turn.

"You lost?" she asked, settling back in her seat as she crossed her ankles.

"I hope not," he said, continuing to slowly drive the vehicle forward. "There's something I want you to see."

Eve's curiosity was piqued. "Okay," she said slowly, appreciating the beauty of the large pots on each street corner filled with plants or colorful perennial flowers.

Soon he was driving the vehicle to a stop with the bright lights displayed against a frozen lake with several people skating atop it. "From what Montgomery told me, although a lot of the townspeople are wealthy, there is a determined effort to keep the charm of a small town, including no apartment or office buildings, no public transportation goes through the town, low population, familiarity, community events and stuff like that," he said, shifting his gaze from the lake to look at her. "The lake is heart-shaped. It's the reason they named the town Passion Grove."

"No," she gasped. "For real. Awww."

"Could you live here?" Lucas asked, his eyes searching hers.

Bzzzz.

Her phone lit up on her lap. She glanced down. "It's Suzi. I'll call her back," she said.

"Is this our compromise?" he continued, still staring at her intently.

Eve played with her engagement ring as she looked at a couple ice-skating. "I guess I only need to be close to the Hamptons during the summer season for work and I could rely on Suzi and my team more and commute when I need to," she said.

Lucas leaned closer to press a kiss on her cheek, then settled back in the driver's seat.

"Can I think about it?" Eve asked.

Lucas froze.

"It's a major decision, Luc. I just want to be sure," she contended, fighting not to get lost or not be seen in the relationship and upcoming marriage.

Any more than I already have.

"Okay," he said, giving her a smile before steering them around the circular drive and back out to the street.

He drove in silence.

Their subtle flirtation had ended.

Several times, Eve glanced over at him and found his handsome face solemn. She was curious about his thoughts but left him to them. When he made another turn onto Belladonna Lane, Eve noticed the homes suddenly were smaller in size, but still grand and beautiful. Not mansions. Not ostentatious.

Soon he was turning up the curved driveway to a two-story home of approximately three thousand square feet. "This is still Passion Grove, right?" she asked.

"It should be," Lucas said, pulling to a stop next to a Jaguar and large SUV. He left the car to come around it and open her door.

"This is very nice," she said as she wrapped her arm around his.

"I'm starving," he told her as they made their way up to the front door and he rang the doorbell.

"And I need champagne," she said, looking up at him coquettishly.

"Really? You don't drink, remember?" Lucas said.

"Yes, but we have to celebrate," she said. "We're moving to Passion Grove."

The front door opened.

Lucas and Eve turned from each other to find Sean, Montgomery and little Morgan all in their winter coats.

"Change of plans," Sean said as Montgomery lifted Morgan onto her hip. "Jillian and Cole are at the hospital. The twins are coming."

Lucas's smile was broad. "We're right behind you," he said without hesitation, holding Eve's hand as he guided her back to his SUV.

"Excited?" Eve asked in amusement as he held the passenger door for her.

"At a new niece and nephew? Always," he told her. "Uncle Luc loves the kids."

Eve laughed as he hurried around the car to climb into the driver's seat.

One week later

"Do you need anything?"

Eve turned away from the window of her bridal suite to look at her mother, and then Nicolette. "Suzi," she snapped, and then became contrite and offered them a smile. "She's running late. She's the only person I wanted in the wedding and she's *not* here."

"She called and said she was tied up in traffic," Joan said. "The wedding is not for another hour, Eve."

Eve smoothed her hands down the front of the sheer white robe she was wearing over her lace corset and thong, before she claimed her seat in front of the mirror to study the soft waves of her hair and the rhinestone headpiece that framed her face. It brought emphasis to her smoky eyes. "I think you were right, Nicolette, that delicate jewelry was better," she said, pressing her nude almond-shaped nails to the simple but elegant diamond studs she had on. "With the beaded gown and the head-dress, it could have been too busy."

Knock, knock.

Eve didn't miss the look Joan and Nicolette shared in their evening gowns in shades of deep purple. She turned on the seat to face the door as her mother moved over to open it. She bit away at her lipstick, feeling anxious.

Suzi rushed in, dressed in sweats and carrying her garment bag over her arm. "Okay, I'm here," she said, crossing the room to hang the bag on the closet door. "The traffic was—"

"Unavoidable," Eve said.

Suzi looked taken aback. "No. No, it wasn't, Eve," she said. "I got here as soon as I could."

Eve arched a well-shaped eyebrow as she eyed her best friend. "No. I asked you to stay last night after the rehearsal and that would have avoided *this*," she said coldly.

"Eve," Joan said in gentle reproach.

Suzi looked confused. "What?" she asked, taking a step toward Eve with a smile.

Eve jumped to her feet in her rhinestone-covered ballet-style slippers. "You're supposed to be helping me," she screamed, pointing at herself. "It's my wedding. My day. What good are you as my *attendant* if you're not here."

Suzi gasped and her big eyes filled with tears. "I'm not your attendant, I'm your friend," she said softly.

"Right not I'm not sure you're either one!" she shrieked at her, feeling her anger and annoyance fully claim her.

"Eve!" her mother snapped sharply, stepping into her path. "Enough!"

She blinked rapidly as her stormy eyes met her mother's.

Eve's heart pounded as she looked at Suzi's hurt, Nicolette's confusion and her mother's concern. She pressed her hands to her mouth and felt the sheer lip gloss stick to them. Her eyes darted about the room as she released a shaky breath—she was ashamed of her behavior.

The luxury surroundings.

Her glamorous dress and expensive accessories.

The tray of treats made with either Iranian Beluga caviar or white truffles.

The nearly empty bottle of vintage champagne she had sipped all morning.

And then down at her engagement ring.

All of the excess and indulgence.

She whirled, causing her robe to dramatically rise, as she stared at her reflection. Her own tears rose because what she saw was everything she'd fought so very hard to leave behind. She gasped and shook her head, wishing she could deny the truth. "No," she said softly.

"Eve, Hank is battling cancer," Suzi said from behind her.

Joan stepped out of the way.

Eve eyed Suzi in the mirror. "What?" she asked, feeling weakened.

"Mon Dieu!" Nicolette said.

"I didn't want to ruin your happiness," Suzi said. "I'm sorry if you think you didn't matter to me. You know better than that…or you did."

Eve dropped to the seat and lowered her head. Her tears welled and blurred her vision—she couldn't even see her engagement ring. The grief and guilt came next, in waves that engulfed her. She tilted her head back with her eyes closed and felt her body sway as she remembered the moments of her life with Aaron leading up to the wreck.

And I'm repeating the same cycle. Where will it end this time?

"Oh, Eve," Joan moaned.

Soon, she felt her mother's arms around her and the scent of her perfume. Eve leaned into her as she released a tortured cry.

"Eve, please," Nicolette begged. "Calm down."

But she was inconsolable.

"Eve, don't ruin your makeup," Suzi added. "It's your wedding day."

She shook her head as she removed the ring and dropped it on the table.

"I'm going to get Lucas," Nicolette said with urgency.

Eve's body was racked with her tears. "I'm sorry, Suzi," she whispered. "I am so sorry. Please believe me."

Suzi kneeled in front of her and swiped at her tears with tissues. "Eve, it was just a misunderstanding. There's nothing to forgive. Don't do this to yourself. Not again," she implored.

"Yes, Eve, please," her mother begged.

Her tears continued relentlessly. "I can't do this," she said looking from her mother to her friend. "I just can't marry Lucas."

"Perhaps you should talk to me."

Her heart slammed against her chest at the sound of Lucas's deep voice.

Eve looked over at him. He was devastatingly handsome in his tailored tuxedo as he stood in the open doorway with her father and his parents behind him. She could not look away from him.

"Perhaps we should leave them alone," Marco said.

And they all did, closing the door behind them.

Lucas walked over to her. His face was unreadable. He said nothing but he looked at her engagement ring on the table.

"This is about me. Not you," she began.

He frowned a bit as he crossed his arms over his chest.

"Over the weeks there were many things I accepted because of wanting to please you…at first. But soon I just enjoyed it all," she said, standing in front of him to grasp at his arms. "And I changed, Luc. I threw away all of the work I did to change. I went right back to that person who was cruel and demanding."

"No one—not even God—expects perfection, Eve," he said. "I damn sure don't."

She shook her head and removed her hands from him to swipe at her tears. "I don't want to be a part of this world—your world, Luc," she said. "It changes me."

She looked up at him just as he closed his eyes and shook his head.

"You're right—this isn't about me," he said, walking away from her to pace in front of the bed. "This is about the ghost of Aaron lingering between us!"

She flinched at his anger.

"You rather punish yourself—and me—for a death *he* caused," Lucas snapped, his eyes fiery.

"I played a role, Luc," she shouted.

"And you still are, by pretending you are alone in the world, not the only daughter—and sole heir—of wealthy parents who also love you very much," he said. "What are you going to do? Give away everything you will one day inherit because you feel you have something to prove? To who, Eve?"

"Myself," she replied.

His face was pensive as he looked down at the floor for a long time.

She walked over to him.

He looked up at her. "You know, if you love him so much that you *exist* as if you wish you had died with him then maybe *I* can't marry *you*," he said.

Eve paused in her steps. "I love you," she insisted.

"Then why is that the first time you've said it?" he asked.

She looked confused. "Neither have you," she countered.

"I proposed!" he retorted with intensity lining his face.

"And I accepted!"

Lucas released a bitter chuckle. "Then why is your ring over there?" he asked, pointing at the table behind her.

Eve crossed her arms over her chest to hold herself.

"Exactly," he snapped. He waved his hand at her dismissively as he turned away from her.

"This is about the death of who I was, Luc. Please understand," she said.

He looked over at her. "And if I marry someone else?" he asked.

That stung. Her face filled with incredulity. "It's always been about that damn deadline, huh?" she asked.

"And if I marry someone else?" he repeated.

"Then I can only hope she loves you as much as I do."

His face hardened and his eyes burned with emotion. With one last look at her, Lucas turned and walked out of the hotel suite.

Eve sank to the floor and let it give her some support, because she had never felt so alone.

Ten

Three months later

"This is ridiculous, man."

From the center of the king-sized bed in his old suite back at his parents' townhouse, Lucas cast his brother Sean a quick glance before fixing his stare back on the television above the fireplace.

"At least open a damn window!" Phillip Junior snapped.

Lucas took another look, and just noticed that Sean was not alone. All five of his brothers stood there looking at him with a variety of expressions. He reached in the torn open bag on his bed for a chip as he glanced at each one.

Lincoln looked confused.

Phillip Junior was disgusted.

Sean was annoyed.

Gabriel was concerned.

Coleman was amused.

"What?" Lucas asked, scratching an itch in his exposed and slightly rounded belly in the T-shirt he was wearing with cut-off sweatpants.

"Listen, I know your heart is broken but the clipper and the shower are not," Coleman said.

Lucas rubbed his beard. "I'm trying a new look," he said, then tossed a goober into his mouth.

Sean threw up his hands in exasperation and stalked away across the suite to the sitting area. "How about some new clothes?" Gabriel gently suggested.

"I'm fine," Lucas lied.

"No," Lincoln said with his thick British accent as he shook his head. "Not at *all,* mate.

In the three months since he and Eve had wasted an ungodly amount of money on a wedding that did not happen, Lucas had plenty of time to think. He had concluded that Eve Villar was the beautiful chaos his brother Coleman had labeled her as in high school.

Same old Eve.

In the end, I still wasn't good enough for her.

Lucas reached for another handful of chips and devoured them all in one bite.

"Let me help you," Phillip Junior said, reaching across Lucas's body to grab the bag of chips.

Lucas reached out for them, but Phillip stepped back as he balled up the bag and all of the chips inside. "Really, dude?" he asked, even as he reached for a snack cake.

Knock, knock.

All the men looked to the door as it slowly opened, and Nicolette entered carrying a tray. They all either shook their heads or threw up their hands at her appearance.

"What?" Nicolette asked. "It's just a little lunch for my son."

"Qu'y a-t-il au menu aujourd'hui, Maman?" Lucas asked of the menu for the day.

"Grilled cheese on freshly made brioche and three-cheese, onion and cheese soup—your favorite, and lavender *crème brûlée* for dessert," she said, moving past her bewildered sons to set the tray on Lucas's lap.

"You made that yourself, didn't you?" Coleman said in an accusatory tone.

The family had a private chef because their schedules were all too busy to cook for themselves.

"Of course," Nicolette said, unfolding a linen napkin and tucking it into the rim of Lucas's shirt. "Anything for my baby boy. He's had his heart broken and he deserves to be cherished right now."

"Merci beaucoup," Lucas said.

Nearly every Cress brother tilted their head to the side to watch as Nicolette sat on the edge of the bed and picked up the spoon as if to feed him.

"Absolutely not!" Gabriel, normally the more sedate of the brothers, exclaimed. He took a step forward to take the spoon from his mother and dropped it on the tray with a clang. Next, he picked up the tray.

Both Lucas and Nicolette released wails of protest.

Sean clapped his hands with intensity. "You are the weakest link, *Maman*," he told her.

"What?" she gasped, pressing a hand to her chest and flashing her massive diamond ring.

"You have helped him pack on half the weight it took him years to lose," Lincoln added.

Coleman gently guided their mother to her feet and took the tray from Gabriel to ease into her hands before steering her to the carved door of the suite.

"How dare you!" Nicolette exclaimed, stomping her foot—other the other side of the door frame.

"Oh, we dare. Or next, you'll try to breastfeed him, *Maman*," Coleman told her, before gently closing the door in her face and locking the door.

The brothers all surrounded the bed.

He fought the urge to reach for one of the dozen or more snack cakes that littered the unmade bed. "I'm feeling judged, and body-shamed," he told them.

He watched them all share looks.

"Fine. I got this one," Gabriel said. "The issue is not being a larger man, Lucas. It's the speed with which you did and that it's clear you are feeding your emotions with food—which is not healthy—and should not be ignored anymore."

"You're acting like I'm ready for that TV show *My 600-lb Life*," he said with attitude.

"We're afraid if we don't step in we will have to roll you out," Coleman drawled.

"Cole," Lincoln reprimanded him sharply.

Lucas sat up straighter in bed and adjusted his shirt over his stomach. He knew his brothers were not wrong. He had not exercised at all during the last ninety days and had slid right back to his old eating habits. His heartbreak had led to a need for a belly full. His heartbreak had led to a need for a full belly. "She didn't want me big or little," he admitted out loud and then regretted the show of vulnerability.

"Dude," Coleman said.

"Nope," Phillip asserted. "Not you. Not yet."

Coleman looked offended, but pressed his lips closed, turned and walked a few steps from the bed.

"I got it," Lincoln said. "It seems more has resurfaced than just the weight. The insecurity is there and possibly never left, and we all say this with love, little brother, you got to heal that wound."

The other brothers nodded or spoke their agreement.

"And that has nothing to do with Eve or anyone else," Phillip Junior added.

Lucas released a heavy breath.

Coleman turned around. "Right, it's—"

"It's not your moment," Gabriel drawled.

"Why am I here?" Coleman muttered under his breath.

"She told you the reason she felt she couldn't marry you—and you took it as she judged you when it seems she's judging herself," Lincoln said. "But that's up to her family to get through to her."

"I'm sure she's just fine," Lucas said, still upset with her.

"You're not," Sean said, with the most concern in his eyes. "Depression is real. Do you need to talk to someone? A professional."

"It's that bad, huh?" Lucas asked.

Sean was the most fun and carefree of all the brothers. If *he* was worried, then there was something to be worried about.

THE MARRIAGE DEADLINE

"Cole," the brothers all said in unison.

He splayed his hands, then cleared his throat, as if relishing his moment to finally contribute.

Lucas actually bit back a smile—perhaps his first in months.

"Three questions," Coleman began.

Lucas felt unsure because this particular brother had some snark that often straddled the line between being funny and rude.

"Do you love her?" Coleman asked.

All of his brothers eyed him and Lucas rose from the bed to go and stand in the mirror above the eight-drawer dresser that matched the slate-gray-and-blue decor. He looked at himself and truly saw the changes. The unruly appearance. The slight weight gain. The dark circles around his eyes from lack of sleep, because he'd been so full of anger.

And hurt.

And where there was hurt, there was love.

"Eve Villar has and will always be a thorn in my ass," he said, rubbing his hand over his full but unkempt beard that had a sandy color because of their mother's blond hair.

"Do you love her?" Coleman repeated.

In the background of the mirror, all his brothers watched him carefully.

"Yeah," he admitted. "Still dumb for her, huh?"

"Does she love you?" Coleman asked.

"Then I can only hope she loves you as much as I do."

Lucas frowned, hating that he still felt so connected and affected by her that the hurt in her eyes the day of their failed wedding sent a pang through him that radiated. In it was his own hurt and disappointment because Eve had made a choice, and it was not him. "Not enough," he finally said.

"Do you want her back?" Coleman continued.

Lucas shook his head. "No more chaos for me," he said.

"Then it's time to get your life off pause, little brother," Coleman said, coming to stand beside him to rub the back of his head affectionately. "You can't live in limbo forever. You deserve more than that and you have to know it."

Lucas shook his head in understanding but lowered his head.

A hand lightly grasped his chin and raised his head. It was Sean. *Chin up*, his eyes said.

Lucas nodded to assure him.

"Shower, shave and we'll all go out to dinner," Lincoln said. "The housekeeper is dying to get in here and clean up."

"Poor Felice," Phillip drawled as he looked at what could be considered a pigsty.

They all chuckled.

"I'm going home," Lucas said, knowing it was time.

"Thank God, before *the* Nicolette Lavoie-Cress tries to push her big baby back into the womb," Coleman said.

The men all laughed at that.

Lucas ran his fingers through his afro of curls, which also had sandy tips. "Call for a barber to come in," he said before he pulled his T-shirt over his head.

"I'm on it," Gabriel said, pulling his phone from the pocket of his khaki shorts.

Lucas jerked down his sweatpants.

"Hey!" all his brothers roared in unison before turning their backs on him.

Lucas chuckled as he removed the sweatpants and kicked them away before, then continued across the suite nude as the day he'd officially become their baby brother. In the en suite bathroom, he started the shower. He could still clearly hear his brothers talking.

"Cole, you did pretty good there," Gabriel said. "With you anything is possible and you chose the high road, little brother."

"That is called growth and maturity, fellas," Coleman said.

"Shocked me," Phillip Junior added.

"Jillian has done wonders our parents could not with the rebel," Sean mused.

"The ways of a woman," Lincoln added.

"I *started* to tell him to find something to get under so he could get over Eve," Coleman said.

His brothers all groaned.

Lucas chuckled before he stepped inside the shower and let the steam envelop him.

One week later

Eve pushed her feet against the bottom of the pool and rode up through the water like a rocket. Her swim cap with her Aquatic Safety Solutions logo protected her long weave. She swiped her eyes with her fingertips before she swam the length of the pool one last time before climbing the stairs out of it.

She was gearing up for the start of a new busy summer season in the Hamptons by enjoying as many as she could at the public swimming pool in East Patchogue. The irony of being a lifeguard was she spent most of her time beside the pool and not in it.

"Thanks, Jim," she called up to the twenty-something blond lifeguard of the beach club who also worked for her during the summer.

"Get home safe," he called behind her.

With one more wave of her hand, she grabbed her towel from atop her duffel bag and wrapped it around her waist, then eased on her swim slippers to make her way to the locker room. With her swimming cap still on, she quickly showered the chlorine from her body before leaving the frosted shower stall to walk to her locker to get dressed. She removed the swim cap and raked her short, almond-shaped nails through the beach waves of the long hair that was past her back.

I wonder if Luc would like my hair.

And then she paused and closed her eyes as her shoulders slumped and she lowered her head.

When will I stop thinking of him?

With a closed fist, she lightly banged it against the door of her locker.

When will I stop loving him?

She took a deep breath that she hoped could relieve her sadness. Because she had to get over Lucas.

I've got to.

They could never be.

After taking a few more deep breaths, Eve finished

dressing in a jean jacket over a white T-shirt dress with navy leather Converses. She grabbed her duffel bag and made her way out of the locker room, then out of the building to her car. She played music as she drove the short distance home. As she pulled up to her house, she spotted her parents' silver Porsche Panamera.

Visits from them were a rarity.

They were the type of New Yorkers to see the Hamptons in the summer. They preferred the faster pace of the city. Most of the time she made the trip to visit them over the years.

She parked on the driveway behind their car and pulled her duffel bag as she exited her vehicle. As she looked out the window to find the vehicle empty, she frowned in surprise and hurried up the rest of the flower-lined drive, the steps and across the porch to open the front door.

"Stay strong, Marco," her mother said.

"I will, Joan," her father replied.

Their voices came from the kitchen. Eve set her bag on the floor and held her keys in her grip as she made her way to join them. "Hello," she said.

Both turned to smile at her in welcome.

Both were wearing jeans and button-up shirts—very casual for them.

She moved to hug her mother, who was pouring herself a cup of coffee she must have prepared, then she moved to the other side of the counter to wrap her arms around her father and squeeze him tightly. She closed her eyes and allowed herself to be transported back to childhood by the familiar scents of cigars and cologne.

"Look, Marco, she remembers us," Joan said.

With the side of her face still pressed to her father's barrel chest, with his hand warmly patting her back, Eve looked over at her mother to find an indulging smile on her face. "I know I haven't been to see you," she said, releasing her teddy bear of a father with reluctance, then removing her jacket. "I've just been—"

"Running," Joan interrupted. "And this time, my beautiful daughter, we are not letting it ride."

Eve's mouth fell open—she was confused.

Joan gave her husband a meaningful stare over the rim of her coffee cup.

Eve looked over at him.

Marco shifted his stance. "Eve, after Aaron's death your mother and I gave you the room to do whatever you needed to feel better," he said, removing his glasses to wipe his eyes before he put them back on. "The trust fund. Moving to East Patchogue. Barely visiting. Damn near cutting us out of your life, *mi hija.*"

Lucas's words resurfaced.

You rather punish yourself—and me—for a death he *caused.*

Had her parents felt punished?

She remained silent and let them speak their piece because they had given her plenty of time and space to seek her own.

"And now that you have walked away from Lucas, you're doing the same thing," Joan said. "We've barely seen you twice since you called off the wedding."

Eve nodded and jangled her keys in her hand.

"Mi Hija," Marco said.

Eve looked up at her father.

"We're not handling grief in the same way as a family," he said, with lots of compassion but firmness. "I have been so intent on giving you the world, that I accept I—"

"We," Joan pressed.

He gave his wife the hint of a grateful smile. *"We* left you alone to figure out a lot of the world," he said.

"And how to handle loss," Joan said. "We didn't realize until the day you were supposed to get married that in the distance between us that we allowed you had not properly healed from Aaron's death."

Aaron's death.

Aaron's death.

Aaron's death.

She winced as the accident replayed in her head. Their screams blended with the squeals of tires and the eventual crush of metal on metal. She wrapped her arms around herself. Tightly. Fighting to console her. To forget. To push it out of the forefront of her thoughts. Her head hung so very low.

"We're *right* here, Eve," her mother said, impassioned.

"Just look up, *mi hija*," Marco implored her.

She heard them but she was haunted by the memories of the excruciating pain of her physical recovery as she continued to struggle with the emotional one.

"And you still are, by pretending you are alone in the world, not the only daughter—and sole heir—of wealthy parents who also love you very much."

As Lucas's words replayed, she raised her head and looked to find her parents standing there, their faces emotional, but seemingly determined for Eve to *allow* them to help. To see them waiting to help—just as they had always been.

With tears, she took a step forward and they both

met her halfway. She could feel their relief as they both wrapped an arm around her. She felt some of the weakness leave her legs as she accepted their love and their strength. For both of her losses. Aaron and Lucas.

In time, Joan eased away. "I'm gonna make some tea for you," she said.

"Come," her father said as he steered her to the living room to settle her on the white linen sofa with oversized navy pillows suited to the coastal design of her home.

Eve kicked off her sneakers and reached for the striped blanket folded over the arm to cover her feet. "I'm okay," she said. "Thanks for coming to check on me."

"We're staying all weekend, *mi hija*," Marco said over his shoulder. "I'm making shrimp-and-pork empanadas, black beans and rice, and coleslaw."

Her mother brought in a cup of tea from the kitchen. "Lavender and lemon tea," Joan said, then kicked off her shoes and curled up into the oversized rattan club chair with navy cushions.

"No surgeries?" Eve asked as she took a sip of the tea.

"We cleared our schedules," Joan explained as she reached for the remote to turn on the television in the bookcase.

"For me?" she asked, hoping to have hidden her surprise.

Joan reached over and squeezed her arm. "For you," she said warmly. "We're going to do it differently this time."

Eve took a sip to hide her smile, feeling childish to be so excited.

"Speaking of different. You've gone back to long hair, I see," Joan observed with the kind of loving smile that was the hallmark of mothers.

"It's a weave, but I am growing my hair out," she admitted. "Time for something…"

"Different," they said in unison before sharing smiles.

"Speaking of which again," Joan said, turning down the volume on a cooking show, *Delphine's Cuisine*, on the CRESSTV channel. "Have you spoken to Lucas?"

"No," Eve said, hating that the very mention of his name made her feel things.

Longing.

Love.

Loss.

"I'm sure he's on the hunt for a new bride," she said.

"You don't believe that," Joan said with a playful chastising look.

"And if I marry someone else?"

Eve closed her eyes as she remembered the moment Lucas had asked her that with his eyes filled with his vulnerability.

And I walked away, leaving him to move on.

"I don't know what I believe," Eve admitted.

"That's a good start," Joan said, looking up as Marco entered the living room to bring her a glass of white sangria with fresh fruit. "Now you can begin to figure it out from a new mindset."

Eve eyed her mother.

"I think once you move beyond the grief and stop punishing yourself by hating the life you were provided, you will not just discover what you believe, but what you *know*," Joan said, leaning over to offer her wine-glass in a toast. "Trust Mama on this, baby girl."

Eve leaned over to touch her teacup to the glass.

Two weeks later

The annual charity gala for UNCF was being held at the Ziegfield Ballroom and the entire Cress family was in attendance. Once Phillip Junior had stepped into the role of CEO of Cress, INC., he continued their parents' legacy of supporting the foundation dedicated to supporting higher education. Lucas stood at the bar looking across the crowded venue at his family spread across two tables.

He felt thankful for them all. Each one—even his nieces and nephew—had poured so much love on him as he recovered from Eve Villar.

Yet again.

"Your scotch and water," the bartender said.

"Thanks," Lucas said, sliding a hefty tip across the bar to the pretty bartender before picking up his drink—something he had come to enjoy more and more since *that* day.

"Enjoy it, Luc," she said.

He paused in taking a sip to give her a longer-than-cursory look. She was cute—petite with a heart-shaped face with skin the color of melted chocolate. She did look familiar. He vaguely remembered a wild party, and an even wilder after-party with just the two of them. "Mandalyn?" he said, not hiding that he wasn't sure that was her name.

She gave him a bright smile. "That's right," she said, leaning on the bar to look up at him. "You're looking good. Maybe we should hit replay on that night."

Lucas smiled into his drink as he felt his interest stir. He wasn't looking to replace Eve—or set a new marriage deadline—but some sexy fun? Why not. "What time you get off?" he asked.

"Ten," she replied.

"Good to set you out and about, son."

"One sec," he said to Mandalyn before turning to find his father standing behind him. "It's a good cause."

Phillip Senior leaned forward as he pressed both his hands on the carved ebony cane he sometimes used if he felt winded. "And lots of good eye candy," he said, leaning to the right of Lucas to give the bartender a brief wave.

Lucas took a deep sip of his drink and ran his free hand down the front of his black-on-black tuxedo.

"But Eve is here," Phillip Senior said. "I thought you should be aware and move accordingly."

Lucas stiffened.

Eve.

His heart hammered so hard he felt like it was ringing in his ears as he looked about the ballroom. And there she was, standing at the entry with Suzie at her side. He was surprised to see she had long hair that she wore draped over one shoulder with a middle part. The rust-colored, off-the-shoulder dress she was wearing hugged her curves, while the short length highlighted her toned legs and the slit exposed a bit of her right thigh. The heavy gold-and-diamond necklace around her neck matched similarly designed pieces that adorned her ears, wrist and fingers.

Stunning.

Always was. Always would be.

He rubbed his free hand over the beard he had decided to keep and have groomed.

Will she like it?

"Luc?" Mandalyn said behind him.

He barely heard her. The sudden reappearance of Eve had taken all of the air out of the room for him. Nothing else existed. Or mattered.

Nothing.

Will I ever be free of her?

His grip on the glass tightened as he watched her move across the room, searching for her seat, until soon she was giving her parents a kiss before claiming her seat with her loyal friend at her side. Suddenly, she looked up and he saw her stiffen and do a double take as her eyes locked with his across the ballroom.

The DJ began to play Usher's "Burn" as Lucas felt like pure electricity sparkled in the air between them.

Neither looked away.

Lucas couldn't. He hadn't seen her since their breakup. Hadn't been this close to her. Hadn't been reminded of their strong chemistry.

"But you know you gotta let it go," Usher sang.

He understood that he should let it go but how could he let his love for Eve burn away when he wanted nothing more than to be consumed by the fire.

Eleven

One month later

"Let it burn, let it burn, gotta let it burn," Eve sang softly as she sat on her back deck looking out at the lake, but only seeing memories of sharing long stares with Lucas across a ballroom.

She couldn't forget it, or the song that had played at the time.

"Good luck with that!" Suzi called out from her office across the hall.

Eve closed her eyes and smiled before she swiveled in her office chair and looked out the window at the lake. Spring was flourishing. Everything was beginning to look refreshed after the onslaught of a northeastern winter. She eyed the lake that had been frozen just weeks ago.

She smiled a little as she remembered a frozen heart-shaped lake.

"What's on your mind?" Suzi asked from behind.

Eve glanced back to find her leaning in the doorway. She just slightly shrugged her shoulder, not sharing her regrets about Lucas.

"How's therapy going?" Suzi said, walking into the office in jean shorts and a white polo shirt with the Aquatic Safety Solutions logo on the top left of it.

During that weekend her parents had spent with her, they had truly dug in on talking…and revealing. She had been stunned to realize that her parents had begun regularly attending couples counseling in the last few years. They eased her concern that they were having difficulties and explained it was just a regular check-in on their marriage that they enjoyed.

Their transparency had left her encouraged to begin counseling sessions that had provided revelations on top of revelations. Limiting beliefs. Emotional blocks. Fears. Inner-child wounds. All of that and more played a role in how she showed up in the world, made decisions, was triggered and handled her emotions.

Who knew?

Eve swirled to face her desk again as Suzi claimed a seat. "Dr. Baugh wants me to revisit the past so that I can release it once and for all," she said.

"Makes sense," Suzi said. "Is there anything I can do to help you?"

"Honestly, the inner child in me wants that so very badly, but I know I have to face this—and conquer it—alone," Eve said.

Suzi nodded in understanding. "Here's to going

straight through it and making it to the other side," she said.

Eve nodded.

Suzi stood up to leave but paused at the door. "It's been one hell of a year, huh?" she asked.

Eve looked at her in confusion. "Huh?" she asked.

"This time last year you were trying to figure out what to wear to your high-school reunion," Suzi reminded her.

"It's been a year!" Eve said softly.

"And you're different. In a good way," she added. "More relaxed. More fun. More open."

Eve's eyes shifted to the dried bouquet she had kept from all of the ones Lucas had sent right after their reunion. As they dried, there was still something hauntingly beautiful about them. She hadn't wanted to throw them away. Not even when she was upset with him after the night of the documentary premiere.

"I would have never guessed that night would lead to you almost getting married," Suzi added, deliberately gentle with her tone.

Eve released a short laugh and then a deep sigh. "It was supposed to be one and done, right?" she asked, thinking of that boldness she had shown to call Lucas to that hotel room. "But…"

I fell in love.

She closed her eyes and allowed herself to think of Lucas—really remembering him and everything they shared. She felt like her soul was warmed. She released a little grunt that was bursting with her appreciation of everything about the man. Big and small.

She felt a chill and she shook her shoulders from the intensity of it.

"He sure looks good with that beard," Suzi added.

Eve opened her eyes to give her friend a wide-eyed stare. "Right?" she agreed with a shake of her head, then covered her face with both of her hands. "Just so good."

Suzi chuckled. "You in the thick of it right now?" she teased.

"He kept staring at me and just felt like he wanted to sop me up with a *biscuit*," she said before releasing a low whistle. "Woo-o-o-oo."

"He wasn't the only one staring, Eve," Suzi said, setting her straight.

"It just felt damn good to see him. Period. Point-blank," she said, lightly tapping the edge of her desk as if to confirm. "And it felt damn good to *be* seen."

"Trust me—I get it. Hank's treatment makes him weak sometimes, but to wake up and find him staring at me is—"

"Amazing, right?" Eve asked.

"Yes!" Suzi said with a body roll.

"How is he?" Eve asked.

"Approved for surgery," Suzi said with her eyes twinkling with happiness—so his recovery was going in the right direction.

"Suzi!" Eve exclaimed, rising from the desk to rush over to hug her close. "Why didn't you tell me?"

"We decided not to share the news yet, just want to keep the energy good, you know," Suzi said, wiping a tear. "But I'm telling you because the love of my life must fight for his to be here to love me and yours is just fine, Eve. Stop wasting time. It's not promised."

Eve shook her head. "Suzi—"

"That's it," Suzi said, holding up both hands. "I have been holding that in. I said it. I won't repeat it."

"Thank you," Eve said, reclaiming her seat.

Suzi left the office.

Eve turned in the chair to look out the window again.

"But I think you need to visit that past sooner than later," Suzi called out. "Okay, *now* I'm done."

Eve chuckled, but she fell into reflective silence.

Sooner than later.

"I'm headed out," Eve said, rising to her feet and leaving the office, but pausing in the hall.

"I just have to finish the expense report for the accountant to do the taxes," her friend said. "I'll lock up when I'm done."

Eve nodded. "Thank, Suzi," she said, then turned to walk away. She paused again. "Suzi?"

"Huh?"

"Thank you," she said.

"You're welcome."

Eve's mood was solemn as she made the nearly two-hour trip to Manhattan. Her thoughts were full and varied. The sun was just beginning to set, casting the sky in shades of orange and lavender, and then an ombré of blues. She lowered the windows and allowed the spring air to blow against her face as she drove up the highway.

She felt anxious as she entered the city limits. She was getting closer to her past. Manhattan West. It was time for a reckoning.

She pulled into the parking lot and made the short walk up Tenth Avenue to the 56-story apartment building.

"Ms. Villar?" the uniformed doorman said in obvious surprise as he opened the door for her. "How are you?"

She gave him a warm smile. "Different," she said. "It's good to see you, Mr. Harris."

"Welcome back," he said with a polite nod. "Let me know if I can get you anything."

As Eve stepped inside the double-height lobby, with its modern design, it truly did feel like stepping back in time. She almost felt out of place as she made her way to the hall where the carved door elevators were lined up. She moved to the one reserved for the penthouse apartment dwellers and entered her code for entry.

As the doors closed, she was able to see her reflection and refused to look away from it. Facing it *all* was necessary. "Forward," she said.

Upon Aaron's death, she discovered there was a trust fund established to automatically pay the monthly fees and utilities on the condo for ten years. There were three more years before she had to decide whether to sell it or not. For seven years she didn't even want to deal with it, even turning down requests to rent it out.

And so it sat.

She used her thumbprint to unlock the door and enter. "Frozen in time," she said aloud, finishing her thought.

Everything was just as they'd left it the night went out to celebrate. The lights were on throughout the three-bedroom condo. Dust coated everything. The air was stale. Draped along the back of the custom sofa were the different coats she had tried on to wear for their celebratory night out. Her iPad was still on the coffee table. A painting of them they'd commissioned in clothing that matched the black-and-white decor still hung above the fireplace. It was still ostentatiously beautiful. Over the top with artwork, wild lighting fixtures and custom furnishing.

She closed the door and crossed the foyer.

Seven years ago seemed more like a hundred.

She eyed the painting again. They stood close, with Aaron's arm around her hip and her hand on his chest. She remembered posing for the photo the painter used for the artwork. It had been a fun day. Laughing. Having fun. Dreaming.

Loving.

Slowly, Eve went through each room and was reminded of not just all she regretted, but of truly happy moments they'd shared in this home they'd built. When they would stay in for the night, order food and just relax around the house. When they talked. When they made plans.

When it wasn't all about excess.

They had converted the two extra bedrooms into walk-in closets for each of them. Both were bursting with clothes. His was neat and orderly. Hers looked like a tornado had blown through it. Back then, she waited for their weekly cleaning service to pick up behind her.

Eve reached for her phone and opened the mobile app she had in a hidden folder on her phone.

Out of sight, out of mind.

She called down to the concierge desk and requested that Mr. Harris bring up boxes. She'd decided to donate all of the clothes, shoes and accessories to charity.

The old Eve surfaced for a moment. It's all outdated, anyway, she had thought.

Eve actually smiled. The old Eve had been fun.

And not all bad, she thought, pausing to look at her reflection in the full-length mirror on the wall.

During one of her counseling sessions, the therapist had her do an exercise where she wrote a letter to her inner child—the part of her stuck at age six when her parents' busy careers had left her in the care of nannies. That part of her is what subconsciously triggered feelings of abandonment and made her far too clingy in her relationships—fearing being left alone, as she had been as a child. She was then guided to visualize joining her inner child in her childhood bedroom and giving her permission to join her in adulthood. To set her free. To merge her into the adult version of Eve.

That session had been a roller-coaster ride of emotions, but it had also been eye-opening as to how deeply the past affected everyone's life and how the best way to move forward was to accept what happened, forgive all involved and be thankful for the lessons taught.

Eve looked back over her shoulder at all the things she once cherished. Things to try to replace feeling unworthy. To feel seen and respected.

None of it had worked.

Losing Aaron had. She had changed for the better.

Eve faced forward, and in the mirror, she visualized herself in her twenties, in a designer dress, hair flowing to her waist, full makeup and expensive jewelry. Sarcastic look. Cold eyes. "It's time for you to join me," she said, beginning the conversation with her younger self, determined to shift *their* life forward.

One week later

Knock, knock.

Lucas looked up from his iPad to find Phillip Junior's wife, Raquel, in the doorway of his offices at Cress, INC. He gave her a smile. "Hey, sis, we rarely see you around here," he said, waving her in.

Raquel entered, wearing a strapless A-line floral dress beneath a tailored blazer, with a fuchsia portfolio tucked under one arm. "I was hoping to talk with you about changing that actually," she said, easing her chic blunt-cut bob behind her ears.

"Me?" he asked, dropping his stylus to give his sister-in-law his full attention.

"I want to apply for a position on your team that best utilizes my creativity and artistic vision," she said.

"Apply?" Lucas balked before laughing. "Your husband's the CEO."

"No," Raquel said in mock surprise as she pressed a hand to her chest, then set her portfolio on the corner of his desk. "Will you hear me out?"

"Yes," he replied, leaning back in his chair and changing his demeanor to honor the seriousness with which she approached him.

"Giving you some help with the design palette for the linen and textiles sparked that light in me to create," Raquel said with enthusiasm, reaching to open her portfolio. "Maybe even do some artwork to use."

Lucas eyed the array of floral watercolors she laid out before him. "They're really beautiful," he said.

"I'm not looking for preferential treatment as Mrs. CEO," Raquel added, also setting her résumé atop the artwork. "I want to use my expertise to help the brand and to reconnect with something I really shouldn't have left behind."

"What does Phillip Junior think about this?" Lucas asked.

Raquel gave him an odd look, then sat in one of the four chairs in front of his desk. "Do you ask every potential employee what their spouse thinks of them wanting to work for you?" she asked.

"But your spouse is *my* brother," Lucas said.

"And my daughter is your niece. We're family. *And*?" she asked.

"Raquel, I just—"

"Just what? Want to send the little wife off to get her husband's permission?" she asked with a raised eyebrow.

"No, that's not what I meant—"

Lucas stopped in midsentence as his assistant, Melvin, entered carrying a large floral arrangement.

"These were just delivered," Melvin said, as he held an arrangement that was wrapped in burlap and tied with a rope into an elegant bow.

"For me?" Lucas asked as the flowers were set on the corner of his desk.

"My, my, my, Lucas," Raquel said, leaning over to smell the flowers. "Who is spoiling you?"

As Melvin left, Lucas reached for the card amid the florals, but Raquel snapped it up before he could. She held it up between her index and middle finger. "Think over my offer?" she asked.

Lucas's eyes shifted from the card to his sister-in-law's face. "I will," he said. "We'll figure out something if this is what you want."

"It is. Thank you, Luc," she said, rising to her feet and handing him the card before easing her items back into her portfolio. "I'll leave you to your mystery."

Before she was out the door, Lucas opened the envelope and withdrew the card.

"'Please meet me where this all began,'" he said, immediately knowing the handwriting.

Eve.

His heart hammered and his hand trembled a bit as he fanned the card like butterfly wings. He looked over at the flowers and studied them. "Wait," he said, taking in the colorful blooms before he picked up his tablet and searched for the confirmation emails from the florist he used.

The arrangement was indeed the first one he'd sent to Eve the day after the reunion.

He dropped the card atop the desk and leaned back in his chair as he stared at it hard enough to bore holes into it, if that was possible.

She's back.

"What do you want?" he asked aloud, as if she could hear him.

He balled his hand into a fist.

As much as he couldn't take his eyes off her at the gala, Lucas had fought not to step back into her life. To observe her. To enjoy her beauty. To give in to that addictive chemistry of theirs. But not to approach. Not to invade her life.

Or have her invade mine.

"I'm done," Lucas said, feeling the lingering sting of her canceling their wedding.

"Done with what, son?"

He looked to the door to see his mother walking over to his desk in a flowing—and rather dramatic, for the office—foil-print caftan that thankfully was not sheer. "You're back from Bali," he said, rising to come around the desk to press kisses to both of her cheeks.

"We came here straight from the airport," Nicolette said, moving from where they stood to study the flowers. "Beautiful. Can I have them? They would look wonderful in my office."

As he watched his mother cradle the bouquet like a baby and dip her head to inhale the sweet scent of them, he was surprised that he felt so territorial. "Uh, actually…no. Those were a gift for me that I am keeping," he said as moved over to her to ease them from her arms.

"From whom?" she asked.

He sat the bouquet atop the card. "Eve," he admitted.

"Oh," Nicolette said.

Lucas turned. "Oh?" he repeated. "That's it? Just… oh?"

Nicolette nodded. "Yes. After your father collapsing and then having heart surgery, we took big steps back from controlling the businesses, your lives and whom you chose to be with," she said. "Near-death experiences—whether you experience them or you deeply love someone who did—can change a point of view."

Lucas turned to view the flowers and thought of the invite that sat beneath them.

"Besides, all of the traveling we've been enjoying—especially visiting Bali—has taught us about grace and going with the flow," she said, reaching past him to quickly pluck a lily from the bunch. She broke off the stem and eased the flower into her hair above her left ear. "Frankly, I don't know how much time I have with the love of my life. He is my focus and we are determined to make the very best of it. *L'amour peut-et mènera-au pardon, mon petit garçon.*"

"*Love can—and will—lead to forgiveness, my baby boy.*"

His eyes eyebrows dipped as she turned seemed to float toward the door with the ends of the caftan rising a bit as she moved. "Are you saying forgive Eve?" he asked.

Nicolette shrugged both shoulders without turning around. "I'm saying whatever you decide will work out just the way it is supposed to," she said before exiting.

"Not helpful," he muttered, then reached under the blooms for the card.

There was no date or time.

She's there. Now.

"Beautiful chaos," Lucas said. "To just drop in my life and demand my appearance. The nerve. And to do what? Blow up my life again?"

He began to pace as he wrestled with his heart and his mind. One wanted nothing more than to race to her and hold her close.

"*L'amour peut-et mènera-au pardon, mon petit garçon.*"

Lucas released a swear before he grabbed his keys

and took long strides out of the office. "I'm gone for the day," he said to his assistant as he blazed a path through his outer office.

"You have a dinner meeting with Phillip Junior in ten minutes," Melvin called behind him.

"Cancel it," Lucas told him over his shoulder.

As he made his way down on the elevator and to his vehicle in the parking garage, Lucas convinced himself that he was just going to make it clear that he was done. It was time they went their separate ways and wished each other well. He loved her—he *adored* her—but he was better without her and all of the drama.

The street outside Manhattan University Prep was nearly empty with the school closed for spring break and the hour being so late in the day. As he walked across the sidewalk and up the stairs to the metal double doors of the formidable 19th-century brick building, he considered that he was wrong and that the building was locked. As he tugged on both doors, he discovered he was right.

He reached into the front pocket of his gray tweed slacks for his phone to call her, but stopped himself.

Maybe this is a sign to let it burn.

He made his way back toward his SUV, determined to drive away and leave Eve Villar alone for good.

"Lucas!"

His hand paused on the handle of the driver's-side door and he looked across the hood at Eve standing just beyond the wrought-iron fence that ran the length of the block and offered the campus security and privacy with the grass hedges directly behind it. She unlocked and opened the gate before stepping onto the sidewalk to beckon him.

He slid his hands into the pockets of his slacks, with his sleeves still rolled up and his tie loosened after a long day of work. As he made his way toward her, the wind pushed her hair back from her face and the sun illuminated the ombré sequins of the long-sleeved mini-dress she was wearing with heels.

Beauty.

"Thank you for coming," Eve said when he reached her.

"I think I'm underdressed," he said, smoothing his hand down the front of his shirt and tie.

"No, you're perfect," she said as she looked up at him. "Always have been. Always will be."

He said nothing.

"I thought it was time we talked," she said.

He nodded, fighting to appear aloof. "How'd you get the school?"

"My parents are both on the school board," she said. "I'm grateful for their help with this."

He paused. In the past, she shunned the opportunities they provided, he observed to himself.

"And what is *this*?" Lucas asked her.

Eve opened the gate farther and waved him in. "Just hear me out," she said.

Lucas walked past her to take the concrete path down the side of the school and around the back of it to the quad. He stopped in surprise at the fairy lights adorning the trees, an abundance of deep rich red roses and lit candles. The massive concrete circular engraved with the school's logo was topped with a table covered in black satin. On it was a silver-domed plate cover.

"I'd figure it was my turn to do something grand for you, Lucas Cress," Eve said as she eased past him to go and stand by the table. "Since the day right here on this quad that you wore your heart on your sleeve to me, I have been too foolish to see your goodness—that I needed in my life. Then…and now."

Lucas took a deep breath and looked pensive as he stared at his feet.

"Lucas, we need to start over," Eve continued. "And what better place to start over than where it first went all wrong."

"Because of you," he said, knowing he still clung to hurt feelings from the past—even if he shouldn't.

"Yes," she said. "And running away from our wedding."

He deeply frowned.

"I love you, Luc," Eve continued.

He dared to look up at her. Her eyes glistened with emotion. "I believe that," he said. "And I love you, but we are not meant to be. We weren't all those years ago on this quad and we're not now, Eve. Let's just let it burn out. It will."

Sadness filled her face before she hung her head.

Lucas turned to walk away.

"I've been in therapy," Eve called behind him. "Luc, *please*!"

He stopped with his hands dug deep into the pockets of his slacks and he looked up at the darkening skies and rocked back and forth on the heels of his handmade shoes.

Damn it.

"I am so sorry that I let my unhealed broken place cause breaks in you and your heart," she said.

Lucas could hear the deep emotion of her regret.

"I thought I didn't deserve anything good, so I pushed you away," she continued.

He turned and hated the tears that wet her cheeks. "Shit," he said as he felt his insides twist from seeing her hurt.

The invisible ties between them remained.

And perhaps always would.

"I've had some time on the couch myself since you called off the wedding," he admitted to anyone else for the first time.

Eve looked surprised.

He nodded and gave her a slightly playful look as he took slow steps toward where she was standing by the table. "I've learned I had to find my more self-love and release issues I put on along with the weight," he said.

"That I didn't help," she said with a wince.

He shrugged one shoulder. "But if I was solid in loving me just as I am, then nothing you or anyone could say or do would sway me one way or the other," he said.

"We both a bunch of work, huh?" she said, her eyes still pleading with him to try again. "Let's work it out together, Luc. Maybe even do counseling together. My parents do."

Lucas raised his eyebrows in surprise at that. "My parents *need* to," he quipped.

They shared a smile.

"Listen, I have learned to accept the parts of my past that were good. It wasn't as horrible as I made it out to be," she said. "Such as this dress that I kept after finally visiting the condo I shared with Aaron."

Lucas looked surprised again. "You still had the condo?" he asked with a bewildered shake of his head.

"Yes, but I have put it on the market and said good-bye with some sadness and some love for the part of my life," she explained, her tone soft.

Their eyes locked.

"I love the beard," she said, wringing her hands together.

Lucas chuckled as he rubbed the beard. "Collateral damage from our breakup that I decided to keep," he said.

Eve dared to take a step closer to him.

Lucas felt pure electricity flow through his body. "Your hair is long," he said, feeling just as nervous as he did back in high school before he built up the nerve to approach her.

"Do you like it?" she asked as she reached up to stroke his beard.

Lucas nodded. "I like it short, t-t-t-too," he told her and then made a face at his stutter. "I haven't done that since high school."

"Don't worry—my heart is doing the same thing right now just being close to you again," she said as she looked up at him.

"Eve," he said, stepping back from her, still hesitant because he felt he was taking the biggest risk—just as he had since high school.

"I get it, Lucas," Eve said as she moved away from him.

The chemistry pulsing between them barely lessened with the sudden distance between them.

I love her.

"We're in the same place we were all those years ago, but this time it's me laying my heart on the line and taking the chance that I will have my heart broken, as you did," she said, looking over at him. Then she removed the lid of the container to reveal a dozen strawberry-shortcake cupcakes topped with cotton candy. She picked up one with her left hand before turning to face him with her arm outstretched.

Lucas removed his hands from his pockets to cross his arms over his chest.

"It was my turn to make you cupcakes," she said, her eyes soft with her hope for them.

For us.

"And hopefully we can start over, but thankful for everything we went through—good or bad—because we will love each on now better than we ever could have before," she said. "This is a choice. It's your right. Toss my cupcakes in the trash or accept them and me."

Lucas's heart was pounding like crazy, but he kept his cool as he walked closer to her to look at the dessert. He bit back a smile because the design left a lot to be desired. The icing wasn't neat. The cotton candy was too large and had crystallized back into sugar in some spots.

He looked at her. "Did you make those?" he asked.

"I found a recipe online," Eve said.

"Not mine," he spouted. "Because I have not made that recipe since you gave them the toss."

"Do you want to eat my cupcake, Lucas?" Eve asked, her voice sexy and her eyes soft with love and desire.

Lucas could not resist the double entendre and freed

his tongue to swipe off the sweet icing, wishing that he was between her thighs instead.

Eve took a step to close the gap, still holding the treat near his mouth. "Bite," she demanded in a whisper.

Lucas gave in to his temptation and took a bite with barely a thought that he may face a fate similar to Adam.

"Careful," she said.

His teeth bit down on metal. With his brow a little furrowed, Lucas removed the item and found it to be her engagement ring. He held the diamond band between his fingers as he cleaned the rest of the cake, strawberry juice and icing from it with his mouth. Her eyes glazed over with the heat he knew he stoked in her.

"We both have worked to go before we're ready for marriage," Eve said with a lick of her lips. "But I promise you if you put it back on my finger, where it belongs, I will *never* take it off again."

"L'amour peut-et mènera-au pardon," he said, feeling his love for her swell in his heart and then warm his entire body.

Eve nodded. "Love can—and will—lead to forgiveness," she translated softly.

With a nod of assurance, Lucas took the rest of the cupcake from her hand to shove into his mouth and then held her hand to slide the band onto her ring finger as he chewed and then swallowed the treat. "Never again?" he told her with a steady stare.

"Never," she promised.

With a slow smile, he wrapped his arm around her waist and pulled her close for a deep kiss that only hinted at the depth of his feelings for the woman who was undoubtedly the love of his life.

Epilogue

Five years later

"Happy anniversary, Mrs. Villar-Cress."

Eve raised her face for Lucas to press a kiss to her mouth as she paused in piping buttercream onto the last of the strawberry-shortcake cupcakes she made for their anniversary—which she'd done for the last four. The act was symbolic of them making lemonade out of lemons. Over the years, with Lucas's guidance she had become skilled at making them. "Happy anniversary, Lucas," she told him, looking up into his eyes.

"We really did it, huh?" he asked her, turning her by her hips to face him in the kitchen of their six-bedroom, five-thousand-square-foot home in Passion Grove— their compromise.

Eve had finally found her way back to the lifestyle she'd grown up in, but maintained the acts of service and giving nature she had acquired after Aaron's death. She had shifted away from running Aquatic Safety Solutions, though, having sold the majority ownership to Suzi and Hank—who had fully recovered and was doing well. The now-married couple had even purchased Eve's little home by the lake.

The diamond of Eve's ring sparkled as she raised her hand to press to his face. "We did," she said. "*Very* happily ever after."

"That was the better goal than worrying about a deadline to get married," Lucas admitted, easing his hands down to cup her bottom.

They shared gentle kisses before both deepened them with a moan.

"Let's sneak away," Lucas said against her lips.

Eve leaned back just enough to see his face. The intense look in his eyes made her consider leading him up to their suite for the real celebration to begin. "We can't!" she said suddenly, remembering they had a house filled with guests to celebrate their wedded bliss—both of their parents, all his siblings and their little families, and plenty of friends, new and old. It had become their tradition for all of the Cress chefs—including the formidable Phillip Senior and Nicolette—to bring decadent dishes to feast upon. "But we can wrap this up early."

"Agreed," Lucas said.

"And maybe one of the grandmothers would love to take Luca with them for the night," Eve suggested.

They both turned to look at their two-year-old son

playing with the other children in the center of the double-height family room.

"That sounds like one hell of a plan," Lucas agreed.

Eve looked around at their beautiful home with the retractable doors opened wide as people flowed effortlessly from the pool area to the family room. She smiled at Hank and Suzi, lost in their own world as they danced near the pool to a slow song played over the home's audio system. While living in Passion Grove, they had made so many new friends and all were in attendance.

And their family.

The Cress family had continued to grow over the years. Coleman and Jillian's six-year-old twins, Christian and Christina, were the same lovable rebels as their father. Phillip Junior and Raquel—Lucas's newly promoted vice president—had given the thirteen-year-old selfie princess, Collette, a baby brother and she loved five-year-old Phillip III. Gabriel and Monica had expanded their family to five with the addition of four-year-old Mona and three-year-old Danni, both curly-headed beauties just like their older sister, Emme. Sean and Montgomery had created future stars in Morgan and four-year-old Lil' Montgomery, who loved the spotlight even more than her father. Seven-year-old Poppy was treasured by Lincoln and Bobbie and perfectly fine being the couple's lone child, because she contained all of the spark and whimsy of her grandmother and namesake.

"Nah, no rush," Lucas said as he also looked across the open living space at his entire family and other gathered guests.

There was laughter. Good energy. Good food. A damn good time. All in celebration of them.

Eve nodded in agreement as she leaned back against her love. "You're right. We have a lifetime to make love," she told him, knowing they would do whatever it took to make that promise a reality.

* * * * *

COMING NEXT MONTH FROM

ⓗ HARLEQUIN

DESIRE

ONE STEAMY NIGHT & AN OFF-LIMITS MERGER
ONE STEAMY NIGHT
The Westmoreland Legacy • by Brenda Jackson

Nadia Novak thinks successful businessman Jaxon Ravnell is in town to pursue a business location. What she doesn't know is that he's also there to pursue *her*. Will Jaxon's plan to seduce the innocent beauty end with a proposal?

AN OFF-LIMITS MERGER
by Naima Simone

Socialite Tatum Haas is strictly off-limits. She's the daughter of the man Bran Holleran needs for his latest deal. But the passion between them can't be denied—even if it burns everything in its wake...

WORKING WITH HER CRUSH &
A BET BETWEEN FRIENDS
WORKING WITH HER CRUSH
Dynasties: Willowvale • by Reese Ryan

Tech guru Kahlil Anderson plans to sell the horse farm he's just inherited. Not that he's confessing that to manager Andraya Walker. He has other plans for the sexy, determined beauty. But when Andraya learns the truth, will forgiveness be in *her* plan?

A BET BETWEEN FRIENDS
Dynasties: Willowvale • by Jules Bennett

When baseball star Mason Clark retreats to a dude ranch in Wyoming, he comes face-to-face with the best friend he left behind. Darcy Stephens has her own ambitions, which don't include an affair with Mason. Until one fiery kiss changes everything...

SECRET HEIR FOR CHRISTMAS &
TEMPTED BY THE BOLLYWOOD STAR
SECRET HEIR FOR CHRISTMAS
Devereaux Inc. • by LaQuette

Actor Carter Jiménez lost his world to celebrity and now avoids it at all costs, protecting his daughter and his still-broken heart. Can billionaire Stephan Deveraux-Smith mend it? Or will the truth about his wealth and his family's public scandals be too much?

TEMPTED BY THE BOLLYWOOD STAR
by Sophia Singh Sasson

Bollywood star Saira Sethi has fame and fortune, but what she really wants is Mia Strome. Yet no matter how much explosive chemistry sizzles between them, will Mia risk her career for the woman who once broke her heart?

You can find more information on upcoming Harlequin titles, free excerpts and more at Harlequin.com.

HD2in I CNM0923

Get 3 FREE REWARDS!

We'll send you 2 FREE Books plus a FREE Mystery Gift.

PRESENTS
His Innocent for One Spanish Night
CAROL MARINELLI

PRESENTS
Bound by the Italian's "I Do"
MICHELLE SMART

FREE Value Over $20

Both the **Harlequin® Desire** and **Harlequin Presents®** series feature compelling novels filled with passion, sensuality and intriguing scandals.

YES! Please send me 2 FREE novels from the Harlequin Desire or Harlequin Presents series and my FREE gift (gift is worth about $10 retail). After receiving them, if I don't wish to receive any more books, I can return the shipping statement marked "cancel." If I don't cancel, I will receive 6 brand-new Harlequin Presents Larger-Print books every month and be billed just $6.30 each in the U.S. or $6.49 each in Canada, a savings of at least 10% off the cover price, or 3 Harlequin Desire books (2-in-1 story editions) every month and be billed just $7.83 each in the U.S. or $8.43 each in Canada, a savings of at least 12% off the cover price. It's quite a bargain! Shipping and handling is just 50¢ per book in the U.S. and $1.25 per book in Canada.* I understand that accepting the 2 free books and gift places me under no obligation to buy anything. I can always return a shipment and cancel at any time by calling the number below. The free books and gift are mine to keep no matter what I decide.

Choose one: ☐ **Harlequin Desire**
(225/326 BPA GRNA)

☐ **Harlequin Presents Larger-Print**
(176/376 BPA GRNA)

☐ **Or Try Both!**
(225/326 & 176/376 BPA GRQP)

Name (please print)

Address   Apt. #

City   State/Province   Zip/Postal Code

Email: Please check this box ☐ if you would like to receive newsletters and promotional emails from Harlequin Enterprises ULC and its affiliates. You can unsubscribe anytime.

Mail to the **Harlequin Reader Service:**
IN U.S.A.: P.O. Box 1341, Buffalo, NY 14240-8531
IN CANADA: P.O. Box 603, Fort Erie, Ontario L2A 5X3

Want to try 2 free books from another series? Call 1-800-873-8635 or visit www.ReaderService.com.

*Terms and prices subject to change without notice. Prices do not include sales taxes, which will be charged (if applicable) based on your state or country of residence. Canadian residents will be charged applicable taxes. Offer not valid in Quebec. This offer is limited to one order per household. Books received may not be as shown. Not valid for current subscribers to the Harlequin Presents or Harlequin Desire series. All orders subject to approval. Credit or debit balances in a customer's account(s) may be offset by any other outstanding balance owed by or to the customer. Please allow 4 to 6 weeks for delivery. Offer available while quantities last.

Your Privacy—Your information is being collected by Harlequin Enterprises ULC, operating as Harlequin Reader Service. For a complete summary of the information we collect, how we use this information and to whom it is disclosed, please visit our privacy notice located at corporate.harlequin.com/privacy-notice. From time to time we may also exchange your personal information with reputable third parties. If you wish to opt out of this sharing of your personal information, please visit readerservice.com/consumerschoice or call 1-800-873-8635. **Notice to California Residents**—Under California law, you have specific rights to control and access your data. For more information on these rights and how to exercise them, visit corporate.harlequin.com/california-privacy.

HDHP23

HARLEQUIN
PLUS

Try the best multimedia
subscription service for romance
readers like you!

Read, Watch and Play.

Experience the easiest way to get
the romance content you crave.

Start your **FREE TRIAL** at
www.harlequinplus.com/freetrial.